When we were Reckless

Copyright © 2021 Emery Rose

All rights reserved.

No part of this book may be reproduced or transmitted in any form or by any means, electronic or mechanical, including photocopying, recording or by any information storage and retrieval system, without written permission from the author.

This is a work of fiction. Any names or characters, businesses or places, events or incidents, are fictitious or have been used in a fictitious manner. Any resemblance to actual persons, living or dead, or actual events is purely coincidental.

Cover Design: Cat Imb, TRC Designs

Editors: Jennifer Mirabelli (Content Edits); Ellie McLove, My Brother's Editor

Dedication

For my readers. Thank you so much to each and every one of you who has ever picked up one of my books. With so many amazing books to choose from, I'm honored and grateful that you chose to read mine. It's because of you that I'm able to live out my dreams and write the stories of my heart. xoxo

Playlist

"You Broke Me First" - Conor Maynard version
"Love Songs Ain't For Us" - Amy Shark, Keith Urban
"Thing Called Love" - NF
"I'll Wait" - Kygo, Sasha Sloan
"Some Say" - Nea
"smile again" - Blackbear
"Biting My To"ngue" - The Veronicas
"Like Lovers Do" - Hey Violet
"Adore" - Amy Shark
"In My Blood"
- The Veronicas
"Slower" - Tate McRae
"What A Time" - Julia Michaels, Niall Horan
"Don't Give Up On Me" – Andy Grammer
"If You Love Her" - Forest Blakk, Meghan Trainor

Chapter One

Quinn

My brothers bought me metallic gold Nikes to coordinate with my blue cap and gown and the gold Honor Society sash around my neck. I *lived* in Nikes. It was literally like walking on air. My collection was huge. A couple of years ago, Mason and Holden, my two oldest brothers, built shelves for me with cubbies to display them all. Whenever I thought about packing for college in the fall, I wondered how I'd cull my collection to fit into my dorm room closet. I wouldn't have the kind of space I did now.

Which ones would I leave behind?

As I was debating this, the guy next to me—Jackson Carter—

nudged my shoulder. I blinked up at him. He was huge, a baller. "You're up."

"Oh. Thanks." Typical. I'd missed my name being called. I grinned, excitement bubbling inside me as I climbed the steps to the stage to accept my high school diploma—one of four hundred and five seniors graduating tonight.

The ceremony was at Maverick stadium, the football field and stands lit up by floodlights. I was the fourth and last Cavanaugh to step onto this stage and receive a diploma. Last time, we were here for Declan. Earlier this evening, Mom had cried that her baby was 'flying the nest.' My family still wasn't sold on the idea of me leaving home or being so far away, but they'd come around. Eventually.

Principal Bradley handed me my diploma and clasped my hand in his. "I do not doubt that you will go on to do amazing things," he said, and I wondered if he repeated those exact words to every student that walked onto this stage. "Good luck, Quinn. You've been an inspiration. Go out and make the world a better place."

No pressure there. My brothers would be laughing at how cheesy this was, but I just smiled and bit my tongue to stop myself from cracking one of my stupid jokes. "Thank you. I'll do my best."

I turned and waved my diploma in the air, my eyes searching the stands for my family. They weren't hard to find. My three brothers and mom held a gigantic banner that said: YOU'RE THE TOP BANANA, CHIQUITA. Someone had painted a fruit bowl with a bunch of bananas. The top banana had a blown-up photo of my face on it. It was so huge they could probably see it from Mars.

I should have known my family would make a stupid fruit joke. It was a tradition. It went with the territory of owning a chain of organic food stores.

They were shouting my name. In a sea of thousands, the Cavanaughs always managed to be the loudest. They were so annoying.

I loved their guts.

I brushed off the disappointment that my dad hadn't made an effort to be here tonight and blew my family kisses as I danced across the stage on sneakers made of air. When I stepped off the stage, I searched for the other family that matched mine in spirit and volume—the McCallisters.

My gaze zeroed in on Jesse McCallister. *He was here.* I'd heard he was coming back. And now, here he was, looking all cool and casual.

It was no exaggeration to say that I have been in love with Jesse my entire life. Too bad he only thought of me as his best friend's little sister. I had one summer to turn things around. One summer to make him see that I was the woman of his dreams.

I'd just have to make sure to keep my plan a secret from my brothers, *especially* Mason.

Jesse's eyes locked on mine. Then he raised his arm, made a fist, and thumped it against his heart. The smile that used to be so quick to form, the brilliant smile that could rival the floodlights for its brightness, wasn't there but the gesture—the fist to his heart—that was for me.

And I died just a little. I was liquid gold, my limbs, and muscles, and bones melting into my sneakers and leaving a puddle on the grass. The only thing left of me was my thrashing heart lying on the ground at my feet.

Unrequited love. Was there anything more painful?

When I was five years old, I asked Jesse to marry me. He said yes. He even went along with the fake wedding ceremony I set up under the giant oak in my backyard. I made him wear a daisy chain around his neck that matched mine. We celebrated our nuptials with pink lemonade and pink-frosted sugar cookies.

After that, I told everyone he was my husband—even the guys at the motocross track where Jesse and my brothers practiced. I was only five at the time, but he was fourteen. A lot of boys that age would have been embarrassed or told me to get lost. But not Jesse. By the time I was twelve, he was already a hotshot in motocross and Supercross with sponsorships and endorsements, his pretty face and cut abs plastered on posters that girls hung on their walls and drooled over. They probably licked them too. Or maybe that was just me.

I filled my journal with stories and poetry and confessions, his name doodled in the margins. At the time, he was busy training and competing, traveling all over the country for races, but he dropped everything for me.

Eighteen months ago, he came home from California to be by my side again.

I'd never told him that his stories about California were one of the reasons I'd set my sights on UCLA. I wanted to live near the ocean. Dance in the sunshine. Learn to surf. Take creative writing classes and psychology classes, and film classes and live every day like it was my last.

Most of all, I wanted to be near him.

At the time, he was living and training in Temecula in Southern California. My overactive imagination had run wild with possibilities. I'd be his ride or die. My arms wound tightly around him on the back of his motorcycle as we zipped up the Pacific Coast Highway. The wind in my hair, sun on my face, his sunshine citrus scent washing over me. Out from under the watchful eye of my overprotective brothers. Not defined by my medical history.

As if a change of location would free me from the ties that bind.

But oh, the absolute irony of my best-laid plans.

In a few short months, I'd be heading to California, and where would he be? Still in Texas?

Was it because of his ex-girlfriend? Had she loved him? Had she loved him the way I loved him? Was that possible? I thought not.

I sighed as I stood with my classmates and watched the other graduates walk across the stage. When they called Ridge McCallister's name, I watched him climb the stairs. His golden-brown hair touched his collar, his cap was askew, and his gown flapped behind him. Despite the predictions that he'd end up in juvie or flunk out, Cypress Springs High's resident bad boy was not only graduating but going on to college where he'd be playing football. I didn't even know Ridge, not really, but I cheered for him and laughed when he turned his back to the crowd, lifted his gown, and mooned the entire audience, eliciting catcalls and shouts, and an *I love you, Ridge McCallister* from the cheering squad.

"That will be enough, Mr. McCallister," Principal Bradley said sternly. But even he was fighting a smile as he shook his head at Ridge's antics. Good for Ridge. He'd turned his life around.

Miracles do happen. I was living proof.

Chapter Two

Quinn

It had been four days since my graduation, and I still hadn't seen Jesse. I didn't even know where he was. I'd driven past his house a few times, low-key stalker that I was, but he wasn't home.

I parked my VW Beetle in the designated employees' parking area—a patch of gravel and grass next to the brewery and grabbed my bag from the passenger seat. According to my brother Declan, I was the world's worst waitress, but since they were family, my brothers had no choice but to hire me for the summer.

Cavanaugh Brothers Brewing Company was the brainchild

of my three brothers and sat on twenty acres of prime Texas Hill Country land. They grew fruits and vegetables for Declan's farm-to-table restaurant and the fruit they used in their craft beers.

A timber and stone barn had been converted into the brewery, and a renovated stone farmhouse housed the taproom and the kitchen—all open and airy with soaring ceilings and wide plank wood floors.

I walked into the taproom, twenty minutes before they opened, and I heard *his* voice. Low and kind of raspy. I'd know it anywhere.

"Holy shit," Mason said. He and Holden were standing in front of a laptop on the oak bar.

"What's going on?"

Neither of them answered, their eyes glued to the screen.

"After months of soul searching," I heard Jesse say as I hurried around to the other side of the bar and squeezed in between Mason and Holden, two walls of muscle, both of them well over six feet tall. At five foot three, I was the family runt. They stepped aside to make room for me, and there on the screen was Jesse.

"I've made the decision to retire."

I stared at the screen in shock. *Retire?* What the hell was he doing? He did not just say that. I must have misheard. No way would Jesse retire. He was only twenty-seven.

Was this because of this past season? It hadn't been *that* bad.

I'd watched all his Supercross races this season and had seen him struggling to get back to the top where he belonged. For anyone else, finishing eighth after coming back from a severe injury would have been admirable. But for someone at Jesse's level--a motocross legend who had won four Supercross championships in a row, not to mention thirty-nine National wins, five AMA moto titles, and three gold medals at the X Game--this past season had been a massive blow.

And yes, I could recite all his stats off the top of my head. I knew every win and every loss, every podium finish, and every injury he'd sustained in his career.

But why was he retiring?

I stared at his gorgeous face. He was wearing a blue button-up that brought out the blue in his eyes. Behind him was the factory team's green and black racing colors and logo. He was standing behind a lectern, speaking into the mic.

There was no smile on his face, but I heard his emotions in every word.

"I want to thank the team and my sponsors for all the support you've given me over the years and for allowing me the opportunity to make a career in the sport I love. My heartfelt thanks go out to my fans. Thank you for sticking with me through all the ups and downs, the serious injuries, and the great successes. I'm grateful to my family, who has always believed in me and encouraged me to give one hundred percent in everything I do. I've been so fortunate to have had so much support throughout my career. This sport has given so much back to me. It has been an honor and a privilege to race against the very best in the world."

He bowed his head and put his hand over his heart. "It has been an amazing ride."

And that was it. When Jesse finished making his announcement, he walked away, not even hanging around to answer any questions.

Mason shut down his laptop, and for a few seconds, we stood

in stunned silence.

"Did you guys know about this?" I asked them. "Did he say anything to you?" I looked from Holden to Mason. They were only a year apart, with the same chestnut brown hair. I was the only one who had inherited Mom's blonde hair.

They both shook their heads.

"I just know he was going through a bad time," Holden said. "He went through so much shit in the past year."

"With his injury, you mean?" Last August, he broke his vertebrae in two places. That would have been enough to get anyone down. But Jesse had always been stubborn and determined. Three months after that crash, he'd been riding again. So none of this added up.

"That had to be rough," Mason said. "But I think it was everything that happened with his ex that messed with his head."

"What did she do?" I gritted out between clenched teeth, my eyes narrowed. Holden's brows shot up.

Tone it down, Quinn. I cleared my throat. "I mean… Do you guys know what happened?"

"He didn't want to talk about it," Mason said. "Can't blame him. If my girlfriend cheated on me, I wouldn't want to talk about it either."

My jaw dropped. "*Cheated on him*? Alessia Rossi *cheated* on him?" My hands curled into fists. If she were standing in front of me, I'd plant one of them in her pretty face. But, instead, I took a deep breath and exhaled. I wasn't usually a violent person, but she brought out the worst in me. "How could she do that to him?"

"Shit. I thought you knew," Mason said. "Do me a favor and just keep it to yourself."

I nodded. "Yeah. Sure. I won't say a word."

Why had he lied to me?

They broke up before he came back home last fall. When I asked him if he was okay with it, he told me the decision was mutual, that they wanted different things out of life. And I'd believed him. Probably because it was what I'd wanted to hear. I'd been so happy that after three years with Alessia, he'd finally figured out what I'd known all along. She wasn't the right girl for him.

And I wasn't just saying that because I was in love with him. I'd met Alessia Rossi. The first time was two years ago when he brought her home for his brother Jude's wedding.

She was beautiful. On the outside, anyway. A tall, willowy brunette with flawless olive skin, and big boobs, she was every guy's fantasy—the opposite of me in every way. Whenever Jesse had looked at her, which was all the freaking time, you could tell that he really loved her. His love for her made him blind, that's for sure.

Alessia was one of those girls who pretended to be sweet and friendly, *especially* around guys, when really, she was cunning and manipulative.

"Your friendship with Jesse is so sweet," she'd cooed, but I could tell she had meant the opposite. Then to further cement my hatred for her, she'd said, "Jesse has such a big heart. Do you know how many charities he donates to?" She'd laughed like it was a bad thing instead of a good one. "I swear, he's the biggest sucker for sick kids. Whenever kids message him and tell him they're in the hospital and they're his biggest fan, he'll drop everything to visit them."

As if I was just another sick kid and not someone special to him. So yeah, I really, *really* couldn't stand Alessia Rossi. And how he could have spent three years with that shrew was a mystery.

She must have a magic vagina, that's all I could say.

"Have you been listening, Quinn?" I looked up at my brother Declan AKA the executive chef. His green eyes flashed in annoyance, and he speared a hand through his dark hair.

Next to me, Aubrey stifled a laugh. Aubrey was the front-of-house manager and worked for my brothers since they opened the brewery last year. The gorgeous curvy redhead knew I hadn't been paying attention to whatever Declan was saying. She, on the other hand, hung on his every word.

Declan was the only one who couldn't see that Aubrey was madly in love with him. Wasn't that always the way?

"Of course, Declan. I listen to everything you say." I batted my lashes and gave him a sweet smile that didn't fool him for a minute.

He exhaled loudly and crossed his tattooed arms over his chest. I guess I could kind of see why women called him hot. But no way would I want a hot-tempered guy like Declan, no matter how 'hot' he might be.

"What are today's specials?"

I peered into the kitchen through the shelves of the pass, searching for a clue. The stainless steel gleamed, and the white subway tiles sparkled. Pans sat on the gas burners, but I couldn't tell what was in them. A few wood crates were on the counter, but I couldn't identify anything inside them. Declan was a forager, so God only knew what he'd dug up today.

The sous chef, Casey, was slicing meat into paper-thin slices.

Bingo. "Carpaccio…" I squinted at the slab of meat. "Wait, no. Is that prosciutto?"

Declan threw up his hands. "I don't have time for this shit," he growled. "Aubrey. Fill her in." I rolled my eyes as he stalked back into the kitchen to lord over his little empire.

Declan was a perfectionist and a culinary genius. Out of my three brothers, he was the most volatile and the one I argued with the most. Pretty sure Declan thought he was Gordon Ramsay. This summer was already shaping up to be a kitchen nightmare.

After Aubrey filled me in on the specials, Mason called my name. I spun around to face him as he came to stand in front of me. "Has Ridge McCallister ever given you any shit?"

Ridge? "No. I've never even talked to him. Why?"

"He's coming in for an interview. Just wanted to make sure you're cool with it."

"Why wouldn't I be?"

Mason shrugged. "Just checking. If he's ever caused you any trouble—"

"He hasn't," I said quickly. "I'm cool with it."

"He'll be helping Holden in the brewery." Holden had a degree in Biology and was the head brewer. He loved nothing more than to experiment with hops and fermentation processes.

I was the odd man out, the only one in my family who wasn't a massive foodie or a beer lover. Not that I'd ever tried more than a few sips of beer.

"Great. Sounds good." Mason looked like he was waiting for me to say more or fill him in on Ridge's character. But since I didn't know Ridge, I had nothing to add.

I highly doubted that it would work in Ridge's favor if I shared what I did know about him. Man whore. The life of every party. He was the guy who always knew how to score the alcohol and drugs. Or so I was told. Not that he did drugs. But rumor had it that he was a supplier.

He'd shocked everyone when he'd not only made it on the football team but had been one of the best wide receivers in the history of Cypress Springs High.

The cheerleaders used to fight over who got to do his homework. That was his superpower. He didn't even have to lift a finger. All he had to do was swagger down the hallway, and girls were falling all over him.

"I'm sure he'll be good at…." I waved my hand in the air. "Carrying oak barrels and stuff."

Mason gave me a funny look.

"He's big. And he looks strong. I mean, he's a baller, so…" I shrugged.

"Yeah, okay." He was still giving me a weird look, but I ignored it.

I couldn't think about Ridge. All I could think about was Jesse. Was he devastated? Heartbroken? Why had he retired from the sport he loved?

So many questions. And there was only one person who could answer them.

Chapter Three

Quinn

Jesse lived in a treehouse. He bought it a few years ago. A retreat from his busy life on the road. But he'd never really lived in this house, except for a couple of months during the off-season. He'd lent it out to friends, though.

For a while, Mason had lived here. I'd heard that Jesse was thinking of selling it so he could buy a house in California. But now I didn't know what he was planning to do with it.

The house was romantic, though. Timber-framed with a wraparound deck overlooking the woods in the back and the river from the front. He had land too—acres and acres of trails for off-road riding.

    The last time I was here, it was Christmas Eve. Which also happened to be my eighteenth birthday. Right after Christmas, he left Texas, and I hadn't been face-to-face with him since.

    On Christmas Eve, something had happened, though. For me, it had been magical, but to him, it obviously meant nothing. So I didn't know why I was here tonight. Eleven o'clock was too late for a social call.

    I peered at his house through the windshield. The lights were on. My heart raced, nerves and excitement making it beat triple time. He was home. He was still awake. He hadn't invited me, but I wanted to be here for him if he needed me. I just wanted to make sure he was okay. Because how could he be?

    Taking a deep breath, I got out of my car, and I climbed the wood staircase. Up and up and up.

    Pine from the Cypress trees scented the air, the night air balmy as I bravely, foolishly followed my stupid heart up the stairs and across the cedar deck. My heart was in my throat, my pulse pounding in my ears. I felt like I was going to throw up.

    Just breathe, Quinn.

    It had been five months since I'd seen him up close. Five months since I'd breathed in the scent on his skin that had made me dizzy with wanting and longing.

    Sucking in a deep breath and squaring my shoulders, I lifted my hand, and I knocked on the wood door.

    Oh God, this was a terrible idea. I should turn around and leave. Get back in my car and drive home. But my feet were rooted to the spot, and I couldn't move. So I just stood outside his door with my shaky hands clasped in front of me.

Moments later, the door opened, and I breathed a sigh of relief.

He squinted as if he was trying to place the face and bring me into focus. He was shirtless and barefoot, sporting only a pair of black athletic shorts.

Jesse had the most beautiful body. He really did. Lean and sculpted, without an ounce of fat. Broad shoulders, narrow waist. I stared at the dips and valleys of his chiseled abs, so well-defined that I could count all six of them. I clasped my hands more tightly and fought the urge to reach out and touch him, to feel the warmth of his skin, the tautness of his muscles under the palm of my hand.

After what felt like forever, I dragged my gaze up to his face. To his summer sky blue eyes and full, sensuous lips. Lips I'd tasted once. They were softer than I'd expected but firm too. Now his face was neutral, devoid of expression.

Jesse roughed his hand through his hair. His messy, disheveled light brown hair that was shorter than it had been at Christmas.

"What are you doing here?" he asked brusquely.

Not exactly the welcome I'd been hoping for, but I was here now, so I had to say something. "I… I couldn't sleep. So I thought I'd take a drive, and I ended up here." Lame, Quinn. Super lame. "Can I come in?"

He studied my face for a moment. Then he swung the door open wider and strode across the hardwood floor on his bare feet. I closed the door behind me and moved farther into the room.

He disappeared somewhere, but he'd opened the door for me. He hadn't asked me to leave, so he must have wanted me here, right?

I walked over to the horseshoe-shaped sofa, butter-soft, caramel-colored leather, and stood behind it, unsure what to do next. The flatscreen TV above the stone fireplace was on, an action movie playing. Empty beer bottles sat on the rustic oak coffee table—a whole row of bottles. I stared at the beer bottles. At the bottle of tequila. Half-empty. There was a pizza box sitting on the coffee table too. If it had been anyone else, I wouldn't even question it.

Pizza, beer, and a movie. No big deal.

But this was Jesse, who had always claimed that his body was his temple. He was a vegetarian. He ate healthy, never touched junk food, and he didn't drink. I mean, I was sure he drank a beer or two sometimes, but this was something different.

My gaze moved around the open-space living area. An oval dining table with six upholstered chairs sat in front of the tall glass windows, affording a view of the river. Framed black and white photos of Alessia Rossi used to hang on the walls. He'd been in some of them too--photos of him doing a double backflip at the Summer X Games a couple of years ago when he won the gold and a few pictures of him racing at the Pala National.

But those photos were gone now.

Ceiling fans hung from the double-height ceiling, an American flag on one of the timber walls. Jesse's older brother Jude had brought that flag home from Afghanistan, and it was one of Jesse's most prized possessions.

I turned as Jesse came back into the room, wearing a fitted maroon Rogue T-shirt, the soft cotton molded to the contours of his body.

He was drunk. I hadn't seen it before, but now I could tell that he was unsteady on his feet.

"Did you... um, have some friends over?" I asked when he plopped down on the sofa and lifted a beer to his perfect lips. I watched him take a pull, his throat bobbing on the swallow, his eyes on the TV that I didn't think he was watching.

He shook his head no but didn't say anything. He didn't tell me to leave, but he didn't ask me to stay. For a moment, I hovered, not sure what to do.

After a few seconds of internal debate, I took a seat in the corner of the sectional and tucked my legs underneath me.

His gaze swung to me, and I saw that his eyes were glassy. "What are you doing here, Sunshine Girl?"

Sunshine Girl. He used to call me that when I was younger. He used to say that I was his sunshine girl because I had the most brilliant smile that lit up my whole face. He used to say it made him smile just to see me. But now, he wasn't smiling. Not even a little bit. "I just came to see how you're doing."

"Doing just fine."

But he wasn't 'just fine.' That much was obvious. So I should have kept my mouth shut. I shouldn't have asked the question that had been running through my head ever since I'd watched his press conference, ever since I'd heard that Alessia had cheated on him.

"What happened? I don't understand. Why would you retire? Why would you give up the thing you love most? Your passion. You're one of the best motocross racers in the country." All the words came out in a rush, my tongue tripping over itself to get them out before I could stop myself. "And you're only twenty-seven... and you always said...."

His eyes narrowed on me, the muscle in his jaw ticking. A

warning that I was venturing into dangerous territory. "What did I always say?"

I couldn't say the words. I'd already said too much. But what Jesse had always said was, "If or when I retire, I'll leave when I'm on top."

He hadn't done what he said. Instead, he'd done the opposite. So none of this made sense.

"I just don't understand."

"There's a lot of things you don't understand. You're just a teenager. You've lived a sheltered life. So how could you *possibly* understand?"

"Was it because of your injury? Does your back still hurt?"

"My back is just fine."

"Okay, so… why did you give it up?"

"I'm done. Don't have what it takes to be number one anymore."

"How can you say that? If you train hard and focus like you always did, you'll come back stronger next season. I know you will."

He drank his beer and didn't comment. I should have stopped, should have kept my mouth shut, but this seemed too important just to let it go, so I persevered.

"You always said that not riding makes you miserable. You live for it. You love it. And you're the best, Jesse. Everyone knows that. *I* know that."

He shook his head, disputing my words. "You've always put too much faith in me. That's your problem, Quinn. I'm not the guy you think I am."

"What happened to you? The Jesse I used to know always said, "If anyone tells me it can't be done, I'll take it as a challenge and prove them wrong." But now you're just giving up?" I threw my hands in the air. "None of this makes sense."

"Why do you even care?"

How could he even ask me that?

"Because I do," I whispered. "I care about you. I've always...." I cleared my throat. "I've known you all my life, Jesse. We've always been friends. And friends care. *I* care."

"You should go home. You shouldn't even be here."

"You were always there for me when I needed you. I can't just leave you like this."

"Like what? I had a few beers. I'm not shooting heroin into my veins. I'm not holding a gun to my head. I told you I'm fucking fine."

"But—"

"Go home, Quinn." He raised the volume on the movie he was watching and focused on the screen.

I stared at his profile. At the set of his clenched jaw. His hooded eyes and shuttered expression. I'd never seen this side of Jesse before and had no idea he could be so mean. So closed-off. Where was the easy-going, laidback guy I used to know?

Where was his smile? Had *she* taken that from him? Was this all because of her? Alessia Rossi. But it had to be something more than that, right? I didn't know what to think.

"Are you acting like this because of what happened on Christmas Eve? Because... I mean, we never talked about it, and I just thought...."

He turned his head and stared at me blankly, with no recollection of Christmas Eve or that kiss.

"You don't remember?"

He shrugged one shoulder, non-committal.

"Just tell me you remember the kiss. We kissed," I whispered.

He ran his hand through his hair and laughed under his breath. "I was hoping you wouldn't go there. You've never been good at taking a hint, have you? I didn't bring it up because I was trying to save you the embarrassment."

"Embarrassment? Why… but…"

"*We* didn't kiss. You. Kissed. Me. You think I never noticed your schoolgirl crush, Quinn?" He was mocking me. "*Everyone* noticed."

Jesse McCallister, the love of my life, the guy of my dreams, was mocking me.

Tears stung my eyes, but I blinked them back and gritted my teeth. That wasn't how it happened. Why was he trying to pretend it was like that? I might have been inexperienced, but I wasn't stupid.

We'd kissed, and he had kissed me back. He'd pulled me close until our bodies were flush, and I had felt him. *All of him.* His body had responded to me just as much as mine had to him.

How could he lie and pretend it had happened differently?

I swallowed past the lump that had formed in my throat and got to my feet. The ground beneath me felt unsteady, but I squared my shoulders, and I looked Jesse right in the eye. Those summer sky eyes that used to make me weak in the knees whenever they landed on me. I steeled myself against the effect he'd always had over me, his words playing on repeat in my head.

You think I never noticed your schoolgirl crush, Quinn?

So hard. So cold. Nothing like the Jesse I used to know. My cheeks flamed with mortification, and I hated the way my voice quavered on the words, but I forced myself to say them anyway. "You were right about one thing. You're not the guy I thought you were. I came over because I thought you might need a friend."

"You came over hoping to get laid. At least be honest about your intentions, Sunshine Girl."

I stared at him, so shocked that those words had come out of his mouth that I didn't know how to respond or what to think. He shrugged one shoulder, so casual, so cavalier as if to say, *Just telling it how I see it*.

And it was that casual little shrug and the look of indifference on his face that made the words sink in and burrow deep inside.

My hands clenched into fists. My chest was heaving.

How dare he say those words to me?

My hand was itching to slap the arrogance off his face. Feel the sting on my palm and leave my handprint on his cheek. His gaze lowered to my clenched fists, and he jutted out his chin. "Go ahead. Punch me."

He probably wouldn't even feel it. If anyone got hurt, it would be me. I took a few deep breaths trying to control my anger and my hurt. Emotion clogged my throat, and I couldn't even speak.

I hated him. I really, really did. I never thought it was possible to hate the guy I'd loved all my life, but somehow, he'd managed to make me do it. If I didn't leave right now, I'd end up crying in front of him, and I didn't want to give him that satisfaction.

So I turned away from him, and I stumbled to the door, my eyes blurry with tears. My heart ached. God, this hurt so much. Jesse used to be so kind. So *good*. How could he have changed so much?

My hand wrapped around the smooth brass doorknob, and I

tried to yank the door open. The palm of Jesse's hand flattened on the wood, his body caging me in. I could feel the heat of his skin, smell the beer and tequila on his breath as he leaned in close to the shell of my ear.

"You might not see it now, but I'm doing you a favor."

I let out an incredulous laugh. "Don't do me any more favors, *asshole*."

"You're right. I am."

"What?"

"An asshole. I am an asshole."

He took a few steps back, taking the heat of his body and the scent of his skin with him. Then, without turning to look at him again, I walked out the door.

I didn't let the tears fall until I was safely inside my car.

How could I have gotten it so wrong? Maybe this was the real Jesse, and I'd just been too blind to see it. But, God, he must have gotten a good laugh at my expense. Poor little Quinn with her schoolgirl crush.

"We *didn't kiss. You. Kissed. Me.*"

How could someone so beautiful be so cruel?

It didn't matter anymore. I didn't care what Jesse thought about me or what he said or did. I was done.

I wasn't going to waste another minute of my precious time worrying about him, or thinking about him, or dreaming about him.

As I drove away, I held my middle finger out my open window and kept it there until his house disappeared from view. It didn't even matter that he wouldn't see it. That small act of defiance made me feel just a tiny bit better.

Chapter Four

Jesse

Never trust a beautiful woman.

Not only had Alessia Rossi shredded my heart, but she had also destroyed my career. Some would say I'd done it to myself.

I'd dug my own grave.

I'd been fucked, literally and figuratively and in every way imaginable.

When you play with fire, you get burned, and I'd been the arsonist. I'd thrown the lit match on the gasoline, and then I stood back and watched my life burn to the ground.

I'd never been one to do anything half-assed. Why start now?

And all because I'd chosen the wrong girl. I'd been naïve and foolish enough to believe that she was my one true love, and I'd turned a blind eye to her flaws and insecurities. I thought that by giving it my all, by loving her with every cell in my body, that would be enough for her. But with Alessia, you could move mountains for her, and it still wouldn't be enough.

Fuck her. Fuck love. Never again would I put my heart on the line only to have it stomped on.

I accelerated into the turn, my leg nearly brushing the tarmac as I leaned into the road. My Kawasaki Ninja ate up the miles, the scenery passing in a blur. The hangover I'd woken up with was all but gone, cured by the rush of adrenaline.

When I returned from my morning ride, my brother Jude was waiting for me. He was sitting on the deck with his feet propped on the wood railing, the sun on his face. I sat in the lounge chair next to him, set my helmet on the ground, and took the cup of coffee he handed me, jerking my chin in a silent thank you.

"You wanna talk about it?"

I ran my hand through my sweaty hair and stared at the dirt trails that cut through the trees. "Nope."

He scrubbed a hand over the dark stubble on his jaw, contemplating my answer, then nodded and took a sip of his coffee. We sat in silence, drinking our coffee while we soaked up the morning sun that filtered through the trees.

When I was a kid, I'd always said I wanted to live in a treehouse. Now I had my very own. I had a garage filled with toys—dirt bikes, mountain bikes, my Kawasaki, an ATV. I'd gotten to the top of my profession. Number Fucking One. I'd even been featured on the back of a Wheaties box.

But nobody ever warned you how hard the fall was from the top.

"Shouldn't you be working? Or with the kids?" Hard to believe Jude had three kids now. But after a rocky road back to the love of his life, he was working on making all his dreams come true.

"Yes, to both."

I took a sip of my coffee. "Then why are you here?"

"The kids are with Lila. The work will always be there. But you're not doing so great. And if there's anything I can do to fix this, say the fucking word, and I'll do whatever it takes."

And that was the thing about Jude. His words weren't empty. He really meant them, and he would do anything it took to fix things for the people he loved.

"Not even you can fix this."

"We're all worried about you."

"Don't be. I'm fine."

"Those words should be outlawed."

A laugh escaped me. "Outlawed? Are we in the Wild West now, Sheriff?"

He snorted. "Whenever I used to say I was fine, Lila wouldn't rest until she got to the bottom of it. So I stopped saying those words a while back. Especially when I was anything but fine."

"What you went through is way worse than anything I could ever imagine. I haven't just come back from a combat zone. I retired from a sport. It's not the end of the world. It's what I want."

"I call bullshit."

"Call it whatever you want. It's the truth."

"Does this have anything to do with breaking your back?"

"Not really." It did, and it didn't. It certainly hadn't helped matters. I squinted at the view in front of me. "This past season, I struggled mentally. Like, I really struggled. I had to push myself to get through every race. And it showed. I don't have what it takes to be a champion anymore."

As much as it pained me to admit it, all of what I'd just told Jude was the truth. Not the whole truth. But it was a big part of my decision to retire. I'd saved face by 'leaving gracefully' rather than having the team publicly announce that they'd fired me.

Maybe I could have tried harder to find another team. But after I talked to two other teams, and they hemmed and hawed rather than jumping at the chance to add me to their roster as they would have in the past, I knew. Word had traveled.

"I always thought that if, *when* I finally retired, I'd go out when I was still on top. But life doesn't always go according to plan."

Jude didn't respond. I could tell he was puzzling over something in his brain, trying to put the pieces of my story together. And I knew he'd figure out that some parts of the puzzle were missing.

My eldest brother was sharp. Nothing got past him. He'd always been my hero, the guy I looked up to as a kid. I used to worship the ground he walked on. Used to confide all my hopes and fears and dreams to him. But now, my pride wouldn't allow me to admit how epically I'd failed. How badly I'd fucked up.

"When you're ready to tell me what happened, you know where

to find me." With those words, he stood up from his chair, bumped his fist against mine, and strode away.

When the sound of his footsteps faded, I sank back in my seat and finished my coffee.

Who was I now, and what the hell was I going to do with the rest of my life?

For twenty years, moto had been my life, the only thing I knew. My passion. My dream. And now… I just felt so fucking empty.

I had no goals. No dreams. Nothing to work toward. I'd sacrificed so much, had worked so hard, and stayed so focused on my career. I'd sustained injury after injury and had ridden through the pain. But the physical pain paled in comparison to this feeling that I had nothing left to strive for.

Even worse than that, the team owners had questioned my good judgment and character.

All my life, I'd tried to do the right things and adhere to a strict moral code. I'd built my reputation on being honest and loyal with a strong work ethic. A true champion in every sense of the word, reporters had always said.

Whenever I lost, I did it gracefully. I was never the guy who lost his temper or stirred up shit with the competitors. Instead, I went home and licked my wounds in private.

So it was shocking how quickly I'd destroyed years of hard work. What's more, I had nobody to blame except myself.

I slid my ringing phone out of my pocket and stared at the name on the screen. Guilt slammed into me. Fuck. I'd been such an asshole last night. I'd treated her like shit. The last person who deserved it. My sunshine girl.

I answered the call. "Hey. What's up?"

"I know you hate being idle, so I've got a job for you," Mason said, making it sound like he was doing me a big favor.

"What kind of job?"

"You are part owner, in case you forgot. I could use your help this summer."

"With what, exactly?" I'd only invested in the brewing company because Mason and Holden were my oldest friends. The brewery had been their dream, not mine.

"You need something to do this summer. And I could use the extra help."

"Is business doing okay?"

"It would be better if the moto legend was behind the bar." He was joking, but every muscle in my body tensed. I rolled out my shoulders and tried to shake it off.

"Sorry to burst your bubble, I'm a has-been. Putting me behind the bar won't help your business."

"First of all, I don't know what the fuck happened because you're not talking. Second of all, I'm not even going to acknowledge that bullshit coming out of your mouth. Third, you can't see me, but I'm over here playing the world's tiniest violin."

I laughed and scrubbed my hand over my face. You could always count on Mason to call you out on your bullshit.

"Are we done with the pity party yet?"

"We're done. I'll continue the pity party for one after we hang up."

"Shit, man. If you want to talk—"

"Nah. I'm good." I wasn't good, but he didn't need to deal with my shit. Self-pity was for losers, as my dad had drummed into my head all my life. "It'll just take some time to adjust."

"All the more reason to hang out with us for the summer. I know it's not what you want to be doing but have you got something better to do?"

"I can think of a million better things to do."

"Name one."

I propped my booted feet on the railing and stared up at the clouds skittering across the blue sky. Mason didn't need me to work at the brewing company. I'd known him for twenty years, so I knew there had to be something more to this. "What's going on?"

"We hired Quinn for the summer."

"And?"

"And… she'd kill me if she found out I told you this."

I sat up straighter. "Told me what? What's going on? Is she sick again?"

"No, nothing like that. Quinn is okay. We want to try to convince her to stay in Texas."

"I thought she was going to UCLA. She has her heart set on it."

"Yeah, I know. It was one thing when you lived out there. We knew you'd keep an eye on her. Be a friend. Drop everything if she needed you. But now that you're back in Texas, we're nervous as hell about letting her be so far away with nobody to look after her. If something happened to her again… fuck, I don't even want to think about it. Last time, if we hadn't found her in time, she wouldn't even be here, man."

I took a deep breath and let it out as my eyes drifted shut. I could envision Quinn in that hospital bed. So pale. So small. Hooked up to all those tubes and machines that were keeping her alive. Quinn had always been so brave, so optimistic.

You're a fucking asshole, Jesse.

I wanted to punch myself in the face for treating her the way I had. Not just last night. But Christmas Eve. I'd kissed her back. I'd kissed a high school girl. My best friend's little sister. I'd kissed her soft, pouty lips as my hands skimmed over her tight little body, and I'd palmed her ass and pulled her closer.

How fucking low could I sink? What kind of man had I become?

But I still didn't get it. "Nobody wants that. We all want her to be happy and healthy. But she has her heart set on going to Cali." I knew this because she'd told me on Christmas Eve. And every other time I'd seen her before that. "It's her dream."

"I know it is," Mason said quietly. "But she can always go live there after college. She's just too damn young to be on her own right now. And you know what a daydreamer she is. So if she forgets to take her meds or doesn't eat right or take care of herself, her body could fail her again."

Her body was fit, and she was stronger than anyone gave her credit for—not only physically but mentally and emotionally. Quinn knew who she was and what she wanted, and at only eighteen, that was pretty damn impressive.

"What does any of this have to do with me working at the brewery?"

"She loves you, man. She's loved you since she was a kid. Remember how she used to follow you around and tell you she loved you? She was like six or seven with those cartoon hearts in her eyes."

He laughed at the memory, and I usually would have joined

him. But now, I couldn't laugh because I'd thrown it back in Quinn's face. And why? Because I was so fucking bitter and angry that I felt the need to lash out at a girl who didn't have a mean bone in her body. Quinn was good and true. Not a liar or a cheat. Not cunning and manipulative. She had never done a single thing to hurt me.

"Holden and I figured if you spent some time with her this summer, it might be easier to convince her to stay in Texas. You said this was home, and you're planning on staying, right?"

It was home, and I was staying. For now, at least. Until I figured out what to do next. "I don't think this is such a great idea." In fact, I knew it was a shitty idea.

"It's the best we've got. I hate to ask for favors. I know you have a lot of shit to deal with, but if you just do me this one solid, I'll owe you."

"Quinn isn't a little kid anymore. Pretty sure she doesn't even like me that much."

He laughed as if I'd just told him the world's funniest joke. "Yeah, okay. But at the end of the day, you've always been a good friend to her. Like another big brother but not half as annoying."

I took another stab at trying to talk him out of this. "Why don't you just tell her the truth? That you're worried about her, and you want her to stay closer to home?"

"We've told her. Pretty sure that's why she's so hell-bent on leaving. She wants her independence, and she wants to get away from her overprotective brothers. But we only do it because we love her."

I knew that. The Cavanaughs, like the McCallisters, had always adhered to the motto that family comes first. We were loyal to our siblings, we did whatever we could to help each other out, and we were always there for each other. So I understood why he thought this was a good idea even though I knew it wasn't. He loved his sister and would do anything it took to make sure she was okay.

"We don't want to play the guilt card. We want it to be Quinn's decision. I know it's a long shot. But it can't hurt to try."

"If it does work…" Which I highly doubted it would. "Then what? She wants to go to a good college. You can't just fuck that up for her."

"Yeah, about that. This needs to stay between us. But you're family, so I know I can trust you. UT Austin is holding a place for her in the fall. My dad knows someone… Anyway, doesn't matter. Quinn doesn't know about it."

"If she ever found out, she'd be pissed." And I wouldn't blame her.

"I know. That's why it needs to stay between us. For now. So what do you say? Will you help us out?"

I should say no. Or tell him the truth. But I couldn't do either of those things. Everything about this was wrong. I didn't know if anyone would be able to convince Quinn to give up her California dream, and in my heart, I didn't believe it was right to play her like this. Yeah, I got it. She'd been through hell, and she was only eighteen.

But did anyone, even the family who loved her, have the right to fuck with her dreams?

If anything, spending time around me would make her want to leave home even more. But maybe this could be a chance to show her that I was still her friend, that I was still looking out for her. I'd let her know that I was sorry for the words I'd said.

Instead of thwarting her plans, I'd find a way to help make her dreams come true. I'd convince her brothers that Quinn wasn't a kid anymore and that letting her go was the best thing they could do for her.

Even as I devised the plan in my head, I knew it was a shitty one. But I told Mason I'd do whatever I could to help and shoved away the guilt when he thanked me for being a good friend.

Chapter Five

Jesse

The following evening, I parked my bike next to Quinn's cherry red VW Beetle and strode across the field to the taproom. As I rounded the side of the building, she came out the front door, her arms laden with plates. I watched her serve a family of four sitting on the front patio. She was wearing orange neon Nikes with shorts so short they should be fucking illegal.

Quinn was tiny. Five-foot three and all legs. Naïve and innocent with the most brilliant smile I'd ever seen. A honey blond with these big hazel eyes that changed from brown to green, depending on the light.

The night she'd come over to my house on her eighteenth birthday, I hadn't seen it coming.

Before that, I'd always thought of her as Mason's little sister. But that night… there was something different about her. I forgot that she was only eighteen, still in high school. Completely off-limits.

I could blame it on a million things. My confidence had taken a hit, and I'd been in constant pain. My back. My heart. Every bone and muscle in my body. I'd pushed my body to the limits. I rode through the pain, kept a grueling practice schedule in anticipation of the upcoming Supercross season.

At my level, the level I'd been at as an athlete, you couldn't afford to sit back. You couldn't afford to lose your edge because then some guy would come along and steal the title right out from under you. So all my life, I'd strived to win, win, win.

After I broke my back and had my third concussion, I was scared to race again. Although I'd never admitted it, I was afraid that I'd fail.

So I had a lot on my mind.

I hadn't even been thinking about Alessia. Not that night anyway.

When Quinn showed up at my door, her cheeks rosy from the cold, her eyes green and filled with stars—that was how she looked—like she had stars in her eyes. Big dreams and hopes and plans for the future. And yeah, maybe I liked the way she looked at me too. The way she stroked my bruised ego and made me feel like I was the guy of her dreams.

She'd been standing right in front of me, her eyes raised to mine when she said, "There's only one thing I want for my birthday. I have one birthday wish, and maybe you can make it come true."

And I think I knew what she was going to answer even before I posed the question. "What's your wish, Quinn?"

"*Kiss me. I want you to kiss me, Jesse.*"

Now she turned, about to go back inside when she caught me watching her. Before she had a chance to escape, I erased the distance between us in a few long strides and stopped in front of her. "Hey, Sunshine Girl."

"Hey, asshole."

Okay. So Quinn wasn't going to make it easy. I smiled because it made me happy that she didn't put up with my shit. She was better than that. Stronger and fiercer.

When she was a kid, I always told her not to settle for any guy who didn't treat her like a queen. She used to tell me I would be her king. But that was a long time ago.

She planted her hands on her hips. "What are you doing here?"

"Didn't Mason tell you? I'm the new summer bartender. I'll be working in the taproom."

Her eyes widened, and she inhaled a sharp breath. "Oh my God. Just when I thought this summer couldn't get any worse. Now I really can't wait to leave for college."

I winced as she bolted toward the front door like she couldn't get away from me fast enough.

If I'd had any doubts before, I knew it with absolute certainty now. This plan was going to backfire in the worst fucking way.

Later that night, I watched her neon orange Nikes through the side windows as she jogged toward her car. No doubt she thought she was getting away from me. Guess she hadn't seen me leaning against my bike. She rounded the hood and stopped short, her hand going to her heart. "Oh my God. I thought you were in the brewery with Holden."

She beeped the locks and yanked open her car door.

"I'm sorry." I advanced on her until I was standing right behind her.

She paused for a moment, her back to me before she climbed into her car and slammed the door shut. When she rolled down the window, it gave me hope that she'd accept my apology.

"Is this what you're going to do with your life now? Serve beer?"

"Just helping out a friend for a few months."

She shook her head. "You never had any interest in working here. Why now?"

"I'm currently unemployed. Thought it would be a fun way to spend the summer."

"Right. Can't wait for all the fun times," she deadpanned as she turned the key in the ignition.

"I'm sorry for the things I said the other night. They were uncalled for."

"Yeah, well, that's the thing about words, Jesse. Once they're out there, you can't take them back. Besides, you did me a favor. You got me over my schoolgirl crush. It's liberating, actually. So, I *should* be thanking you. You were so right. You're not the guy I thought you were. The Jesse I used to know was never a quitter. And he wasn't a coward or a liar. But people change." She shrugged one shoulder. "Or maybe I never really knew you at all. Maybe I was just in love with the idea of you. A fantasy I'd conjured up in my mind, an ideal version of you that had never really existed."

My jaw clenched, and I took a few deep breaths through my nose.

Fuck, she'd wielded her words like weapons.

She smiled as if she knew they'd hit their mark, and she was happy about it.

Then she drove away and left me standing there, wondering where the hell my sunshine girl had gone.

But I knew. I'd crushed Quinn with my words and actions, and instead of taking it lying down, she came back swinging.

It was going to take more than *I'm sorry* to regain her trust.

But I was determined to win back her faith in me. I needed Quinn to believe in me again.

Chapter Six

Quinn

If my eyes could shoot actual daggers, the brunette would be writhing on the floor in pain, gasping for her last breath.

Oh my God. I did not just think that. But yes, yes, I did.

If she giggled or reached across the bar and touched his arm one more time, I was going to fly across the room and plant my fist in her pretty face.

My hands curled into fists at my sides, ready for action.

Try me, bitch. Push me and see what happens.

Oh my God. There I went again. I needed to get this under

control. Deep breaths, Quinn. You're not a violent person.

But wow, she looked a lot like Alessia Rossi. Was that what he went for? Girls who looked like his ex-girlfriend? This girl looked like a Gianna. Or a Gabriella. Where did she even come from?

And why should I care? I hated Jesse McCallister. So why was my traitorous heart sending my brain all the wrong signals?

"Quinn. What the hell are you doing?" Declan shouted.

I spun around to face him. He threw up his hands, his anger barely contained.

"Do you see this food?" He pointed to the plates sitting on the pass. "It's been sitting there for five minutes."

"Do you see this face?" I pointed to my face. "Ask me if I care."

His eyes narrowed on me. "What's with the attitude?"

My shoulders slumped, my misplaced anger immediately dissolving. "Sorry. I'm just..." I sighed loudly, expelling all my pent-up frustration.

"Are you feeling okay?" His dark brows furrowed, concern replacing his anger as his eyes flitted over my face. "Why don't you take a break. Carly can cover for you."

"I'm okay. I feel fine." He needed more convincing. I held up two fingers. "Scout's honor. I was just... doing that thing I do."

"Daydreaming."

"Yeah." I smiled. Better to let him think that than know the truth.

Sometimes Declan was annoying and quick to anger, but I knew this was important to him, and I didn't want to mess up his beautiful creations by leaving them sitting on the pass for too long. Not like I was being run off my feet like Carly, who had gotten slammed earlier. Unlike me, she was an excellent waitress.

"I'll do better," I promised. Declan gave me a skeptical look and shook his head, resigned to the fact that he was stuck with me for the summer.

I grabbed the plates and delivered them to a couple sitting outside. Unfortunately, they ordered two more beers which meant I had to deal with the asshole behind the bar.

I leaned my hip against the end of the bar and drummed my fingers on the wood while I waited for him to stop flashing his smile at the brunette and fill my order.

When he finally set the two draft beers in front of me, I should have taken them and run, but no, I had to open my big fat mouth. "Sorry to interrupt your social hour."

He gave me a slow, easy grin and leaned his forearm on the bar, getting all up in my space. Even though I wanted to back away, put some distance between us, I forced myself to hold my ground.

Now that I knew how he could flip the switch on his emotions, his smile didn't look as charming as it used to. In fact, I was completely immune to his charms now.

"You don't sound too sorry."

I shrugged one shoulder. "I don't care one way or the other."

"We went to high school together. So we were pretty close."

I bet they were. "Good for you. I'm sure you can rekindle that old flame."

He chuckled, amused, and I wanted to kick myself. Why couldn't I just walk away? Why did I always have to say too much?

I grabbed the beers, spun around, and slammed right into a wall. Oomph. Holden steadied me with his hands on my upper arms. Beer sloshed over the rims of the pint glasses and onto his T-shirt.

"Jesus, Quinn." He released me and caught the bar towel Jesse tossed him, wiping it over his wet T-shirt to sop up the beer before he threw it on the bar. "Watch where you're going."

"Well, I didn't expect you to be creeping up on me, did I?"

He sighed and took the beers out of my hands. "Hey man, two beers on the house."

I turned to look at the guy who had just joined the brunette, his arm wrapped around her shoulders. I recognized him. It was their high school friend, Tanner.

Jesse smirked as he set two new beers in front of me. It took all my self-restraint not to roll my eyes.

I didn't know if it was a coincidence, but this was my third shift this week, and Jesse had worked the same hours as me. If I complained to my brothers, they'd want to know why I had a problem with Jesse. Since I couldn't tell them the truth, I had to keep it to myself.

But the truth was that I hadn't felt a sense of victory after I'd said those words to him last week.

I'd hurt him, I could tell.

And hurting Jesse made my heart hurt too. That was how I knew my words had been empty. No matter how much I tried to convince myself otherwise, I was still in love with him. Probably always would be.

But I needed to protect my fragile heart.

If I put myself out there again, only to get knocked down, the only one who would get hurt was me.

My words might have hit a nerve, but the most they'd done was bruise his ego, not break his heart.

Every Rose

Jesse was waiting for me when I came out of the restroom after my shift. On the way out, I said goodbye to Mason, who practically lived here. I didn't say anything when Jesse walked me to my car. Maybe he wasn't even walking me to my car. His motorcycle was parked right next to it.

"Since you're stuck with me all summer, how about we call a truce?"

Instead of getting into my car and driving away, I leaned against the side of it, facing him, arms crossed over my chest for protection.

Why did I have to love him? Of all the guys in the world, why had I fallen for him? None of my old feelings had gone away either. But I shoved them deep inside and vowed not to let them resurface.

"A truce?"

"Before I said all that shit and before… the kiss… we were friends, right?"

The kiss. So Jesse *did* remember it.

I lifted one shoulder, schooling my features so he couldn't read my expression. "I guess so." To me, we were so much more than just friends, but I guess that's all we'd ever been. *Friends*.

"I know it's not a good excuse, but I've been going through a rough patch. It's been a shitty year. Not a matter of life and death like what you went through."

It was his vulnerability that got to me. Jesse had always been so confident, so sure of his path in life, and so focused on his career that I couldn't imagine how empty his life must feel without it. "There are all different kinds of deaths. The death of a dream is just as bad. And I'm... I'm sorry. I don't know what happened, but I know how much your career meant to you. You wouldn't just walk away without a good reason."

He gave me a small smile, but to me, it looked so sad. "Is California still your dream?'

I nodded. "Yeah. I... still want that. I know my family isn't thrilled. But I just want something of my own, you know. I feel like they've done so much for me, and it feels important that I don't waste this opportunity. I mean, I've been given a second chance at life, and I want to live it fully." That sounded dramatic, but that's how it felt. "And I want them to see that I'm okay. I can take care of myself."

"I know you can." He said it without a moment's hesitation like he genuinely believed that.

That was the thing about Jesse. He always used to believe in me. Never made fun of my dreams or belittled them or me. So that's why it had been even more hurtful that night when he'd say those things to me.

"Do you still want to be a writer?"

I smiled because he remembered. He remembered when I told him that was my dream. "Yeah. It's all I've ever wanted. And to travel and see the world. I still want to do all those things."

"Then I hope all your dreams come true."

He sounded so sincere that I believed him. And the part of me that had always cared about Jesse prompted me to ask, "And what about you?"

"I guess I need some new dreams."

"Yeah, I guess you do. Because a life without dreams is just too sad for words."

There was that smile again. The one that looked so sad. The one that made me want to wrap my arms around him and tell him everything would be okay, that he'd find a new dream, and someday he'd forget all about Alessia Rossi. But I stayed where I was, my arms still crossed over my chest, and made no move to comfort him.

"So… friends?"

"Sure. Friends." But even as I said it, I knew we'd never be friends like we used to be.

Deep down, I knew he was still good. That he was still the guy I'd fallen in love with forever ago. But now, I also knew how easy it would be for him to break my heart.

So I entered this truce, this friendship, a little wiser and a little more jaded than I'd been before that kiss and before that night I'd shown up at his house a week ago only to be crushed by his words and actions.

The only flaw in this plan? Now that I knew the feel of his lips against mine, all I wanted was to kiss him again.

Which probably made me a masochist.

I shouldn't waste any more of my wishes on Jesse. I needed to save them for more important things than just a kiss from a beautiful boy who could be so kind one minute and so cruel the next.

Chapter Seven

Quinn

"Are you sure you'll be okay?" my mom asked for the millionth time. It was Monday morning, my day off, and I'd woken up early to say goodbye.

"I'll be fine." I poured my breakfast smoothie into a tall glass and took a sip, my eyes on her as she slid her laptop into her bag and double-checked that she had everything she needed. My mom was super organized, so I had no doubt that she did.

"No parties while I'm gone. I want the house to still be standing when I get home."

"I'm not Declan."

"Oh. Declan. I prefer to forget his teen years." She sighed. "He's responsible for all the gray hairs on my head."

"You don't have any gray hair." My mom's hair was a lighter shade of blond than mine, and unlike me, she blow-dried it and styled it every morning before she left for work. Today she'd pulled it back in a smooth chignon.

"Because I spent three hundred bucks on highlights. Now don't forget to take your—"

"Mom. I take my pills every single day. Stop worrying. You'll only be gone for a week."

"I know that. But your father is… God." She massaged her temples. "Why he chose this week to be on the West Coast is beyond me."

As if it even mattered whether he was on the West Coast or thirty minutes away in his luxury high-rise in Austin. My dad wasn't around much anymore, so I'd stopped relying on him. Far better to pretend I didn't care than to set myself up for more disappointment.

I had no idea how my parents ran a business together. Neither of them was willing to step down or give up their share of a company they'd built from the ground up almost thirty years ago. They'd started with one farm stand. Then they opened their first store in Austin. And now, they had one hundred and twenty-seven Green Fields Markets across the country. Mind-boggling that they'd accomplished so much, and yet they couldn't even be in the same room together.

"He knew I was meeting with the Northeast regional offices this week. It's been on the calendar for months."

My mother was a workaholic. Always had been. My father had gone so far as to blame his infidelity on her crazy work schedule. He wasn't getting enough attention. Boohoo, you big man-baby.

So I would never hurt my mom's feelings by pointing out that even when she wasn't away on a business trip, she was rarely home. My mom was great, I loved her, and she didn't need that kind of guilt.

"I love you, Mom. I promise not to burn the house down." *I'm not Declan.* "No crazy parties. I'll take my meds every morning and eat healthy. So just trust me, okay?"

"I do, baby. I trust you completely. I just worry."

"I know. But lucky for you, I have three annoying brothers, and two out of three of them worry just as much as you do. Declan, on the other hand, would sell me to the highest bidder."

My mom laughed. "Even big bad Declan loves you." She checked her phone. "Okay. The car is here." She came around the granite counter, her heels clicking on the limestone tiles, and I met her halfway. She pulled me into a hug, then kissed my forehead before she released me and rubbed her fingertips over my forehead to erase the traces of her lipstick kiss.

"Pillow Talk," she said with a smile, referring to the nude pink lipstick she wore. "I'll be home early Sunday evening. We'll have a nice dinner together."

"Sounds good."

After my mom was gone, I carried my smoothie, peanut butter and honey toast and my laptop outside to the patio and set myself up at a round glass table overlooking the pool. The green and white striped awning provided shade from the morning sun.

What I loved most about writing was that I could explore all the different sides of my personality, dig deep inside, and let my imagination run wild.

"Summertime Sadness" by Lana Del Rey piped from the surround sound speakers as I stared at the deep blue swimming pool, the morning sun reflecting off the water, the same shade of blue as Jesse's eyes.

I envisioned a girl floating in the pool. A beauty queen in a red dress, her eyes staring blankly at the night sky, face cast in shadows from a silver moon. Blood trickled from the corner of her mouth.

All around her, a party raged, the music pulsing, bodies gyrating. Nobody noticed that the girl in the swimming pool was dead. Not even the guy with summer sky eyes and disheveled brown hair. He was dancing with a blonde, slow and sensual, his hands skimming over the curves of her body, his perfect lips spewing lies.

"*I love you. It's only ever been you.*"

Embracing my dark side, I spun a tale of lethal love. My fingers flew across the keyboard, and words filled up the blank pages as I completely lost myself in the story.

Later that evening, I pulled over in front of the house next to Evie's and sent her a text. Then peered through the windshield at her house. What little of it I could see beyond the overgrown bushes and scrubby trees. The paint, once white, was peeling away to expose the gray underneath, the front porch sagging under the weight of an old sofa, the chain-link fence around her property rusting.

I wanted to whisk her away from this world and give her the

kind of life she deserved. But Evie was too proud to accept help, and the one time I had offered to give her money, she refused to speak to me for two weeks. She forbade me to tell my parents or anyone else about the way she lived. It was part of our friendship pact, and if I didn't honor her wish, I'd risk losing Evie's friendship.

Rock meet hard place.

A few minutes later, she sauntered toward my car in cut-offs and a thin-strapped black tank top. The wedge sandals on her feet accentuated her mile-long legs.

Evie was gorgeous. Hands-down the most beautiful girl I'd ever seen in real life. Waves of raven black hair, olive skin, and jade green eyes slanted like a cat's. We'd been best friends since sixth grade when she transferred to my middle school. I'd thought she was the coolest girl in the world and made it my mission to befriend her. At first, she'd kept me at arms-length, but as the years went on, she started to trust me enough to let me in, and I'd learned that distancing herself was a self-preservation tactic.

Too many people in Evie's life had fucked her over and let her down. It took a lot for her to trust someone.

She slid into the passenger seat and heaved a weary sigh as she pulled the door shut. "Don't drive past the house. My mom might throw shit at your car again."

Not needing to be told twice and not wanting to deal with her psycho mom's tantrums, I turned the car around and drove in the opposite direction, avoiding the potholes in the road as I took her away from her shitty run-down house in the shitty run-down neighborhood.

To say that we lived in different worlds was a massive

understatement.

Her mom made her life a living hell, so I didn't get to see her as much as I would like. When Evie wasn't working, she looked after her baby sister, Wren, who was only two years old. So whenever she got some free time, I wanted to make her life just a little bit better. But I knew her limits, and I could only push them so far.

"We're going for tacos," I told her a little while later as we cruised the winding roads with the summer breeze whipping our hair around, music blasting from the speakers. It was the golden hour, the limestone cliffs and rolling green hills bathed in a warm glow. It made me wish I was a cinematographer to capture this on film and use it as a backdrop for our life story.

"And then we're going to hang out at the pool and do each other's nails, watch movies and eat ice cream."

"Sounds like heaven. Have I told you lately that I love you?"

"It's been a while. I was starting to worry that the honeymoon was over."

She laughed. "Never. You're my one true love." She kicked off her shoes and planted her bare feet on the dash, her right arm hanging out the window to capture the warm breeze. Her toenails were painted black cherry, like her lips.

"So, what's been going on with you?" she asked. "I feel like we haven't talked in ages. Tell me everything."

I'd called Evie after the Jesse incident, but she was dealing with her mom's junkie boyfriend and trying to keep him away from Wren. So I hadn't even told her what happened. Evie had real-life problems, the kind of problems I'd never had to deal with. She'd been forced to grow up faster and become tougher than I'd ever had to be.

On the way to the taco place, I filled her in on the Jesse drama. When I finished talking, she smacked my arm.

"Ow. What was that for?"

"What's wrong with you? Why didn't you tell me?" She sounded hurt. As if I'd purposefully kept something important from her.

"You were dealing with—"

"I'm always dealing with something, Quinn. But that's no excuse. You need to tell me shit like that. I'm your best friend."

"I know you are. That's why I haven't told anyone else."

"Next time something important happens in your life, don't keep it to yourself." She chewed on her lip, thinking about the story I'd told her. "What a fucking asshole. How could he say those things to you?"

She was angry on my behalf, and I loved her for that. Evie was a fierce ally, and trust me, you didn't want to get on her bad side. She'd rain holy terror on anyone who hurt the people she cared about. "I don't know. He wasn't himself. Or maybe he has another side to him that I'd never gotten to see before."

"You always see the best in people. Even when they don't deserve it."

I got the feeling she wasn't only talking about Jesse.

Evie thought she was terrible because of some of the things she'd done in her life, but I thought she was a warrior. A survivor who did whatever was necessary to protect herself and Wren. In my eyes, there was nothing bad about Evie except for the life she'd been thrust into.

"I don't know what to think. Supposedly, we're friends again, but now that I saw another side of him, I'm scared to let him in again."

"*Let him in again*? Are you insane? One strike, he's out." She sliced her hand across her neck to punctuate her words. "He doesn't deserve you. Not after that shit he pulled on you. We need to find you someone new. You've wasted too many years obsessing over that loser."

I opened my mouth to protest, to tell her that Jesse wasn't a loser and that I didn't obsess over him, but then I shut it instead. She was the only one who knew how I felt about him, and I guess it was a borderline obsession. I'm sure if I told a shrink, they'd call it unhealthy. Good thing I only confided in Evie.

Maybe she was right. Maybe I needed a distraction—a summer fling. I almost laughed at the thought. Was I even capable of having a fling?

"I think you need someone too."

"No, thank you. Been there, done that."

"They're not all like Trevor," I said, referring to her ex. "There are plenty of good guys out there."

"Sure there are."

My eyes zeroed in on Ridge as I parked in front of the taco place, just a shack on the side of the road that served the best tacos I'd ever eaten.

Ridge and his friend Walker were sitting at one of the picnic tables under the trees. When we got out of the car, Evie didn't even glance their way. Maybe she hadn't seen them. But Ridge saw Evie. His eyes tracked her every move, this intense, thoughtful expression on his face that I'd never seen on him before. The way Ridge looked at Evie wasn't like the way other guys did.

It felt like he saw beyond the gorgeous face and the hot body and recognized that she was someone special. And I didn't think he looked at other girls that way.

Ridge and I weren't total strangers now. Since he'd started working for my brothers, I saw him around. We made small talk, joked around a little. Neither of us was attracted to the other, so that made it easy. He wasn't my type, and I wasn't his. Don't get me wrong. Ridge was gorgeous. But I didn't think I could handle a guy like Ridge. He was just too much of everything. He looked like a Viking and made me feel like a shrimp when I stood next to him. The guy had to be at least six-four. Big hands that could easily palm a football. Broad, broad shoulders. Abs for days. And then there was his reputation. But I doubt that Ridge cared what people said about him.

If anyone could handle a guy like Ridge, it was Evie.

Walker turned in his seat to see who Ridge was looking at, a slow smile forming on his face like he was let in on a secret.

Okay, that was encouraging. This plan could work. Maybe Ridge just needed to find the right girl, and maybe he and Evie would be perfect for each other.

As luck would have it, all the picnic tables were full when we carried our food outside. So, without consulting Evie, I made a beeline for Ridge and Walker. I wouldn't usually be so ballsy by barging in on two guys I barely knew, much less two popular football players, but I was doing this for Evie, so that made me braver.

Evie grabbed my arm to stop me. "What are you doing?"

"Just finding a place to sit." I smiled at her, the picture of innocence.

"Let's just take the food home."

"I'd rather eat here."

Her brows creased like she was trying to figure out my ulterior motive. Then her gaze drifted to the guys, and when it returned to me, her lips tugged into a devious smile. "Good plan. Walker seems okay. Not a total douche. He's kind of cute too. He'd be a good starter boyfriend. I'll be your wingman."

I nearly laughed in her face. I had no interest in Walker, but okay, I'd go with it. "You're too good to me."

"What are friends for? I'll take one for the team and deal with the asshole."

By asshole, I assumed she was talking about Ridge. Thinking she was doing me a favor, Evie led the charge. Two seconds later, we were seated at the picnic table with Ridge next to Evie and Walker next to me. It couldn't have worked out more perfectly if I'd planned it.

"Don't get any ideas," Evie told Ridge. "We just needed a place to sit."

Ridge gave her a slow, easy grin. "Whatever you say." He grabbed her drink and took a sip through the straw.

"What are you doing? That's my drink. Get your filthy lips off my straw."

He handed it back, not the least bit apologetic. "Just checking to see if it was a Cherry Cola, *Cherry*."

Evie's eyes widened, and her jaw dropped. "You're... no." She shook her head, her voice faint. "No way. It can't be you…"

Ridge winked at her. "Been in Dallas lately, Cherry Bomb?"

"Oh my God," Evie said under her breath. I'd never seen her this frazzled before, and I had no idea what was going on.

I looked at Walker, thinking he might have some insight. He was cute and kind of hot, with short dark hair and warm brown eyes, so I was kind of disappointed when his nearness didn't make my pulse race. Dammit.

But right now, I was more curious about whatever was happening between Evie and Ridge. "Do you know what's going on?"

Walker laughed and shook his head. "No clue." He gave me a conspiratorial wink. "But I'm here for it. I can't wait to see how this thing plays out."

Neither could I.

Chapter Eight

Jesse

Quinn wasn't answering her phone. My calls went straight to voice mail, and my texts went unseen. So I was just going to check on her, make sure she was okay like a big brother would do. That was what I kept telling myself as I rode over to her house at eleven o'clock on Friday night. We'd worked three shifts together this week, but she'd barely spoken to me. So much for our truce.

As I got closer, I saw that the brick courtyard in front of her house was jam-packed with cars.

The fuck? Quinn wasn't a party girl, but this sure as hell looked like a party.

I parked behind a black pickup truck that looked familiar. It looked a hell of a lot like Brody's old truck that he'd given to Ridge.

Since when did Quinn hang out with my cousin? Last I'd heard, they ran in different circles and barely knew each other.

Was it any of my business who she hung out with? I rubbed the back of my neck, debating.

I'd always been cool with Ridge, but I knew what he was like. A lot like his older brother Brody had been at eighteen. Before I could stop myself, I strode to her front door and rang the bell.

Minutes later, the door swung open, music blasting from inside, and there was Ridge. Shirtless and barefoot in black swim trunks, his longish hair still wet from swimming.

"Well, shit. Didn't expect to see you." He held up his fist and bumped it against mine. "What are you doing here, bro?"

"I could ask you the same question."

"Just chillin'. This house is sick, man."

Couldn't deny that. The Cavanaugh house was 'sick.' It looked like a Tuscan villa, stone with archways and a terracotta roof. But I was more interested in his definition of 'just chillin'.' "Are you in charge of this party?"

He rubbed his hand over his washboard abs. Ridge never missed an opportunity to display his bare torso. "You could say that. We're keeping it low-key. Nobody gets in without getting through me first. Quinn's cool, and I don't need any aggro from her brothers."

That was for damn sure. Thanks to me vouching for Ridge, Quinn's brothers had given him a job. If he fucked this up, he'd lose it.

"Where is she?" I asked, brushing past him.

"Dunno. The pool, maybe."

It wasn't exactly a rager, but about twenty people were hanging out in the kitchen and around the pool. Beer cans, vodka bottles, and mixers littered the countertops, and a girl with long dark hair was mixing blender drinks at the island. I'd met her a couple of times before. Quinn's friend, Evie. She didn't notice me because Ridge came up behind her and squeezed her ass. She spun around and smacked his bare chest. I didn't hang around to see what happened next. I was just relieved he hadn't gone after Quinn. Because then we'd have a problem.

I stopped in front of the open French doors, and my eyes zeroed in on the tiny blonde, effectively blocking out everyone around her. Her hair flew around her face, her arms in the air, hips swiveling to the beat of the music. For a few moments, I just stood there, hypnotized, watching her dance.

Fuck, she was beautiful like this. Barefoot in a thin white tank top and tiny orange terry cloth shorts. Quinn was built like a ballerina. Flat stomach, small breasts, toned legs.

When she lost her balance and stumbled, I strode toward her. The guy she was with—I hadn't even noticed him before—caught her in his arms and pulled her against his chest. She looked up at him, laughing, and then his lips met hers, and she wrapped her arms around his neck.

My hands clenched into fists at my sides.

Motherfucker was kissing her. Touching her. *My* sunshine girl.

In two seconds flat, I was at her side and pulling her away from him.

"Hey. The fuck are you doing?" The dude was pissed. Too fucking bad.

Ignoring him, I grabbed Quinn's hand and dragged her away from the party.

"What are you doing?" she asked as I strode across the kitchen with her in tow, her shorter legs having to jog a little to keep up with me. She tried to yank her hand out of mine, but I kept it firmly clasped. Not happening.

We stopped in a dimly lit terracotta-tiled hallway at the bottom of the staircase, and she pressed her back against the wall and crossed her arms.

I planted a hand on either side of her head, caging her in, and leaned in close. "What do you think you're doing?"

The real question was, *What the fuck was I doing*?

She looked up at me from under her long dark lashes, with those big hazel eyes of hers. "I'm having fun. Just being a teenager. Because that's all I am. Right, Jesse? A sheltered girl who couldn't *possibly* understand anything about the real world."

She swiped her tongue over her pouty lips.

Lips that had just been kissing someone else.

Tempting lips that beckoned and teased. I wanted to crush my mouth against hers, bite and suck on that plump bottom lip. Keep kissing her until I sucked all the oxygen from her lungs, and her lips were so swollen and bruised, the memory of that other kiss would be forgotten.

My gaze lowered to her tank top, the outline of a purple bikini top visible underneath, her chest rapidly rising and falling on each breath as if she'd just finished a 200-meter dash. Then up to her mouth again. She tugged her bottom lip between her straight white teeth, and I didn't know if it was a calculated move, but it was fucking hot.

I took deep breaths through my nose, trying to get my body in check, and inhaled the scent of grapefruit. Quinn wasn't allowed to eat grapefruit, so she chose to wear it on her skin instead.

The forbidden fruit was always the sweetest, wasn't it?

"You let someone else kiss you." I lifted my hand to her face and swept away a lock of honey blonde hair, tucking it behind her ear. The backs of my fingers brushed over her jawline and traced the curve of her cheekbone.

So young, so innocent, so fucking beautiful.

"What's it to you, *friend*?"

Cupping her chin in my hand, I slowly dragged my thumb over her pink, pouty lips and wiped away all traces of that other guy's mouth on hers.

Her eyes drifted shut, and a small breath escaped her lips as my hand moved to the side of her neck. I could feel her pulse thrumming beneath my fingertips. I leaned in closer, close enough that her chest heaved against mine, her tits crushed against my hard chest.

"Did you enjoy it? Did you enjoy that kiss?" I asked, my voice low and husky. I wrapped my other hand around her hip and made lazy circles with my thumb on the soft skin just above the waistband of her shorts.

I shouldn't have been touching her like this.

I shouldn't have been jealous of an eighteen-year-old guy for kissing a girl who wasn't mine. But I couldn't fucking stand the thought of anyone else touching her. Kissing those bee-stung lips. Watching her dance like she was putting on a private show just for him.

"What are you doing here, Jesse?" Her voice no louder than a whisper as my fingers tangled in her soft, silky hair. Just as if I had any right to be doing that. "Why are you here?" she asked again.

I wanted to tell her that I came over to see her. That my whole fucking world had fallen apart, and I felt hollowed out and empty. I wanted to tell her that I'd taken my bike to the track every morning this week and raced against a stopwatch just to prove to myself that I could still do it. But every fucking time, I'd failed to get even close to what I used to be able to do.

For the past two days, after I finished a thirty-minute moto, I had arm pump. I'd never had that before. It was this mysterious ailment that happens to motocross racers sometimes. When your arms go numb, and they feel like concrete blocks and fly right off the grips.

And I wanted to tell her that when I saw her with another guy, it felt like she was cheating on me. Like the sight of her dancing and kissing another guy was a betrayal. Which made zero fucking sense.

So I didn't say any of that.

"You didn't answer my question. Did you enjoy kissing him?"

Her eyes met mine, and they flared with defiance. "Yes. *He* kissed me, and I kissed him back. Do you want to kiss me, Jesse?" She taunted, sweeping her tongue over her lips. "Or did you come over here to get laid? At least be honest about your intentions."

When had Quinn become so bold? So brazen? She was giving me a dose of my own medicine. "You want honesty?"

She nodded, clamping her lip between her teeth again.

"You were right. I kissed you back. I remember every little detail of that kiss. I remember the feel of your lips against mine. Pillow soft. You tasted edible, like honey and brown sugar from the lip gloss you wore that night. And I remember the way your tongue darted out to take a small taste of me, and I let you in."

Sliding my hand around to the small of her back, I skimmed it over the curve of her ass and pulled her against me. "And you wrapped your arms around my neck."

As if on cue, she lifted her arms and wrapped them around my neck. I stared down at her upturned face, her pert little nose, and big eyes and lush lips, her apricot skin flushed a pretty pink, then dipped my head and hovered there, our lips a mere fraction of an inch apart but not touching.

Her lips parted, and her soft breath mingled with mine. It smelled sweet, like fruity summertime cocktails. With her arms still looped around my neck, she tugged on the ends of my hair like she was giving me permission to make the next move.

I could kiss her right now, and she'd probably let me.

"And I kissed you back." I dropped my forehead against hers, my fingers biting into the soft flesh of her ass. A reprimand for grinding her little body against mine. For making me get hard for her. For making me want her in a way I shouldn't. "But then I remembered that you were only eighteen, and you were still in high school. My best friend's little sister."

"So you pushed me away."

I released her and took a step back, putting some distance between us. She was still eighteen, and I was twenty-seven, old enough to know better.

She was still my closest friends' little sister, the girl we'd always tried to protect. The girl they'd entrusted me to protect from guys like me. Guys who were looking for a sunshine girl to make their world a little brighter. Guys who would take advantage of her naivety and innocence to stroke their bruised ego and make them feel like they weren't total losers.

"Because you felt guilty?" She couldn't meet my eyes.

"Yes."

"And now?" She pressed her body against the sunflower-yellow wall behind her. Her palms pressed flat against it, her fingers curled, gripping the wall as if she was fighting the urge to reach out and touch me.

"And now... I don't want you kissing anyone else."

"Why not?"

"Because I don't fucking like it," I growled.

She flinched a little, her eyes wide. I carved my hand through my hair and tried to get myself under control.

Fuck. I really was an asshole.

"I'm not yours, Jesse. So I can *kiss* anyone I want to. It's my body to do what I want with." She lifted her chin, her eyes defiant and her words taunting. "So I don't even have to stop at kissing."

My jaw clenched, and I took a few breaths through my nose. "You're going to give it away to some high school asshole?"

"Who's the asshole here?" she accused. "You might have been my first kiss, but I'm not saving any of my other firsts for you."

My eyes narrowed on her. "Is that right? And you think that guy has the first fucking clue how to make you—"

"Quinn? Are you okay?"

She dragged her gaze away from me to the guy standing at the end of the hallway—short dark hair, a few inches shorter than Ridge, and built like a linebacker. I knew who he was. Austin Armacost's nephew, Walker. Ridge's best friend. That's who she'd been kissing.

"Yeah, it's all good." She turned her bright smile on for Walker, a smile she hadn't bestowed on me in far too long. "Jesse was just checking up on me. He's good friends with my brothers. Just give me a minute, okay?"

He hesitated a moment, his gaze darting to me then back to her as if trying to determine whether she was in danger. She gave him an encouraging smile, letting him know she was okay. Reluctantly, he nodded. "Yeah. Sure."

When he was gone, she refocused on me. "I'm being rude. He's a good guy." She raised her chin and stabbed her index finger at me. "And *you* need to go."

I had no intention of going anywhere. I crossed my arms over my chest and widened my stance, pinning her with my gaze. "How well do you know him?"

She shrugged. "What does it matter? We're just having some fun. It's harmless. And it's safe."

"Safe?" I laughed at her naivety in believing a horny eighteen-year-old who looked at her like she was an ice cream sundae with a cherry on top was *safe*. "You think he's safe?"

"Yes." She looked me right in the eye. "He doesn't have the power to break my heart. And not that you deserve an explanation, but just so we're clear… I'm saving myself for someone who treats me like a queen. And that's. Not. You."

Having delivered her message, she turned and walked away, and this time, I let her go. Fuck, that hurt.

Quinn was stronger than she looked. Braver than she knew. What was braver than admitting that *he* didn't have the power to break her heart which implied that *I* did? Nothing. And maybe it was the alcohol that had made her so honest, but I didn't think so. She was just being Quinn. And Quinn had always been honest.

As I strode to the front door, after yet another failed attempt to pick up the pieces of my life, someone grabbed my arm to stop me. I turned to look at Quinn's friend, Evie.

She poked her finger at my chest and narrowed her eyes on me. "If you ever hurt my friend again, I'll cut off your dick, spit-roast it, and force-feed it to you until you're gagging on it."

Jesus Christ.

I needed to get my act together. Losing my shit over a girl who was barely out of high school was not cool. Not to mention getting told off by her best friend.

It was official. I had reached an all-time low.

But her friend's loyalty put a smile on my face. Evie, of course, mistook it for arrogance.

"You think that's funny?"

I shook my head. "No. Not at all. I think you're a good friend. And nobody deserves a good friend more than Quinn."

"You get as good as you give," she threw out before she turned and sauntered away.

She was wrong about that, but I didn't bother setting her straight.

At eighteen, I used to believe the same thing.

Chapter Nine

Quinn

On Sunday morning, I drove to the track. I didn't know what had compelled me to come here this morning. Last week at work, I overheard Jesse telling Mason he did moto laps every morning against a stopwatch. So maybe I just wanted to see for myself.

As if watching him ride would help me figure out who this other Jesse was.

Why should it even matter?

I rubbed my lips together, remembering the feel of his thumb brushing over them on Friday night. The tremors that had gone through my body, making it quiver and sing. His rough, calloused thumb gliding over my skin. The almost kiss, when our lips had been so close, and he told me all the things I'd wanted to hear the night I went to see him.

Even though he'd made me angry on Friday night, I couldn't deny the thrill that had shot through me. He'd been jealous.

His touch had ignited my body in ways that Walker's kisses never could. Not that Walker was a bad kisser. He wasn't. It had been nice kissing someone who wanted to kiss me. A part of me had hoped and prayed that Walker's kisses would erase the memory of Jesse. But they hadn't.

The party had been a bust. Thirty minutes after Jesse left, Holden and Mason had turned up and shut it down. Then they'd lectured me about the perils of underage drinking. As if they'd never done it when they were my age.

But I couldn't stay mad at them. My brothers were just looking out for me and trying to keep me healthy. I knew I wasn't supposed to drink alcohol. Not excessively, anyway. It weakened the immune system. I was on a daily cocktail of immunosuppressants and had to watch my diet. There was a whole list of foods I wasn't even allowed to eat.

My brothers agreed not to tell Mom as long as I promised to stay away from alcohol. It was an easy promise to make. I could live without it, not to mention the headache and nausea I woke up with on Saturday morning.

I got off easy.

Ridge, however, was still on shaky ground. He'd accepted full blame and told my brothers that the party had been his idea. Just as if he'd forced me into doing something I didn't want. I'd jumped to his defense and told my brothers the truth. The party had been my idea. My house, my responsibility, and no one else's. After my brothers had kicked everyone else out, Ridge stayed behind to clean up. He did such a thorough job it was like the party had never happened.

For now, Ridge still had a job, and I'd fight tooth and nail to make sure it stayed that way. None of what happened on Friday night had been his fault.

I walked around the side of the garage that held all the rental bikes and waved hello to Mick. He used to coach Jesse and my brothers when they were kids. Until Jesse had gotten so much better than the other racers and needed a new coach. Mick had coached me when I was eight and begged my parents to let me do what my brothers did, ride dirt bikes just like the boys. My brothers said I wasn't terrible at it, but I think we all knew that was a lie.

As soon as I entered my first race, I was done. I officially hated it.

One year later, I was diagnosed with kidney dysplasia, which explained why I'd felt so tired and so sick all the time. But I was so determined to be as strong and healthy as my brothers that I tried to hide it from my parents.

"Hey, Mick." I stopped in front of him.

"Hey, doll. Haven't seen you around in a while. How've you been?"

"It's all good." My gaze wandered to the track. We'd had rain last night, so the ground was muddy with a lot of ruts in the turns. It was still early, and the track was empty, but I knew Jesse was here. The gunmetal gray Silverado that he used to haul his bike was parked right out front.

"Are you here to watch Jesse?" he guessed, because what else would I be doing at eight o'clock in the morning with a thermos of herbal tea in my hand.

I nodded. "Yeah. I just... I haven't seen him ride in a while. I miss watching him." I used to love watching Jesse ride. He rode standing up, which was so hard to do.

"How's he doing?"

Mick stroked his beard. It matched the red hair on his head, shot through with gray now. "He's better than anyone else who practices here."

That went without saying. Most of the guys who practiced here were amateur racers. There were a couple of former pros, but they'd retired from the sport years ago and weren't up to a competitive standard anymore. "But?"

"He's holding back. And Jesse was never one to hold back. Something is blocking him." Mick tapped his temple. "Pretty sure it's all up here."

"He's too much in his head, you mean?"

"I think so, yeah." He shook his head. "But that's not an easy fix."

"Do you mind if I hang out and watch?"

"Be my guest. I've got some work to do. See you later."

I walked over to the bleachers and climbed to the top for a better view. A few minutes later, I heard the quiet roar of a dirt bike as Jesse came into view from behind the trees. I watched him fly up and over a jump, his bike parallel with the ground to shave off a few seconds before his tires hit the dirt.

When he finished his final lap, I climbed down the stairs and waited for him at the bottom.

He stopped a few feet away from me and climbed off his bike, setting it in a folding metal stand to keep it upright. His dirt bike was splattered with mud, as were his moto boots and trousers.

He took off his goggles and helmet, then peeled off his gloves and ran a hand through his hair. Sweat dripped down his face, and he wiped it on the back of his arm as I came to stand in front of him.

The old Jesse used to come back from a ride with a big smile on his face, like nothing in the world brought him more joy than riding. But today, Jesse's face looked grim, his lips pressed into a firm, straight line.

"Hey," I said.

"Hey." His eyes roamed over me from head to toe, taking in my retro black and white Good Vibes T-shirt with an orange and yellow rainbow and white denim mini with a frayed hem before returning to my face.

He looked exhausted. Motocross was a demanding sport, especially in the Texas heat, but still, it bothered me that doing laps had sapped all his energy.

"What are you doing here?"

It was starting to feel like we asked each other that question every time we saw each other. "I wanted to see you ride." I nudged the toe of his boot with the toe of my Nike. Black with fluorescent coral, yellow and teal. Jesse had given them to me for my seventeenth birthday.

"When did it stop being fun for you?"

"Why would you ask that?"

"Because it's obvious."

He squinted at something over my shoulder, then his gaze

returned to me and dipped to the sterling silver heart, the charm that looked like a bean, and the medical spiral on a silver chain I always wore around my neck.

I tucked the necklace inside the collar of my T-shirt.

"What happened to you, Jesse?" Instead of answering, he grabbed a water bottle that he'd left on the bleachers and drank his fill, then wiped his mouth with the back of his arm. He chewed on the corner of his lip, and even though I was desperate for information and that's why I was here, I couldn't stop staring at his face. The sexy way he was chewing on the corner of his lip while he debated whether he should tell me what was going on with him. He grabbed the back of his neck and studied my face for a moment.

I smiled, hoping it would encourage him to talk.

Finally, he gave me a slight nod as if he'd made up his mind and was ready to share. "Do you know who Nate Hutchins is?"

"Sure. He was your teammate. And your friend." Although I didn't know why I used the word friend. They were rivals, and Nate won the Supercross title this year.

And now that he'd mentioned Nate, I was reminded of another side to Jesse. Despite always appearing to be laidback and easygoing, Jesse was highly competitive. He *hated* to lose. Thinking back, that had always been his tragic flaw. He always had to be the best, and nothing less would suffice.

"The team appointed me the leader. That pissed Nate off. He was tired of coming in second. Last summer, we were battling for the championship. He wanted to steal it from me. He wanted to steal fucking *everything* from me."

"Everything?" I was playing dumb. I had a feeling he was

talking about Alessia, but I wasn't supposed to know that she'd cheated on him.

Was she the *everything* he was referring to?

"Ever since I was sixteen, I'd been focused on riding, training, and racing. That was the year my dad asked if I was planning to go to college or if I was going to make a career of it. I chose my sport. And luckily, it paid off. On the flip side, I knew that I'd have to make it in motocross because I wouldn't have a college degree or anything else to fall back on."

"So it was a lot of pressure."

He nodded. "Yeah."

I was eager to get to the heart of the story, but I waited for him to continue, stupidly happy that he was confiding in me.

"When you reach the top, everyone expects you to keep winning. Your team. Your fans. Your sponsors. Anything less than number one feels like a failure. And the competition got so fucking intense." His jaw clenched. "But Nate... he was my biggest competitor, and he was hungry for a win." He shook his head and laughed harshly. "It was the last race of the season when it all came to a head. I'd just bought a ring. I was planning to propose to Alessia after I won the championship."

My heart sank. Jesse was going to propose to Alessia. He'd even bought a ring. How had he planned to do it? Would he have gone down on one knee? Would it have been intimate and romantic, or would he have made a grand gesture in front of his fans on national television? I was so stuck on the thought of him proposing that I missed some of what he was saying.

"... and I knew. I fucking knew. She was cheating on me."

Oh crap. I'd missed something important, but I couldn't ask him to rewind and repeat his words.

"With Nate? Alessia cheated on you with Nate?"

He nodded.

Oh my God.

How dare she do that to Jesse? He'd been so good to her. He had loved her. I remembered thinking that he would have done anything for her. And I'd been so envious. She'd had something so good, and she took it for granted. No, worse than that. She'd betrayed him.

"And you had no idea?"

"None." He scrubbed his hand over his face. "I'm usually good at blocking out all the noise and getting into the right headspace before a race, but that day I just couldn't focus. I couldn't get the vision out of my head. Of the two of them together. As soon as the gates dropped, I had only one thing on my mind. To beat Nate Hutchins. And fucking Nate, he cut into my line on the face of a jump."

Another rider had crashed into him from behind. I watched that race. I had watched him lying on the ground, so still and unmoving, and for a few long moments, I'd feared the worst. I'd barely been breathing. My heart had been in my throat, and I'd been frantic, continually updating social media until I found out he was okay.

"And Alessia, she rode in the ambulance with me, and she was crying. No idea why the fuck she was crying." He rubbed his hand over his heart like it hurt too much to talk about, even now.

A stab of pain shot straight to my heart at the expression on his face. He was devastated. All these months later and he was still devastated over losing her. I couldn't even understand how or why he could have loved her, but he had loved her enough to want to marry her. And she'd betrayed him in the worst way possible. Had broken his heart. It had shattered his confidence to the point where he wasn't the same rider he used to be.

Of all the guys Alessia could have been with, she'd chosen another rider. Not just another rider. Jesse's nemesis.

Jesse had always put a premium on loyalty. He was loyal to his friends, to his family, to the woman he loved. So this kind of betrayal would have shaken him to the core. And now that I'd heard the story—I didn't even think it was the whole story—I was starting to understand why he seemed so different.

What happened to him would have made anyone bitter and angry. And now, even though he'd retired, it looked like he was trying to prove something to himself. He was trying to get back to being the rider he was before, but he couldn't get in the right headspace, which had to be so frustrating for a guy like Jesse who was used to competing at the highest levels. Not just competing. *Winning*.

I wasn't a professional athlete, but even I knew if your mental game wasn't strong, you'd already lost before you left the starting gate.

"Fuck him." My voice was hard and cold, my body vibrating with anger. "And fuck her."

Jesse's eyes widened, and then a laugh burst out of him. "Holy shit." He scrubbed his hand over his face. "I've never heard you curse."

I shrugged one shoulder. "I save special words for special occasions."

"And you think this is a special occasion?"

"Yes. I also think your ex-girlfriend is a bitch."

He crossed his arms over his chest and tilted his head. "Is that right?"

"That's right. I always did. But I kept it to myself."

"Why did you keep it to yourself?"

"Because you loved her. And I thought that if you loved her, she had to have some redeeming qualities. Deep down. *Really* deep."

He laughed softly. "The first time I met her, I thought, 'This is it. She's the one for me. I've met the girl of my dreams.'"

Jealousy reared its ugly head. Jesse would never think that way about me. I'd never be the girl of his dreams, the only one for him. And I shouldn't care, and it shouldn't hurt to hear those words, but when it came to Jesse, I was still a lovesick fool.

Despite giving me no reason to care what he did or what he was going through, I couldn't stop myself from caring about him.

"Obviously, I know better now," he said.

Love really does make people blind.

I wondered what had hurt him more. The fact that Alessia had cheated on him or that his teammate had wanted to win so badly that he was willing to do whatever it took to eliminate the competition.

"Good. Then don't let her fuck with your head anymore."

He smiled, and it was genuine, just like the old Jesse used to smile. And then he was laughing, and I didn't know why he was even laughing, but I joined him, and it felt good. Easy. Carefree.

"What are you doing later, Sunshine Girl?"

I considered lying and telling him I was wide open and had no plans. But I didn't want to lie to him or rearrange my life for him on the off chance he wanted to spend time with me. Besides, I was looking forward to hanging out with Evie and Wren. "Evie is bringing her little sister over. We're going to take her in the pool. And my mom's coming home this evening, so we're doing dinner and a movie."

"Shit. It's Sunday, isn't it?" He grimaced. "I promised I'd be at the family dinner."

"That should be fun. You'll get to spend time with your niece and nephews."

"Yeah," he said with a smile. "They're cool."

"Will Ridge be there?"

His eyes narrowed. "Have you got a thing for my cousin?"

I shrugged. "I thought I'd make my rounds through the football team before I head to Cali," I teased. "Get a few notches in my bedpost."

He grabbed my hand and held it over his heart. "Don't play with my heart." He was joking, or at least it sounded like he was.

I smacked his chest with my free hand, the memory of how he'd played me on Friday night running through my head. "Stop playing with mine."

"I'm not." He released my hand. "I won't."

I raised my brows, skeptical, but he ignored it.

"I'd like to spend more time with you before you head to college. Just hanging out. As friends," he added, emphasizing friends.

I considered his words. Maybe we could make this work. Maybe we really could be friends. "Hanging out and doing what?"

"You were always asking for a ride on my motorcycle... Still interested?"

My eyes widened, and I clapped my hands together. Jesse laughed. I probably looked like a kid, but at this point, I didn't care anymore. "You'll take me on the back of your bike? Really?"

"Mmhmm. You just have to promise to hold on tight. If anything happened to you, your brothers would kill me. And I'd never forgive myself."

"I don't want your guilt on my hands. Or my brothers' wrath. I promise I'll hold on tight." Like that was such a hardship.

"How's tomorrow?"

The brewing company was closed on Mondays, so I had the day free. But I tried to hide my excitement at the thought of spending the day with Jesse.

I gave him a casual little shrug and kept my tone breezy. He didn't need to know that my stomach was doing somersaults. "Tomorrow works for me."

Chapter Ten

Jesse

"You're late," my dad grumbled when I stepped onto the back porch of our stone and timber farmhouse and joined my family. They were already seated at the long oak table, casserole dishes filled with Cajun food down the middle of it, and by the looks of it, halfway done with dinner.

I put my hands on my mom's shoulders and leaned down to kiss her on the cheek. "Sorry I'm late."

She patted my hand. "I'm just happy you're here."

I greeted my family—my dad at the opposite end of the table, Jude and Lila across from Brody and Shiloh—and got a chorus of hellos. The newest addition to our family, my niece, Gracie, was in Jude's arms, her head resting on his shoulder while he ate with his free hand. She was four months old with silky, dark hair and rosy cheeks. So fucking cute and tiny.

"She's asleep, Jude," Lila stood from the table and reached for her daughter. "Let me put her in her—"

"I'm good." He put his hand on Lila's shoulder and pushed her back down in her seat. "Eat your dinner. My baby girl's happy right where she is."

Lila rolled her eyes but couldn't hide the smile on her face. We all grew up together, and I'd always considered Lila to be the older sister I'd never had. Still pretty with long dark hair and big green eyes. "Someday, you'll have to let her go."

"Never."

"You're ridiculous."

"You love me anyway."

Jude and Lila had the kind of love I'd always wanted for myself. The type of love that transcended time, that rose above every obstacle and grew stronger and deeper with each passing year.

"Hi, Uncle Jesse," Noah yelled as I circled the table to take my seat.

My nephew was in the backyard chasing his two-year-old brother, Levi. "Hey, buddy. How's it going?"

"Good." He bobbed his head and pushed his sweaty dirty-blond hair off his forehead. He looked so much like Brody there was no doubt the kid was his son. I had no idea how Brody, Jude, and Lila had moved on from that betrayal, but they'd found a way. "I'm babysitting. I get a dollar an hour. So I'm gonna be rich real soon."

"You sure are. I might have to borrow money from you."

"Oh. Okay." His brow furrowed. "I'll have to charge interest, though. Uncle Gideon said you never just *give* someone money. You have to make a profit." He shrugged his shoulders and held up his hands as if to say, *I didn't make the rules.*

We all laughed at that one. My brother Gideon was a venture capitalist and lived in New York City. Money was the only god he worshipped, so his advice to my seven-year-old nephew didn't surprise me.

Noting that Ridge was absent from the family dinner, I took the empty seat next to Shiloh. It still blew my mind that Brody not only had a girlfriend but that his girlfriend was Shiloh Leroux, the rock star.

He slung his arm around her shoulder and leaned around her to speak to me. "Shy made the dinner." I heard the pride in his voice.

"Then I know it will be amazing."

"I made red beans and rice especially for you. And a big salad," she said with a smile as she dished up some food for me. She wore a loose black tank top that exposed the tattoos on her left arm, her black hair in a messy topknot, and no makeup. But even so, she had an aura about her, like you could tell she had star quality.

Shiloh was the whole package. Gorgeous, sexy, edgy, and a good person. Brody had lucked out when he'd met her. Not that their road to true love had been smooth, but they'd made it now. They'd reconciled the night before Ridge's high school graduation, and Shiloh was taking a break from touring to work on her next album.

"Thank you," I said when she set the plate in front of me. It was a Brody-sized portion—double the amount of what I'd typically eat for dinner.

"You don't have to serve everyone," Brody grumbled.

She arched her brows. "You don't complain when I serve you, Cowboy."

"Because you're mine. And don't you forget it."

"You're so bad at sharing. You need to work on that," Shiloh teased.

"Bad enough I have to share you with the whole fucking world. I'm not gonna share you with my family too."

She just laughed like she found his jealousy adorable. I wonder if she'd told him that she hooked me up with concert tickets and backstage passes in April. The concert was at the Staples Center in L.A., the final show of her world tour. I'd been a fucking mess, and she hadn't been much better, but when she'd been up on that stage, you never would have guessed she was having personal problems.

Fake it 'til you make it, she'd said after the concert when I'd asked her how she was holding up.

No sooner had I taken a few bites of food when my dad spoke. "So when were you planning to tell us you were walking away? I didn't raise quitters."

"Oh hell, here we go," Brody said with a loud sigh.

Not like I hadn't been expecting this. Growing up, my two older brothers, my cousin Brody, and I had heard those words more times than I could count. It was why I'd been avoiding Sunday family dinners. I wasn't ready to explain my actions. Maybe I never would be.

"Patrick," my mother said sternly, a warning in her voice. "Let's just enjoy a nice family dinner."

"Did you know he was planning to retire? Did he discuss this with you?" he asked my mom.

My mother pursed her lips. "I'm sure Jesse had his reasons." She gave me a little smile, trying to be supportive. Unlike my old man, my mom loved us unconditionally. "You've had so many injuries. I, for one, am relieved you won't be racing anymore. It's such a dangerous sport."

As the youngest of four—Brody was my cousin, but he'd lived with us since I was three—my mom had always treated me like the baby of the family. At twenty-seven, that still hadn't changed.

When I was seven, my dad asked me what sport I wanted to do. I was obsessed with motorcycles, so motocross seemed like the obvious choice. I'd also wanted something that would set me apart from my older siblings. Jude was the football god, Gideon had a genius IQ, and Brody was the rodeo king.

As a kid, I'd been a show-off and a daredevil. But my mom hadn't been too happy about the sport I'd chosen, and my dad had had to fight tooth and nail to let her 'baby' compete in motocross.

So far, she was the only person happy about my retirement.

"You can't up and retire at twenty-seven," my dad said. "And you sure as hell can't do it after a losing streak. Makes it look like you're giving up. You need to get back out there and show them what you can do."

I gritted my teeth and took deep, steadying breaths, trying my damnedest to let his words slide off my back. In the past, I'd never had any trouble doing that. But now, he was rubbing salt in an open wound. "Thanks for the advice. Appreciate it. But I'm done. It's over. And now I'm just looking to move on." I took another bite of food, hoping he would just drop the subject.

"This is delicious, by the way," I told Shiloh.

She smiled and gave my arm a little squeeze. "Thanks, Jesse."

"Move on to what?" my dad asked, picking up right where we'd left off. Should have known he wouldn't give up so easily. "Have you got a backup plan? I hear you're serving beer now. So is this what you're planning to do? Be a bartender? After I spent all those years lugging that damn bike around to every race? After I spent all that money getting you the best coaching and—"

I cut him off before he could say more. "I'm happy to pay you back for your investment in my career." I held his gaze, trying my best not to lose my shit at a family dinner. I'd never been a hothead. Had never been the fighter in the family. I'd left that to Jude and Brody. But this past year had turned me into someone I barely recognized. So if my dad pushed me too far, I *would* fucking lose it. "Just tell me how much I owe you, and I'll deposit it into your account."

My dad's jaw clenched. "This isn't about the money. I don't want your damn money. This is about you."

"I'm fine. Don't worry about me." That should have been the end of it, but unfortunately, my dad couldn't let this rest.

"You don't look fine to me. And walking away when you still have something to prove is *not* the way I raised you."

Fucking hell. I clenched my jaw so tightly I was surprised my molars didn't crack. Breathe, Jesse. In. Out. In. Out.

He was kicking me when I was already down. And he had no fucking idea what he was talking about.

"You think I wanted to walk away when I wasn't on top?" I gritted out. "You think this was *easy* for me?"

"I don't know what the hell to think. Why don't you tell me

what the hell happened?"

I shook my head and snorted in disgust. "I don't feel like I should have to explain myself. It was my career. My choice to leave. And it doesn't have a damn thing to do with you."

"Have you ever been a professional athlete?" Brody asked. He aimed the question at my dad, and it was rhetorical. "No, you sure as hell haven't. So you don't know the first fucking thing about the demands of a sport like motocross. It's *almost* as demanding as bareback bronc riding."

I snorted. It was an age-old battle between us.

"Sometimes, you just gotta know when it's time to walk away," Brody said. "And Jesse feels that time has come. So leave him the hell alone and enjoy the dinner my girlfriend cooked for you."

My dad opened his mouth to speak, but the baby started crying, and Jude narrowed his gaze on my dad. "You've upset Gracie."

"It's not my fault you insist on carrying her everywhere you go," he muttered.

But Jude was too busy fussing over his baby girl to respond. Usually, he would have been the one standing up to my dad. Which just went to show how distracting this parenting gig was.

Just then, Noah climbed the porch stairs, carrying his little brother under the armpits. When he set him down, he wiped the sweat off his forehead and leaned over, his hands on his bent knees while he panted. "Levi's getting too fat. He weighs a ton."

Lila laughed. "You don't have to carry him. He can walk."

"I'm working on my muscles so they can be as big as Dad's." He made a muscle. "See? Big guns, right?"

"Put the guns away, and nobody will get hurt," Brody said.

Noah cracked up. He was laughing so hard he doubled over. When he pulled himself together, he wrapped his arm around my mom and patted her cheek. "Hi, Grandma. You're so pretty. Can we have dessert now?"

My mom laughed. "You must have learned a thing or two from your Uncle Jesse."

Noah's brows furrowed. "Huh?"

"He was a charmer, just like you."

Not so much anymore, but I kept my mouth shut. I'd said enough.

I loved my family, and I usually enjoyed spending time with them, but this dinner couldn't be over fast enough.

A crushing weight pressed down on my chest, making it hard to breathe. Every time I thought about the way my career ended, the way I'd sabotaged my future, shame and anger warred inside me.

I had to get out of here. So I made my excuses, and I strode away, ignoring the look of disappointment on my mother's face.

The Texas Hill Country had some of the best back roads for motorcycle riding, and this road was one of my favorites—a winding, two-lane road with switchbacks and blind turns that cut through the trees and had little traffic on it. I'd been riding for two hours ever since I walked out on my family dinner.

The sun was setting, the sky painted orange and pink as I headed back home, calmer and more focused, feeling more relaxed now that I'd had a chance to clear my head.

I didn't need drugs or alcohol. I was an adrenaline junkie, and nothing gave me a bigger rush than speed. Nothing made me feel more alive than being right on the edge of losing control.

I leaned into the turn and straightened up when I hit a straight, flat section.

Up ahead, a few cars lined the shoulder of the road, and loud music drew my gaze to the grove of live oaks, where I caught a glimpse of blonde hair. It could have been anyone. No reason to think it was her.

Was that Ridge's truck? As I zoomed past, I checked my rear-view mirror. Sure as hell looked like it.

It was none of my business. *Just leave her the fuck alone, Jesse. Just friends, remember?*

Besides, it couldn't have been Quinn. She was hanging out with her mom tonight.

So why the fuck had I pulled over onto the shoulder?

I backed up my bike until it kissed Ridge's bumper and looked down the hill through the trees. A dirt path led to the swimming hole where I used to hang out in high school. I took off my helmet and ran my hand through my hair, straining my eyes to catch another glimpse.

Fuck, I was acting like a creepy stalker.

There was a group of teens hanging out, but my eyes homed in on her. Quinn Cavanaugh. The girl who used to follow me around since she was Levi's age. The girl I'd known since she was Gracie's age. Weird to think about that now.

My eyes narrowed on Walker as he slung his arm around her shoulders just like it belonged there.

I couldn't read the expression on her face. She was too far away.

It didn't help that Ridge blocked my view of her either. Now all I could see was his back.

I slid my ringing phone out of my pocket and checked it. *Mason.*

"How's it going?" he asked.

Fucking great. Just stalking your sister. I laughed under my breath. "It's all good."

"You wanna head up to the lake tomorrow? We thought it would be fun if we all hung out together. Take my dad's boat out. Ride the Jet Skis. We'll take Quinn too. You in?"

I heard a shriek and glanced over at the trees again. *Quinn.* Barefoot in cut-offs and a tank top, she darted through the trees with Walker chasing after her. Son of a bitch. Without thinking, I was off my bike and striding along the shoulder for a better view.

Did she need my help?

"Jesse? You there?"

"Yeah, sounds good. I'm in the middle of something. I'll call you—"

"Oh shit. Why'd you answer your phone? Catch you later."

I cut the call and pocketed my phone just as Walker caught Quinn around the middle, tossed her over his shoulder, and jogged toward the water.

"No! Put me down." I couldn't tell if she was laughing. Was she enjoying this? "Ridge! Help!"

"Hell no. Not after that prank you pulled on us."

"Evie!" Quinn yelled. "Watch out."

Ridge pulled the same trick as Walker and threw Evie over his shoulder. Two seconds later, the girls were flying through the air and hit the water with a splash. When their heads emerged, they were laughing. They weren't in any danger, so I headed back to my motorcycle before they noticed me watching.

Quinn had obviously gotten over her crush on me. She was having fun, being a teenager, enjoying her summer just like she should be doing. It should have been a relief. We'd stay in the friend zone, where we belonged.

She was too young for me, and I wasn't the same guy I used to be. So she was right to protect herself from me.

"I'm saving myself for someone who treats me like a queen. And that's. Not. You."

I rubbed my hand over my heart. Those words shouldn't have hurt as much as they did. And I sure as hell shouldn't want her the way that I did.

My sunshine girl with her pouty lips and star-filled eyes.

Tomorrow we'd find out just how honest Quinn was. Maybe I'd gotten her wrong too. But no, she'd tell me the truth when I asked her what she'd been up to today.

Chapter Eleven

Quinn

Declan slid the omelet onto a plate and set it in front of Jesse, sitting at the other end of the island.

I drizzled honey on my berries and Greek yogurt and jammed a spoonful into my mouth. It was still too tart, but maybe that was just the bad taste in my mouth from this unexpected turn of events.

"Sure you don't want an omelet, Bean?" Declan asked. He was at the stove again, his back to me while he made another omelet. He was shirtless in boardshorts and a backward ball cap.

"I'm sure. And don't call me Bean," I muttered.

"*Little* Bean," Holden said, shoveling a forkful of eggs into his mouth. "Damn, that's good. I can taste the cilantro."

"I can't see how. You've put so much hot sauce on it. You've probably killed off your tastebuds."

"Love me some hot sauce." To prove his point, he doused his eggs in more sauce, completely ignoring the heat warning on the label.

I checked my phone as a text came in from Evie. I'd messaged her for backup. **Sorry, can't. I have to work today. If J gives you any shit, kick him in the balls.**

After texting a response, I pocketed my phone with a sigh. Looks like I was on my own.

"So, what's the plan?" Carly asked, pulling her dark hair into a ponytail. She was wearing a tiny bikini top with shorts, just like her friend, Tasha. I had no idea who had invited them, but with each passing minute, my mood plummeted.

I'd been so excited about spending time with Jesse today. Just the two of us. Until my brothers had shown up with girls in tow and hijacked my plans. Shortly after, Jesse had arrived, but unlike me, he hadn't been the least bit surprised.

Had Jesse planned this?

I side-eyed him. He was talking to the blonde. Tasha. With all that hair flipping and giggling, I couldn't imagine she'd have anything of interest to say.

Salty much, Quinn?

Ever since he'd arrived, he'd barely glanced at me. And why should he? Tasha's boobs were practically spilling out of her tiny bikini top, and she was leaning into him, giving him the perfect view of her cleavage.

Could she be any more obvious?

"My dad keeps his Jet Skis and boat up at our lake house," Mason told Carly. "It's about a forty-five-minute drive...." I tuned him out while he discussed logistics. Mason was big on logistics.

I loved the lake. I loved going out on the Jet Ski and hanging out on my dad's pontoon.

Or, at least, I used to. I rubbed my hand over the jagged scars on my abdomen hidden under my white t-shirt. The black script across the chest said: Perfectly Imperfect. Wasn't that the truth? A heart punctuated the words.

My scars, though... It looked like a shark had attacked me.

Mason nudged my arm. "Hey. Nobody cares." He kept his voice low, for my ears only. My brothers knew about my insecurity. It had been the topic of a family discussion last summer.

I cared. Because Jesse was here, and these two girls were flaunting their perfect skin.

Mason lifted the hem of his T-shirt to show off his scar. He only had one where they removed his kidney. I had four—two eight-inch scars on each side.

My stomach looked like a road map.

"I wear mine like a badge of honor," he said quietly.

Tears sprang to my eyes. He gave my shoulder a little squeeze as if he knew the effect his words had on me. My brother had given me a kidney. Every single one of my brothers had volunteered. Even Declan. Surprisingly, he had been the first to offer. And that was just so amazing that they loved me enough to do that.

I lowered my head, a curtain of hair falling to cover the side of my face. Tears brimmed in my eyes. It was so stupid. I didn't want to cry in front of everyone. I didn't even know why I felt like crying.

After my second kidney transplant a year and a half ago, I was so depressed that Mom took me to a therapist. Logically, I knew it wasn't my fault that my body had rejected the first kidney. My dad had donated it when I was twelve. But still. I felt like such a failure.

I always tried to put on a brave face, but deep down, I was so scared it would happen again. So afraid I'd have seizures and convulsions again and that I'd have to go through yet another surgery or be put on dialysis.

You couldn't live like that, though. You couldn't live in constant fear of what *could* happen. The therapist helped me deal with my fears, and for the most part, I felt optimistic about the future. But sometimes, my fears and doubts still surfaced.

I shouldn't care about the scars or how they looked. It was the least of my worries. The important thing was that I'd gotten another chance, and I was alive and well. Obsessing over something so trivial, so superficial, was a waste of time and energy.

But I couldn't help it. No matter how many times I told myself that it didn't matter, that today I'd be brave enough to bare my stomach to people other than Evie and my family, I couldn't bring myself to do it.

I always kept my tank top on. If I wanted to go in the water, I wore a one-piece that made me look like a twelve-year-old.

Mason nudged my arm. "Go get your stuff, Bean. We're heading out."

"Stop calling me Bean."

He ignored me and told Jesse they'd see us up there. I didn't hang around to listen to his warnings to keep me safe. Like I was a china doll. Fragile and breakable.

On my way out of the kitchen, I glanced at Jesse. He was too busy talking to Tasha to even notice me. It felt like the old days, just as if Friday night had never happened.

I would forever be the little sister.

As I threw a few things into my bag, I heard the floorboards creak outside my bedroom.

"Are you wearing the purple bikini today?" Jesse asked.

What the…

I lifted my head. He was gripping the top of the doorframe. There was so much to look at I didn't know where to look first. His biceps were flexed, and the thick veins in his forearms were so pronounced that I knew this was what they called vein porn.

Why was that even sexy? No idea. But it was.

My gaze lowered to the strip of suntanned skin just above the waistband of his jeans where his gray T-shirt rode up.

He had a V cut. Oh God. It was too much. My mouth gaped.

"Quinn?"

My gaze snapped to his face, and his brows raised, prompting me to answer his question. *Are you wearing the purple bikini today?*

"No," I snapped.

He advanced into my room, his gaze roaming over the bookshelves that spanned an entire wall. I was an avid collector. Hundreds of books filled the shelves, and at last count, I had twenty-seven Funk Pop! figures. Notorious B.I.G. and Baby Yoda were my newest additions to the collection.

"Why not?"

Why was he even asking me that? Was this friend-zone appropriate? "I'm wearing a one-piece. It's better for watersports."

"Huh." He picked up a framed photo from my white lacquer dresser. I watched him in the round gold-framed mirror above it as he studied the picture—our annual family Christmas photo taken when I was thirteen. Six weeks later, Dad moved out. After that, Mom stopped sending family photo Christmas cards.

Jesse set it down and turned to face me. He leaned against the dresser and crossed his arms over his chest, and when he spoke, his voice was filled with accusation. "So you only wear the bikini for Walker."

I wore the bikini under a tank top and shorts, neither of which I'd taken off. "I didn't..." I pursed my lips. He didn't even deserve an explanation. "Why are we even having this conversation?"

He didn't bother responding. His gaze roamed over my body and down my bare legs, but it wasn't heated, and his eyes weren't hooded like they'd been on Friday night. "You need to wear jeans. Or long pants."

I looked down at my shorts and then at his jeans. Faded denim hung low on his narrow hips. I knew for a fact that Jesse sometimes wore shorts and Vans when he rode, but today, he was wearing jeans and black motorcycle boots, so I couldn't even put up a protest.

"I brought an extra jacket for you."

"It's going to be in the nineties today," I argued.

He shrugged one shoulder. "If you want to ride on my bike, you need protection."

I needed protection, all right. *From Jesse.*

"Wear a bikini."

My jaw dropped. Who the hell did he think he was, coming into my bedroom and making demands on what I wore?

Why was he doing this to me? Why was he sending mixed signals and messing with my head? Anger and frustration had me planting my hands on my hips and narrowing my eyes to slits. "I thought you said you weren't playing games anymore."

"I'm not playing with you," he said calmly.

I snorted. This guy was unbelievable. "But you want to see me in a bikini. Why? To see if I measure up to Tasha and Carly? I'm sure you'll get your fill of Tasha in a bikini."

He laughed. The asshole was laughing at me.

I brushed past him and stepped into my walk-in closet, slamming the door shut behind me.

When I returned to the bedroom in ripped black jeans and leather high tops, Jesse was checking his phone. I stuffed the shorts into my bag, slung it over my shoulder, and marched out of my room with him right behind me.

"Quinn."

"What?" I snapped as I automated our security system on the touchscreen in the foyer on our way out.

"You've got it all wrong. I just wanted—"

"Yeah, okay. Whatever." I didn't want to listen to any of his excuses. "Save it for someone who cares."

He sighed loudly, echoing my own annoyance with the way this day had started.

When we got outside to his bike parked on the brick courtyard, he stowed my things in the saddlebag and handed me a black and white motorcycle jacket. It was summer-weight, mesh, with padded elbows. It was a little big for me but fit better than I would have expected. He put on his own—a black, red, and white jacket—and put a white Arai helmet on my head.

"How does that feel?" he asked after he'd adjusted the chin strap, his fingers brushing my skin and making the hairs on my arms raise. God, why did my body have to react so strongly to his every touch?

His knees were bent so we were eye-level, and I averted my gaze. He was standing too close. I couldn't think straight. "It feels fine."

I didn't even want to know whose helmet and jacket this used to be. I wasn't even sure I wanted to spend the day with him anymore.

"How was dinner with your mom last night?"

"We ordered pizza and watched a movie." Her flight was delayed, so she hadn't gotten home until nine-thirty. "It was fun."

His eyes narrowed on me like he didn't believe me. "Fun, huh?"

"Um, yeah? I like hanging out with my mom." What was his deal?

"And how were Evie and her sister? Was that *fun*, too?"

"Why do I feel like you're interrogating me?"

He shrugged one shoulder. "Just making conversation. Friends tell each other things, right?"

"Yeah, sure." But this conversation didn't feel all that friendly.

I would have told him that I hung out with Walker, Ridge, and Evie at the swimming hole but not when he acted like this. The only reason I'd gone yesterday was to help Ridge and Evie. I'd kind of tricked Evie into thinking I wanted to be with Walker. Otherwise, she would never have agreed to it.

We had fun, something Evie didn't get enough of in her life. So it was worth it.

"Was this your idea? The lake and my brothers…." *And the girls.* I waved my hand in the air.

"Mason called me yesterday. He thought it would be *fun* if we all hung out together. Is that a problem?"

"No. Why would it be?"

"I don't know." He jerked his chin at me. "You tell me."

God, he looked so arrogant. And so beautiful. With the morning sun on his golden-tanned face and his eyes so blue. His jacket fit like a glove, molded to his broad shoulders and tapering down to his narrow waist, and he was standing in front of his big black motorcycle, looking so impossibly cool.

I just wanted him all to myself. But I couldn't say that, could I?

I couldn't tell him that I dreamed about him last night. Or that he was the hero in the story I was writing. Or that I'd killed off his ex-girlfriend, cackling like a lunatic while I'd been writing that scene.

I took a deep breath and let it out, gearing up to make myself vulnerable and be honest with him. "Yesterday when I saw you… you were nice. And today… you're acting like…" I averted my face to hide the hurt expression. I didn't even have a word for it. Had Jesse always been this moody? I guess I'd never noticed it before.

He crossed his arms over his chest, so closed-off and aloof with that same arrogant look on his face like he was looking down his nose at me. "How am I acting?"

How could I talk to him when he was acting like this? I couldn't. "Just forget it. Let's just go."

Without further prompting, he put on his helmet, straddled his bike, and started the engine.

Two minutes later, we hit the road, and I vowed just to enjoy the day. So what if it hadn't gone according to plan? So what if he was acting like a dick again? It would be fun to spend the day with my brothers. If worse came to worse, I could always catch a ride home with them.

The sun was shining, the sky was blue, and I was on the back of Jesse's bike, so I needed to shake it off and channel all my good vibes.

My arms were wrapped tightly around his middle, my chest pressed against his back as we took the winding back roads instead of the highway. Although I suspected he was holding back, not riding as fast as he usually would, we were still going fast.

I'd wanted to ride on the back of his bike for so long, and it was just how I imagined it would be.

I felt so wild and free. Reckless and a little bit dangerous.

Holding onto Jesse like this, straddling a bike, with all this power between my thighs and the vibrations of the engine shooting straight to my core... God. Now I understood why motorcycles were so sexy.

For a moment, I closed my eyes and pretended that he was mine and I was his. And that he'd look at me and think, *"She's the one. The girl I've been waiting for all my life. And all along, she had been right in front of me."*

When I opened my eyes, reality hit me.

I needed to get it through my head that I would *never* be that girl to him. And with the way he'd been acting lately, I shouldn't even want that.

When we got to the lake, I would just do my own thing and

avoid him as much as possible. If he'd rather hang out with a bikini-clad blonde with big boobs, far be it from me to get in his way.

I deserved better, and that's what I had to keep reminding myself. I refused to become one of those girls who let herself get treated like dirt just because they had a stupid crush on a hot guy.

If he wasn't going to play nice, then why should I?

Chapter Twelve

Jesse

Quinn had lied to me. She. Lied. To. Me. I fucking hated being lied to.

Of all the people in the world, Quinn was the last person I'd expected dishonesty from. But history had proven that I wasn't the best judge of character.

"He… he forced me," Alessia said, her chin quivering, eyes filled with tears as she stood in front of me on the driveway, wringing her hands.

I still had the condo in Temecula, the one we used to live in together. She'd been waiting for me when I got home from a thirteen-mile trail ride on my mountain bike. I'd been trying to shake off the dejection of my second eighth-place weekend in a row. To say that my Supercross season wasn't going well was a massive understatement.

And now she was telling me this?

"Nate wanted to win so badly that he would have done anything. And he knew... he knew that if he went after me, it would mess you up." She wrapped her hands around my biceps and looked up at me with her big brown eyes, pleading with me to believe her.

Her dark hair was pulled back in a ponytail, her face makeup-free, just the way I'd always liked it. My gaze lowered to her white crop top and high-waisted shorts that showcased her suntanned stomach. I used to think Alessia was stunning, but deception had painted her in an ugly light, and I still didn't know if I should believe her.

My eyes narrowed on her. "Why didn't you tell me this when it happened? Why did you wait all these months to fucking tell me?"

"You wouldn't even speak to me, Jesse. You wanted nothing to do with me."

How could she blame me for that? She'd cheated on me. "I fucking loved you. I would have done anything for you."

"Loved?" Tears streamed down her cheeks. I'd always hated when Alessia cried and had wanted to do everything in my power to make things better for her. "I don't want to lose you. I can't lose you, Jesse. I love you so much. You have to believe me. I would have never..." She exhaled a ragged breath. "I would never have done that to us."

I didn't know what to believe. I knew Nate was aggressive. He'd always tried to provoke me before a race. But this was a serious allegation. "Look me in the eye and tell me that what you're saying is the truth."

She raised her eyes to mine, her voice faltering on the words, but her gaze didn't waver. "Nate forced me into having sex. I said no, and I tried to fight him off. But he…" She lowered her eyes then raised them to mine again. "He wouldn't take no for an answer."

I studied her face, searching for the truth.

"I swear on my life that's the truth, Jesse."

That son of a bitch. This was all my fault. If it hadn't been for my rivalry with Nate, he would never have gone after her.

I would fucking kill him for what he did to her.

I pulled Alessia into my arms and held her close. It had been months since I'd held her like this.

Her whole body was shaking, and she was crying so hard her tears soaked my T-shirt. "Everything is going to be okay," I promised. "I'll take care of everything."

How fucking wrong I'd been.

And how fucking stupid to have ever believed her.

How had I never noticed that Alessia was so cunning and manipulative? How had I spent three years with her, fucking her, loving her, sharing a life with her without really knowing her at all? She'd sworn up and down that she was telling the truth, and I'd believed her. Like a fool, I'd let her back into my life.

Fucking hell. I'd even apologized to her. I told her how sorry I was for putting her into that position.

All because she'd lied to me.

And now I was wound so tightly I felt like I was going to snap.

My grip was too tight, and I needed to loosen up. That's where I'd been going wrong in my moto sessions.

Shake it off. Put it out of your head.

I relaxed my shoulders and wiggled my fingers, loosening my death grip on the handlebars.

As if Quinn sensed that something was wrong, her arms tightened around me. Was she scared? I eased up on the throttle and kept to the speed limit.

I needed to put this in perspective. So what if Quinn wanted to keep secrets from me? We weren't in a relationship. She owed me nothing. Her lie of omission didn't even come close to the lies that Alessia had fed me.

Was it any of my business what Quinn had been doing yesterday? Or who she had been doing it with?

No. It sure as hell wasn't.

So why was I so pissed at her for hanging out with Walker? Was she going to give him her virginity? Was she going to let him touch her in places where nobody ever had?

Fuck. Just the thought of them together made my stomach churn.

She's not yours, Jesse, and she never will be.

The last thing I needed or wanted right now was a relationship.

The very last thing I needed was an eighteen-year-old virgin fucking with my head.

Quinn

Thanks to Declan, the pontoon had turned into a party cruise. He'd invited a bunch of friends I didn't know, and now one of the girls was climbing him like a monkey. He carried her through the lower deck, his hand on her ass, a beer in his other hand.

They disappeared to the upper deck where Declan was hosting his party. He and his friends were planning to stay the night at the lake house. No doubt they'd trash it by morning.

I pulled my knees to my chest and wrapped my arms around them, my eyes on the crystal blue water. Two Jet Skiers zipped past the pontoon, and a few kids were diving off the rocks into the lake. When my brothers and Jesse were in their teens, they used to dive off those rocks. One time Jesse did a double backflip, and Mom nearly had a heart attack.

We used to have some good times at this lake. Back when we were a family and did everything together. Earlier, when I'd walked into the lake house to change out of my jeans, it had smelled musty from being closed up for so long. When my parents were still married, Dad used to take his girlfriend to that house. Not that anyone had told me that. I'd overheard them arguing about it the night Dad packed up his things and moved out.

"You good, Bean?" Holden asked, jolting me back to the present. He was behind the wheel, Ray-Ban aviators shielding his eyes from the sun's glare while he navigated. I was sitting across the aisle from him in a horseshoe-shaped booth with a bottle of water on the kidney-shaped table in front of me.

"Never been better." I ignored the sound of Jesse and Tasha's laughter that carried through the breeze. Even though the music was pumping—Dominic Fike's "3 Nights"—I could still hear them. They were hanging out with Mason and Carly on the sun deck in the front of the boat. Lounging on the plush vinyl sofas. Jesse, in all his shirtless glory, his golden skin kissed by the sun. Tasha with her big boobs in a fluorescent orange string bikini. Earlier, I'd been treated to the sight of Jesse rubbing sunscreen onto her back.

So I'd gone for a swim in the lake with Declan and his friends, and then I'd hitched a ride on the Jet Ski with a tattooed guy, Thor. I didn't know if Thor was his real name, but he was a funny guy, the size of a mountain, and claimed he had a big hammer. I didn't stop laughing for most of the ride.

"Enjoying your summer?" Holden asked.

I didn't even know how to answer that. I'd had such high hopes for my last summer before college. But so far, nothing had gone according to plan.

While I debated how to answer, I watched Holden maneuver around a fishing boat, giving it the right of way.

My brothers were all handsome. Mason looked like a younger version of Dad, and Declan was the dark-haired, tattooed bad boy. But in my opinion, Holden was the best looking out of the three. He wore his hair a bit longer, the ends curling up a little where they hit the collar of his T-shirt, and his eyes were the clearest shade of green.

Holden knew how it felt to have his heart broken.

Last summer, his girlfriend of six years left him for a job in New York City. Avery told him she needed space and needed to figure out who she was without him.

I was tempted to confide in him. Tell him that I was in love with someone who would never love me back. But that someone was his friend who was currently getting cozy with Tasha. And even though Holden wasn't quite as overbearing as Mason, he still thought of me as his baby sister and felt it was his duty to protect me.

So I kept it to myself. "Yeah. It's been good."

"And what about this guy, Walker? Do you like him?"

My eyes sought out Jesse, although I didn't know why I needed to look at him to answer the question. His hair was all messy, ruffled by the breeze, and he was sitting on the sofa like a king on his throne, his arms draped across the back, and Tasha nestled against his side as if she belonged there. She was looking up at him, her lips moving, face animated as if she was telling him an exciting story.

But he wasn't looking at her. Instead, he was looking directly at me. His eyes narrowed as if he knew what I was talking about, even though he couldn't hear me from where he was sitting. "He's a good guy. He's cool."

"Better be. Or he'll have me to deal with."

I rolled my eyes. "You and Mason made that pretty clear on Friday night."

"We can't have some douche messing with our little sister."

Which proved my point. No way could I confide in Holden. Why would I have even considered doing anything so idiotic? Better to let him think I liked Walker than to guess the truth.

Jesse extricated himself from Tasha and stalked toward me. There was something a little bit dangerous about him now. It should have scared me, but it had the opposite effect. My body was humming at his nearness.

He reached into the small fridge next to the booth where I was sitting and pulled out a bottle of water, his back to me.

"Walker's fun to hang out with, and he treats me right," I told Holden, noting the way Jesse's muscles tensed and his body stiffened. I'd felt how tense he was on the motorcycle ride earlier.

I saw it yesterday at the track when I watched him ride too. So if we were on friendlier terms, I'd ask him to do yoga with me just to loosen him up. It might even help his riding.

"I like Walker. I like him a lot," I added for Jesse's benefit.

I was laying it on thick, but Jesse had been getting cozy with Tasha since we left the boat ramp, so he deserved that and more. "I might as well enjoy my last summer before college, right?"

Holden nodded. "Right. Glad you're having fun."

"Yep. It's been a fun summer so far. Lots and lots of fun."

Jesse turned to face me, and I gave him a big smile he didn't return.

"How's your summer going, Jesse?" I asked, my smile still firmly in place. I repositioned myself, so I was sitting the way he had been, my arms stretched out across the back of the booth, cool and casual as you like.

So what if I was wearing a one-piece? I'd own it. Make it my bitch. I wasn't going to let him undermine my confidence. "Are you having fun?"

He unscrewed the lid of his water bottle and drank before answering. It was a power play. He wanted to keep me hanging. Make me sweat it out. I stared at his throat as it bobbed on a swallow and dug my nails into the plush vinyl.

Even his throat was sexy. God. I hated him for making me feel this way. My fingers itched to touch his skin. To feel his taut muscles under my fingertips. To run them through his messy hair and trace his squared jawline.

I wanted to feel those lips on mine. I wanted to feel those lips on every inch of my skin. Biting, sucking, teasing, tasting.

He lowered the bottle and raked his eyes over my face, dragging his gaze down my body. It felt like he was stripping me bare, just with his eyes. My cheeks flushed with heat, and not even the breeze off the water could cool my overheated skin.

But I held his gaze, faking a confidence I didn't feel as he flattened his palms on the table in front of me and leaned in close, his voice low, so his words were for my ears only.

"I don't fucking like being lied to, *baby* sister."

I stared into his baby blues. They looked darker. Angrier. Like the sea being churned up during a storm. I was so mesmerized by his eyes that it took a moment for his words to register. "*Baby sister*? Don't call me that," I hissed. "And what are you talking about?"

He laughed harshly and shook his head as he straightened up to his full height, legs slightly spread, eyes hooded. I opened my mouth to speak, to protest his words, but he turned and walked away before I got a chance to say a word.

Just then, two of Declan's friends headed toward us on the Jet Skis, and Holden cut the motor so they could pull up next to the pontoon. That was why Jesse had moved to the back of the boat. He had seen them coming.

I jumped up from my seat, ready to snag one of the keys. Too late. Jesse had already claimed them and tossed one to Mason.

"I'm going to beat your ass," Mason said.

"Good luck with that," Jesse said with a laugh. So cocky. Such an arrogant asshole.

So why couldn't I stop staring at him? I watched the muscles in his arms flex as he fastened his life vest, and then he climbed onto the Jet Ski and put the key in the ignition, ready to take off.

Tasha and Carly scurried to the back deck where the Jet Skis were parked alongside, and Tasha called to Jesse, "Can we ride on the back?"

"We're going to race. It's not safe with a passenger."

Tasha's shoulders slumped in disappointment. Internally, I cheered that he'd dismissed her. But really, what did it matter? Just because he'd shot her down didn't mean he wanted me.

Why had he been so angry? And what was he talking about? I've never lied to him. Unlike him, I've always been honest.

"Jesse's gonna leave Mason in the dust," Holden said with a laugh.

"I don't know about that. I think Mason has a good shot at winning."

Holden snorted. "We haven't beaten Jesse at any motorsport since we were thirteen."

I shrugged one shoulder. "Jesse's not the guy he used to be." Talk about an understatement. "My money's on Mason."

While Tasha and Carly raided the fridge for beer and flirted with Holden, I moved to the sofas in the front and caught some sun, my eyes on the Jet Skis. Jesse rode standing, just like he did on a bike. I watched him jump a wake, flying up into the air before landing vertically, and then he was racing across the lake like a madman, and I lost sight of him.

I really, really wanted Mason to win.

Unfortunately, none of my wishes were coming true this summer.

Chapter Thirteen

Jesse

"Shit, man. I almost had you," Mason said when we climbed onto the pontoon.

Declan snorted. "You weren't even close." He held up his hand, and I tossed him the lanyard with the key attached.

"Who else wants to ride?" Mason asked.

Quinn jumped up and lunged for the lanyard, but Mason yanked it back, earning a scowl from her. I tried my damnedest not to notice her tight little body in a red Speedo. It wasn't designed to be sexy but fuck me, that suit was a hell of a lot sexier than the bikini Tasha wore. The Speedo was cut high on the legs and fit her like a second skin, molded to every curve. But it left plenty of room for the imagination.

"Sure you can handle it?" Mason asked.

She planted her hands on her hips. "Dad taught me how to ride. I can handle a Jet Ski."

Mason shrugged, still not giving up the key. "Just trying to look out for you."

"I appreciate it, but I can look out for myself." She snatched the key out of his hand and looped it around her wrist.

"Hey Declan, how about a race?" she asked after she put on her life vest.

"I'm not racing you."

"Scared you'll lose?"

He snort-laughed. "Hardly."

"Then you have nothing to worry about."

"Okay, you're on."

"Hell no," I interjected, beating Mason to the punch. I grabbed her arm before she climbed onto the Jet Ski. Her eyes narrowed on me. "You're not racing."

She glared at me and yanked her arm out of my grip.

"Quinn," I said as she punched the start button on the Jet Ski. She looked up at me, annoyed.

"What?" she gritted out.

"Be careful."

She snorted. "Yeah, okay. I'll be just as careful as you always are."

Just then, Tasha sauntered over to me and put her hand on my chest. She was one of those touchy-feely girls. Pretty, I guess. Blonde-haired and blue-eyed. But not my type. Her tan was as fake as her boobs. I'd never been a hit it and quit it guy, but I'd thought maybe it was what I needed. Just fuck a random girl and get Quinn out of my system. If Tasha's body language was any indication, she'd be up for it.

"Hey, Jesse. I brought you a beer." She put the cold beer in my hand, a beer I didn't want, and smiled at me.

Quinn's eyes narrowed on us just before she pushed the throttle and veered away, chasing after Declan, who had gotten a head start.

"Is she okay on a Jet Ski?" I asked Mason, keeping my eyes on Quinn. He'd taken over the wheel and was following behind the two Jet Skis.

"Guess we'll see. She's been acting weird today. Like she has something to prove."

Tasha handed me a bottle of sunscreen and fluttered her lashes at me. I guess it was meant to be sexy, but it just wasn't doing it for me. "Do you mind doing my back?"

Oldest trick in the book and the second time she'd used it today. Mason chuckled under his breath as Tasha pulled her hair over one shoulder and turned her back to me. While I rubbed the sunscreen into Tasha's back, she let out a little moan, but I barely noticed. My eyes were on Quinn up ahead.

"Fucking Declan," Mason said.

He was playing a game of chicken with two other Jet Skis headed toward them. My gaze swung to Quinn. She veered around them, narrowly missing one of them. Shit. She'd turned too abruptly.

Her Jet Ski flipped over, tossing her into the water, the kill switch bringing the Jet Ski to a stop a few feet away from her.

"Jesus Christ. Quinn!" Mason yelled. But his voice got lost in the wind, and it was already too late.

I shoved the bottle of sunscreen into Tasha's hand and dove off the starboard, swimming toward Quinn in long strokes.

She was floating on her back when I reached her side, buoyed up by the life vest.

I wrapped my arm around her waist and pushed the hair off her face with my other hand, my legs treading water to keep us afloat. "Are you okay?"

Before she could answer, she started coughing. "I'm good. Just a little…"

"Shaken up?"

She nodded. "I'm usually a better driver… I don't know what happened."

I wouldn't call her a good driver by any stretch of the imagination, but I kept that to myself. "That wasn't your fault. Those guys were assholes."

Declan turned in a wide arc and came back to check on Quinn. "Shit. You okay, Bean?"

"No thanks to you."

"I thought you knew how to drive a Jet Ski," he scoffed.

She glared at him. "I was doing just fine until you decided to mess with those two guys."

It was a stupid-ass thing to do, but we'd all done stupid shit like that. The difference was that Declan knew how to handle a Jet Ski better than his sister.

"You should have been looking out for her," Mason yelled. "What the fuck, Declan?"

He held up his middle finger then focused on me. "You good

to deal with her?"

"Nobody has to *deal* with me," Quinn said, pulling out of my grasp and swimming toward the Jet Ski.

"I've got this," I told him.

"Cool," he said before he took off.

I swam around to the back of the Jet Ski and read the instructions on the sticker. Clockwise.

"I can do it," Quinn said, swimming around to the right side with me.

"I've got it. Stand back."

She rolled her eyes but gave me some space. I reached up on the hull and grabbed the intake grate, pushing down on the rail with my feet and rocking the Jet Ski back and forth until it flipped right side up again.

"You wanna drive that back to the boat ramp for me?" Mason yelled.

I gave him a thumbs-up and turned to Quinn to get the lanyard from her. "I'm driving," she said, trying to pull herself up and onto the Jet Ski. From the water, it took a lot of upper body strength.

"You can ride with me," I told her.

"Fuck that."

My brows shot up. "Is it another special occasion?"

"No. It's just being around you. You bring out the best in me."

Quinn was so fucking cute with such a determined look on her face that it made me laugh. She glared at me, which only made me laugh harder. Still cute. Not the least bit threatening. Normally, I would help Quinn, but I was enjoying the show too much to lift a finger.

She grabbed the back of the seat, and after a few more tries, she managed to lever herself up and onto the Jet Ski.

"Impressive."

Quinn made a muscle and smirked at me. "I do a lot of planking."

Huh. It was only then that it dawned on me. She was in the driver's seat.

"You want *me* to be a passenger?"

"You don't have to ride with me at all. You can ride on the boat." She shrugged one shoulder like it didn't matter to her one way or the other.

"Jesse," Tasha called.

"Go finish your beer," Quinn said.

I ignored Tasha and climbed on behind Quinn, then put on the life vest Mason tossed me. With the way Quinn drove, I'd need it.

"If you insist on riding with me, make sure you hold on tight." Now she was giving me orders.

"You don't have to tell me twice. I've seen how you drive." I placed my hands on her hips.

"This feels weird." She looked at me over her shoulder.

I dug my fingers into her hip bones, wishing I could feel her skin instead of nylon and Spandex. "Feels pretty good to me."

Her eyes locked on mine for a moment—the sun highlighting the green and gold in her irises. "You need to loosen your grip, Jesse. That's your problem, you know. You're holding on too tight."

The way she said it, I knew she wasn't only talking about my hands on her hips. How did she know I was holding on too tight?

"Maybe I don't want to let you go. Maybe I want to hold on tight."

Her lashes lowered, and she let out a breath before she turned and faced forward again.

"Get ready. I'm going to take you for the ride of your life, racer boy."

I was laughing when she pushed the throttle in. This girl. She was so damn cool.

I forgot she'd lied to me. I forgot about the boundaries. I forgot all my problems.

"It feels like we're flying," she yelled. The joy and sheer excitement in her voice put a smile on my face.

I didn't point out that 25 mph wasn't even close to flying. If I did, she might be tempted to go faster, something I wanted to avoid at all costs.

Let's face it, Quinn was a shitty driver, barely in control of the Jet Ski. I was so tempted to wrap my hands over hers and show her how to steer into a turn and increase the speed. But I didn't want to curb her enthusiasm. She was having too much fun, and I loved seeing Quinn happy and loving life. And if this guy, Walker, made her happy, I guess I'd have to find a way to live with that.

But that didn't mean I had to like it.

The sun was setting behind her as she walked out of the cedar-shingled lake house. The lighting made her hair shimmer gold. She smiled, her teeth so white against her lightly tanned skin, cheeks slightly flushed from all the sun she'd caught today.

"See you tomorrow," Mason told me. Thankfully, he hadn't

caught me staring at his sister. "Drive safe."

I nodded to acknowledge that I'd heard him and understood. I was carrying precious cargo.

Mason fist-bumped me before he walked over to Quinn. He pulled her into a hug and kissed the top of her head. "It was fun hanging out with you today, Bean."

She tipped back her head and gave him a big smile. "Yeah, it was a good day. I'm glad we did it."

That put a smile on his face. Earlier, he'd asked me if I thought she'd change her mind about California. I'm sure it wasn't the only reason he'd come up with the plan to spend the day at the lake, but I suspected it had played a part.

He'd also thanked me for being a good friend and looking after her. A reminder that it was the way things needed to be between Quinn and me.

She gave him a little slug on the shoulder before she sauntered over to my bike. I handed her the jacket, and she threaded her arms through the sleeves and zipped it up.

Just then, Holden, Tasha, and Carly came out of the house, the girls giggling. "See you soon, Jesse," Tasha called, blowing me a kiss before she climbed into the back seat of Mason's Jeep.

Quinn scowled at the Jeep as they drove away. "She seems… friendly."

"Uh huh." Couldn't deny it. Tasha was *friendly*. In Mason's words, "*She's the perfect rebound girl. Sex. No strings attached.*"

"Are you… planning to see her again?"

I had no intention of seeing Tasha again. Hadn't even asked for her number. "Would it bother you if I said yes?"

She shrugged one shoulder. "No. Why should it?"

"Exactly. You have Walker, right?"

"Yeah, Walker…" She exhaled a breath and smoothed her hands over the jacket, looking down at it. "Was this Alessia's?"

I got rid of all traces of Alessia. Every item of clothing, every tube of lipstick, every photo and text message, and every physical reminder that I had shared a life with a liar and a cheat. "No. It's yours."

Her gaze snapped to mine. "You bought this for me?"

I nodded.

"You bought me a jacket and a helmet?"

"If you're going to ride on the back of my bike, you need protection."

"Thank you." She smiled. It was bright, and it was beautiful. Glorious, really. I hadn't seen that smile aimed at me in a long time. I'd missed it. I'd missed the way she used to look at me like I was someone good and not a total fuck-up.

I wanted to believe her smile was genuine. That *she* was genuine. That I hadn't gotten her all wrong. "I saw you yesterday. At the swimming hole."

"You saw me…" Her voice trailed off, and she sucked in a breath. "Oh. Right." She nodded as if she got it now. "You thought I lied to you."

"You *did* lie to me."

"I didn't lie. I just didn't tell you everything."

I grabbed her hand and tugged her toward me. "Why not?"

Without thinking, I stroked the underside of her wrist with my thumb. She looked down at our joined hands then up at me again. My dick twitched. I was getting a semi just from this simple touch.

I had to stop touching her.

I released her hand, and she tucked her hands into her back pockets and took a step back.

"You were acting weird. And I didn't feel like you deserved to know. Not after the way you were badgering me about wearing a bikini." She lowered her eyes to the ground.

"You didn't let me explain. Have you seen how many scars I have on my body?"

She muttered something under her breath I didn't catch. I hooked two fingers under her chin and lifted her face to mine. "Quinn... the scars don't matter."

"Maybe to you they don't. It's different for you. Yours are sports-related and...." She sucked in a breath and averted her eyes. "You're a guy, so you wouldn't understand...." Her words trailed off, and she stared at the boat ramp, not meeting my eyes.

I wrapped my hands around her upper arms, feeling this constant need to touch her, to bring her closer to me so I could make her understand. It felt important, somehow, to help her see her scars the way I would. "You know how I would look at your scars?"

"How?"

"Like they're beautiful." Her eyes locked onto mine as I skimmed my hands down her arms and took her hands in mine. "Because they are. They tell part of your story, but not all of it. You're more than your scars. But those scars just prove what a warrior you are. They're like samurai sword wounds. Be bold. Be strong. Wear them proudly."

"Samurai sword wounds?" She laughed softly and blinked back the tears in her eyes. "Really?"

"They make you a badass."

"You think I'm a badass?" she whispered, her eyes on my mouth, our bodies moving imperceptibly closer.

"Mmhmm." I released her hands and traced the curve of her jaw with the backs of my fingers. "And one day soon, you're going to show me your scars."

"You… you want to see my scars?" She placed her hand over my heart, and I covered it with mine.

I wanted to see more than her scars. I wanted to see all of her. Every inch of skin. Every curve and dip and valley. I wanted to drag my tongue through her soft folds. Taste her sweetness on my lips. Lick the sweet juices of the forbidden fruit.

I wanted to be the one to show her how good a guy could make her feel. I wanted to hear her scream my name when I gave her an orgasm that would rock her fucking world.

Fuck. I shouldn't want any of this. I shouldn't even be thinking dirty thoughts about this girl standing in front of me, looking like an angel.

So sweet and young and innocent.

"You're going to bare your stomach to me. Only me." I was doing this for her, I told myself.

I held out her helmet, ready to put it on for her, but she took it from my hand and did it herself.

"How do I know I can trust you with something like that?"

"Guess you'll have to be brave. Take a leap of faith." I snapped down her visor and straddled my bike, putting my helmet on. Then, kicking up the stand, I started the engine, and it roared to life. Fuck, I loved that sound. "Ready to ride?"

If only she'd ride me.

Jesus Christ. I needed to get this shit out of my head.

In answer, she hopped on behind me and wrapped her arms around my waist.

By some miracle, my body was loose and relaxed on the ride home. It gave me hope. Maybe I'd do better at the track tomorrow. Maybe I'd be able to ride the way I used to.

Chapter Fourteen

Quinn

Declan glared at the empty breadbasket then turned that glare on me. "You missed a few crumbs."

I offered him a piece of the baguette in my hand. It was only a small piece because I'd eaten the rest. He huffed out a loud breath and checked his phone for the time again.

"Where the fuck is he?" he growled, draining the rest of his drink and slamming the empty glass onto the table. Fittingly, Declan had ordered the Dark & Stormy, a fiery ginger beer cocktail.

"He's not going to show up, is he?" I took a sip of my sparkling water with a twist, hoping it would stave off my hunger and disappointment.

"He'll be here," Mason assured me. "The dinner was his idea. He made the reservation."

It was a belated graduation dinner, and my dad was already fifteen minutes late. When had he become so unreliable?

The restaurant was long and narrow, dark wood with French posters on the exposed brick walls and jazz music piping from the speakers. I craned my neck, looking past the suits hanging out at the long, glossy wood bar toward the front door.

No sign of Dad.

"Let's order without him," Holden said. None of us put up a fight when he flagged down the server who appeared at our table within seconds.

"We're ready to order," Mason said, gesturing to me with his hand, *Ladies first*.

"I'll have the burger, please," I told the server, who wore a white tuxedo shirt and black pants. "It comes with fries, right?"

"Pommes frites," he said.

I nearly rolled my eyes. Same thing. This might be a French bistro, but we were in Austin, not Paris. *Get over yourself, dude.*

"Can I get it without the aioli and just have American cheese instead of this…" I glanced at the menu in my hand. "Whatever this cheese is…."

"Gruyere," the server said.

Declan lost patience and threw up his hands. "Just give her the damn burger that's on the menu."

I scowled at him. "I don't want all that weird stuff on it."

"This isn't McDonald's," he said. "Who orders a burger at a

French restaurant?"

He looked so scandalized I had to laugh. Then I redirected my gaze to the server. "Can I please just have a plain burger with nothing on it?"

Five minutes after we ordered, my dad waltzed through the front door. For a moment, I wasn't even sure it was him.

For the past five years, my dad has been having a midlife crisis. Or, at least, that was what Mom called it. It all started on his forty-fifth birthday when he traded in his SUV for a Porsche 911. I still remember when his idea of fun was an annual fishing trip with his college buddies. Or his monthly poker games in the den.

He used to be a good dad, the kind of dad you could rely on to be there for you when you needed him.

I don't think I ever really got over him leaving. And I'm not sure I ever truly forgave him for cheating on Mom. But my relationship with my dad was complicated. He gave me a kidney when I was twelve, and even though I hated the things he'd done, I still loved him. Because he was my dad and hello, he gave me a kidney.

Now I watched him escort a leggy brunette to our table, his hand on her lower back, a broad smile on his suntanned face. He was wearing a dark tailored suit and a white dress shirt with the first two buttons undone. He looked as if he'd just stepped off a yacht after a holiday in the Caribbean. So it took me a few minutes to fully process that this was indeed my fifty-year-old father.

"Holy shit," Mason said.

"Well, damn," Declan said. "Daddy-O's doing all right for himself. I'd tap that."

"Now I can see why he was late," Holden muttered.

With long dark hair and caramel skin, this woman looked like she could be a Brazilian supermodel. She couldn't have been much older than Mason.

My dad was handsome. I'd never really thought about it until Evie had called him a DILF. And I hated that. I hated that everything had changed and that now I felt like I was looking at someone I used to know and vaguely remembered.

My dad had a big smile on his face when he stopped in front of our table—two small tables that had been pushed together to accommodate our party of six, although I'd thought we were going to be a party of five.

"There's my Bean." He pulled me out of my seat and into a hug. My dad used to smell clean, like soap and peppermint gum. Now he smelled like expensive cologne. Nothing about him was familiar except for his voice. "How are you doing, kiddo?"

"Great. I'm doing great." *Other than the fact that you missed my graduation and now you brought a date to our family dinner, everything is just great.*

He released me and pulled out a chair for the woman. I don't remember him ever doing that for Mom. I stared at the woman across from me. She was beautiful. Sexy. Exotic.

She wore a black silky wrap dress with a plunging neckline and a gold medallion around her neck. Her hair was dark, cut in long layers, and her eyeliner was winged, but the rest of her makeup was minimal.

My dad made the introductions. Her name was Camilla, and she ran her own PR company, which my dad had hired to do some campaigns for Green Fields Market. At second glance, she was probably in her early thirties, if I had to guess, but still too young for my dad.

When she picked up her menu, I saw it. The diamond on her ring finger was the size of a small asteroid. It felt like such a punch in the gut that I was having trouble breathing.

My brothers and I exchanged looks, raised brows, and expressions that said, *What the fuck?*

My dad waited until he and Camilla had put in their orders to drop the bomb.

"Camilla and I are getting married. We wanted you to be the first to know." He beamed like he was doing us a big favor by telling us he'd proposed to a woman that none of us had even met.

For a few moments, my brothers and I sat in stunned silence. I mean, I'd seen the ring. We all had. It was hard to miss. But those words sounded so wrong coming out of my father's mouth. *Camilla and I are getting married.*

For the first thirteen years of my life, it had been Abby and Mark. Mark and Abby. Whenever their friends used to say it, it almost sounded like one word. That's how close they were. Now it was Mark and Camilla. It didn't sound right.

"When's the wedding?" Mason asked.

"October."

October? I'd be in California in October. That was only a few months away. How long had they been dating? It couldn't have been that long unless he'd kept it from us. "Isn't that… kind of sudden?"

"When you know, you know." He winked at Camilla. *Winked.* My father never used to wink like that. I was so tempted to punch him in the face and tell him I wanted my old dad back. Not this suave stranger in a tailored suit who winked at sexy women who were too young for him.

"I want to make her my wife before some other rogue comes along and claims her," he said with a chuckle.

"Never." Camilla placed her palm on his cheek, a loving gesture and a little too intimate for a family dinner. My father wrapped his hand around her wrist and looked at her like she was the only woman in the world. "You're the only man for me."

Suddenly, I'd lost my appetite.

The dinner was a disaster, and not only because my French burger was so rare, it could have practically walked off my plate, but because I just felt so betrayed.

My dad and I used to be close. I was his Bean, and he was my hero. When I was a kid, I'd been a daddy's girl. I used to believe he could fix anything, make everything better.

But I didn't even know who he was anymore. It felt like one day, my dad decided he didn't want to be a family man anymore. When Dad left, Declan was in his first year of culinary school in New York, and Holden and Mason were in college. So it was just me and Mom in that big old house that felt so empty without my brothers and dad.

"Remember how Mom and Dad used to slow dance in the kitchen?" Mason asked on the drive home.

We were reminiscing about some of our happiest family memories. Annual camping trips, summer beach vacations, birthdays and anniversaries, and holidays. I felt like I'd missed half of them. And I didn't even remember them dancing.

"It was always that one song," Holden said.

"I fucking hate that song," Declan muttered.

"Which song was it?" I looked at Declan, who was next to me in the back seat. He didn't even bother answering.

"A Bryan Adams song," Holden said.

"'Everything I Do, I Do It For You,'" Mason said.

A wave of sadness washed over me.

My brothers had memories of my parents slow dancing in the kitchen, like two people who were so in love that even years later, they were still keeping the romance alive. They'd been together since their freshman year at UT Austin. So how could they erase all that history?

"When did they stop dancing?" I asked because it seemed important.

"I don't know." Mason glanced at Holden before returning his eyes to the road.

"We must have been young," Holden said.

Declan snorted. "We used to make gagging noises and tell them it was gross."

My brothers laughed, but I couldn't join in. After Dad left, I remember thinking that maybe I really had been an accident. I was so much younger than my brothers, and whenever I used to annoy Declan, he *told* me I was an accident.

What if I had been the one to kill the romance?

Now I was home, sitting cross-legged on my bed, my fingers flying over the keyboard. Fiction was a good escape from the real world, from the anger I felt inside, and this story was shaping up to be a good one. I was wearing my headphones, the Bryan Adams song playing on repeat. I'd never listened to it before, but now I thought it was just about the most romantic song I'd ever heard. It made my heart ache, and I poured all those emotions into my story.

My music cut out, and I answered my phone without even checking the name on the screen.

"Hey. You okay?"

I'd expected it to be Evie calling me back. But the low voice was definitely male and definitely not Evie. "Jesse?"

"Yeah, it's me. Sorry. Did I wake you?"

"No. I wasn't asleep."

"Are you okay?"

"I…" He was calling to ask if I was okay? I didn't even know what to think about that. I pushed my laptop aside and leaned back against the pillows propped against my headboard. It had been almost two weeks since we'd gone to the lake, and I'd only seen him a few times at work. There had been no motorcycle rides. No intimate moments. No almost-kisses.

Jesse was busy. Mason had told me that when I asked why he hardly ever came to work anymore. But he hadn't told me what Jesse was so busy doing, and I hadn't bothered asking. Maybe he was busy hanging out with Tasha or some other random girl. So I'd been too scared to ask.

"I'm okay. Why are you calling?"

"I talked to Mason. He told me about your dad. Do you feel like talking about it?"

Right now, he sounded so much like the old Jesse that it made my heart hurt. He cared. He was calling to make sure I was okay. He wanted to know if I wanted to talk about it. And maybe I did. Maybe I wanted to tell him how I was feeling. Just get it all out there and untangle my mixed-up emotions.

"This whole thing is so... I don't know... it feels like it came out of left field. I just... a big part of me has always been holding out hope that maybe my parents would settle their differences and get back together," I admitted. "I guess... I just wanted things to go back to the way they used to be. Which sounds stupid."

I sounded exactly like the naïve eighteen-year-old sheltered girl he'd accused me of being, but I didn't really care right now. I just wanted to be honest and tell him how I was feeling.

"I know life doesn't work that way," I went on. "But I never thought my dad would become this kind of guy, you know?"

"I know. But people change. Life changes them."

It sounded like he was talking about himself, too, and I'd seen how much Jesse had changed.

"I guess. My mom didn't even know. So we had to be the ones to tell her." My brothers and I had decided that it would be best rather than have her find out from mutual acquaintances or someone at work. "He didn't even have the decency to tell her himself. That's just... so low. They have four kids together, and now it's like he forgot how happy they used to be. He said that he's never loved anyone the way he loves Camilla."

"And I just... I can't understand how my dad could say that. I don't understand how he could lie to us... lie to himself like that." The more I thought about it, the angrier I got. Because it wasn't true, it couldn't be. How could he possibly love this woman more than he'd loved Mom?

"How did your mom take the news?"

"She didn't say much. She drank a glass of wine then went

to bed. But I think… I feel like she still loves him. I just had this feeling that she never really got over him, even after what he did… she still loves him."

Jesse was quiet for a moment, and I thought about what I'd just said. Was that how it was for him? Did he still love Alessia, despite what she'd done to him?

"Love is fucked up," he said a few seconds later as if he'd been giving it some thought. "I don't think you can ever truly know what another person is capable of, no matter how many years you've been with them."

My breath caught in my throat, and I squeezed my eyes shut as if that would block out the pain his words had caused. When had Jesse become so cynical?

"But… I mean… you still believe in love, right?" I don't know why I asked him that, except that I needed to hear him say he did.

"Not really, no. I don't believe there's one true love for everyone if that's what you're asking."

How could he not believe in love anymore? How could he believe that you could never truly know another person? What about soul mates? What about true, deep, *real* love? I needed to believe that it was real, that love was worth finding and keeping and fighting for.

But now he was saying he didn't even believe in it.

I sagged against the pillows, my heart sinking to my stomach. Everything felt so hopeless.

Yet another sucker punch in the gut for me tonight. It felt like I'd not only lost my dad, but I'd lost Jesse too. Not that Jesse had ever been mine, but I'd been holding out hope that one day he *could* be.

Optimism was so overrated.

"Do you feel like going for a ride?" His question took me by complete surprise.

My brow furrowed, trying to make sense of this.

I should have said no.

But I was still that stupid girl with hope in her heart who believed in true love. And despite all the odds stacked against us, Jesse was still the only guy I'd ever loved.

So I said yes. Another leap of faith.

Maybe I should be looking at this differently. If Jesse didn't believe in true love, there was no point in sitting around, wishing and hoping for something that could never be.

Maybe I'd channel the fearless heroine from the story I was writing. Tonight I'd be reckless and daring. Throw caution to the wind without worrying about the consequences.

I was tired of waiting for something to happen. So why not take charge and *make* it happen?

I had some things I needed to learn, and who better to teach me than a guy who was no stranger to risk-taking.

Chapter Fifteen

Jesse

I don't know why I asked her to go for a ride. Maybe it was because she sounded so sad on the phone. I knew how much she loved her dad and how much she looked up to him. When Quinn was a kid, her dad doted on her like Jude did with Gracie. Being the only girl and a lot younger than her brothers, I suppose it was only natural that he'd treated her like a little princess.

So finding out that her dad had cheated on her mom, and now this… it had to have hit her hard. I could empathize. I knew how it felt to be betrayed by someone you loved. Or, in my case,

I thought I'd loved.

She came out through the garage and walked toward the motorcycle I was straddling. She was wearing the jacket I bought her with tiny shorts, the little rebel, and carrying the helmet I told her to keep for the next time we went for a ride.

"Hey Jesse," she said with a little smile when she stopped next to me.

My eyes roamed down her legs, over the toned calves, and to the cheetah print Nikes on her feet, then back to her face. "Why are you wearing shorts?"

"I was hot."

When I rode on my own, I wore a T-shirt and jeans. Sometimes I wore shorts. The truth was that if you were in a motorcycle crash, covering your legs in denim wouldn't do jack shit to protect you. But with Quinn, I wanted to minimize the risks as much as possible.

"You need to change into jeans."

"I'll be fine." Quinn was so stubborn. Always had been. "Besides, I trust you."

"You trust me."

"You know how to handle a motorcycle. You've been riding forever. So we're not going to crash."

She sounded so sure of herself, so sure of *me*.

I glanced at her dark house. When I'd invited her to go for a ride, it hadn't even occurred to me that she'd have to sneak out. "Would your mom be okay with this?"

I vaguely remembered Abby telling me that if Quinn asked for a ride, I should say no. But that had been years ago when Quinn was just a kid.

She shrugged one shoulder. "She'd be fine with it. It's no big deal. Let's just go somewhere, okay?"

"Where do you want to go?"

"I don't know. Just..." She rocked back on her heels. "Where do you go when you want to get away from it all? Do you have a special place?"

I thought about it for a minute. There was a place I used to go sometimes. Just to decompress and get in the right headspace before a race. But it would be a stupid thing to do late at night.

"Take me there," she said as if she'd read my mind.

"You have to hike to get there. It's too dark. It would be too dangerous."

"I have my phone flashlight, and I'm wearing high tops. Let's go there. Take me to your special place. Please," Quinn pleaded.

I studied her face. My sunshine girl should never look this sad. I opened my mouth to say no, but she held up her index finger to indicate that I should wait a minute. Then she handed me her helmet and hurried away. A few minutes later, she returned with a triumphant smile on her face and two head torches in her hand.

I had to give it to her. Quinn was one of the most determined people I'd ever met.

I held her hand for the entire trek to the waterfall, the head torches guiding the way. The first part of the hike was mostly flat, the dirt path surrounded by a few scrubby bushes and sparse trees. Toward the end, the descent was steep, bordered by cypress trees with Spanish moss hanging from the branches. The night air was musky, scented with earth and pine, but I could still detect Quinn's citrusy scent. I inhaled it with every breath I took.

She smelled like summertime, like hope and possibility.

It was easy to envision Quinn on a SoCal beach, her blonde hair bleached lighter from the sun and saltwater, her apricot skin bronzed and glowing. She would probably love California as much as I did. I'd moved to Temecula because it was a motocross hotbed, and last summer, I'd been house-hunting, all set to sell my place in Texas and make Temecula my permanent home.

But in May, when I moved out of the condo I was renting, all I wanted to do was get the hell out of there and never look back.

I guided her down the steep incline, keeping her right behind me so my body would block her fall. Rocks skittered beneath our feet, and when she stumbled and slammed into me, my arm snaked around her back to steady her, a reminder that this was a stupid-ass thing to do late at night.

I've done a lot of stupid shit in my life. I had taken a lot of risks without giving it a second thought. I dove off cliffs in Mexico. Jumped out of an airplane without a parachute. I'd done more tricks and stunts on a dirt bike than I could count.

So this wouldn't have been a big deal if not for the fact that I was responsible for Quinn's safety.

The sound of rushing water grew louder, and a few minutes later, we came into the clearing at the base of the waterfall. The moon was big and bright tonight, shining on the water cascading from the sixty-foot travertine drop in front of us.

"Oh," Quinn breathed, stopping in her tracks to take in the sight. Now that we'd reached our destination, we removed our head torches. "I love this."

"I thought you would." It was hard to see at night, but that didn't dim her joy.

She dragged her gaze away from the waterfall to me. Her hair paled in the moonlight, face cast in shadows. Then she walked to the edge of the water pooling at the base of the falls. I grabbed her waist and pulled her back against me, my mouth close to her ear and my arms circling her middle. "Don't get so close. I don't want you to fall."

"Too late. I already have," she said quietly, her words barely audible over the sound of the rushing water.

Maybe I'd imagined those words. Maybe Quinn had said something completely different. But that was what I'd heard.

I moved her back a safe distance and took off my jacket, laying it on the ground for us to sit. She did the same with hers, and we sat side by side, her shoulder leaning against my upper arm, knees hugged to her chest.

"Have you ever brought anyone else here?"

I turned my head to look at her face in profile, her straight nose, and the long sweep of her dark lashes. "No."

She smiled like that made her happy. "Have you... I haven't seen you much." She cleared her throat, her words hesitant like she was afraid of the answer. "What have you been up to?"

I didn't mention the night I'd gone out with Tanner and ran into Tasha. I could have taken her home and fucked her, but I didn't. Instead, I'd gone home and jerked off to the vision of Quinn in my head, which had pissed me off. I'd also spent countless hours watching and analyzing my races, pinpointing where I'd gone wrong and what I could have done better.

"I've been working out a lot. Mountain biking. And I've been doing a lot of dozing."

What I hadn't been doing was going to the track.

"Dozing?" Her brow furrowed. "Sleeping?"

I laughed and rolled out my shoulders. They were stiff from all the hours I'd spent clearing my land. My dad had been so thrilled with my plan he'd offered to send me an entire crew from his construction company, but I'd declined. I wanted to do most of the work myself. "No. Bulldozing." I smiled at her confusion. "I'm building a playground."

"A playground."

"Mmhmm."

"What kind of playground?"

"The kind with dirt jumps and ramps."

Her whole face lit up, and her mouth formed a comical O that made me laugh again. "That's so exciting." She hesitated a moment before she asked, "What made you decide to do that?"

"You." It was true. Mostly.

"Me?"

She looked so fucking pretty and so hopeful, I couldn't stop myself from touching her. I wrapped a lock of her hair around my fingers and gave it a gentle tug before I released it. "Yeah, you. Because of what you said that night… about a life without dreams being too sad for words."

"So this is your new dream?"

I shrugged one shoulder, my gaze on her face. She wasn't my dream, but she looked like one with her skin bathed in the moonlight. She was glowing, a hazy halo of blonde hair framing her perfect face, and I couldn't tear my eyes away.

"An old dream revived. I haven't competed in FMX in a few years. Looking to get back into it."

She nodded, taking a few moments to think about it before she asked, "Are you scared?"

"Scared of what?" I hedged.

"Everything."

"Not everything, no."

"What scares you most?"

"That I'll fail," I answered honestly. "That I'll get injured again and suffer another setback. But mostly... I'm scared I'll fail."

In the past, I'd never thought about failing. That word hadn't even been in my vocabulary. But now that I'd failed at fucking everything, it haunted me.

"You won't fail. You're going to soar so high you'll touch the sun."

There she went again, putting too much faith in me. "That's what Icarus tried to do. And look what happened to him," I joked.

"Moral of the story. Don't make your wings out of wax."

We were both laughing, and the tension in my body melted away, replaced by hope and possibility. So maybe that was why I wrapped my arm around her shoulders without giving it a second thought.

"Jesse," she whispered.

"Hmm?" I turned my head to look at her.

She pointed to the sky. "I made a wish. Now it's your turn."

Chapter Sixteen

Jesse

Quinn was straddling me. How the hell had we gotten here? My brazen sunshine girl was a magician. So bold. So fucking ballsy that it made me question whether she truly was as innocent and naïve as I'd thought.

"What do you think you're doing, Sunshine Girl?" I inhaled the scent of her hair. The scent of *her*. Flowers and citrus.

"I don't know. I just want… I need…" She grabbed my shoulders to steady herself.

"What do you want?"

She swallowed, her eyes searching mine as she lifted her hand to my face and tentatively traced my cheekbone and then my jaw with her fingertips. Her touch was light, gentle as a soft breeze, but it ignited something inside me. Made me burn for her.

My hands cupped her ass and squeezed. I didn't know if it was a warning or permission to continue rocking against my erection, making me impossibly hard.

"It's easier to be brave in the dark," she said.

"Is it?"

"For me, it is. Do you want to kiss me, Jesse?" She swept her tongue across her lower lip. "Do you want to touch me?"

The answer was *Fuck, yes*. I wanted to touch her everywhere. Kiss her lips and her silky soft skin and the jagged ridges of her scars.

But Quinn was looking for something I couldn't give her. She wanted love. Something real and strong and true. She still believed in happily ever after and fairytale romance. She still had stars in her eyes and wore her heart on her sleeve, and I knew with absolute certainty that if she gave me that heart, I would break it.

I wasn't in the right place in my life to make her dreams come true or to open my heart to her. Right now, I was too fucked up. Still hanging on to so much bitterness and anger that I'd never be able to give her all of me. And Quinn shouldn't have to settle for less.

"If I kissed you… if I touched you in all the places I wanted to, it wouldn't mean anything. It would be purely physical. It would be meaningless sex."

"I don't believe you. You're lying again." Her touch grew bolder, and she traced my lying lips with her index finger.

"I'm not lying." I didn't want to be careless with Quinn's feelings or promise her something I couldn't deliver.

"You lie to yourself all the time. You're lying now. Otherwise, you wouldn't be so scared. If it meant nothing to you, you'd kiss me dizzy, and you'd… you would do the things I imagine and dream about. I want to know what it feels like."

"What happened to waiting for the person who treats you like a queen?"

"Why can't that be you?"

"Because it can't be."

"And yet… you don't want me to be with anyone else."

Yeah, I couldn't explain that one either, so I remained silent.

"You don't want me, but you don't want anyone else to have me."

"I never said I didn't want you." My erection was proof of that. My hands cupping her ass, holding her in place, was further proof. But lust was completely different than love.

"How can I write something that I've never experienced?"

My brows shot up in surprise. "You write about sex?"

"Well…" She chewed on her lower lip. "I had to skip those scenes. I need to do more research. I…" Her eyes lowered, and she averted her face. "I watched some things on my laptop.…"

I couldn't help it. A laugh burst out of me.

She huffed out a breath and tried to climb off me. I should have let her go, but I held on tighter so she couldn't escape.

"What did you watch, Sunshine Girl? Did you watch porn?"

She nodded, shocking me into silence. This girl was full of surprises. I would never have guessed that sweet, innocent Quinn Cavanaugh would even consider watching porn.

"And did you like it?" I squeezed her ass, prompting her to answer my question. My dick twitched just thinking about her lying on her bed, watching porn on her laptop while she touched herself. "Did you touch yourself?"

I shouldn't be asking her this, but she'd been the one to bring it up, and now it was the only thing I could think about.

"Yes. But it's not the same." She rocked her small body against my erection, and I should have stopped it, but I didn't, which seemed to be a recurring theme whenever Quinn and I were together.

"Tell me. Tell me how you imagine it."

She shook her head. "I don't want to imagine it. I want you to show me." She got up on her knees and rubbed against me, her breasts pressed against my chest. Taunting. Teasing.

"Don't play these games with me, baby girl."

"Or what? What will you do, Jesse? Will you take my virginity and show me what it's like to be with a man? Or maybe you're not brave enough for that. Maybe you're just a scared boy—"

I grasped her chin and crushed my lips against hers, effectively shutting her up. She'd played me, and I'd fallen for it, but I didn't give a shit right now. I was kissing Quinn, and she was right. I didn't want any other guy to have that privilege.

Her lips parted on a gasp, and I slid my tongue inside her mouth, stroking the deepest recesses.

She tasted just as sweet as I remembered. She tasted like sunshine and summertime and long-forgotten innocence.

I didn't know what made this kiss so different from the others, but it felt like the first time I'd ever been kissed. Heady and intoxicating, like an adrenaline rush that zipped through my veins and ignited every cell in my body.

All the blood rushed to my dick, rock hard and threatening

to burst through the zipper of my jeans. She was rocking against me, her pace more frantic, her inexperience evident in her clumsy movements. But my body responded just the same, and for some reason, her inexperience was an even bigger turn-on.

It was all I could do not to come in my jeans as she dry-humped me beneath a waterfall under the light of a silver moon.

It felt like high school again. Oh right. This girl was barely out of high school.

Fuck me.

"Jesse…" she panted. "I'm almost… Oh God…" She moaned, the sound shooting straight to my cock. I can't remember the last time I'd been this hard.

It was fucking agony not to give in to the overwhelming urge to rip off her clothes and give her exactly what she wanted.

I moved my mouth lower and guided her tit into my mouth, my teeth nipping and biting her nipple through her thin cotton tank top. She wasn't wearing a bra, my brazen sunshine girl, as if she'd been planning to seduce me in her tiny shorts and her braless tank top.

Her hands grasped my shoulders, her short nails digging into my skin, and I wondered what had changed. It wasn't that long ago she told me she was waiting for someone to treat her like a queen, and that wasn't me.

She was panting, her chest heaving, sweet little moans and whimpers falling from her pouty lips. I moved my mouth to her other breast, giving it the same attention as the first one, my hand kneading her ass cheek, squeezing it roughly in my palm as she rode me.

I wanted to slide my hand inside her shorts. Squeeze her clit between my fingers. Shove two fingers inside her and stretch her tight walls to make room for me. To create a space that only I could fill.

"Oh God. Jesse," she rasped.

I didn't even want to think about how wet she must be. How easy it would be to unzip my jeans and glide inside her, breach her tight walls. Feel her muscles clench around me, milking an orgasm out of me that would go on and on. She would be tight as a fist. Her virginal pussy pink and swollen, so dripping wet that her juices would coat my dick and make it so easy to slide into her and bury myself to the hilt.

My cock was throbbing. So hard it was painful.

She should be punished for this. She should be punished for being so bold and brazen, for making me so hard for her that I had to jerk off in the privacy of my own home instead of letting Tasha ride my dick like she'd offered.

I fisted her hair and yanked it hard, exposing the column of her neck that begged to be marked by my lips and teeth. I left purple bruises on her skin while she shuddered and screamed my name, her body convulsing with an orgasm that I hadn't even given her.

"Can I touch you?" she asked a few seconds later, her voice hushed, her hand drifting lower to the button of my jeans. "Can I see you?"

I squeezed my eyes shut while she fumbled with the button. My cock was screaming yes, but my brain was telling me it was a bad fucking idea. I was a grown-ass man, and she was still a girl pretending to be bold and brazen, so much braver in the dark than she usually would be.

"I don't want to be reckless with you."

"I want to be reckless."

"No, you don't," I said gruffly.

It damn near killed me to do it, but I shoved her hand away, the hand that was rubbing against my hard cock, and lifted her off me. For a moment, she looked dazed, like she was still coming down from her orgasmic high and couldn't figure out how she'd gotten there, sitting next to me instead of in my lap.

Then she said, her voice so soft and sweet, "I don't think you're a failure, Jesse. And I don't think you're an asshole either."

But she didn't know. She didn't know the half of it.

I was both—a failure and an asshole, but not a complete bastard.

Which was why I drove her home and dropped her off, safe and sound. This whole night had been a mistake.

I told myself that I would stay away from her, that from now on, we really would be *just friends* and nothing more.

As it turned out, she was right. I lied to myself all the time.

Chapter Seventeen

Quinn

"Hold the bottom and wrap your lips around the top. Take it as far as it can go and slide it in and out. No teeth, though. Just lips. Unless he deserves it, then feel free to sink your teeth in."

I was laughing so hard I nearly choked. "I can't do this. This cucumber is too fat."

Evie shrugged. "You said he felt big."

"Yeah, but… I mean…" I stared at the cucumber in my hand. We'd peeled the top half but left the skin on the bottom. Evie claimed it would make it easier to grip. I wrapped my lips around the cucumber again and sucked on it before I bit off the top, making Evie laugh.

"Do you think this is dick-sized?" I waved the cucumber in the air as I floated past her on my giant inflatable donut. Pink with sprinkles. Evie was on the chocolate donut with sprinkles.

She grabbed the cucumber from my hand and studied it before taking a big bite. "It depends on the guy," she said. "But don't get your hopes up. He won't taste like a cucumber. We should have rolled it in salt. How weird is it that we're expected to suck on something that guys pee with?"

My nose scrunched up. "Ew. And how weird is it that you're eating something I was sucking on?"

She wrapped her lips around the cucumber and pushed it into her mouth as far as it would go, her cheeks hollowed before she slid it out. "I'm deep-throating a cucumber. This has to be an all-time low." She shook her head like she couldn't believe it and tossed the cucumber across the pool. "Look. It's a floater."

We both cracked up as we watched the cucumber bob past us in the water. I was laughing so hard my stomach hurt, and I nearly capsized my donut.

"Have you given Ridge a blow job yet?" I asked a few minutes later. Obviously, I had sex on the brain.

"I'm not going there. Too many girls have already been up close and personal with his dick."

I thought about that for a minute. "So you want to be someone special to him?"

She shrugged and trailed her hand through the water, staring into the blue depths. "I shouldn't even be hanging out with him."

"Why not?"

"We're too alike. We come from similar backgrounds. It could never end well."

"But that's a good thing that you're so alike." The fact that she knew that about Ridge meant that they must have talked about important things. They'd opened up to each other enough to know that they had a lot in common. "Who says it has to end?"

She sighed. "He's going to San Marcos State to play football. This is his big opportunity. His chance to do something better with his life. I don't want to be the girl standing in his way." She spun around on her donut and then faced me again. Her green eyes were almost translucent in the sunlight, dark hair slicked back from her face. "Besides, I have my own plans for the future, and I can't get sidetracked by some guy."

In the fall, Evie was starting the nursing program at the community college in Austin. She didn't want to leave Wren, so she'd be living at home and commuting. She wanted to be an ER nurse, and I knew she'd be amazing at it. Evie was tough and strong, but she was caring too. When I had my second kidney transplant, she was there for me. That's how you learned who your true friends were. They were the ones who showed up in good times and bad, and they lifted your spirits even when you weren't much fun to be around.

"San Marcos is only a forty-minute drive from Cypress Springs," I pointed out. "Why couldn't you have it all? The future *and* the boy."

She shook her head, empathically denying my words. "Life doesn't work that way. You can't have it all."

Sometimes she was so pessimistic, and it made me want to shake some sense into her. I wanted her to dream big, to believe that anything was possible, but I knew it was hard for her to see a bright future for herself. "You *can* have it all, Evie. You like him, right?"

She shrugged one shoulder. "Meh."

I splashed water at her. "Lie to yourself all you want. But admit it to me, at least. I'm your best friend," I reminded her. "I told you all about Jesse."

"Fine. He's okay, I guess." But a little smile tugged at her lips, giving her away.

I grinned. "Oh my God. You're such a liar. You really like him."

"Shut up." She rolled her eyes, but she still couldn't hide the smile. "I don't want him to know. His ego is already as super-inflated as this donut."

I laughed. "You're ridiculous. So… are you going to have sex?"

"I'm not… we're not… Quinn, he's…" She clamped her mouth shut and pursed her lips like she was trying to keep the words inside and regretted saying as much as she did, which had told me absolutely nothing.

"He's what? What is Ridge?"

Evie studied her nails, painted black cherry, her signature color, and refused to meet my eye. "You know how he is. He's a total player."

That wasn't what she was going to say, but I didn't push it. "Do you know that for a fact? Or are you just basing it on the rumors?"

"It doesn't matter. I barely know the guy. It's just a summer fling. No harm, no foul. It means absolutely nothing."

Despite her breezy tone, I could tell she was lying. Evie liked Ridge, and I could tell he was crazy about her. It was so obvious it was laughable. "What time is he picking you up?"

"Not for a few hours." She pushed my inflatable with her foot and sent me drifting across the pool. With my eyes closed, I hung my arms over the sides, my fingertips skimming the water while the hot Texas sun beat down on my face and bronzed my skin.

"You should come with us," she said a little while later.

I snorted. "As a third wheel? No thanks."

"You wouldn't have been a third wheel if you would have said yes to Walker."

"I couldn't do that. You know I couldn't. Not after—"

"After what, Quinn? I don't trust Jesse. He's running hot and cold, and he's playing you."

"Maybe he is. But I'm the one who initiated it."

I was referring to three nights ago at the waterfall when I'd climbed on top of Jesse and straddled him. So shameless. I had no idea how I'd had the guts to pull a move like that, but I'd done it, and the following morning, in the harsh light of day, I'd felt like an idiot. So embarrassed that I threw myself at him. Had begged him to touch me. I must have reeked of desperation.

What was wrong with me?

But last night, he showed up for work, and I caught him watching me a few times. Not only that, but when he walked me to my car, he kissed me. He pushed me against the stone wall of the brewery, and he'd kissed me in the dark, his lips firm but soft, his arms caging me in, his tongue stroking mine and setting off tiny explosions inside me.

And I knew why he'd kissed me. He hadn't been too happy when Walker had stopped by and asked me to the Fourth of July fireworks. Not only had Walker invited me to the fireworks, but he'd done it within earshot of Jesse and Mason.

I'd lied and told Walker that I already made plans to spend the holiday with my family. It wasn't a total lie. My brothers were working, and Mom asked me to eat dinner at the brewery with her. Our way of being together as a family. So I *was* spending the holiday with my family. But I still could have gone to the fireworks with Walker afterward. I'd just chosen not to.

I didn't want to lead Walker on. I could barely handle one guy, let alone two. And the guy I wanted was playing head games with me. Did he want me or not? I was so confused. I don't even think *he* knew what he wanted.

"Just be careful, okay?" Evie said later after she'd gotten ready for her date with Ridge. Although she refused to call it a date. Allegedly, they were just 'hanging out.'

He was picking her up at my house instead of hers because her car had broken down again. At least, that was the reason she'd given him. But I knew the truth. She didn't want Ridge to see where she lived, and she didn't want to subject him to her mom or her mom's boyfriend, who was now living with them.

"I don't want you to get hurt."

I wrapped my arms around her. "I love you. And don't worry about me. I can look after myself."

She raised a skeptical brow, but she hugged me and told me she loved me too. "Make him work for it. Seriously, Quinn. He needs to prove himself to you, not the other way around."

I knew she was right, and maybe I needed that reminder.

"Ridge is here," Evie said, sliding her phone into her pocket after checking it. "Is it okay if I crash here tonight?"

"You don't even have to ask." She smiled and headed for the front door. "But Evie…"

She spun around to face me and waited for me to tell her what was on my mind.

"You should let Ridge in. Let him see the real you."

Evie gave me a sad smile. "I can't do that."

"Why not?"

"Because he'd try to fix things."

Before I had a chance to respond, she walked out the front door. My curiosity got the best of me, so I moved to the window and watched her and Ridge. He circled the hood of his pickup and pulled her into a kiss. Then he did the most amazing thing. Ridge opened the passenger door for her. Like a gentleman. Like Evie's knight in shining armor. My hand went to my heart. He treated her like she was his queen, and he was her king.

I didn't care what Evie said. That looked like the real deal. It put a smile on my face and made me feel less guilty for deserting her to run off to California. Even though she'd always encouraged it, had told me she'd disown me if I didn't, I still worried about leaving her behind. But if Ridge were here for her, she'd have someone who cared about her the same way I did.

I was still smiling when I walked into the kitchen and found Mom working on her laptop. I grabbed a bottle of water from the fridge and sat across from her at the island. I sat there for five whole minutes before she even noticed I was there.

"Hey, baby." She shook her head as if to clear it. "Are you—"

Her phone rang on the countertop, and she held up one finger, indicating that she needed a minute. I grabbed my phone and took yet another virtual tour of UCLA. Then I scrolled through my Instagram and liked all the photos my brothers had posted. Jesse hadn't posted anything in months and had deleted all the photos of Alessia.

My thumb hovered over the search bar. Then, taking a deep breath, I typed her name. It had been a while since I'd stalked Alessia Rossi's Instagram. Her feed used to be filled with photos and reels of her and Jesse—#couplegoals—and my stupid heart had been crushed every time I'd seen their smiling faces. So I didn't know what had possessed me to look her up today.

I scrolled through her photos and stopped at one that caught my eye. I checked the date then double-checked it. She'd posted this photo in April. I stared at her face, the big smile on it as she posed for the camera. Then I studied Jesse's face, his casual posture, his arm draped around her shoulder. A smile on his face that didn't quite reach his summer sky eyes. At least, that was what I needed to believe.

And finally, I looked at Shiloh Leroux, standing next to Jesse, his other arm around her shoulders. She was smiling too, but like Jesse, her smile wasn't as bright as Alessia's.

I didn't follow celebrity gossip, but Shiloh Leroux and Brody McCallister's relationship had been one of the most talked-about stories in the school halls, so it had been nearly impossible not to hear the rumors about Ridge's brother, Brody. I knew Shiloh was Brody's girlfriend, so obviously, Jesse knew her too.

But none of this made sense. Why would Jesse have taken Alessia to Shiloh Leroux's concert in L.A.? In April. *After* she'd cheated on him. *After* he'd kissed me on Christmas Eve. Like I needed more proof that the kiss had meant nothing to him.

"Looks like I have to go to New York next week," my mom said with a sigh.

I lifted my head from my phone and tried to focus on her words. But my mind was elsewhere, still puzzling over why Jesse and Alessia were together as recently as April when he'd told me their relationship had ended last August. He'd lied to me. Why would he do that? "Sorry. What?"

She laughed. "Let's go to the brewery. We'll talk over dinner."

Chapter Eighteen

Quinn

Ripping off a piece of flatbread, I dipped it into the hummus—I practically lived on this stuff—and continued reading my paperback, doing my best to block out Carly and Aubrey's conversation. They were discussing Declan, and I'd rather get lost in fiction than hear about the sexy chef's 'heat factor.' I was tucked away at a table in the back of the taproom, eating a late lunch before my shift started.

"Next time, you'll have to come up to the lake with us," Carly said, just as if the lake house and the pontoon and Jet Skis were hers, and she had every right to extend the invitation.

Pretty sure Carly and Mason were sleeping together, but I didn't want to know about that either.

I looked up from my book as Ridge set down a plate with his lunch and took a seat across from me. He'd cut the sleeves off his dark green Cavanaugh Bros. Brewing Company T-shirt, showcasing his biceps, and the collar was ripped. Ridge always looked as if he'd just come out of a street fight.

Without asking for permission, he grabbed a cucumber spear off my plate. We'd gotten familiar enough that he felt like he could do that.

But all I could think about was that cucumber Evie and I had been deep throating in the pool last week, and I started laughing.

The more I thought about it, the harder I laughed.

"What's so funny, Bean?" He ate the cucumber in two bites, then took a huge bite of his sandwich, his brows cocked in question, prompting me for an answer.

Still laughing, I shook my head, unable to get the words out. Finally, when I pulled myself together, I took a sip of water and set my glass down on the zinc-topped table. "Nothing. It's just something stupid. And don't call me Bean."

"Why not?" He grinned. "It's cute."

"Just like that mayo on the corner of your mouth," I pointed out. Unfazed, he wiped it off with the back of his hand and took another bite of his BLT. If anyone had told me before this summer started that Ridge McCallister and I would become friends, I'd have called them crazy. But here we were.

"You've been hanging out with my brothers too much. That nickname is *not* cute."

"Why do they call you Bean?"

"Because a kidney looks like a bean." I pulled the necklace out of my T-shirt collar and showed him the silver charm. "I've had two kidney transplants."

Someone must have already told him, either Evie or my brothers because he didn't look surprised. "You good now?"

"Yep. All good."

He nodded and took another bite of his sandwich. A slice of tomato fell onto his plate. "What are you reading?" He jerked his chin at the paperback next to me.

I held it up so he could see the cover. "It's called *Bonjour Tristesse*."

His brows shot up. "You're reading in French?"

I laughed softly. "No. It's in English. The author was only eighteen when it was published, and it's so good," I said with a wistful sigh as I set the book next to my plate.

"Pretty sure S.E. Hinton was only sixteen when she wrote *The Outsiders*."

I tried to hide my surprise that he knew that, but I must have failed because he laughed. "Yeah. I'm not much of a reader. But that book…" He shrugged one shoulder. "It wasn't total shit."

By saying it wasn't total shit, I got the feeling he meant that it was pretty great.

"Evie thought so too. In fact, it's her favorite book."

She'd started reading it when I was recuperating from my kidney transplant. She'd loved it so much that I tracked down a signed limited-edition copy and gave it to her for her eighteenth birthday.

The part that had resonated with her, though, was the famous quote: 'Nothing gold can stay.'

I should have expected that, but it still made me sad.

Ridge gave me a crooked grin that was disarmingly boyish. "Yeah, I know. She loves that book."

And then it hit me. Ridge's nickname for Evie was Cherry. Cherry and Dallas. They both loved *The Outsiders*. They came from similar worlds. They belonged together. How much more perfect could they be for each other?

Ridge took another huge bite of his sandwich, completely oblivious to the fact that I was plotting out his future with my best friend.

"Shit. This is good. Best fucking BLT I ever ate."

"Declan would be thrilled to hear it. He bakes his own bread. The mayo is homemade. And I wouldn't be surprised if he slaughtered the pig himself." When I'd gone into the kitchen to get my hummus, he'd been slow-roasting pork belly for tonight's special and making 'country pâté' out of pork. He'd tried to get me to sample it so I could answer customers' questions, but no thanks. When I said it looked and smelled like dog food, he'd kicked me out of the kitchen.

"He uses every single bit of the pig from nose to tail." I pulled a face because that was just gross.

"A vegetarian's nightmare," Jesse said, taking a seat next to me.

I side-eyed him. Since when did he come to work early? My gaze dipped to the plate he set on the table in front of him. Goat's cheese salad with mixed greens.

"What are you doing here so early?" I blurted. So much for playing it cool and ignoring him. Which I'd been trying to do for the past week, after deciding that Evie's advice was good. Not to mention what I'd seen on Alessia's Instagram that I'd had no business stalking.

"It's the only way I get to see you." His voice was so low I wasn't sure I'd heard him correctly. More head games. Great. Just what I needed.

I wasn't even going to analyze or dissect his words. Nope. Not going there.

I looked across the table at Ridge, but he was too busy eating to pay us any attention. He finished his sandwich in two more bites and pushed back his chair, his eyes on me as he stood up. "If you need a ride to Walker's party, let me know."

I opened my mouth to ask him what he was talking about but shut it when he winked at me. Like we were in on a secret.

Was he doing this on purpose? Trying to make Jesse jealous? Had Ridge noticed that something was going on with Jesse and me?

"Catch you later, bro," Ridge told Jesse before he swaggered away, chuckling under his breath.

Was it obvious to everyone? My gaze drifted to Mason behind the bar, talking to a customer. He caught me watching and smiled at me before he went back to his conversation, not the least bit suspicious that Jesse was sitting right next to me.

Probably because nothing was going on with Jesse and me, except in my overactive imagination. Oh yeah, and the time I got myself off at the waterfall while he hadn't even been an active participant. Thinking about it now made me cringe.

"How's that story coming along?" Jesse asked.

My cheeks flushed with embarrassment. Yet another

humiliation to endure. Why had I told him about the story I was writing? "Fine."

"What's it about?"

"None of your business," I muttered.

He laughed and took a sip of his water. I ate my hummus and tried to ignore him, which was virtually impossible. He was sitting right next to me, so close that I could feel the warmth radiating off his skin. See the tendons in his arm flex when he speared his fork into the greens. God, I loved his hands. I loved how big they were with these thick veins that were obviously so fascinating I couldn't tear my eyes away.

"There's somewhere I want to take you after work."

"Where do you want to take me?" I dipped a carrot stick into the hummus and studiously avoided him.

My stupid heart was thrashing, just as if he'd said he was in love with me and couldn't live another day without me.

God, I needed help. I needed to stop looking at his veiny hands and his lean, muscular arms. I needed to stop noticing the way his throat bobbed on a swallow when he took a sip of water.

All my best intentions to avoid him and play it cool were being shot to hell just because he wanted to take me somewhere.

"It's a surprise. Mason said he's cool with letting you leave work early."

"You discussed this with Mason?" My gaze snapped to my brother again. He flipped the caps on four bottles of pale ale and set them in front of Carly, too busy flirting with her to notice me staring at him.

What the hell was going on? Obviously, Mason assumed Jesse

was just being a good friend, looking after his little sister while our mom was away. Maybe that was exactly what Jesse was doing.

"Is it a good surprise?"

He smiled. "You're going to love it."

So arrogant. So sure of himself. I needed to shoot him down. "I'm busy tonight. I'm going to Walker's party. So I'm not free." I stood up from the table, ready to make a dramatic exit.

If I'd expected him to look forlorn, I was sadly mistaken. He smirked at me. "Walker isn't throwing a party. And even if he was, it wouldn't matter."

"It wouldn't?"

He shook his head. "Nope. Because you're coming with me."

"Sorry to burst your bubble, racer boy. It's not happening." It was my turn to smirk.

Ha! That would show him. When I walked away, I had a smug smile on my face. I gave myself a mental pat on the back. *Good going, Quinn.*

Evie would be so proud.

"Why is this movie so funny?" I asked, laughing as I grabbed another handful of kettle corn from the tub in my lap.

Okay, so I'd ended up doing exactly what Jesse had wanted. But for the record, it was Mason and Holden's fault. They'd threatened to come over to the house and babysit if I didn't hang out with Jesse. And yes, they'd used the word babysitting.

Little did they know what they'd gotten me into. If my brothers knew, they'd be trying to keep me away from Jesse instead of pushing us together.

"The Dude abides." Jesse mimicked The Big Lebowski's voice and had me cracking up.

"That rug really ties the room together."

We went back and forth, reeling off quotes we'd committed to memory, laughing at each and every one as if it was the first time we'd ever heard them.

I'd watched "The Big Lebowski" so many times with my brothers and Jesse when they were in their teens. I was just a kid, and I was supposed to be asleep, but I'd sneak out of my room so I could hang out with them in the den and watch movies and eat pizza.

Declan was always trying to get rid of me, and sometimes Holden and Mason did too, but Jesse always told them it was cool. He let me sit next to him on the sectional and always shared his popcorn with me. And nine times out of ten, I'd fall asleep, my cheek pressed against his chest, and he'd carry me up to my bedroom and tuck me in.

Sometimes I'd pretend I was asleep so that he'd pick me up and carry me.

Now we were sitting side by side, watching the movie on a fifty-foot screen at the drive-in one town over. Jesse drove his Silverado tonight and had reserved a spot right up front. Then he'd set up two striped beach chairs in front of his truck with a cooler filled with drinks. Like he'd planned this whole thing. Which he had.

Was this a date?

Sweat slicked my skin and gathered at the backs of my thighs. I lifted my hair off my neck and gathered it into a high ponytail, securing it with the elastic band on my wrist. It had been a hundred degrees today, and although it had cooled off after the sun went down, it was still hotter than balls out here.

Jesse took the tub of popcorn out of my lap and handed me a cold drink from the cooler. I thanked him and pressed the bottle against my forehead before I unscrewed the lid.

I side-eyed him. He was looking all chilled and relaxed in a Quiksilver T-shirt, shorts, and Vans. He still dressed the same as he did as a teen. I kind of loved that. Even though he had changed a lot in the past year, I took comfort in the fact that his fashion sense hadn't. His T-shirts were always faded and so soft. I had to wrap both hands around the bottle to keep myself from reaching over and touching him.

"Why did you bring me here tonight?"

"I thought you'd like it." He leaned his head against the back of his chair and turned his face toward me. "And I missed hanging out with you. You've been avoiding me, Sunshine Girl."

He hadn't posed it as a question, but he was waiting for an explanation. As if he didn't know why I'd been avoiding him.

I took a swig of Arizona Iced Tea to buy me a little time. Green tea with honey, my favorite. He knew that too, which was why he'd brought them for me. "Can you blame me?"

He smiled a little. "No. But that doesn't mean I have to like it."

"You can't always get what you want."

"I know that."

Yeah, I guess he did. But for a while, he had everything he'd always wanted. The career that had earned him millions. The jet-set lifestyle. And the girl of his dreams.

Was it better to get what you want, only to lose it all? I wouldn't know.

I faced the screen again, a small smile playing on my lips when I saw in my peripheral that he was watching me and not the movie. I wish I knew what he was thinking. I wish I could get into his head and read his thoughts.

Were they dirty? Sweet? Did he ever dream of me the way I dreamed about him? Of course, he didn't. I sighed. Stupid heart.

Time was moving too quickly. At the end of August, I'll be headed to college.

The closer it got to leaving, the more nervous I felt. I had these butterflies in my stomach that never seemed to go away. It was a big step, the first time I'd be away from my home and my family—the start of a whole new adventure.

It felt like I was standing at the edge of a cliff, about to jump off. So, I was excited but nervous and scared too.

And then there was Jesse.

Every time I thought about leaving him, it made me sad. A guy who wasn't even mine. A guy who was sitting right next to me. So it was stupid that I missed him already.

When we were at the waterfall, and I'd made that wish on a star, I wished that Jesse would move back to California. A lot of freestyle riders lived there, so my wish wasn't entirely selfish. It was for him too.

Had he made a wish that night? If he had, I wondered what it had been. His wish probably had nothing to do with me.

Chapter Nineteen

Quinn

"You planned this whole thing," I accused as he followed me up the stairs to the second floor. When I reached my bedroom door, I whirled around to face him.

"It's hot. What better way to cool off than a dip in the pool?" He smiled at me, feigning innocence, and held up the boardshorts in his hand, jerking his chin toward the end of the hall. "I'll change in the bathroom."

"I'm not wearing a bikini."

He pressed his lips together and crossed his arms over his chest like I was unreasonable. "It'll be dark. And it's just the two of us."

"Exactly." I slammed my bedroom door shut, not sure why I was so angry.

"After I change, I'm going to dive in the pool," he called like he needed to report his every move to me.

"You do you."

I heard him chuckle on the other side of my closed door. Two seconds later, he said, "I promise you that the only thing I'll be thinking about is that your scars are beautiful. That's if I even notice them at all. Which I probably won't." He lowered his voice before he delivered his final words. "Be brave, Quinn."

I squeezed my eyes shut and listened to his footsteps retreating.

Should I be brave? I was making a big deal out of nothing. I'd already made such a big deal out of it that now it was a *huge* deal. If only I'd acted like it didn't bother me, he never would have brought it up in the first place. But I got the feeling that Mason and Holden must have discussed my insecurities with him, which made me feel even more embarrassed. What else had they told him about me?

I changed into a coral pink bikini, my favorite one, and stared at myself in the full-length mirror on the back of my closet door. Thanks to Pilates and yoga, my stomach was flat and toned. I put a lot of work into my core strength, and except for the scars, my stomach was suntanned. I ran my finger over the raised scars that sliced up my stomach. Tonight they looked red and angry.

Slipping a white cotton cover-up over my suit, I walked out of my bedroom.

After grabbing a couple of beach towels from the laundry room, I crossed the limestone tiles to the French doors and stood in the dark kitchen. The pool lights glowed, illuminating Jesse, who was swimming laps, his strokes long and powerful, his arms slicing smoothly through the water, barely making a splash. When he reached the pool edge, he did a flip turn and pushed off the wall with his feet.

Stepping outside, I dropped the towels on a lounger and turned on some music from my phone, trying to reason with myself as the music piped from the surround sound speakers.

I was hot and sweaty. There was nothing I wanted more than to dive into the water and cool my heated skin. So that's exactly what I should do. It was my pool, and I'd been planning to take a swim when I got home. The fact that Jesse was currently swimming in my pool should not deter me one little bit.

Be brave, Quinn.

Sucking in a deep breath, I pulled the cover-up over my head and tossed it on the towels. My first instinct was to cover my stomach with my arms.

But Jesse didn't even look at me when I walked to the pool's edge and dove into the deep end, which was exactly how it felt. Like I was diving into the deep end.

I think I already knew that I would get in too deep, and he was going to break my heart, but I did it anyway.

Love makes you reckless. All logic and reason flew out the window, and you let your emotions take the driver's seat.

You took your chances, pretending to be brave while you ignored the consequences.

That's how it was for me, anyway. But as I swam underwater, bubbles floating to the surface, my hair fanning around me in the cool depths of the pool, I remembered Evie's words about making him work for it. If he wanted me, he'd have to prove himself. Because I wasn't chasing after him anymore.

A hand wrapped around my ankle and dragged me down. I kicked out of Jesse's grasp and swam to the surface. When my head emerged, I started swimming toward the side of the pool, trying to get away from him. Too late. He yanked me back, wrapped his hands around my waist, and tossed me halfway across the pool. I was laughing when I came up for air.

I'd barely had a chance to catch my breath when he grabbed me again. I let out a yelp and struggled to break free of his hold, but I didn't fight that hard, and my feeble attempts were laughable. Seconds later, I was flying through the air again.

"You're going to pay for this, Jesse McCallister," I spluttered, launching my body at his back and pushing my hands down on his shoulders, attempting to dunk him.

He just laughed, all boyish and playful and adorable, and hooked his arms under my thighs, hoisting me up and onto his back. Seconds later, he dove under the water and swam the length of the pool, with me riding his back, my legs cinched tightly around his waist, my hands gripping his broad shoulders. I could have let go if I'd wanted to, but I didn't. I hung onto him and let him take me for a ride.

Skin against skin. Our bodies slippery. His head underwater for the entire length of the pool.

When he reached the edge, his fingers gripped it, and his head emerged. I unhooked my legs from around his waist and slid off, moving next to him while he took deep breaths of air into his lungs.

I rested my forearm on the side of the pool, and he did the

same, so we were facing each other.

Water spiked his long lashes, and his hair was slicked back from his face, making his high cheekbones appear sharper, his face more angular as the pool lights danced across it. For a long moment, we just stared at each other.

My gaze dipped to his mouth, and he licked his lips, just the bottom one.

I didn't know who made the first move. I think it was both of us, gravitating toward each other.

My back hit the side of the pool, and he caged me in his arms, his palms flattened on either side of my head. Then, as if they had a mind of their own, my arms looped around his neck and my legs wrapped around his waist, my ankles locking me firmly into place. Like this was exactly where I belonged. With my body wrapped around him after a late-night swim with Camila Cabello's "Never Be the Same" piping from the speakers.

And it was true. Even if I never saw Jesse's face again, I would never be the same. Because for a little while, I'd known the feel of his skin against mine. I'd known the feel of his lips and his hands. The heat of his gaze when he looked at me like he was doing now. Like I was his favorite food, and he was dying of starvation.

"What are we doing?" I whispered as his eyes lowered to my mouth and my lips parted.

"No fucking clue." His voice was low and rough, his blue eyes darker.

My eyes drifted shut when his mouth captured mine, and a deep guttural groan ripped from his throat that shot straight to my core.

A person could drown in a kiss like this. My head was

swimming, and my body turned to liquid heat as his tongue stroked mine and his hand kneaded my ass cheek, his other hand holding the back of my head to keep me where he wanted me. With my lips pressed against his, our tongues tangled in a crazy dance that stole my breath and made me dizzy and lightheaded.

Maybe we kissed for hours. Or only minutes. I couldn't say. But when he pulled back, my lips were swollen and bruised, and I still wanted more. So I told him that. So bravely, and so boldly.

"I want more," I whispered, rocking my hips, seeking the friction. I could feel his erection, and I wanted to shove my hand into his swim trunks and wrap my hand around his hard length. Test it. Squeeze it. Rub the head against my entrance and sink down on him.

"How much more?" he murmured, his lips pressed against my neck, his fingers digging into my soft skin. I arched my neck, giving him better access, and he kissed his way up my neck to the sensitive spot just below my ear.

I shuddered, my chest heaving. My nipples strained against the confines of the two triangles of my bikini top, and my breasts felt so heavy, they ached.

"I want it all." I arched my back, rubbing my breasts against his chest, my nipples so sensitive, so needy. If he didn't touch me, if he didn't ease this ache inside me, I felt like I might die. "It doesn't have to mean anything."

"You think you can do that?" He grasped my chin in one of his big veiny hands, forcing my eyes to meet his. "You think you can separate the physical from the emotional?"

"Yes," I lied. Jesse's eyes narrowed in disbelief. Obviously, he needed more convincing. "I know you're not looking for a relationship. Neither am I. At the end of the summer, I'm out of here. This will never be more than a summer fling."

"Is that right?" He bit my earlobe then sucked on it to ease the sting, sending a delicious shiver down my spine. I wasn't fooling him any more than I was fooling myself, but I persevered.

"I'm over you, Jesse." I dug my fingers into his shoulders. God, I loved the feel of him. His rock-hard chest against mine. The tautness of his muscles under that warm golden skin. I reveled in the fact that I got to touch him like this where before he'd only been a dream. Now he was solid, real, so deliciously perfect.

My core clenched, the tight bundle of nerves between my thighs throbbing, and even if we hadn't been in a swimming pool, I knew that I'd be dripping wet for him.

I wanted him so badly I would have said or done whatever it took to have him, so I was willing to play dirty if it got me what I wanted. "Before I head to California, I'm planning to lose my virginity, so if it's not you, it will be somebody else. I'll give it to someone who isn't you."

His body stiffened, shoulders tensing under the palms of my hands.

I knew that Jesse didn't want me, but he didn't want anyone else to have me either. So why not use that to my advantage?

Maybe I should have been ashamed of stooping to conquer, but I wasn't. Right now, I couldn't even think straight. I ached for him. Craved him like a junkie in need of a fix.

"Don't play these games with me," he rasped, his teeth sinking into my bottom lip. I didn't even care if his teeth drew blood. I loved the pain he gave. I loved this side of Jesse that I'd never gotten to see before. "That's not something you give away to just anyone. Not until they earn it."

I loved how hard he was working to fight this, but at the same time, he was still holding onto me like he couldn't let me go.

It was a game of push and pull, and for the first time in my life, I knew which buttons to push. In some ways, I knew Jesse better than he could ever know. The result of a lifetime of loving him and watching him and dreaming about him.

"I'll show you my scars," I said finally, tossing my last bargaining chip onto the table. "I'll let you trace your fingers over them. Or your lips…" I traced his lips with my fingertip, noting how his eyes were hooded and his big hands squeezed my ass. "If you want to," I whispered, my eyes locked on him. "I'll let you do that. Because I trust you."

I was offering myself up to him on a silver platter.

That's how desperate I was. And that did it.

My words, my promise to bare myself to him and nobody else, to make myself so vulnerable for him and him alone, loosened every last bit of resolve he was still desperately trying to cling to.

"Fuck," he growled, knowing he'd been beaten.

Without letting me go, he waded through the water to the steps and climbed out of the pool, carrying me with him, my body clinging to his.

I'd expected him to keep going, to stride into the house and across the kitchen floor and up the stairs to my bedroom. But he didn't do that.

When we reached the loungers on the side of the pool, he laid me down on one and leaned over me. I moved my hands to the back of his head and pulled him down to me for a kiss.

"I'm not going to fuck you tonight."

Disappointment and hope warred within me. He wasn't going to fuck me, but he'd said *tonight*. Which implied there'd be other nights.

"What are you going to do?"

He gave me a wicked grin. "I'm going to use my fingers and lips and tongue to fuck that virginal pussy of yours."

He grabbed my ass and dragged me to the end of the chaise. Then he wrapped his hand around my left ankle and bent my knee, planting my foot flat. "I'm going to lick you from slit to crack and everywhere in between, Sunshine Girl…." He did the same with my right foot, and I pushed myself up on my elbows to watch his face. That beautiful face that I loved so much.

"I'm going to shove my fingers into your sweet pussy and imagine it's my cock that you're clenching." He dropped to his knees at my feet and knelt before me, pushing my thighs flat against the lounger before he moved up my body.

"You're wet for me, aren't you?" he murmured, hooking his finger around the string that held up my bikini top and sliding it up and down. "So wet it's dripping down your thighs."

Oh God.

I was going to die.

Sliding the fabric aside, his lips latched onto my nipple, his teeth grazing the sensitive peak while he squeezed and twisted the other one with his fingers. My back arched off the seat, and I held his head to my chest, my body writhing underneath him.

I wanted everything right now, but he tortured me, taking

his time, and when he released my nipple, his lips moved down my body, over my stomach, his fingers trailing behind, touching everywhere his lips had. Lips and fingertips traced my scars. So gently. So reverently that I nearly cried.

I sucked in my breath. It was too much. I wanted to tell him to stop, but no words came out.

"Fucking beautiful," he said, his voice low and husky, bringing tears to my eyes.

How could he say this meant nothing?

I wanted to cry, and I wanted to laugh, and I wanted to moan with pleasure. I think I did all three at once when his fingers and lips brushed over every inch of my skin and reached my bikini bottoms. Magically they disappeared.

No, that's not true. It wasn't magic that did it. It was his teeth. He tugged the string that was tied in a bow with his teeth, and oh God, this was happening. I was bare to him, and he sat back on his heels to take in the sight of me.

"Fuck, you're perfect."

My thighs trembled under his touch. My whole body was shaking. I pushed myself up on my elbows again because I wanted to see him. I wanted to see his beautiful face and his lips and fingers, and I wanted to watch him perform magic.

"Jesse," I whispered as he dipped his head, ready to take the first taste of me.

He paused and lifted his head, his eyes meeting mine. He must have heard the tremor in my voice. "Do you want me to stop?"

I shook my head. "No."

"Stop thinking so hard. Just relax."

I nodded. "I… I will. I just… I never did anything like this…."

He smiled, and it was such a sweet and tender smile. "I know. I promise I'll make it good for you."

As if I'd expected anything less.

When his tongue brushed my clit, my hips bucked against his face, and a whimper escaped my lips.

My fingers gripped his hair and tugged as he did what he'd promised he would. He fucked me with his fingers and his tongue and his mouth.

Licking, tasting, teasing.

"You're so fucking wet."

One thick finger slid inside me, and I gasped at the intrusion as it reached and curled and hit a spot that made me scream his name so loud that I was glad we didn't have any neighbors close by. I wasn't in control of my own body or the sounds that came out of my mouth. I wasn't thinking about anything at all, except how good this felt.

"That's it, baby. Fall apart for me. Fuck my fingers."

He pumped his finger in and out, his eyes locked on mine, gauging my reaction before he replaced his finger with his tongue. And oh my God, when he pressed his thumb against my clit and rubbed the tight bundle of nerves, that did it.

My vision blurred, and I was crashing, falling, flying.

The orgasm built and built and built like a wave, and then it crashed over me. Light splintered behind my closed lids, and my body was shaking uncontrollably, my muscles clenching.

When I thought I couldn't take anymore, he licked me with the flat of his tongue, and it was too much. Almost.

"So fucking sweet."

I scooted back on the chair, and he moved up my body and settled between my thighs, kissing me hard so I could taste myself on his tongue.

I reached down between us and rubbed my hand against his hard length. Then, feeling braver, I slid my hand under the waistband of his swim trunks. He hissed when I wrapped my hand around him, and oh God, it felt so big and so hard in my hand, the skin velvety soft and smooth. I wanted to make him feel just as good as he'd made me feel. I wanted to wrap my lips around it and suck on it.

"Fuck." Jesse pulled away abruptly and got to his feet, leaving me confused. What had just happened? He tossed a towel at me. "Cover up."

It took me a second to realize why he did that.

Chapter Twenty

Jesse

Fuck. My orgasm came quickly and suddenly. I flattened my palm against the limestone tiles, the water cascading over my head as I came.

Breathing hard, I took a moment to steady myself before rinsing off and stepping out of the shower.

At this rate, I was going to set a Guinness World Record for jerking off to the thought of my sunshine girl sucking my cock with her pouty lips and warm mouth. Or this time, I'd envisioned her on all fours, her muscles clenching around me, my hand fisting her hair as I rammed into her from behind.

This needed to stop. I needed to stop fantasizing about Quinn. Why had I let her get into my head like this?

I carried my breakfast outside—avocado, tomato, Swiss, and a fried egg between two slices of whole wheat—and sat on a deck chair. My deck overlooked the trees and, beyond that, the dirt jumps and metal ramps with airbags to cushion my landing.

It was a great set-up. I'd designed the jumps so they'd have a nice flow. Just thinking about getting out there for a practice session put a smile on my face. It made me feel like I used to, back when moto made me fucking giddy with excitement.

My phone rang as I was putting on my body armor. I answered Mason's call and sat on my bed to pull on my moto boots.

"I need a favor," he said. "Can you cover the bar for a couple of hours this afternoon? I just spoke to Mike, but he's out of town for the day. A family thing. So he can't cover for me."

I planned to spend the day working on my jumps, but I could still get in a few hours this morning. The brewing company was a cool place, chilled and laid back, so I didn't mind working there. "No problem. What time do you need me to come in?"

"Three fifteen. Second thought better make it three in case the traffic is bad. Knowing Bean, she'd leave it until the last minute, and then she'd drive like a maniac. Probably miss her exit too," he said with a chuckle.

"Where does she need to go?"

"Doctor's appointment in Austin. Declan can't take her. He needs to prep for dinner and Holden's meeting with the distributors."

Had something happened after I left her last night? Or had I done something... *Shit.* "Is she okay?"

"Yeah, yeah. It's just a routine check-up. She has to go every few months to make sure everything is okay with the transplant. My mom usually takes her, but she's in New York, so she called me. I have a shitload of work, but I don't want her to be alone."

"I'll take her," I volunteered as I jogged down the stairs to my garage.

"Nah, man, you don't have to do that. It's a lot to ask."

"It's not a problem. I'll take her. And you didn't ask. I offered."

"You sure?"

"Positive."

"Thanks. Appreciate it. I'll text you the details. I owe you one."

If only he knew how untrue that was. On top of everything else, I was a shitty friend too.

I pulled on my helmet and gloves, mismatched because I was always losing one, and climbed onto my dirt bike. A two-stroke I'd modified for freestyle. A real beast. Cool as shit with custom orange, black and white graphics.

No sooner had I gotten my bike out of the garage than my mom turned up, sporting a visor, a polo shirt, and shorts. She was carrying a jug of water, and a gigantic tote bag was slung over her shoulder as if she was planning to stay the night.

"Did Dad kick you out of the house?" I joked as she marched right past me and grabbed a beach chair from the back of my garage.

"If you insist on risking your neck for this sport, I'm not going to let you do it without supervision, now am I?"

"So you're going to sit in the heat and watch me do jumps? What if you get heatstroke?" We'd had thunderstorms last night, but now the sun was burning through the clouds, and it was going to be another scorcher.

"I won't get heatstroke," she scoffed. "I'll sit in the shade, and I brought my Kindle and snacks." She patted the bag on her shoulder. "So, don't you worry about me."

"You do know I'm twenty-seven, right?"

"It doesn't matter how old you get. You'll always be my baby. So I'll always worry about you. I worry about all my kids. But right now, I'm especially worried about you."

I knew this because she'd told me at Sunday dinner last week. "I'm getting back on track." I rolled out my shoulders. "Getting my life back together. So you don't need to worry about me."

For the first time in months, it felt like I was telling the truth. I smiled at her just to prove it.

She nodded, a slow smile forming on her face. "Good." She patted my shoulder. "Because I can always tell when you're lying. You've never been very good at it."

About an hour later, when I stopped for a water break, my mom looked up from her Kindle. "So... have you met anyone special? A nice local girl, maybe?" She sounded so hopeful. My mother's greatest wish was to have all her kids married and settled and living within a ten-mile radius.

"You need to stop reading those romance novels."

"When the right one comes along, you'll know it. And just like Jude and Brody, you'll be a goner," she said with a knowing smile.

I didn't want to crush her hopes by telling her that I'd given up on love, so I remained silent.

I decided to drive my pickup. It didn't seem like a good idea to rock up to a doctor's office on a motorcycle.

"This was really unnecessary," Quinn said on the way to Austin. "I'm perfectly capable of going on my own."

I side-eyed her. She was staring straight ahead, her eyes hidden behind sunglasses. My gaze lowered to her crossed legs. When she caught me staring, she tugged down the hem of her little white dress. It was so short it barely covered anything.

"Yeah, well, you don't have to go on your own because I'm taking you."

"Watch the road."

Reluctantly, I returned my gaze to the road.

"We're going to be early," she complained.

When I'd shown up, she had just gotten home from the gym, and I'd given her exactly ten minutes to shower, change and get in my damn truck. She hadn't been too happy about that. In fact, I'd never seen her this grouchy.

"What's wrong?"

"Nothing," she mumbled.

In my experience, when a woman said nothing was wrong, it usually meant the opposite.

"Come on, Sunshine Girl. Tell me what's going through that pretty head of yours."

She sighed loudly. "You'll think it's stupid."

"Try me."

"Declan's moved back home."

I kind of figured that out after the way he'd crashed our little party for two last night and left his duffel bags on the kitchen floor.

If he'd shown up a few minutes earlier, he would have gotten a hell of a show. Thankfully, he hadn't seen me going down on his baby sister. He'd strode right past us and dove in the pool. My cue to get the hell out of there.

"And why is that a problem? You think your house isn't big enough for both of you?" I joked.

"It's not. He'll get all up in my business. Last night, I wanted to do more... I wanted to...."

"What did you want to do?" I knew what she'd wanted, but sick fuck that I was, I wanted to hear her say it. "What did you want to do?" I asked again.

"You know..."

"Not really. No idea what you're talking about." She exhaled loudly. "Say it."

"I wanted to see you... touch you... taste you," Quinn said, her voice low.

"See what? Touch what? Taste what? I thought you wanted to be a writer. Use your words."

She huffed out a breath. "Your..." She cleared her throat and averted her gaze. "Penis."

A laugh burst out of me. "My *penis*? I haven't heard that word since Sex Ed in middle school."

"Ugh." She reached across the center console and smacked my arm. "Stop making fun of me."

"Nobody says penis."

"I just did. It's a penis."

"Is that what you call it in this story you're writing? Do you say... I want to touch his penis. I want him to put his penis inside my... *vagina*?"

"No."

I glanced at her. She was blushing. It was so fucking cute that I couldn't stop teasing her. "Oh, wait. Do you use other words? His throbbing member?" She shook her head and pursed her lips, barely holding in her laughter. "His joystick? His trouser snake? Oh, I know." I snapped my fingers. "You call it a hot sausage, don't you?"

She burst out laughing. "Oh my God. Ew. No. Who calls it that?"

"The same people who use the words penis and vagina, probably."

"What should I call it?"

"It's your book. Call it anything you want. Unless you're asking for my help to write the sex scenes? Do you need my help, Bean?"

"You're not allowed to call me Bean."

"Then say it. Tell me what you wanted to do last night."

"No." She crossed her arms over her chest.

"Okay, Bean. Your call, Little Bean."

"You're such an ass," she said, but she was laughing.

I flicked on my turn signal and waited for the light to change before turning into the medical complex and pulling into a parking space right near the entrance.

"We have twenty minutes to kill, *Bean*. And we're not getting out of this truck until you say it."

"I don't have to say it."

"Come on. You can do it. You know you want to," I goaded.

"I want to suck your cock," she muttered, the words all jumbled together, her voice too low to hear it properly.

"Sorry, Bean." I cupped my hand around my ear and leaned

toward her. "I couldn't understand what you were trying to say. A little louder for the people in the back."

"Oh my God. You're so annoying. Fine. You asked for it." She unfastened her seat belt, and it flew into the holder as she turned in her seat and glared at me.

"Ooh, look at you." I held up my hands and pretended to cower. "You look like you mean business. Please don't hurt me, Bean," I said in a falsetto voice.

Her eyes narrowed on me, and her chest was heaving. It was all I could do not to laugh in her face. "Come on, Little Bean. You can do it. Use your words."

Her hands balled into fists, and she took a deep breath before she shouted, "I want to suck your big, beautiful, hard cock."

Well, damn, she went there.

Guess she hadn't noticed I'd rolled my window down after I'd pulled into the parking space and cut the engine.

I grinned and waved at an older woman walking past the front of my truck. She shot me a dirty look and shook her head before she hurried away, her bag clutched to her chest.

Quinn slid down her seat and covered her face with her hands. "Oh my God," she groaned.

I was laughing so hard I could barely breathe. This was entertainment gold.

"I can't believe you made me do that," she hissed, slinking even lower in her seat. "I'm not getting out of this truck."

"Oh, come on." I wiped my eyes. Shit, that was hilarious. "It was funny."

"No, it wasn't." She gestured toward the windshield. "That

woman is Dr. Greenbaum's receptionist."

"Oh shit." That made me laugh harder.

While I sat in the waiting room, I flicked through a *Sports Illustrated* under the watchful eye of Glenda the Good Witch. Every now and then, I heard her tskk. It was all I could do not to start laughing again. Tossing the magazine onto the table next to me, I slid my phone out of my shorts pocket. A message that had just come through.

Colby Deegan. I hadn't talked to him since last summer.

Hey dude, where you been? You still riding?

I texted a reply. **Laying low. Back home in Texas. Just built some sick ramps in my backyard.**

No shit. Me and Knox were just talking about that time you did a front flip on a 4-stroke. Fucking epic. You thinking about coming back to Cali?

Not sure yet.

We've put together a freestyle team. DirtDevilz. Got a nice ring to it, amiright?

I chuckled and watched the dots form on my screen while he typed. Colby was a cool guy. So was Knox. Two of the craziest guys I'd ever met and also two of the best freeriders in the country. It seemed the two went hand in hand. Nobody had ever called FMX riders sane.

The bubbles stopped and then started again. **Shit. I got a lot to say. You good to talk?**

I stood up from my seat and walked up to the receptionist.

"Hey, Glenda." She couldn't meet my eye. I bit my tongue to keep from laughing. "I need to take a call. If Quinn comes out and I'm not here, tell her I'm waiting for her outside by my truck."

"She's only eighteen," she said with a lift of her brow. "She's a good girl." It sounded like a reprimand, like I was the bad guy who was making the good girl dirty. Which was accurate, I suppose.

I tipped my chin to acknowledge that I'd heard her and stepped outside to make my call. I opened the glass door and held it for a man in a suit. It took me a moment to realize who it was.

"Thank you," he said and then did a double-take. "Jesse?"

"Hey, Mark."

"I haven't seen you in years."

We stepped aside to let a woman pass. "Yeah. It's been a while. You're here for Quinn?"

He nodded, his eyes darting to the door of the doctor's office. "I didn't know she had an appointment until I saw it on Abby's calendar." He frowned, clearly not impressed that he hadn't been apprised of Quinn's doctor appointment.

"I'm sure she'll be happy to see you."

He grimaced. "Not so sure about that. I haven't been the most reliable father lately."

"It's never too late. She has a big heart. Doesn't hold grudges."

"You know my daughter well. But then, you two have always been close." He clapped me on the shoulder and smiled at me. "Thanks for being here for her. Appreciate it."

Another Cavanaugh thanking me for being here for Quinn. Not sure any of them would be quite so grateful if they knew the truth. "Anytime."

Chapter Twenty-One

Quinn

When I walked into the waiting room after my appointment, I'd expected to see Jesse waiting for me. Instead, my father stood up from his chair and walked toward me, a big smile on his face.

"How's my girl? What did Dr. Greenbaum say?"

"Um, yeah. Everything is fine. All good." My gaze darted around the waiting room, but there was no sign of Jesse. "What are you doing here?"

"How about an early dinner?" He held the door for me, and I stepped out of the air conditioning into the heat. "Thought I'd take you to that teppanyaki place you used to love."

"I… I can't." I gestured toward Jesse, who was leaning against the side of his truck, talking on the phone. "Jesse brought me."

"How about I take you both?" My dad slid his phone out of his pocket, and knowing him, he was already making reservations. "It's the least I can do to thank him for being there for you."

"Um, I don't think…"

Jesse ended his call and walked over to us. "Everything okay?" he asked, his gaze focused on me.

I nodded, not sure if he was asking about my doctor's appointment or the fact that my dad had turned up.

"I'm taking you two out to dinner. How does Japanese sound?"

"Jesse probably already has plans—"

"I'm free," he said with an easy smile. "And Japanese sounds great."

"Jesse, you don't have to—"

"It's cool. What's the place called?" Jesse asked my dad, his thumb poised over his phone screen, ready to search for the restaurant's location.

Guess we were doing this.

Dinner lasted two hours. It was nice. Kind of weird to be with my dad and Jesse but in a good way.

By the time we said goodbye outside the restaurant and got in Jesse's truck to go home, I was in a food coma. I wouldn't need to eat again for an entire week.

My dad had spent a good part of the dinner extolling the virtues of Austin. I got the feeling he was trying to sway me. Convince me to stay in Texas. But Jesse had been talking about the merits of California, fully supporting my decision and me, I guess, which had felt good. Like we were a team.

I told my dad that I'd already committed to UCLA, so there was no point in trying to talk me out of it. He'd just laughed and said, "I know, Bean. I know how you are. So determined. You remind me so much of your mother." I'd given him a funny look, not sure how to take that. "I meant that as a compliment. We always said you got the best of both of us."

It had been a nice evening, so I didn't know why I felt the need to ask Jesse about Alessia. Maybe it was because I still couldn't wrap my head around the fact that my dad was remarrying, which had nothing to do with Jesse. But my relationship with my dad confused me. He'd betrayed my mom, and in a way, he had betrayed all of us. Yet in my heart, I'd forgiven him. Because he was trying. And my good memories outweighed the bad.

And maybe I didn't understand the first thing about love.

When we left the city limits, headed west as the sun was setting, the sky awash with pink and orange, I asked Jesse, "Why did you lie to me?"

"You'll have to be more specific. What exactly do you think I lied to you about?"

He'd been in a good mood today, I could tell, and he'd been his old charming self all through dinner, so really, I should have let it go. But I couldn't. "You told me you broke up with Alessia last August."

"I did."

"But you got back together with her?"

He glanced over at me. "Why are you asking this?"

I shrugged one shoulder. Now that I'd broached the subject, I'd have to come clean. "I saw a photo on her Instagram. You were at Shiloh Leroux's concert."

He cursed under his breath. "Why the fuck were you checking her Instagram?"

"I don't know. I guess I was curious." I chewed on my lip.

Just shut up, Quinn. You've said enough already.

But I couldn't let it go. I needed to know.

"Are you still with her? I mean… Do you still love her? I just…" I took a deep breath and let it out. "I can't understand how or why you could take her back after what she did to you."

Maybe I was overstepping. Was it really any of my business? He'd made it clear that he wasn't looking for a relationship. But we were still friends, right? And hadn't he been the one to accuse me of lying to him by omission that day we went to the lake?

He drove in silence, and I had all but given up waiting for an answer when he finally spoke. "It's complicated. The reason I took her back. And no, I don't love her anymore. She made damn sure to destroy every last ounce of love I'd ever had for her."

There was no anger in his voice when he'd said that. Instead, he'd sounded a little bit sad, and it made my heart hurt for him. I stared at his profile. We'd rolled down our windows after we'd gotten off the highway, and now the breeze ruffled his hair, made it all messy and disheveled. His jaw was clenched, and the muscle in his cheek ticked. Like he was trying to hold in his anger, keep it in check, and bottle it all up inside.

"What did she do to you?" I asked softly. "Sometimes it helps to talk to a friend."

He chuckled under his breath. "And you think that friend is you?"

"Why couldn't it be me? Have you talked to anyone else about this?"

"No," he said flatly.

"So… you can tell me. I… I showed you my scars. I made myself vulnerable to you and…."

"That was your choice," he bit out. "I never forced you to do anything you didn't want to." He narrowed his eyes on me.

"I know. But… Please tell me, Jesse. Tell me what she did to you. Tell me what happened to you."

He raked his hand through his hair, his eyes on the road, and it looked as if he was trying to decide whether to tell me. So I waited, giving him some time and space, and I was rewarded for my patience.

"I got fired. I got fired from my team."

My jaw dropped. Oh my God.

I didn't want to say the wrong thing or make him regret telling me, so I remained silent. I didn't know if he would tell me the rest of the story, but I silently prayed that he would. I knew it was important. I knew it was the reason he'd been acting so differently. And it also explained why he'd retired from the sport he loved. Not because he'd wanted to quit, but because his team had fired him.

Which was so unbelievable. Jesse had always been the poster boy for good sportsmanship, so he had to do something really bad to get fired. I couldn't hold it in anymore. I had to know the rest of the story. "Why did you get fired?"

He glanced at me, then returned his gaze to the road, his grip on the steering wheel so tight that I could see the whites of his knuckles. Even from my spot in the passenger seat, I could feel the tension rolling off him. But I got the feeling that he wanted to tell me, and maybe if he said the words aloud, he could start to let go of some of that anger he was hanging onto.

"I got fired because I beat up Nate Hutchins, and I falsely accused him of sexual assault." He laughed harshly. "What kind of an idiot would do that?"

Oh my God.

All the missing pieces of his story slotted into place. My poor sweet baby Jesse.

No wonder he was so bitter and angry. No wonder he didn't believe in true love anymore.

How could he, after what she'd done to him? She'd ruined him. Destroyed his career. She would have had to know that Jesse would have done anything for her. She'd known that, and she'd found a way to get back in his good graces. To cover her tracks and pretend that she hadn't really cheated on him, she must have lied to him.

What kind of a person would lie about something like that? Had she really believed that would work, that she'd get away with it, and he wouldn't confront Nate?

If she had ever believed that she didn't know Jesse at all.

"There's your truth, Sunshine Girl. I jeopardized my entire career because the woman I thought I loved lied to me. But guess what? Nate had texts and voice mail messages saved on his phone. Imagine the joy he took in showing them to me. Imagine the joy he got out of proving that it had been going on behind my back for *months,* and I'd been none the wiser." He laughed bitterly. "Things were going too well for Alessia and me, and she couldn't trust that. So she thought she'd fuck it up by fucking me over and fucking another rider. Makes complete fucking sense, right?"

My hands curled into fists, and I gritted my teeth. "I hate her. I hate her so fucking much."

"Join the club, baby. Join the fucking club."

If I ever came face to face with Alessia, I wouldn't hold back. I'd tell her exactly what I thought of her. I'd find a way to make her pay for hurting Jesse. For destroying his faith in love.

I would never forgive her for that.

But conjuring up all the things I'd say and do if I ever saw Alessia was pointless. I would never come face to face with her again.

Chapter Twenty-Two

Quinn

"*I want to suck your big, hard cock.*"

Ugh. Would she really say that? I stared at my laptop screen, the words dancing before my eyes. I deleted the sentence and chewed on my lip. Then I typed it again. And deleted it. Again.

Outside, the music grew louder, thanks to DJ Declan. No wonder I couldn't focus. I pushed my laptop aside and hopped off my bed, searching my room for my noise-canceling headphones.

Where had they gone?

After checking my dresser and bookcase, I slid open the

top drawer of my bedside table and rummaged through it. No headphones. I opened the bottom drawer. Bingo. I grabbed them, ready to shut the drawer, when my eye caught on a glass jar lying on its side in the back. I stared at it for a moment before I pulled it out.

My childhood wishes. I couldn't even remember the last time I'd read these.

Sitting cross-legged on my bed, I unscrewed the lid and upended the jar. Folded-up pieces of sherbet-colored paper fluttered onto my blush pink comforter. I plucked one off the bed and unfolded the pink slip of paper.

Kiss a boy (J.J.) in the rain.

I grabbed another one. Orange.

Dance in the moonlight and sleep under the stars.

Refolding it and returning it to the jar, I selected a yellow one.

Travel the world and seek adventure. Be bold and daring. Always.

One by one, I unfolded each slip of paper and read all the things that my younger self had wished for and dreamed about.

Dive off the cliffs at the lake and show my brothers (and J.J.!!!) that I'm not a baby:(

Find a way to make Mom and Dad ~~stop fighting~~ love each other again.

Ride on the back of J.J.'s motorcycle (keep it a secret so Mom doesn't worry).

Find a new BFF. Someone fun and nice who doesn't make fun of me and talk about me behind my back like Lexie does. I don't even care that she didn't invite me to her sleepover party. I don't even care that she gave Mia a friendship bracelet and not me. Someday I'll have a BFF who thinks I'm cool. <u>Don't be a sheep. BE YOU.</u>

I read that note a couple more times. Back then, in fourth grade, losing my so-called best friends felt like the end of the world. Lexie and Mia had gone on to become the 'popular, cool girls' while I'd continued being the biggest nerd on the block. I'd cried so hard over losing them. But two years later, Evie had come along and shown me what it was like to have a true friend.

I popped it back in the jar and chose a lilac one.

Write a book with lots of kissing and sexing. DO RESEARCH.

Be J.J. 's queen and live happily ever after in our enchanted kingdom AKA Narnia (<u>make sure there's a good motocross track!!!</u>).

Ten years later, and I still wanted most of the same things. What a joke. Laughing at myself, I unfolded a piece of paper that looked like it had been ripped out of a spiral notebook and folded into a football.

Smoothing out the wrinkles with my hand, I read the note I'd written.

Dear J.J. (that's what I call you, so my brothers don't know it's you. They tease me all the time and I hate it. Sometimes I call you racer boy too but only in my head),

Why did you kiss that girl in my pool? Do you think she's pretty? I heard Declan say she's hot. He said something about eating a pussy. Is that her nickname? She doesn't even look like a kitten. And why would you want to EAT a cat???!!! SO gross.

I heard her talking to her friend too. You were swimming. (It was a race, and Holden won) She kept saying the word S-E-X. She said YOU are hot. Are you sweaty? It's not that hot today. And the water is cool.

I know what sex is. I asked my mom about it. Are you going to have a baby???? Are you going to MARRY her???

If you do, I will cry forever and ever.

I love you with all my heart. Why do I have to be 8 years old? It's not fair. I HATE being treated like a dumb kid.

Love forever and ever,

Your Sunshine Girl

P.S. I made you a new friendship bracelet. It's orange. Your favorite color. And yellow. My favorite color.

P.S.S. You kissed her AGAIN!!! I'm throwing this letter in the trash. Stupid Kitten. I hope she chokes on a furball.

Oh my God. Could I get any more embarrassing?

I covered my face with my hands. I didn't know whether to laugh or cringe. Thank God I hadn't given him that note. Just thinking about what his reaction would have been made me laugh.

In the midst of my laughter, my door flew open, and a bikini-clad blonde stumbled in. "Oops." She giggled and then hiccupped. "I thought this was the bathroom."

I rolled my eyes. "There's one at the end of the hall."

No sooner were the words out when Thor appeared in my doorway and tossed the girl over his shoulder. Then, grinning at me, he spun around and charged out of my bedroom, the girl over his shoulder shrieking with laughter. "I'm going to throw up."

If she threw up, I sure as hell wasn't going to clean it up.

Just as I'd suspected, living with Declan was already a nightmare, and it had only been three days. Scooping up all the folded papers on my bed, I returned them to the jar and set it on my bedside table.

I crossed the room and flung open my window. Resting my forearms on the windowsill, I watched the pool party. The scent of weed drifted up in the heavy, muggy air, and I inhaled deeply.

It was sweeter than cigarette smoke. Not unpleasant.

When Declan was in high school, he'd been the biggest pothead. At twenty-four, I guess that hadn't changed.

When I'd spoken to Mom on the phone yesterday, I bemoaned the fact that Declan had moved back home. "It will be a good time for you two to bond," she'd said. "You used to be so close."

Was she high? "Um, no. Declan and I were never close."

"Oh honey, yes, you were. Remember when we dropped him off at culinary school? You cried all the way home."

"That's an exaggeration. Crying from New York to Texas would have made me an Olympic gold medalist in crying."

She'd just laughed and said it would be nice to have him around for the summer. I wholeheartedly disagreed.

Before Declan had moved back home, he'd been sharing an apartment with his friend Joe. Apparently, Joe's new girlfriend kept turning up in Declan's bed. She'd even walked in on him when he was in the shower of his en suite bathroom.

"I don't need that kind of shit in my life," he'd told me.

And I didn't need him sticking his nose in my business. "Did you talk to Joe about it?"

Declan had laughed and patted me on the head like I was a puppy dog. "You don't get it, Bean."

So here he was, invading my space. When I had suggested he move in with Mason and Holden, who had tons of space, he shot me down. "I spend enough time with them. I don't need to live with them. Besides, they don't have a pool."

"Well, just… you know… stay out of my business." Wrong thing to say.

"Well, damn," he'd said, suddenly taking an interest in me. "What's baby sister been getting up to?"

"Nothing. I just like having my own space, that's all."

He'd given me an evil grin like he was onto me and knew exactly what I'd been getting up to. "You don't stand a chance with Jesse. You do know that, right? You're just the rebound girl. The one he's going to use to get him over whatever shit went down with his ex."

I guess he had seen more than I thought when he caught Jesse and me by the pool. "Jesse and I are just friends."

"Yeah, okay. Whatever you say. I'm just trying to look out for you." He'd shrugged and held out his hands. "Just telling it like it is. No point in sugarcoating it."

That conversation had taken place yesterday morning over breakfast while he was making espresso with the fancy Italian machine he bought Mom for Christmas. She never used it. Mom preferred filtered coffee to espressos and cappuccinos, but she never told him that because she hadn't wanted to hurt his feelings.

Which was ironic, really. Declan never cared about sparing anyone's feelings, least of all mine. And I hated that he'd said that about Jesse. I hated that he'd put the seed of doubt in my mind. I'd been dwelling on it ever since the words had come out of his mouth.

Was I the rebound girl?

The stupid girl who would help Jesse get over all the crap Alessia had put him through.

When he was done playing with me, he'd dump me and move on. He'd be perfectly fine, whereas I'd be devastated.

But maybe it wouldn't go like that. We were friends, right?

He confided in me two nights ago on the way home from dinner, and he hadn't spoken about it with anyone but me.

So that had to mean something. It had to mean I was special to him.

But what if Declan was right?

From my bedroom window, I watched the party, bodies moving to the beat of the house music, my tattooed brother shirtless and barefoot with his arm slung around a brunette while he did shots with his friends, their laughter echoing over the music.

Maybe it was time to join the party. Far better to take action than to spend my summer sitting on the sidelines, waiting and hoping for something that would never happen.

Chapter Twenty-Three

Quinn

"You good?" Thor asked.

I didn't even know what was so funny, but I couldn't stop laughing.

"I'm great. I've never felt so... so..." I waved my hand in the air, trying to find the word, but it escaped me.

It reminded me of that time I'd gone to Pleasure Pier in Galveston with my family and rode the roller coaster six times in a row. Dizzy and lightheaded. Slightly nauseous. Those butterflies were swarming my stomach. "I've never felt so..."

"High?" he asked with a laugh.

I leaned down to where he was sitting on the grass and smacked his shoulder. "Yes! That's the word. I'm so high. So, so high…" I was spinning and spinning like a ballerina, and then I collapsed on the ground, laughing so hard tears sprang to my eyes.

"Weed usually chills people out," he said with a shake of his head.

"I'm chilled. Cool as a cucumber." That got me laughing again. Cucumbers reminded me of penises, which reminded me of that penis conversation with Jesse. "Why did I wait so long to try this?" I sat up and plucked the joint out of Thor's hand and brought it to my lips.

Closing my eyes, I took a hit and held it in my lungs the way he'd told me to do before letting it out. This time I didn't even cough. I was practically an expert now.

I was so freaking cool. Look at me, smoking a joint with a guy named Thor.

Smoke drifted into the air, forming a hazy halo above my head. The bass from the music was thumping, and the party was raging by the pool. But over here in the grove of trees, the sounds were muffled.

Everything was moving in slow motion, all the edges fuzzy.

I leaned my back against the giant oak, the one where I'd conducted that fake wedding ceremony all those years ago. God, that was so sad. So sad and so unbearably sweet. Five-year-old me wearing a white sundress and fourteen-year-old Jesse in a backward ballcap and a daisy chain. I still had the photos from that day, tucked in the pages of *The Lion, the Witch, and the Wardrobe*. When I was a kid, The Chronicles of Narnia were my favorite book.

Now I was sitting under my favorite tree getting high, high,

high and Jesse was… what was he doing right now?

My sweet baby Jesse.

I broke into an impromptu version of "Jessie's Girl," changing the words to suit my needs.

"I wish that I was Jesse's girl," I sang. "I wanna be Jesse's girl. And he's watching me with those eyes. And loving me with that body… doo doo doo… Jesse's girl. You know I feel so dirty when you start talkin' cute."

Joint in hand, I got to my feet and danced in the grass under the tree. I whipped my hair around and swiveled my hips. "Dance with me, Thor."

He snatched the joint away from me and smoked it while I shimmied in front of him, my arms reaching for the sky. "How low can you go, Thor?"

Thor laughed, but he was game, so we shimmied low. My thighs had turned to Jell-O, and we both collapsed on the grass, laughing our asses off. I looked over at Thor on his back, smoking the blunt and laughing at the moon.

"Let's do the worm." So I showed him how, and he tried to imitate me, this tattooed mountain of a man with arms the size of the oak tree and a big hammer. It was probably the funniest thing I'd ever seen—Thor doing the worm in my backyard.

I was crying with laughter. "Is your hammer really that big?"

"Not to brag, but hell yeah. It's not just about size, though," he said thoughtfully.

"What's it about?" I rolled onto my side and propped my head on my hand.

"You ever see the way a jackhammer works?"

"Is that the way you use your hammer?" A laugh burst out of me. "Like a jackhammer?"

"Yeah. I'm like one of those Energizer bunnies, you know. The ones that keep going and going…"

"So you're saying your hammer is battery-operated?"

He choked on a laugh, smoke billowing out of his lips. "Shit. I don't know," he said, his voice strained, trying to keep the smoke in his lungs before he exhaled. "What were we talking about?"

"Sex. We were talking about sex."

"Shit, yeah. Sex is… it's a beautiful fucking thing." He smoked the joint that was so small now it probably burned his fingers. When it was done, he tossed it in the grass and tucked his hands under his head. "I remember this one time me and Dec picked up these girls at a bar—"

I slapped my hand over his mouth to stop the words. "I don't wanna hear about my brother's sex life. Are you trying to make me throw up?"

A little while later, he said, "You got any chocolate? Or Doritos? Damn. I love me some of them spicy hot chili ones."

"Cool Ranch is the only way to go. We should go get some."

"Yeah, we should."

Neither of us made a move to get up. We stayed where we were, too lazy to move. Thor made a great pillow. I was lying on my back now, resting my head on his chest while I stared at the sky. So many stars tonight.

What was the meaning of it all? Why were we even here? Maybe I'd just hang out here for a while and contemplate life and "The Big Lebowski."

"'The Dude abides,'" I said.

"Hell yeah, he does." Then, after a beat, he asked, "What does abide mean?"

My brow furrowed, and I tried to come up with the correct answer but drew a blank. "I don't know. That movie doesn't make sense. Neither does life. It's complicated, you know?"

"Life?"

"Yeah, life. Have you ever been in love, Thor?"

"Love." He stroked his beard, contemplating my question. "That's some heavy shit, little sister. Love really fucks you up, you know? It's like…" He exhaled a heavy breath. "Damn. Love is deep."

I snuggled up against Thor, and he draped his tree-trunk-sized arm across my middle while we contemplated life and love and dicks that operated like jackhammers. I couldn't stop thinking about that jackhammer.

"*The fuck do you think you're doing*?"

My head jerked up, and I tried to bring him into focus, but his face was blurry. Didn't matter if I could see him clearly. I'd know his voice anywhere. "Jesse? What are you doing here?"

He glared at Thor, who removed his arm that had been around me. I sat up and ran my fingers through the tangles of my hair as Thor got to his feet and held up his hands, weaving a little on his feet before he draped his tree-trunk-sized arm around my shoulders. "Just looking after Dec's little sister."

"Stay the fuck away from Dec's little sister."

I burst out laughing at Jesse's words and his tone of voice. "Stay the fuck away from Dec's little sister," I mimicked, my voice low and gruff. "Oh my God. You're ridiculous, Jesse James."

I love you so much, you big idiot.

And that was actually his name. Jesse James McCallister. Like the outlaw Jesse James. Except that he wasn't named after the outlaw. James was his grandfather. Why did I even know that? Because I knew everything about Jesse, that's why.

"I'm going to find some Doritos," Thor mumbled.

When he had wandered away, headed back to the party or in search of junk food, Jesse's gaze swung to me, and he planted his hands on his hips. "You texted me. Three times." It sounded like an accusation. One I wasn't even guilty of.

I waved my hand through the air. "No, I most certainly did not, Duderino." Duderino. That was so funny it made me laugh again.

He grabbed my hands and pulled me to my feet. I swayed before him, and he wrapped his hands around my upper arms to steady me, his eyes peering into mine. "Jesus Christ. You're high. He fucking got you high?"

I started laughing again. I was laughing so hard, I couldn't stop. This was the most fun I'd had in forever.

"I got myself high. So high I can fly, baby. Like Icarus with his wax wings, flying too close to the sun." Pulling out of his grasp, I flung my arms in the air and danced in front of him. "Do you wanna dance with me, Jesse? Do you wanna fly with me? I'll take you for a ride you'll never forget."

One minute, I was swaying my hips and dancing for my sweet baby Jesse and the next minute, I was on the ground, lying in a heap at his feet.

Wow. How had that happened?

I rolled onto my back and closed my eyes. I just needed some rest. A little nap.

Oh God, I shouldn't have closed my eyes. Everything was spinning now, and I let out a little whimper. This ride wasn't so fun anymore.

"Get me off this Tilt-A-Whirl," I muttered.

"Open your eyes, baby."

I did as he said. That was a little better but still not great.

Jesse swooped me up and into his arms, and he carried me, his strides long and purposeful. Jesse was carrying me like he was the groom, and I was the bride.

It was just like our fake wedding day. "You're not wearing your daisy chain," I murmured, looping my arm around his neck and tracing the outline of his soft T-shirt collar with my index finger.

He tipped down his chin to look at my face. "Neither are you."

"Why are you carrying me?"

"Why did you send me those messages?"

"Messages? What did I say?"

He just shook his head. Guess I'd have to check my phone later. Another humiliation to endure, no doubt.

"Maybe I'm trying to be your knight in shining armor, riding in to save the day. That's what you've always wanted, isn't it? The stuff of fairytales and legends. A knight in shining armor to swoop in and rescue you."

"Rescue me from what? I don't need to be rescued from anything but you." His hold on me tightened, and his shoulders went rigid. Oops. Shouldn't have said that. I stroked the stubble on his jaw with my fingertips. Gosh, he was so pretty. "What was I saying? Oh right… Now I remember. And furthermore, if you were the white knight, that would make me the damsel in distress. That's never been me. And that's not what I've always wanted. I've never wanted a knight in shining armor."

"No?" he asked as he carried me up the stairs to the second floor. He pushed open my bedroom door and kicked it shut behind him, feeling his way in the dark, the silver moonlight casting my room in shadows. He laid me down on my bed, on top of my blush pink comforter, and leaned over me.

"What is it you've always wanted?"

"All I've ever wanted was the impossible." I fisted his T-shirt in my hands and pulled him down to me.

When our lips met, my eyes drifted shut, and my tongue peeked out to taste him.

Pink lemonade and sugar cookies. Sunshine and daisy chains. Wishes on stars and slow dancing in the rain.

"Never change to fit in, Sunshine Girl. Don't be a sheep. Be your own person. You'll find your tribe."

That's what he'd told me all those years ago when I was broken-hearted, trying to figure out what was so wrong with me that my friends didn't even want to hang out with me anymore.

How could I not love him? The boy I'd grown up with. The man who had given his heart to the wrong girl. My Icarus who flew too close to the sun.

"What's so impossible?" he asked me now as if he didn't know. He was staring up at the ceiling as if it had the answers to all our questions.

Without his weight on top of me, I felt unmoored. Dizzy. The room was swimming, and I told him that.

So he pulled me against him, my back to his chest, and I fit so perfectly into the curve of his body. I really did. Two pieces of an unfinished jigsaw puzzle. That was Jesse and me. "The Sun and the Moon. It's the greatest love story ever told. It blows Romeo and Juliet out of the water."

"Tell me the story," he said, stroking my hair, holding me close against his warm, strong body.

So I did. I told him the story of the Sun and the Moon and how the Sun was like a god and everyone admired him. Worshipped him, even. The Sun and Moon were lovers but only had rare chances to meet.

All the Moon wanted was to be loved. The Sun loved the Moon so much that he gave up his light so that she could glow.

The Sun made the ultimate sacrifice for his beloved Moon. He gave up everything so that she could shine.

"Is there anything more heartbreakingly beautiful than a love like that?" I answered my own question. "No. No, there is not."

"You have two choices," Evie said the next day when we were poolside. I'd filled her in on the ongoing Jesse drama, the parts of the story I remembered, that is. "Either you forget about him and move on. Or you forget about him and move on."

Her advice didn't surprise me. Evie wasn't exactly Jesse's biggest fan. I tossed a grape into my mouth and stared at the swimming pool from the green and white striped cushioned lounge chair. The same chair where Jesse had given me an orgasm three nights ago.

When I checked my text messages this morning, I saw what had prompted him to come over last night.

I'd sent him long paragraphs, reminiscing about my childhood summers. Talk about embarrassing.

Like the time I was eight, and I'd been messing around on a penny board on the pool deck. Trying to show off for Jesse, of course, who had just turned up to hang out with my brothers and their friends.

I'd fallen and scraped my palms and knees. Jesse had been the one to clean my bruises and bandage them up because Mason, Holden, and their friends had been drinking beer. My parents were at work and had left my brothers in charge. Big mistake.

Afterward, Jesse had taken me for ice cream and sweet-talked the girl behind the counter into letting me choose just about every flavor they had.

"If it was that easy, I would have done it years ago," I told Evie. "And maybe…" I rolled my head on the back of the seat to look at her. "What if I don't want to forget about him?"

What if I can't forget about him?

Evie frowned. "As much as I hate to side with Fuck-a-duck Declan…."

I snort-laughed. "Fuck-a-duck Declan?" I offered her the bowl of grapes in my hand. She plucked out a few grapes and tossed them into her mouth.

"Declan has a point, babe."

I knew that, but I hated to admit it.

A small cry drew our attention to Wren, asleep on the lounge chair under the shade of the umbrella. Instinctively, Evie's arm shot out just as Wren flipped from the spread-eagle position on her back to her stomach.

Wren tucked her legs underneath her tiny body and shoved her thumb in her mouth, sucking on it like she needed another fix. Her eyes rolled back in her head before they drifted shut again. She was so pretty, so much like her big sister with her dark ringlets and long lashes, her cheeks rosy from the heat. So worn out from our morning swimming session.

After Evie made sure Wren was okay, she grabbed the tube of sunscreen off the round table next to Wren and returned to her seat. Squeezing some into her palm, she applied it to her face and shoulders, bronzed from the sun. Evie looked like a Greek goddess in her black bikini. Even with her dark hair in a messy bun on top of her head and the kohl eyeliner smudged under her cat-green eyes, she was stunning. Sexy in a way I'd never be. If she weren't my best friend, I might be jealous.

"Okay," she said, slipping on a pair of oversized black sunglasses to ward off the glare of the sun. "Let's go with option number three. If you stick to the plan, I know you can pull this off."

"This I'd love to hear." After checking the time on my phone, I settled back in my seat and closed my eyes, soaking up the afternoon rays. I still had an hour before I needed to get ready for work.

Plenty of time to come up with a new plan of action.

"Fuck him out of your system."

I turned my head and cracked one eye open. "Fuck him out of my system? What does that even mean?"

"Just tell yourself it's for this summer and this summer only. If you're going to obsess over him, you might as well get something out of it. Then, when the time comes to go to California, I want *you* to be the one to walk away from him. Leave him wanting more. And I can guarantee that by the time you're gone, he's going to realize what he's lost, and he's going to regret it. *Big* time."

I kind of liked the sound of this plan.

"You're special, Quinn. And if he can't see that he's a bigger idiot than I thought. I won't stand by and watch him hurt you. But I will help you come up with a way to avoid that."

This was one of the many reasons I loved Evie. She acted tough, okay, so maybe it wasn't an act… She was tough and strong. But she was loyal to a fault and had the biggest heart.

"So… there's more to this plan?"

"This is the most important part," she cautioned. "If he comes for you and tries to win you back, slap him down. Don't take him back until he earns it. We're talking about some *major* groveling here. And even then, unless he's ready to declare his undying love and fall on the sword for you, he doesn't deserve you."

I popped another grape into my mouth, mulling over her cunning plan.

Hope stirred inside of me. This could actually work. It was all about adopting a different mindset. I'd just have to think of it as a summer fling. I'd get what I wanted from Jesse, and then I'd head to California to live out my dreams.

I'd be daring and brave and adventurous, and I'd call all the shots. "You're like an evil mastermind, you know that?"

She shrugged one slender shoulder. "Treat 'em mean, keep 'em keen."

My brows lifted. "Is that what you're doing with Ridge?"

"We're a different story. Like I said, Ridge and I are just a summer fling. When the summer's over, so are we."

"You're going to break his heart. You do know that, right?"

"He's not in love with me, Quinn. Guys like Ridge love the thrill of the chase. Once he thinks he's caught me, he won't be interested anymore."

She was wrong. I didn't believe that for a minute. But I let it go. For now.

It was only the middle of July. We still had the rest of this month and most of August. Anything could happen in six weeks, and I was counting on Ridge to prove her wrong.

But I had to admit she gave good advice. I'd take what I wanted, and then I'd leave.

Later that afternoon, when I walked into the brewing company, I was feeling like a badass. Ready to put my plan into action.

"Where's Jesse?" I asked Mason about two hours into my shift, trying to act all cool and casual like I wasn't disappointed that I'd been hyping myself up all afternoon, and he wasn't even here.

Mason set two pilsners and two lagers on the bar in front of me. I transferred them to my tray and waited for his answer. "He said something about a family dinner."

I let out a breath of relief. Okay, I could work with that. At least he wasn't on a date.

I'd just have to go and see him tonight after work before I lost my nerve.

Chapter Twenty-Four

Jesse

I took off my motorcycle jacket and cuffed the sleeves of my button-down. Grabbing my helmet, I strode to the front door of the modern timber and glass restaurant.

"Good evening, sir," the hostess greeted me when I stepped inside. "Are you here for the bar or dinner?"

"Dinner. The reservation is under McCallister." My gaze roamed around the restaurant with timber-clad walls, soaring ceilings, and a wall of metal-framed glass doors that opened onto a deck. More upscale than the places my family usually frequented.

That should have been my first clue that something was off

about this dinner.

She checked her tablet and gave me a big smile. "Your party is waiting for you. Right this way."

I followed her outside to a deck overlooking the rolling hills, an awning shading it from the evening sun, and to a table at the far end, slightly separate from the other diners. Most likely, they'd made special arrangements for Shiloh, who got mobbed by fans wherever she went.

Jude and Brody had claimed the two heads of the table—typical—and Shiloh and Lila were seated next to each other. Across from them sat a brunette who appeared to be in her mid-twenties.

Oh, hell no.

The rest of my family was notably absent.

It didn't take a rocket scientist to recognize that I'd been played.

Guess I should have questioned Lila's motives for arranging a 'family dinner' on a Friday night. She claimed they'd barely spent any time with me this summer, and they missed me. I'd been showing up for the family Sunday dinners, so that wasn't entirely accurate.

Even my mom had called earlier to make sure I would be here tonight. She had an ulterior motive—to keep me in Texas. She'd also taken it upon herself to make sure a family member was watching over me at all times while I practiced my jumps. *"Just in case someone has to call an ambulance."*

If that didn't instill confidence in me, I didn't know what would.

I should have never told her about my conversation with Colby Deegan. She'd pursed her lips and remained silent. I knew she wasn't thrilled about my plans, but she'd have to learn to deal with it. After my crash last summer, she'd begged me to give up motocross. I'd tried to explain to her that it was more than just a sport for me. More than just my livelihood.

It's who I am. And now that I had another shot at pursuing my dreams, I sure as hell wasn't going to give it up. And do what? Serve beer? Play it safe? Not happening.

"Hi, Jesse." Lila gave me a big smile, the picture of innocence.

Shiloh bit her lip, trying to contain her amusement. I shot Jude and Brody a look. They both held up their hands as if to say they had nothing to do with this.

Now that I was here, there was no way to get out of this gracefully.

Left with no other choice, I took the only empty seat at the table, next to the brunette. She was gorgeous. Stunning, even. Exactly my type, with almond-shaped brown eyes and long wavy hair. Curves in all the right places.

A woman. Not a girl barely out of high school.

And she was obviously my date for the evening.

Camryn was a physiotherapist specializing in sports-related injuries. Lila joked that we were a match made in heaven. Wouldn't go that far, but Camryn was hot. I'd give her that.

She was also smart, with a Master's degree from UT Austin and a sports fanatic. She lived in Austin and met Lila through her sister, who had gotten married in October. Lila had done the flowers for the wedding, and she and Camryn had kept in touch.

It could have been a lot worse. Conversation flowed. Food was good, and so was the company.

When dinner was over, I said goodbye to my family outside

the restaurant and turned to Camryn. In heels, she was only a few inches shorter than me. Tall and willowy with mile-long legs and a plunging neckline that showed off her cleavage. Perfect tits, more than a handful, and a hot body that was fit and toned.

And yet, my dick didn't even stir at the sight of her.

Fucking hell. There was obviously something wrong with me.

"Where did you park?" I asked her.

"In front of that row of shops." She pointed a manicured finger in the opposite direction of where I'd parked.

"I'll walk you to your car." It was dark, and my mother had always instilled good manners in us. Not that you'd know it. I've done a shitty job of remembering them lately.

I walked Camryn to her car, an Audi A5 Cabriolet. Fuck me. It was the same model Alessia drove. Silver with a black convertible top. The quintessential hot girl car.

Her car was the only one in the lot, partially lit by the dull light of a streetlamp, so I waited until she dug her keys out of her purse.

Keys in hand, she leaned against the side of her car and faced me. "Was this dinner totally awkward for you?"

"Nah. It was fine. I had a nice time." *Nice.* The kiss of death.

"I thought you knew about it," she said ruefully.

"They were probably worried I wouldn't show up if they told me in advance," I answered honestly.

She nodded, not the least bit offended by my bluntness. "Yeah, I get that. I was the same way for months after I broke up with my ex. My friends kept pushing me to get back out there. But I'd been burned once, and I wasn't ready to put myself on the line again. So I figured I'd be better off alone. Just focusing on my career and binge-watching Netflix with my cat."

We both laughed. Somehow, I couldn't imagine this girl sitting around watching Netflix with her cat. "What changed?"

She shrugged one shoulder. "I got lonely. I like being in a relationship. I like having someone …" She let her words trail off. "Okay, let's be real. I missed sex, and I'm not a one-night stand kind of girl."

I laughed at her candor. "Yeah, I hear you. Sex is pretty fucking fantastic."

My thoughts drifted to Quinn. Not for the first time tonight either. Which pissed me off. I needed to get her out of my head. Last night after I'd carried her to her room, we kissed. That was it. Nothing more.

That wasn't entirely true. With Quinn, it was always something more.

I'd held her, and she'd fit so perfectly into the curve of my body. She'd told me that if I held on to her, I'd keep her grounded.

I listened to her stories. All of them. Just like I always had when she was a kid. I loved the way her brain worked, spinning tales and bouncing from one idea to the next. Still a romantic who painted pictures with her words. Fairytale worlds that only existed in her imagination.

When she'd fallen asleep, I should have left, but I stayed to make sure she was okay. At least, that's what I'd told myself. Truth was, I liked watching her sleep and loved the feel of her body. Loved the scent of her skin and her silky hair, the little sighs that fell from her lips while she drifted off to dreamland.

Once again, our physical proximity had made me hard, my

cock prodding her ass while she'd slept, blissfully unaware of my predicament. And once again, I'd gone home and jerked off, coming so hard I'd felt like a teenager again.

Fuck my life. Fuck her for making me fantasize about her. Worry about her. Want to do everything in my power to protect her.

"*The only thing I need protection from is you.*"

She wasn't wrong. Thank fuck I had new goals and had set my sights on new adventures. That's what I needed to focus on. My career. My future. Not an eighteen-year-old girl who had somehow managed to get into my head and crawl under my skin.

An eighteen-year-old girl who had sent me the sweetest text messages last night, reminding me of how close we'd been and how I'd always looked out for her. I'd always wanted to protect her innocence and her childlike wonder.

And now… What the fuck did I want now?

"Can I ask you a favor, Jesse?" Camryn asked, dragging my attention back to her.

Shit. I'd zoned out. "Sure."

She opened her car door and tossed her purse on the driver's seat. Then she turned to face me and squared her shoulders like she was preparing for battle. "Will you kiss me goodnight?"

Not what I'd expected to hear. I stroked my jaw and studied her face, the streetlight casting a faint glow on her features. The determined look in her eyes and the set of her jaw made it feel like a challenge. I very much doubted that she'd ever had to beg for a kiss. "Why does this feel like a test?"

"Because it is. Kind of." She moved a couple of steps closer. Close enough that I could smell her perfume. Floral and spicy. "I just want to see something."

I knew what she wanted to see. If there was any chemistry.

"Humor me?" she asked with a smile.

Kissing a beautiful woman was not exactly a hardship. Part of me hoped that I would feel the spark that had been missing all night. The other part of me knew with absolute certainty that I wouldn't.

I set my helmet on the ground, framed her face with my hands, and I kissed her. Then I waited to feel something.

Nothing. Not a goddamn thing.

When I pulled away, I raised my brows, waiting for her verdict.

"Whoever she is, she's a lucky girl."

"What makes you think there's someone else?"

She laughed and shook her head. "For the sake of my ego, let's go with it. Better to think there's a good reason you're not into me."

"It's not you. You're—"

"A great catch. I know." She winked and got into her car. I liked that she was confident and didn't make this awkward. "Take care, Jesse. And be careful on that motorcycle. They're the leading cause of…." She clamped her mouth shut and shook her head. "Sorry. Occupational hazard. Just drive carefully, okay? No speeding."

"Wouldn't dream of it."

"Liar."

"Occupational hazard."

Camryn gave me a little smile and threw her car into reverse. "See you around, Jesse," she called out her open window before she drove away.

You couldn't force something if it wasn't there.

Chapter Twenty-Five

Jesse

Twenty minutes later, I pulled into my driveway, my headlight illuminating the cherry red VW Beetle parked in front of my garage.

My sunshine girl.

Who was nowhere to be found. I'd expected to see her sitting on the deck, waiting for me but nope.

I turned on the outdoor lights and searched my property from up above. Then, through the trees, I caught a dim glow of light and jogged back down the stairs, my phone flashlight guiding my way along the dirt path.

I found her lying on the 45-degree ramp—the long ramp I used for distance rather than height—staring up at the sky. It put a smile on my face.

My little dreamer. She was probably wishing on stars like she'd been doing ever since she was a kid. When we'd been at the waterfall, and she told me to wish on a star, I'd made a wish for her. That her brother's kidney wouldn't fail and that she'd be able to make all her dreams come true. That she'd head to California, travel the world, and become a bestselling author.

It was a tall order, but I had faith that if anyone could make their dreams come true, it was Quinn Cavanaugh.

When she heard me approaching, she pushed herself up on her elbows and smiled at me. Just like it was perfectly natural for her to be lying on a metal ramp in my backyard. "Hi."

"Hi." I stopped next to her, my phone flashlight casting light on her as my gaze roamed over her orange Adidas T-shirt tucked into a short off-white skirt, down her legs to the cheetah print Nikes on her feet. On her left wrist, she wore a stack of bracelets.

Beaded bracelets, rose gold, and silver ones engraved with messages. Even though I couldn't read it in the dark, I knew that one of them said: Keep Smiling.

It was cheesy, but when I'd given it to her after her first kidney transplant, she'd loved it so much that she said she would never take it off. Since then, her brothers had been adding to her collection. I knew this because Mason had asked me for the name of the store where I'd bought it.

This was the first time this summer I'd seen her wear the bracelets.

I'd barely noticed what Camryn was wearing tonight. A skirt?

A dress? Blue? Black? Shit. But when it came to Quinn, I noticed every detail.

"What are you doing here?"

"I came to play on your playground."

"At ten o'clock at night?"

"Actually, I came to see you." She climbed off the ramp and came to stand in front of me. "There's something I want."

"Another girl asking for a kiss?" I teased. "Must be my lucky night."

"Another girl…" Her smile slipped, and her eyes narrowed. "You were with a girl tonight? I thought you had a family dinner."

"What did you want, Quinn? The same thing you wanted last night?"

"What did I want last night?"

"You don't remember?"

"Last night is kind of hazy." She chewed on her lip. Those poor damn lips. "Did I… um, say or do anything embarrassing?"

Quinn looked so fucking pretty in the moonlight, her hair falling around her shoulders. Those lush pink lips that tasted like brown sugar tempting and beckoning.

"I wouldn't call it embarrassing. Just honest. You told me you wanted to suck my big, fat cock."

Her jaw dropped, and her eyes widened. "I called it *fat*?"

I stifled a laugh. Funny how she took exception to the word fat, but the rest of it didn't seem to bother her. Guess she wasn't as shy or as easily embarrassed as I'd thought. "You did."

I didn't mention that she'd been telling me about a scene in the book she was writing.

"And… what did you do?" She flattened her palms on my chest

and slid them down and over my abs. I wrapped my hands around her wrists to stop her from moving any lower. Bold, brazen Quinn.

Last night she was getting high, and tonight she was seducing me. Guess Quinn was spreading her wings, ready to fly.

"I got so hard, I had to fist my big, fat cock in my hand and imagine it was you with your pouty lips wrapped around it, your cheeks hollowed while you sucked it."

"Oh," she breathed. She licked her lips. "So I made you hard…"

"And it pissed me off."

"Why did it piss you off?"

"Because I shouldn't be thinking about you when I'm jerking myself off. I shouldn't be thinking about you that way at all."

"Why not?" She slid her hands up my chest and looped her arms around my neck. I palmed her ass and pulled her body flush against mine. Whenever she was near me, I couldn't stop myself from touching her from wanting more.

Why couldn't I stay away from her? I had no answer for that.

"What's so wrong about thinking about me that way?"

"Everything." Dipping my head, I pressed my lips to her neck, inhaling her summertime citrus scent. How could something so fresh and innocent be so fucking sexy? And maybe that was it. I was drawn to her innocence, her unfiltered honesty, the way she so bravely wore her heart on her sleeve.

"I was on a date tonight."

"You went on a date?"

"Mmm hmm. She was a brunette." I kissed the corner of her mouth. Her jaw. The sensitive spot just below her earlobe. Her body yielded to mine, a soft sigh escaping her lips, and she pressed her tits against my chest.

"She wasn't a teenager." Sliding my hand through her hair, I fisted it and yanked on it, causing her to gasp. "She wasn't my best friend's sister."

My lips coasted over her clavicle and up the column of her neck, my fingers biting into her soft flesh. I was pulling her against me even when I should have been pushing her away.

"She wasn't me," Quinn whispered.

When I reached her mouth, I slanted mine over hers and patiently traced her lips. Those soft, lush lips that tasted so fucking sweet. She grabbed the back of my head, her fingers tugging at my hair, impatient for more. But I continued my slow, gentle assault.

"She wasn't you," I murmured against her lips.

"Then it's a good thing I'm here now," she said breathlessly.

"Taunting and teasing me in your little skirt."

"I'm not wearing anything underneath."

I reared back at her words. The fuck? "You came over here tonight in your little skirt with nothing underneath?"

She bit the corner of her lip. I reached down and coasted my hand up her inner thigh, stopping at the place between her legs. Fuck me. She hadn't been joking. She was bare underneath this skirt. I dragged my fingers through her soft folds, dripping wet with her arousal and so fucking ready for me, I nearly wept.

"And here I thought you were so sweet and innocent."

"Guess I had you fooled," she panted, her thighs clenching and her chest heaving as I rubbed the tight bundle of nerves.

My hard cock swelled in my jeans.

"Is this your idea of seducing me, Sunshine Girl?"

She smirked and rocked her hips against my erection. "It seems to be working."

Coming to my senses, I pulled my hand away and took a few steps back, putting distance between us. "We can't do this. You're—"

She moved closer and placed her finger over my lips. "Shh. Save the speech. I've heard it all before."

I grabbed her hand and dragged her up the dirt trail toward the garage where her car was parked. "You need to go home. This shit needs to stop. You can't come over here—"

"Jesse, stop." When we reached her car, she dug in her heels and yanked her hand out of my grasp. "Just listen to me, okay?"

I crossed my arms over my chest and clenched my jaw.

She took a deep breath and exhaled. "I'm here for the rest of the summer, and you're here too. So… I thought we could make a deal."

"A deal."

She nodded. "We'll be together for the rest of the summer. Just sex. No strings attached. And when the summer ends, so does our little arrangement."

My eyes narrowed on her. Where had she come up with this crazy idea? It didn't even sound like her. "That's not what you want."

"It's *exactly* what I want. We both want the same thing. So it's perfect. Why fight it?" She shrugged one shoulder, so casual and nonchalant like this was no big deal. "Let's just go with it."

Her smile was so genuine, and she sounded so confident that it was hard to tell if she was lying. But she had to be. I didn't believe for a minute that Quinn would settle for an arrangement like this.

It was a trick. She'd insinuate herself into my life, and then she'd expect more. And more. And more.

Been there. Done that. And had no intention of ever going down that road again.

"I'm leaving in a month, Quinn."

Her face fell, but she quickly recovered. "In a month? Where are you going?"

"California."

She smiled. That big, brilliant smile that told me my answer made her happy. Knowing her, she was already making plans for the future. I wanted to be completely honest with her and squash any notions that this meant we could be together. Giving her false hope and unrealistic expectations was the last thing I wanted to do.

"I'll be on the road a lot, and my sole focus will be on my career."

"What will you be doing?"

"I'm joining a traveling circus."

She laughed and smacked my arm. "Seriously. What will you be doing?"

"Some guys I know have put together a freestyle team, and they've invited me to join them." I couldn't hide my smile. For the first time in a long time, I was excited about the future. Fuck Nate Hutchins. And fuck Alessia Rossi. I wasn't going to let my past stand in the way of my future.

"They've got sponsors and shit. We're going to compete, freeride in the desert, put on stunt shows across the country. So yeah, it's kind of like a traveling circus."

The joy on her face reflected mine.

"That sounds amazing, Jesse." She threw her arms around me, her enthusiasm so great that she almost knocked me over. I staggered back, my arms wrapping around her to keep us from falling.

She tipped her face up to mine. "You're making your dreams come true."

Her smile didn't falter. If she was disappointed that I was leaving soon, she didn't let it show.

Quinn was genuinely happy for me. There was no trace of jealousy, no whining about how I was never around or complaining that I always put my career first. Alessia used to make me feel guilty for spending so much time training and traveling for races. She was always complaining that I didn't give her enough attention.

I had no idea how I could have ever thought she was the one for me. Even before all that shit went down with Nate, Alessia had never been a supportive partner. Everything had been about her. Considering that she'd built her career as a social media influencer on the back of mine, you would have thought she'd be my biggest cheerleader.

When we met, she was a fitness model with a small following and only a few modeling jobs here and there. I'd been the one to encourage her to dream bigger, shoot for the stars. I'd been the one to introduce her to the energy drink company that sponsored me. And to all my other sponsors who could help her career. They'd used her in their campaigns. Her career had taken off, and now she was a lifestyle guru and a social media influencer with hundreds of thousands of followers.

In front of the cameras, she always played the part. But, behind closed doors, it was a different story.

I could have destroyed her career the way she'd destroyed mine. And don't think I hadn't thought about it. But in the end, I decided to rise above. Karma is a bitch, and I had faith it would bite her in the ass. But, until then, sabotaging her career and reputation would make me no better than her and Nate.

Unlike them, I had a conscience.

"So you see… it's all turning out the way it's meant to," Quinn said. "I want to lose my virginity, and who better to teach me about sex than you?"

My determined sunshine girl. Sexy one minute. Sweet and innocent the next. Completely disarming me and knocking down my defenses.

She shouldn't feel so right in my arms. She shouldn't stir something inside of me that had been dormant for too long. But she did. And I was finding it impossible to fight the way she made me feel, the way I wanted her.

"What am I going to do with you, Sunshine Girl?"

"Whatever you want. Let's just have fun and live in the moment."

I couldn't deny the appeal. I couldn't deny that I wanted her. But I needed to be sure that she understood the deal.

"Promise me that this is what you really want. Because I can't promise you more than this. I don't want you to get your hopes up. This doesn't mean we'll be standing under an oak tree with daisy chains around our necks, pledging to love each other until death do us part."

She laughed, the sound sweet and sultry at the same time. That was Quinn. The sweetest temptation. "I'm not five years old anymore, Jesse. No weddings. Fake or otherwise." Her gaze never wavered. "I know the score. I'm not looking for love. Just sex."

Just sex. No strings attached. It couldn't get more perfect than that.

I followed Quinn up the stairs and opened my front door.

"Are you going to punish me, Jesse?" she taunted. "Punish me for making you think about me tonight when you were on your date?"

So bold. So brazen. In her tiny skirt with nothing underneath. Looking up at me with her big hazel eyes. So deceptively innocent.

"Is that what you want? You want to be punished?"

"Yes."

I knew this was wrong. I knew I shouldn't go along with this plan, but I wanted Quinn. I wanted to be inside her. I wanted to hear the little sounds she made when I fucked her. I wanted to be the one who took her virginity. Not some asshole who didn't know what the fuck he was doing.

Fuck it. I was done fighting it.

I grabbed her hand, pulled her inside, and slammed the door shut behind us.

Chapter Twenty-Six

Quinn

"Is that what you want? You want to be punished?"

"Yes." I was feeling so bold tonight. So brave and daring. I shoved away my inhibitions and doubts. All I wanted to do was live in this moment.

He grabbed my hand, pulled me inside, and pushed me against the wall. His big, warm, calloused hands skimmed over my bare skin, sending delicious shivers up and down my spine as he pushed up my skirt so it was bunched around my hips. Then he lifted me off the ground and slammed me against the door. My lips parted on a gasp.

God, I loved this side of Jesse.

He traced my lips with his tongue before sliding inside my mouth and kissing me like I'd always wanted to be kissed with wild abandon. Like he'd given up the fight and had surrendered.

I loved the taste of him. The feel of him. His hard body, muscles taut, pressed into mine.

My blood ran hot, a jolt of adrenaline coursing through my veins that ignited every cell in my body and made me burn for him.

I rocked my hips and ground my bare pussy against the hard ridge of his cock. God, I was so wet and so needy and aching that I couldn't think straight. I wasn't thinking at all. I was just chasing the high, reveling in the feel of his mouth taking command of mine. The lash of his tongue like we were dueling.

"Look what you do to me," he growled, his lips finding my neck and leaving their mark. My back arched off the wall, and I dug my fingers into his shoulders, remembering something he'd said earlier.

"*Another girl asking for a kiss?*"

"Did she make you feel like this? That other girl you kissed tonight."

"Definitely not." That put a smile on my lips. "You make me so hard for you," he rasped.

"What are you going to do about it?" I asked breathlessly, my confidence bolstered by his confession. Whoever he had kissed hadn't made him feel like I did. It made me feel like I had some power, like the playing field was more level now. "You can have me. Right here. Right now," I taunted.

"Fuck. You think I'd take you against a wall your first time?"

"I don't care."

"I fucking do."

He spun us around and carried me across the living room, guided by the light of the moon streaming through the windows, bathing the room in blue. I clung to him, my legs cinched tightly around his waist, my lips crushed against his in a kiss that made me breathless and hungry for more.

Blindly, he made his way down a hallway and took a left turn into his bedroom, where a wall of tall windows overlooked the trees and his backyard. He tossed me on the bed, practically throwing me off him, and I bounced a little on the mattress and stared up at him, waiting for his next move. My skirt was still bunched around my hips, and I was needy and wet and aching for him. Completely exposed. I resisted the urge to pull down my skirt while he removed my left Nike and then my right. They hit the floor with a thud, and then he moved up my body, his hands skimming up my thighs, his lips trailing behind until he reached the place between my legs.

Using his forearms to pin down my thighs, he gave me a few shallow licks. My body jerked at the contact, at the delicious feel of his tongue where I needed him most.

"So fucking sweet," he murmured.

My fingers dug into his hair, and I tried to pull his head up to mine. "This isn't what I want," I whimpered.

"So impatient."

He grabbed the waistband of my skirt and slid it down my legs, then tossed it aside and tugged up the hem of my T-shirt. I sat up to help him, although he didn't need it. He reached behind my back and unclasped my bra with one hand. Two seconds later, I was completely naked on Jesse's bed.

Raw and vulnerable and exposed. When his eyes roamed over my naked body, I resisted the urge to cover myself with my arms. It was so hard to do, but I forced myself to be brave even as my body trembled.

"Jesse," I whispered.

"Quinn. You… are so fucking beautiful." His voice was low and husky, and it was impossible to miss the sincerity. *He* made me feel beautiful. Tears stung my eyes, a lump of emotion forming in my throat.

"I want to see you," I whispered. He was still fully dressed while I was naked. It hardly seemed fair. "Feel you inside me…"

He peered at my face for a moment, and I thought he would prompt me to say the words like he had that day in his truck. But he didn't. "This is your first time. I want to take my time with you. Make it special for you."

The sincerity in his voice made my heart squeeze. Maybe he didn't love me the way I loved him, but I knew he cared about me. What I didn't tell him was that it wouldn't take much to make this special. The fact that it was him already made it special. But if I said that, he might think I wanted more than just sex, so I gave him a slight nod.

We'd do this his way.

Without warning, he grabbed my ankles and dragged me to the edge of the bed, so my ass was practically hanging off it, and my feet were planted flat on the mattress. He knelt in front of me, dragged two fingers through my folds, and guided his fingers to my mouth. "Taste yourself."

With my eyes locked on his, I wrapped my lips around his fingers and sucked, my cheeks hollowed, his fingers coated with the taste of me.

He groaned and slid his fingers out of my mouth, adjusting himself in his jeans before he lifted my left foot off the mattress and draped my leg over his shoulder. I pushed myself up on my elbows, my chest heaving as he used his thumbs to part my lips and drove his tongue inside.

Oh my God. My arms gave out, and my back hit the mattress, all logical thought flying out of my head as he used his tongue and his fingers to fuck me.

When he pinched my clit between his fingers, his tongue still delving deep inside me, my legs started shaking uncontrollably.

He replaced his tongue with one thick finger, pumping it in and out before adding a second one. Oh my God. My muscles clenched around his fingers. "That's it. Fuck my fingers. Fall apart for me."

And I did. I fell apart at his command, and I lay on the bed, boneless.

He kissed the inside of my thigh and stood up from the bed. I scooted back on the mattress and watched him unbutton his charcoal gray button-down. When he got halfway down, he reached behind his head, grabbed the collar, and pulled it off.

In the moonlight, he looked like a god. Lean and lithe, with those broad shoulders and chiseled abs, that perfect V cut of his Adonis belt. He toed off his black leather high tops and pushed down his dark jeans and boxer briefs.

Oh God. I got onto my knees and scooted to the edge of the mattress, my hand reaching for his thick, hard cock that jutted straight up.

It was beautiful. It really was. I wrapped my hand around it and heard Jesse inhale sharply as it twitched in my hand. The thin skin wrapped around his hard length was silky soft, like velvet. I gave it a squeeze, testing it, and he hissed as I dipped my head and licked the drop of liquid off the slit.

"Fuck," he rasped, grabbing the back of my head as my tongue peeked out for another taste. I watched him from underneath my lashes as I took him into my mouth and sucked on him, reveling in the fact that I had this kind of power to make him so hard. To make his hips thrust and his breathing shallow.

But he didn't let me finish. Instead, he put his hands on my shoulders and pushed me against the mattress, then reached into the drawer of his bedside table and grabbed a silver-foiled wrapper. I watched him tear it open, then roll the condom over his erection before he climbed up my body and settled his narrow hips between my thighs. His heavy cock rested against my stomach, arms braced on either side of me to hold his weight.

"Are you sure about this?" he asked, giving me a chance to back out.

"Yes. This is what I want."

Lifting my hips, I urged him on. Instead of pushing inside me, he glided through my slick folds. His hard cock cradled in my wet pussy. Dipping his head, he teased my nipple with his tongue and teeth, and my back arched off the mattress, my fingers digging into his hair as he rocked against me, still gliding but not making any move to push inside me.

When he released my nipple, he stared down at me, and our

eyes locked. "It's going to hurt."

I didn't care. I'd never wanted anything as much as I wanted him right now.

"That's okay. The pain will go away." *Just like you.* I shoved that thought out of my head. This was no time to think about the future. I needed to stay in the here and now.

Reaching down, he guided his tip to my entrance, his eyes still on me, watching my face so intently it was impossible to hide my reaction. The first thrust stole my breath and every muscle in my body tensed.

It burned like fire. I bit my lip to hold back the whimper. Evie warned me that the first time would hurt, but she assured me it got better.

My hands gripped his biceps, and I dug my fingers into his warm skin.

"Breathe, Quinn." He slanted his mouth over mine, caressing my lips with a kiss that was so sweet and so gentle, his soft breath mingling with mine as if he was giving me the air I needed to breathe.

Taking a shaky breath, I nodded, letting him know I was ready for more. After giving me a moment to adjust, he thrust in deeper. Oh God. It felt like he was stretching me out, ripping me open, and creating a space that only he could fill. This fullness… It was too much. I couldn't breathe. I couldn't move.

"You have to relax, baby." He brushed a lock of hair off my forehead and smoothed it back with his hand. "Take a deep breath."

I did as he said. I took a deep breath and let it out, trying to ride through the pain.

"Look at me. Look at my face."

I opened my eyes and stared at his face. His blue eyes and full lips, a lock of brown hair falling over his forehead. This was really happening. Jesse was inside of me.

"Don't hold on so tight," he whispered, brushing his lips across mine.

I knew what he meant. He was trying to get me to relax the tension in my body, so I loosened my grip on his biceps.

"I need to move," he said, his voice strained. "But I don't want to hurt you."

And that did it for me. His face looked so tortured, his voice raw like he was scared of hurting me. Something loosened inside me, and I felt my body relaxing and melting into his.

I lifted my hips, urging him on again, and he started moving, gliding in and out while I did my best to stay as relaxed as I could.

"I knew it," he said. "I knew you would be fucking perfect."

His words put a smile on my face. I was perfect for him. I'd known it all along.

He brought his hand down to where we were joined and rubbed his thumb over my clit. I didn't think I could come. Not like this. So it surprised me that it could feel so good. His thumb rubbing my clit while he thrust in and out. A shot of pleasure laced with pain had me writhing beneath him, rocking my hips and taking him in as deep as I could.

We found a rhythm then, our bodies moving together as he glided in and out, his thumb still rubbing my clit, and I was chasing the high, lost in the moment.

I barely felt the sting now.

"Fuck. I can feel you clenching my cock. You like that?"

"Y-yes. Oh my God," I panted. "I'm... I'm going to come." He pressed his thumb against my clit at the same time that he captured my mouth with his, and he kissed me hard.

Liquid heat poured through my veins, and I was crashing, falling, my muscles clenching his cock as I screamed his name.

It was all the permission he needed to chase his own orgasm, and he was thrusting faster now, more erratically, a guttural sound ripped from his throat when he came.

His body shuddered, and he collapsed on top of me, his sweat-slick forehead dropping against mine.

For a long moment, we just stayed like that. My legs cinched around his waist and the weight of his body on top of mine. And it was all so perfect.

A few tears slid down my cheeks.

Tears of joy mingled with all these overwhelming emotions.

Because I'd given him my virginity. The guy I'd been in love with all my life.

Nobody had ever warned me how intimate it was to let someone inside your body. To be joined so closely. Our hearts beating in sync.

He lifted his head and pushed himself up on one arm, so it bore his weight. When he pulled out of me, I nearly cried. I felt so empty now. So bereft.

He stood up from the bed and removed the condom that had traces of my blood on it. "Be right back."

Wordlessly, I nodded.

When he walked into the bathroom adjoining his bedroom, I squeezed my eyes shut and tried to keep the tears at bay.

I heard the water running in the bathroom, and a few seconds later, he returned with a towel in his hand. Then he proceeded to wash away any traces of blood, being so sweet and gentle with me that I really did start crying this time.

"Shh. It's okay." He tossed the towel on the floor and climbed on the bed next to me, then pulled me against him and kissed the side of my neck. "It won't always hurt so much." He was talking about the physical pain, but that wasn't why I was crying.

He stroked my hair and peppered me with soft kisses, our naked bodies fitting into the curve of each other's, and it made my heart ache for reasons I couldn't fully grasp.

I'd promised myself I would live in the moment, but all I could think about was the future.

How would I ever say goodbye?

I crept up the stairs on my bare feet, trying to be as quiet as possible as I passed Declan's bedroom door. Almost there.

"Where the hell have you been?"

I jumped at the sound of his voice. Great. Perfect. Just what I needed.

Keeping my back to him, I pushed open my bedroom door. "I stayed at Evie's last night."

With that, I closed my door, changed into shorts and a tank top, and threw myself on my bed. It was still early, too early to start my day, and I just wanted to hang out on my bed and relive every moment of last night.

After he'd cleaned me up and kissed away my tears, he'd held me, and we'd talked for hours about everything and nothing. I'd made him promise that this would stay between us. In other words, I didn't want my brothers to know.

"You want me to lie to my best friend?"

"You don't have to lie. Just don't say anything. They don't need to know every detail of my life. This is none of their business."

Later, when I was still too sore to have sex again, he gave me an orgasm with his tongue, and we fell asleep on his king-sized bed with charcoal gray sheets that smelled like him, my body tucked into him, and it was all so perfect.

I'd woken up when the sun was rising, giving his bedroom a golden glow, and slipped out before he even noticed I was gone. It was better that way. It made me feel like I was in control of this situation. Like maybe I could always leave him wanting more instead of feeling like I'd overstayed my welcome.

My door burst open, and Declan strode into my bedroom.

I jackknifed off my bed and scooted back until I was leaning against my headboard. He was wearing boxers and nothing else. I'd forgotten what it was like to live with my brothers. At least he wasn't naked.

"You can't just walk into my bedroom like that."

He stood over me, glowering, arms crossed over his tattooed chest. "You never stay at Evie's."

"Well, last night I did."

"You're a shitty liar."

"I'm not lying." I couldn't even meet his eye. I really was a shitty liar.

"Look me in the eye and swear on Mom's life that you stayed at

Evie's last night."

I rolled my eyes and tossed a pillow at him. "Get out of my room."

My brother didn't budge. He ran his hands through his hair, making the dark strands stick up all over. "You were at Jesse's, weren't you?"

The expression on my face must have given me away.

He cursed under his breath.

"You're going to get hurt," he said softly, so unlike the gruff tone he usually used with me that it made my heart squeeze.

It sounded like he actually cared. I hugged my knees to my chest for protection. "I know what I'm doing. I can handle this."

"No, you can't. Take it from a guy who sleeps with girls and moves on without a backward glance. You're *not* that kind of girl."

I jutted out my chin, attempting to look tough. "You have no idea what kind of girl I am."

"You haven't changed, Bean. I can see right through your tough girl act. You're the kind of girl who falls in love and dreams about her wedding day. The kind of girl I avoid at all costs."

"Why do you avoid girls like me? Are you scared you'll fall in love?"

He huffed out a breath. "We're not talking about me. Stay away from Jesse. It won't end well."

I studied my sky-blue painted nails. "Are you going to say anything to Mason and Holden?"

"I'm not a snitch," he scoffed.

It was true. Declan never told us anything, and he kept everything a secret from us. He'd never introduced us to any of his girlfriends. Probably because they came and went so quickly, there was no point in getting to know them.

"Stay away from him, Quinn. You'll only get your heart broken." Those were his parting words before the door closed behind him.

He was probably right. But it was too late. Now that I'd gotten my first taste of how good it could be, there was no way I'd give him up before I absolutely had to.

Jesse was the Sun, and I was the Moon. Our time together was fleeting. This little arrangement had an expiration date. But I didn't want to think about any of that now.

I just wanted to enjoy this ride for as long as it lasted.

Chapter Twenty-Seven

Jesse

I raced up the ramp and flew off the lip of it.

Leaning back on my bike, I gave it some gas, and on the first rotation, I let go of the foot pegs and kicked both legs straight back, hovering above the ground. My hands gripping the handlebars, I got my feet back under me just in time, and both wheels hit the dirt.

Shifting into second, I cruised past the dirt jumps and popped a wheelie.

I rode over to Mason on my rear wheel and dropped both tires into the bike stand.

"Still a show-off," Mason said with a shake of his head as I climbed off my bike and pulled off my helmet. He'd parked his Jeep under the shade of the trees and was sitting on the tailgate.

With a chuckle, I grabbed a bottle of water from the cooler and guzzled it.

"You're fucking crazy," he said with a laugh. "You know that, right?"

I grinned and doused my head with cold water. Steam poured off me. It had to be close to a hundred degrees in the sun, and I was soaked in sweat, the layers of my riding gear sticking to my skin. But this was the most fun I'd had in a long time. So making the switch to freeriding had been a good call.

It was easier on the body than motocross, and it gave me the kind of freedom I didn't have when I was racing.

"You act like you didn't already know that."

"It's been a while since I've watched you ride," Mason said. "The first time you tried to pop a wheelie, you ran into a fucking tree."

I chuckled at the memory. It had been a dare. My dad had been so pissed I'd wrecked my bike that he'd put me on laundry duty for the entire summer. With four boys in the house, we had a shit ton of laundry.

"But this shit... what you're doing out there... it's next level." Mason eyed my bike. "That's a sweet bike." I heard the longing in his voice as I removed my jersey and body armor and leaned against the tailgate next to him.

"If you ever wanna ride with me, just say the word. I can hook you up."

"Tempting. But I haven't been on a bike in ten years."

I couldn't imagine giving up the way he had. I wiped my face with a sports towel and threw it on top of the cooler. "Do you ever miss it?"

"Nah. Yeah." He laughed a little. "Sometimes."

"Why'd you give it up?" I'd always been curious. Mason had been good, but one day he'd just decided he had enough and walked away.

He squinted at the trees in the distance. "Honestly? I gave it up because I was never going to be half as good as you."

"That's bullshit. You could've been just as good."

He shook his head. "It wasn't my life. It was just a hobby. A fun way to blow off steam. Yeah, I liked it, but I didn't love it the way you do. I wanted to go to college and do other shit with my life. You made a lot of sacrifices to get where you are."

It had never felt like a sacrifice. While I was training and competing in high school, my friends were partying. Did I feel like I missed out? Hell no. If I had to do it all over again, I'd still choose moto.

"And I sure as hell didn't love the injuries."

"They're no fun," I admitted, rolling out my shoulder. I'd been battered and bruised, but despite all the injuries, nothing had ever stopped me from riding, and nothing ever would. Not my retirement. Not the injuries. Not the team that had fired my ass.

"When you headed to Cali?"

"Mid-August." I took another swig of water. I was looking forward to getting out there to train with the team. There would be twelve of us. It was going to be a hell of a stunt show. Every single one of those guys was batshit crazy. In a good way. A few of them, including Knox and Colby, were Hollywood stunt riders. Next year we were doing a live tour of North America, and Colby said they'd been talking to some execs at MTV. Everything was falling into place, and I was getting my life back together. It felt good to be excited about something again.

"Are you going to see your ex when you're out there?"

"Not if I can help it." Last I'd heard, she was living in L.A. I didn't care what the fuck she was doing in L.A. or who she was doing it with. Alessia was the queen of shitty life choices, but she wasn't my problem anymore. As long as she stayed out of mine, she could do whatever the hell she wanted.

"When's the last time you talked to her?"

"It's been a while." Back in May, she was calling and texting all the time. I never answered. Deleted her texts without reading them. "I blocked her number on my phone."

"Sucks that she did that to you."

"Tell me about it." Mason didn't even know the half of it. Only Quinn knew. I hadn't even told her everything, but I'd given her the Cliff Notes version, which was more than enough.

"Takes time to move on from something like that."

"I've moved on." I grasped my jaw in my hand and twisted my head, cracking my neck on one side and then doing it on the other to alleviate the tension that was starting to build there. Every time I thought about Alessia, it fucked with my head, so I tried my damnedest not to think about her at all. "I've put it behind me."

He gave me a skeptical look. I hopped off the tailgate and rolled out my shoulders before I threw on my riding gear. Time to get back out there and work on my jumps. The last thing I wanted to do was sit around and talk about my ex-girlfriend.

"All I'm saying is that you loved her, and those feelings don't just magically disappear."

My jaw clenched, and I snapped. "Why the fuck are we talking about Alessia? I told you I'm over her," I gritted out.

"Yeah, okay. But as soon as I mentioned her—"

"I don't even know why you brought it up."

He rubbed the back of his neck, his eyes not meeting mine. I knew Mason. He was hiding something. I crossed my arms over my chest and waited for him to speak.

Mason winced. "I talked to her yesterday."

I stared at him, trying to process what he'd just said. "You *talked* to Alessia. Why the fuck would you do that?"

"She called the brewery. It's not the first time she called either."

"So what? You've been chatting with my ex all summer?" My eyes narrowed on him. "How fucking cozy. Are you having phone sex too? Did you two make plans to hook up—"

Mason held up his hand, cutting me off. "Stop right the fuck there. You know damn well I'd never go there. But like I said, feelings don't magically disappear. Otherwise, you'd have a completely different reaction."

Chastised, I lowered my head and rubbed the back of my neck. I knew he'd never do something like that, but I wouldn't put it past Alessia to insinuate herself into Mason's life just to get closer to me. Knowing her, she was probably plotting new and innovative ways to fuck up my life.

"Why didn't you just hang up on her?"

"I don't know. She was crying and shit. She kept going on and on about how she fucked up and how much she loved you—"

"*Love?*" I asked incredulously. "She doesn't know what love is. All she ever did was use me."

I worked my jaw, trying to contain my anger. I didn't even know who I was angry with. I thought I'd put all this behind me, but just the mention of her name made all the muscles in my body tense and my hands balled into fists. I flexed my hands and shook out my arms, attempting to loosen up.

"Sorry I mentioned it."

I was sorry I ever met her. "Sorry you had to deal with her shit."

"No problem."

I pulled on my helmet and gloves. Time to ride.

It was the only way to get this shit out of my system.

"Uncle Jesse!"

My gaze swung to Noah as he darted through the trees. He came to a stop in front of me, a big smile on his face. I took a deep breath and forced a smile. "Hey, buddy. What's up?"

"We came to watch." He jerked his thumb over his shoulder at Jude, trailing behind with Levi riding on his shoulders. When Jude set him down, Levi ran over to us on his little toddler legs.

He barreled right into me and wrapped his arms around my legs, looking up at me with his big blue eyes. I knew what he wanted. I lifted him off the ground and over my head, then dipped him down low and spun him around, pretending he was an airplane, sounds and all.

Levi loved this game. He was laughing so hard his whole body shook.

So carefree. So filled with joy. Not a care in the world. Some days I'd give anything to be a kid again.

When I set him on the ground, he stumbled around like a drunk for a minute before he landed on his butt, kicking up a cloud of dust. A second later, he was back on his feet again, running in circles with his hands balled into fists, pretending to rev the engine. "Vroom, vroom, vroom."

We all laughed at his antics.

"Jump! Jump! Jump!" Levi jumped up and down, clapping his hands. Purple stains decorated his yellow T-shirt, and I suspected they were from a grape popsicle, his favorite flavor. He looked so much like Jude, with the same shade of brown hair that curled up at the ends and dimples in his cheeks.

"I think he wants you to do some jumps," Noah said, speaking for his little brother while Mason and Jude exchanged greetings.

I chuckled. "Yeah. I got that."

"I'm gonna take off. I need to get back to work." Mason bumped his fist against mine, and I felt a twinge of guilt. He was my closest friend, and he'd been forced to deal with my ex. Meanwhile, I was going behind his back and fucking his little sister.

Shit.

I watched him drive away, the dust kicking up from his tires as he followed the dirt lane that led out to the road before I returned my attention to Noah.

"I'm gonna make a video on Daddy Jude's phone."

I ruffled his dirty blond hair. It touched the collar of his T-shirt and was thick and wavy. Someday my nephew was going to be a heartbreaker. "Thanks, buddy. I can use that to figure out where I need to improve."

He nodded. "Yeah. Your jumps were okay last time, but maybe

you'll do better today."

I laughed. "I'll try my best. Okay isn't good enough, is it?"

"Nope. You need to be number one," he said with all the confidence of a seven-year-old who'd already been indoctrinated into the McCallister way of life. There was no such thing as settling for second best. We had to be number fucking one.

"But you'll get better."

"Thanks, Noah," I deadpanned. "I appreciate your confidence in me."

He held out his hands. "That's what I'm here for."

Jude and I laughed. The kid was so fucking cute. A little comedian and a charmer.

Jude crossed his arms over his chest. "Show us what you got, Evel Knievel."

I snorted at his old nickname for me. "Is this gonna be a daily thing? A show before dinner?"

He set up the beach chairs my mom had left leaning against a tree, then helped himself to a bottle of water from the cooler before he took a seat, lounging in the shade under the trees like he had all the time in the world. Which he didn't. Jude was the CEO and co-founder of a disaster relief non-profit organization, so he worked a shitload of hours and had three kids and a wife to look after.

"Someone needs to watch your crazy ass."

Someone was always there, watching my crazy ass. Pretty sure my mom had set up a rota like she used to do with chores when we were kids. At some point or other, every single member of my family had shown up to watch me ride.

Even Ridge had stopped by to talk about motorcycles. He was

saving up for a Harley. It wouldn't be my first choice, but Brody had already cautioned me to go along with it and not try to talk Ridge into a racing bike.

"That's the last fucking thing he needs," Brody had grumbled. "He's gonna finish college in one piece if it's the last thing I fucking do."

As if Brody had the power to protect Ridge from every danger. As if a Harley was a 'safe' choice. But who was I to talk about playing it safe?

I shook off my fucked-up feelings about Alessia, and I gave my family what they came for. A show.

But even after I finished riding for the day, I was still keyed up. I needed to shove Alessia so far out of my head that she couldn't mess with it anymore.

My sunshine girl could help me do that.

Three nights ago, I took her virginity. She'd been tight as a fist, and it had been exactly how I'd imagined. She'd milked an orgasm out of me that had seemed to go on and on, temporarily blinding me. It had been *that* good.

Yesterday, we did it again. It had been just as good as the first time. Better, even, because I hadn't been hurting her.

I couldn't remember the last time anything had felt that fucking good. I wanted to *live* inside her.

Not even my guilt over keeping this a secret from Mason was enough to stop me from wanting her.

But I guess I'd always liked playing with fire.

Chapter Twenty-Eight

Quinn

"Change your shirt." Mason tossed a T-shirt to Ridge, who caught it in one hand. But instead of going to the bathroom to change, he pulled off his ripped T-shirt right in front of everyone.

I couldn't help but stare. Wow. Ridge's muscles had muscles.

A group of middle-aged ladies sitting at the bar was watching the whole show, their eyes bulging. He gave them a big grin and a wink, taking his sweet time to get dressed in the T-shirt. It was two sizes too small and fit him like a second skin.

"Jesus Christ," Mason muttered. "Don't make me regret putting you behind the bar."

I snort-laughed. This should be fun. Ridge was saving up for a Harley and was looking to get some extra hours before he left for football training camp in August.

"You won't regret it." He puffed out his chest. "Business will be booming. I'm catnip for the cougars." He kept his voice low so the 'cougars' at the bar wouldn't overhear.

With that, he swaggered over to the group of ladies who were practically swooning off their bar stools and leaned across the bar, oozing charm and swagger. "What can I get you, ladies?"

I didn't have a chance to hear their response. It was the dinner rush. A group of eight sat at one of my tables, and for the next couple of hours, I was run off my feet.

"You've been spending a lot of time with Jesse this summer," Mason said when I stopped for a break. I guided the straw to my mouth and took a sip of my Sprite. My gaze drifted across the taproom to the kitchen, where Declan was visible on the other side of the pass.

Had he said something?

"He's... Jesse and I are friends." I cleared my throat and took another sip of my drink. "I mean, he's practically like a brother to me." *Lies.*

Mason nodded, not the least bit suspicious. I exhaled a breath of relief and ignored the twinge of guilt.

"He's always thought of you as the sister he never had."

If only Mason knew. I remained silent. It was the safer choice. I didn't want to put my foot in my mouth and say the wrong thing.

"I think Alessia was always jealous of his relationship with you," he mused.

My eyes widened. Mason had never discussed Alessia with me. So why was he bringing it up now? "Why would you say that?"

He shrugged. "Just a feeling I got."

"Do you…" Unable to meet his eyes, not wanting to give myself away, I toyed with my straw and summoned my courage to ask a question I wasn't sure I wanted the answer to. "Do you think he still loves her? I mean… does he talk about her with you?"

"I don't know if he still loves her. But I know he's not over her yet."

My stomach dropped, and disappointment punched me in the gut. Had Jesse told him that? Had he told Mason that he wasn't over Alessia? "Oh. Well, yeah… I guess it would be hard to move on from something like that."

Mason nodded. "Look at Mom. It's been five years, and she's still having a hard time moving on."

"That's different, though," I protested. "Mom and Dad were together forever, and they had kids and a whole life together. And Mom… she's moving on." Even as I said the words, I knew it wasn't true.

Mason shook his head, disputing my words. "All she ever does is work. That's not moving on. She's not dealing with it at all."

"Mom's doing great," I insisted. But, once again, I was lying. Yesterday, when we'd spoken on the phone, Mom complained that Dad was on yet another vacation, his fourth one this year. When I told her that she should take a break, she brushed me off and said that someone had to pick up the slack at work.

Just then, my phone buzzed. I slid it out of my shorts pocket and read the message as Mason moved further down the bar to wait on a few customers.

>Jesse: I'm hungry. Ravenous, even.

>So you should eat something.

>Jesse: How about you bring that sweet pussy over here tonight so I can feast on it.

Oh my God.

My cheeks flamed. I used my hand to fan myself. Why was it so warm in here?

He definitely didn't think of me as a little sister anymore. I looked up to make sure Mason wasn't watching and caught Ridge's eye. He smirked as if he knew exactly who I was texting.

"Is it getting hot in here, or is that just me?" He puffed out his chest. Ridge had a giant-sized ego to go with those big muscles of his.

"It's just you." Ridge barked out a laugh as I turned my back to him and texted a reply, a smug smile on my face as I tucked my phone in my pocket and crossed the room to check on my customers.

"Why are you looking at me like that?" I asked Jesse when he opened the door, shirtless and barefoot in faded denim, the Weeknd's "Can't Feel My Face" blasting from inside. His gaze was predatory, and I saw his eyes darken as they roamed down my body, leaving a trail of heat in its wake.

"How am I looking at you?" He braced his arm on the doorframe, and I stared at the thick veins. Vein porn at its finest. My gaze lowered to the obvious bulge in his jeans and stayed there a moment before returning to his face. His gaze was so heated I was surprised I didn't burst into flames.

Our text messages must have had the same effect on him as they had on me—the ultimate foreplay.

"Like you're the Big Bad Wolf, and I'm about to become your next meal."

He bared his teeth and let out a low growl. Oh God. Excitement had me squirming and rubbing my thighs together, but I kept my hands clasped like a good girl. In his text messages, he said I wasn't allowed to touch him.

Why would I have ever agreed to that? The urge to touch him was so intense now that I could feel my hands itching to do it.

"Pretty accurate." With a wicked grin, he grabbed my hand and pulled me inside. The door slammed shut behind me, and he pushed me against it, pinning my hands to the wall above my head. The only light in the room was from the moonlight streaming through the windows and the light spilling from the kitchen.

"Are you sure you want me bare?" he asked, pushing his body into mine and capturing the underside of my jaw with his mouth. He bit and kissed his way down my neck, and I arched it, allowing him free rein.

I wanted to feel *all* of him.

I already told him that in my text message, so we'd gotten that whole awkward conversation out of the way. He was clean. I was on birth control. So we were good to go. "Positive."

Jesse kept my hands pinned above my head with one hand and dragged his fingers down my throat, playing with me, a wicked gleam in his eyes like he knew he could do anything he wanted, and I would go along with it.

Goosebumps raised the hairs on my arms, and a chill ran through me, anticipating what was to come.

"Do you trust me?" he asked, tracing the hollow at the base of my neck. Then, when I didn't respond, he pressed against it, feeling the thrum of my racing pulse under his fingertips.

This felt like a test, and maybe I should have said no, but I found myself nodding.

"Use your words, Sunshine Girl."

"Y-yes."

I gasped when his hand wrapped around my throat, and he squeezed lightly, testing how far he could go, his eyes never leaving my face as he tightened his hold.

I was breathless, nervous and excited. The fear factor only heightened my enjoyment. Maybe I shouldn't have liked this, the way he was taking command, being so possessive, but I did. My core clenched and the ache built inside me, my clit pulsing between my legs. I could feel how wet I was, so needy and desperate for him. My body hummed, and my heart pounded in my ears, drowning out the music.

With his hand still wrapped around my throat and both of mine still pinned to the door, he dipped his head and traced my lips with his tongue, then dragged it over my jaw, slowly, ever so slowly. My eyes drifted shut, and I could feel my nipples growing hard, sending tingles up my arms.

He released my throat and slipped his hand under my T-shirt, and I pushed up on my tiptoes as he palmed my breast and guided it into his mouth, biting my nipple through the fabric of my lacy bra.

I moaned, writhing against the door and panting as he lavished the same attention on my other breast. I struggled to free my hands so I could touch him, but he tightened his grip.

"You don't get to touch me."

I whimpered, and he silenced me with a bruising kiss, his mouth crashing down on mine, his tongue hot and demanding. A jolt of adrenaline shot through me, and my whole body was buzzing. Every nerve ending in my body felt lit up.

I wanted more. More pain. More pleasure. More everything.

Without breaking contact, our lips still sealed in a kiss, he yanked down my hands and twisted them behind my back. Then, turning us around, he walked me backward across the living room, my feet stumbling when my legs hit the back of the sofa.

Then, suddenly, he spun me around, and with his hand on my lower back, he folded me over the arm of the sofa. My cheek pressed against the soft leather, and he pushed my hands into the sofa cushion.

"Don't move," he commanded.

With rough hands, he yanked up my skirt and fisted my panties, ripping them off my body. Oh my God. I heard the lace tear, and then they flew across the room.

Behind me, I heard him unzipping his jeans, building anticipation. I lifted my head and looked back at him, watching him fist his cock before he dragged it through my slick folds, up and down, over and over until I was squirming.

Without warning, he pushed inside me, the move so swift and powerful that he was buried to the hilt in one fluid motion. My breath seized in my lungs, and he groaned.

"Fuck. You feel so good."

God, he felt so good too. So hot and so thick, and he was in so deep. It felt different too. Not just the fullness but that he was bare, no barrier between us.

"Do you like that?" he rasped. "Do you like it when I'm raw? Do you like feeling my hard cock inside your sweet pussy?"

I could barely speak. I moaned, letting him know that I did like it. I loved it. He pulled out then, teasing me, and waited for my response. I knew that was what he was doing. Punishing me for not answering.

"Yes. I like it."

"Good." He rammed into me again, his dick so deep it hurt. But I loved the pain he gave. I wanted everything he had to give me.

With one hand gripping my hip, he wrapped his other hand around my throat and squeezed, holding it there while he thrust in and out, skin slapping against skin, his warm breath on my neck.

His hand moved to the place where we were joined, and he rubbed my clit while he thrust in and out, hard and deep. Releasing my throat, he fisted my hair and yanked my head off the sofa, his teeth grazing my neck and shoulder as I came, crying out as my muscles clenched his cock and I screamed his name.

With one more hard thrust, Jesse came on a roar. A guttural sound was ripped from his throat, and his body shuddered, liquid heat filling me up as he collapsed on top of me. Boneless.

After, spent and breathless, he entwined our fingers and kissed the side of my neck. I stared at his hands, the thick veins, and inhaled his scent--citrus and woodiness. Masculine. *Jesse.*

"Are you okay?" he asked. "Was I too rough?"

"No. I loved it. It was…" I didn't even have a word for it. "Can we do it again?"

"You're too good to be true, Sunshine Girl."

The next morning, Jesse showed up for our yoga session. I'd invited him last night before I left. I wasn't sure he would come, but I was secretly thrilled that he did.

Turns out he was *very* flexible. Not to mention his core strength which put mine to shame. Motocross racers had to be strong but light, so his muscles were lean and toned, not all bulked-up.

He could probably plank all day long, and his arms wouldn't even shake the way mine did.

"Look straight ahead and relax your shoulders," I commanded as I held my warrior position, my eyes on the swimming pool, my feet grounded on the mat, arms stretched out.

"I thought yoga was supposed to be relaxing," he complained. "You're barking out orders like a drill sergeant."

"If you'd stop looking at my ass, I wouldn't have to," I sassed.

"If you didn't want me to check out your ass, you shouldn't have worn that little bikini."

I tried my best to ignore how he was staring at me and guided him through the poses. Not gonna lie. I was enjoying the view too. Jesse, shirtless and barefoot in maroon boardshorts, his golden skin glistening with sweat in the morning sun, was a beautiful sight.

"I'm feeling all Zen and relaxed," I said about twenty minutes later when we were lying on our mats. I turned my head to look at him. His blue eyes met mine, and he gave me the sweetest smile like he was just as blissed out as I was.

"Hi," I said softly.

"Hi." He rolled onto his side and propped his head on his hand, his gaze dipping from my face down to my bare stomach where my scars were on full display. He slowly trailed his fingers over my lips, down my neck, and over my breasts. My breath hitched when he reached my scars and traced them with his fingertips. His touch was gentle as a soft breeze, but it burned, leaving a trail of heat.

"Look at you," he said quietly. He leaned over me and slid his hand under my lower back, then dipped his head, his soft, warm lips taking the place of his fingertips. My eyes drifted shut. All the breath seized in my lungs as he brushed his lips over every inch of my jagged scars. "Being the true warrior that you are."

When I opened my eyes, I was met with a gaze so intense it put a lump in my throat. I swallowed hard, trying to push down my emotions so I could speak.

"It's no big deal." But instead of sounding cool and casual like I'd hoped, my voice shook, giving me away.

He smiled, so much tenderness in his expression that it had me averting my face so he couldn't read it.

Because it was a big deal, and he knew it.

At the beginning of the summer, I never would have felt comfortable enough to bare my scars. Especially not to him. But he'd made me feel beautiful, and no matter what happened with us at the end of the summer, I'd never forget that.

I let out a yelp two seconds later when he lifted me off my yoga mat and tossed me over his shoulder. "What are you doing?" I pounded his back with my fists, but he just laughed.

I hit the cool water, and he dove in after me. "So much for my Zen. You can't just…" I threw up my hands. "Throw me around like a ragdoll."

He advanced on me, and I backed up until my back hit the wall, and I was caged in his arms. "Can't I?"

"No."

There was a gleam of amusement in his summer sky eyes and a sexy smirk on his face. God, he was so beautiful. I wanted to lick him all over. Lick off the beads of water trailing down his chest. But I forced myself to stand my ground as if this was a matter of huge importance. Which it wasn't. I loved it when he played with me. "I'm not your little plaything."

He grinned. "You…." He dipped his head and rubbed the side of his nose against mine, all playful and adorable. "Are my favorite little plaything." The next thing I knew, his hands were on my waist, he spun me around, and I was airborne.

When I came up for air and swiped my hand over my face, a movement from the corner of my eye had me turning my head. Declan was standing on the patio, an espresso in his hand and a scowl on his face. He just shook his head and gave me a look that said, *"You're playing with fire,"* before he went back inside.

Chapter Twenty-Nine

Jesse

At this point, showing up for work wasn't necessary. I had other shit to do with my time, and Mason didn't expect me to be here. But after another poolside yoga session this morning, I worked on my jumps all afternoon, and then I had the evening free. So here I was.

What I didn't want to admit, even to myself, was that I liked being around Quinn, and working at the brewery was just another excuse to hang out with her.

We'd spent the past week talking, laughing, *fucking*.

It was starting to feel like a lot more than just sex, but there was no point in turning it into something it wasn't. When we got to California, we'd both be pursuing our dreams. Vastly different dreams, I reminded myself.

So when the time came to go our separate ways, I would let her go. It was the right thing to do. But for now, I was going to enjoy the ride.

I watched her from behind the bar as she chatted with her customers, a big smile on her face. Declan was always bitching about what a shitty waitress his sister was, but it didn't seem to matter to the customers. They loved her.

I cleared some empties and wiped down the bar for a middle-aged couple who had just come in.

They ordered two beers on tap, and I filled the pint glasses, set them on the cardboard coasters in front of them, and turned to go.

"Are you from around here?" the woman asked.

I turned back around to face her. "Yes, ma'am. Born and raised."

"We're not from around here," the man said, taking a pull of his beer. "But we sure do like what we've seen so far."

The woman nodded. "It's beautiful country. We like it so much we're even thinking about moving here."

"It's a beautiful place to call home."

We talked about what they'd seen so far, and I gave them recommendations on other spots they might enjoy. It was easy to extoll the virtues of Texas Hill Country. I loved California, but whenever I was away from home, I missed it.

Mason had disappeared with Carly, not sure what was going on there, so I moved down the bar to two guys who had just come in. The guy in a Troy Lee trucker pointed to one of the beers on tap.

"Give us two IPAs."

"What are you doing behind a bar?" he asked when I served their beers.

"Everyone's gotta make a living somehow." I'm not sure why I'd answered that way, but something about the way he'd asked rubbed me the wrong way. Like he knew who I was, and he was digging for information. His next words confirmed my suspicion.

"Guess so. Looks like you had a rough year," he mused. "Couldn't have been easy to settle for an eighth-place finish. But to just up and walk away like that." He shook his head and let out a low whistle. "Kind of dramatic, wasn't it?"

My jaw clenched, and I rolled out my shoulder, the one that still gave me trouble after an old injury to the rotator cuff.

"Do I know you?"

"We're big moto fans. Been to a lot of your races." His friend nodded in agreement. "But nah, you don't know us."

"Then I'd appreciate it if you would mind your own business."

He held up his hands. "Didn't mean to hit a nerve. Just curious is all." He took a pull of his beer and watched my face as if he was waiting for an explanation. I didn't owe him a damn thing, so he wasn't going to get one from me.

"Hey, Jesse."

I turned to look at Quinn, who gave me a big smile as I walked over to her. She tucked a few loose strands of blonde hair back into the messy knot on top of her head and jabbed a hairpin in it to keep it in place.

"What can I do for you?" I leaned my hip against the bar and resisted the urge to grab the back of her head and pull her into a kiss. Didn't think Mason would be too impressed if he came back to the bar and caught me making out with his baby sister.

She smiled and licked her lips, her voice low and seductive. "Well, I can think of a few things." Her gaze darted around the room before returning to my face. "But we might get arrested."

I laughed. "Then we'd better just stick to your drink order and save the fun for later."

She lowered her lashes and bit her lip. "Yeah, we'd better do that."

Quinn put in her order, and I filled three glasses with ice and Coke and grabbed two bottles of beer from the cooler. Flipping the caps, I slid them across the bar along with two glasses.

"Do you know that guy you were talking to?" she asked, transferring the drinks to her tray. "The guy in the ballcap."

"No. Why?"

"No reason. It didn't look like a friendly conversation."

Quinn was perceptive. "He seems to have some opinions about my career."

"You know what they say about opinions. They're like assholes. Everybody has one."

A laugh burst out of me, alleviating some of the tension.

She smiled. "That's better. You were looking a bit tense. Thanks to my yoga sessions, you should be all loosened up by now." She gave herself a little pat on the back and sashayed away in those fucking tiny shorts she loved to wear. As if she felt my eyes on her, she put a little extra sway in her hips, and I kept my eyes glued to her ass until she disappeared onto the patio to deliver her drinks.

Damn. That girl. She was so cool, and I was dreaming up all the different ways I could get her screaming my name later.

A few minutes later, I was washing glasses when trucker hat asked for another round. I finished the task at hand before I served their beers.

"Is it true what they're saying?" he asked.

I should have let it go. I shouldn't have taken the bait. If this had been a year ago, none of this would have fazed me. I wouldn't have been concerned about what anyone was saying about me.

"You'll have to be more specific."

He rubbed his hand over the stubble on his jaw. "They're saying your team fired you."

My whole body tensed, but I schooled my expression, so it was neutral and didn't give me away. After I cleared a few empties from the bar, I wiped it down before I asked, "Where'd you hear this?"

"Guess you don't check the moto forums."

"Nah. Never put much stock in them. Just a bunch of trolls talking shit."

"Yeah, guess that must be it. Because there's no way the moto legend would do something bad enough to get fired." He shook his head and took another pull of his beer. "Just seems like you had it all, and then poof, it was gone. But that's life, ain't it? When you're down on your knees, life kicks you in the balls."

He had no idea how accurate that was.

I had never paid much attention to what they said about me on social media or those moto forums. If the information hadn't come directly from my mouth, I chalked it up to idle gossip and brushed it off. But now, someone had leaked information that had some truth to it, and I couldn't help wondering who it had been. It wouldn't have been the team owners. So it had to have been Nate. Or Alessia.

Trucker hat was typing something on his phone and nudged his friend's arm, showing him the screen before looking over at me. "I'll take care of it. Make sure they stop talking shit about you. The discussions get pretty heated. Like you said, there's a lot of trolls talking shit."

Too bad the shit they were saying about me was true.

Mason returned and joined me behind the bar, and we watched a very pissed-off Carly storm past. "Asshole," she hissed, giving him the middle finger. "I quit."

He winced and rubbed the back of his neck. Looked like his night wasn't going much better than mine.

"You good?" I asked, knowing damn well he wasn't.

"That was a mistake," he muttered under his breath as Carly stormed past again. This time she was on her way out the door with her bag over her shoulder. "I thought she understood the deal. I made it clear as fucking day."

"What exactly was the deal?"

"Sex. No strings attached." He scrubbed his hands over his face and groaned. "Shit. Now I have to hire a new server."

A laugh burst out of me. "That's your main concern? That you have to hire a new server?"

He stroked his jaw, thinking about it for a moment before he responded. "Now I understand the saying, Don't shit where you eat."

"Nice."

"Yeah. I'm an asshole." Mason shook his head and sighed as he moved down the bar to wait on a few customers.

Shortly after, I was refilling the ice when Mason muttered, "Huh.

I thought that was over. Guess not. You think that guy's okay?"

"What guy?"

I followed his gaze to the front doors that were open onto the patio. *The fuck?* I thought it was over too.

My blood pressure spiked when he leaned down and said something in her ear. A little too close for comfort. Quinn had her back to me, so I couldn't see her face, but the guy—Walker—had a smirk on his. My hands balled into fists when he wrapped his arms around her and pulled her against him.

Get the fuck away from my girl.

Quinn wasn't my girl, but I couldn't deny that I felt like she was mine.

The middle-aged couple I'd waited on earlier asked for another round.

Tearing my gaze away from Quinn, who was still talking to the fucking baller, I poured two beers from the tap and set them on the bar in front of them.

When I glanced outside, Quinn was nowhere in sight, and neither was Walker. With my back to the doors, I rang up two more beers at the register. "You think there's a chance Quinn will stay in Texas?" Mason asked, coming to stand next to me.

I set the tab behind the bar next to the register. "Nope."

"Yeah, guess it was a long shot. Thanks for trying, though."

I didn't try at all. Quite the opposite, in fact. I'd been encouraging her to go to California. "Not sure how much I helped."

"You're here, though, aren't you? You don't have to keep working at the bar. I know you have other things you'd rather be doing. But now that you'll be out in Cali, I feel better about her going. I'm

Every Rose

hoping you can keep an eye on her."

Guilt slammed into me. He trusted me, and I was betraying that trust. I rubbed the back of my neck. "I'll be on the road a lot. And I'll be living eighty or ninety miles away. Not sure how much help I'll be."

"Yeah, but ninety miles is nothing to you. If she ever needs you, I know you'd drop everything to be there for her, wouldn't you?"

I didn't even have to think about it. "In a heartbeat."

"That's what I thought. You're like family. And like you always said, she's the little sister you never had."

Not anymore.

"I don't need anyone babysitting me." My gaze swung to Quinn. Had she heard the entire conversation? Judging by the look on her face, I'd say it was a yes.

"I can take care of myself. So if you two are done talking about me like I'm a five-year-old…." She glared at me. "I need some drinks."

Chapter Thirty

Quinn

I pulled my arm out of his grasp, climbed into my car, and slammed the door. Or I would have slammed the door if he hadn't blocked it with his body.

"Do you mind?" I huffed.

"Yeah, I mind." He crossed his arms over his chest and widened his stance. His eyes narrowed to slits. "The fuck is going on, Quinn?"

"You tell me. You were the one discussing me with my brother like I was—"

"I'm talking about Walker," he gritted out.

"And I'm talking about the way you agreed to help Mason. Is

that the only reason you've been hanging out with me? What did you think? I'd stay in Texas just because you and Mason decided it was best for me."

"That's bullshit, and you know it."

Right now, I didn't know what to believe. "Just get out of my way."

He smacked the palms of his hands against the roof of my car, making me jump. God, he was so angry. He glared down at me as if I'd been the one who had hurt *his* feelings. As if I had been the one making excuses about how busy and how far away I would be. Only to turn around and say that he'd be there if I needed him. But what he'd meant was that he'd be there in case of an emergency.

I should have known he had an ulterior motive for working at the bar. But, god, how stupid could I be?

"Are you hooking up with Walker?"

"That depends." I crossed my arms over my chest, not giving an inch. "Are you done acting like a jackass?"

"Don't play these high school games with me."

"*You're* the one acting like you're in high school." I was being petty and maybe immature, but I didn't care. I jutted out my chin. "Why do you even care who I hang out with?"

Jesse shook his head in disgust and pushed away from my car. Then, with one more scathing look, he turned and walked away like it wasn't even worth fighting over. Like *I* wasn't worth fighting for.

Still fuming, I slammed my door shut. I wanted to be the first to drive away, but he beat me to it. Of course, he did. I tailed his motorcycle but quickly lost him when he shot ahead. Whenever I wasn't riding on the back of his bike, he was a speed demon.

Jesse would never fight for me. That was the sad truth, wasn't it?

I'd given him an easy option, and he'd taken it.

Sex. No strings attached.

What guy wouldn't jump at that chance?

When this was over, he'd just waltz right out of my life without a backward glance, and I'd be left to pick up the pieces of my shattered heart. How could I have ever thought this would work?

Thunder rumbled in the distance, interrupting my thoughts, and only moments later, the heavens opened up. I flicked on my wipers and peered through the windshield, straining my eyes to see the road. The rain was coming down so hard and heavy I could barely see the yellow lines. It battered my roof, the sound almost deafening. My wipers were doing double-time, but they might as well not have been working at all for how little it helped.

Then it hit me. Jesse was riding in this storm.

My heart was pounding in my throat, and my mouth went so dry I couldn't even swallow.

I pulled into the garage and cut the engine, relief flooding my body. I'd made it home in one piece. *Jesse.*

With shaky hands, I pulled my phone out of my bag and took a few deep breaths, trying to calm the jitters. I fumbled with my phone and snatched it up from the footwell.

Pull yourself together, Quinn.

I finally managed to press the speed dial. The call rang out and went to voice mail. A few minutes later, I tried again, and once again, it went to voice mail. He should have been home by now.

Why wasn't he answering his phone? My mind raced, my brain conjuring up a vision of Jesse on the side of the road, his bike mangled and twisted, his body trapped under the steel frame.

If anything happened to Jesse, I would lose my fucking mind.

Get your shit together, Quinn. Stop thinking of worst-case scenarios.

Sometimes an overactive imagination was a curse.

My car felt too small and suffocating, so I grabbed my bag from the passenger seat and went inside. I was hoping to escape to my room.

"Oh good, you're home," Mom said from the kitchen, relief filling her voice as I walked through the laundry room. She was sitting at the island with a glass of wine and her laptop open in front of her. "I was worried about you." She studied my face as I paused in the doorway. "Are you okay? You look pale."

I was tempted to flee. To run up the stairs to the privacy of my bedroom. But the concern in her voice prompted me to tuck my phone in my bag and set it on the counter. I pulled up a stool across from her and wedged my shaky hands under my thighs, forcing a smile. "I'm fine."

"Are you sure?"

"Yep. All good." No sense in getting her worried for no reason. My thoughts returned to the conversation I'd overheard earlier. "Did you know Mason was trying to keep me in Texas?"

She sighed and closed her laptop screen. "Your brothers are worried about you being in California on your own."

"*All* my brothers?" I knew Declan wasn't worried about me. When we'd talked about my housing assignment in the family group chat, Holden and Mason had expressed their concern. Declan's response?

It's fucking California, not a combat zone. Good riddance, Bean.

"Two of them. And your father," she added.

I snorted. "Like he gets a vote."

"Your father and I may not agree on everything, and there have been a lot of changes over the past few years, but one thing will never change. He loves you. He loves all four of you. But you're his special girl. Our little miracle."

"Declan always called me an accident."

Mom laughed, but she didn't even try to deny it. "You were the very best kind of accident."

"So I *was* an accident?"

"After Declan, I didn't think I could have more kids. So that's why we always called you our miracle. You were wanted. And you were loved even before you were born. Don't ever doubt that."

I brushed away a few tears. This night had turned me into an emotional wreck. "Do you..." I chewed on my lip, not sure if I had the right to ask this question or if it was even any of my business. But I was curious, so I asked anyway. "Do you still love Dad?"

My mom took a sip of wine and set down her glass, twirling the stem between her fingers. She didn't answer right away, and I could tell she was thinking about her response, searching for the right words, so I waited. "Your dad was my first love. My only love," she said with a soft laugh. "You never really forget your first love, and I'm not sure you ever get over it either. But you do move on. And you can find another love. Just as good, maybe even better, but different."

She hadn't really answered my question, but I let it go and didn't push for more. Maybe that was the answer. She still loved him, but it was time to move on. My father was getting married again, and whether she liked it or not, my mom had to find a way to come to terms with it.

While I pondered that, the door from the garage opened, and Declan strode into the kitchen, running his hand through his wet hair. He'd left after me, so he would have gotten caught in the rain on the way to his car. Which, once again, reminded me that Jesse was riding in the rain.

He hadn't called me back yet. Maybe he was still annoyed with me about Walker, so he wasn't answering my calls or returning them. Would he do that?

"How is it out there?" I asked Declan.

"Wet." I rolled my eyes. Such a smartass. "Some of the roads are already flooding."

Flash floods were common in these parts. Jesse lived near the river, so it would be especially bad.

My mom stood up from the island and rinsed her wineglass in the sink before she turned to us. "I'm just glad you're both home safe and sound. Now I can sleep in peace. Goodnight. Love you."

"Love you," Declan and I said in unison. For all his wicked ways, Declan loved Mom and wasn't afraid to say it. Guess he had some redeeming qualities.

He grabbed a beer from the fridge and walked out of the kitchen without saying a word to me. Typical.

Left alone, I tried calling Jesse again. This time I left a voice mail.

"Hey. I'm just... I was worried about you. Call me and let me know you got home okay. Please," I added before I cut the call.

As I passed the den on my way upstairs, Declan called my name.

I doubled back and poked my head in the doorway. He was holding the remote and flicking through the movie selections. I stupidly thought he might invite me to join him. "Yeah?"

"Jesse make it home okay?"

"I don't know. I can't reach him."

Without another word, he hit play on the movie he'd selected and settled back to watch it. Since he didn't invite me to join him, I climbed the stairs to my room. I'd rather be alone anyway.

I changed into sleep shorts and a T-shirt and brushed my teeth. Still nothing from Jesse.

I sat on my bed, leaning against two pillows propped against the headboard, and stared at my phone screen, willing it to light up with his name.

When my phone rang in my hand, I jumped, and my hand flew to my heart.

But it was Mason, not Jesse. I considered not answering, but that would just be immature. I knew he had been the one behind this whole plan, so I wasn't too happy with him. But if I didn't want to be treated like a five-year-old, I couldn't act like one. So I answered my phone.

"You made it home okay?" he asked.

"Yep."

He was quiet for a moment, and I waited for him to speak. "I don't know what you heard, but don't take it out on Jesse. It was my idea."

"But it sounds like he went along with it."

"Because he's a good friend, and I asked him for a favor."

I chewed on my thumbnail and thought about that for a minute. None of this should have surprised me. After Dad moved out, my relationship with Mason changed. It was almost like he felt the need to fill Dad's shoes. Like it was his responsibility to look after me. "I just wish you guys believed in me more."

"We do. We all believe in you. But can you blame us for being worried about you?"

After my body rejected my first transplant, Mason had been my rock when I went into kidney failure. It was a pretty big deal to be a living organ donor. Not something to be taken lightly. While I was on dialysis, he underwent surgery and had to stay in the hospital for four days.

Afterward, I think he felt a huge responsibility, almost similar to the way I felt. He didn't want to fail me. He didn't want to see me have to go through another transplant. And I felt a responsibility to him to keep this kidney healthy.

Those were the kind of ties that bind. No matter where I went or what I did with my life, I would be carrying a piece of him with me. It was a privilege and a burden. I'll never forget what Mason said after he found out we were a perfect match.

"Even if it hadn't been the perfect match, I still would have donated my kidney to you."

"I guess not," I admitted grudgingly in answer to his question. "But you have to let me go sometime, you know."

"I know. Maybe I was just being selfish. I'm gonna miss you like hell."

"I'll miss you too," I said softly, already feeling a pang of homesickness even though I hadn't even left yet. "All of you. Even Declan the butthead."

Mason laughed. "He really is a butthead. But he's a damn good chef."

I sniffed. "If you say so."

"If you had a more refined palate, you'd know so," he teased.

It was a running family joke, but I knew it was good-natured. For all the teasing I got from my brothers, their hearts were in the right place. It wasn't always easy having three older brothers, but I wouldn't trade them for anything in the world.

I wiped away a tear. God, I hated being so overly emotional.

"We good now?" Mason asked.

I sighed. "Yeah, we're good. Just stay out of my business."

"Not happening. I'll be calling you every day when you're in California."

"That's a bit extreme." He didn't call me every day now, so I knew he was joking. At least, I hoped he was.

"See ya, Bean."

"Stop calling me Bean," I muttered.

He was laughing as I cut the call. Two seconds later, my phone rang. *Jesse.*

"Hi. Are you okay?"

In the background, the music was pumping, and it sounded like a party was going on.

"I'm fine." His voice was clipped, and he sounded angry. Was he still dwelling on that stupid Walker thing?

"Are you home now?"

"I'm at Brody's ranch. The road to my house was flooded, so I had to take a detour. I'm shacking up with your buddy Ridge."

"Huh. That's interesting." The loud music faded, and then it was quiet. "Jesse? Are you still there?"

"Yeah, I'm here. I just came out on the back porch. Ridge is living in the guest house this summer, and he thinks he's a DJ."

"Is he any good?"

"If you ask him, he's the best. But he's a McCallister, so what do you expect."

I smiled. "McCallisters have big egos."

"Not the only thing about me that's big. Do you need a reminder?"

The tone of his voice sounded like a warning, so it probably wasn't the right time to tease him, but I couldn't seem to help myself. "Since I don't have anything to compare it to, how do I know yours is big? I mean, it could be average-sized. Or even—"

"Don't go there. Answer my question. What the fuck is going on with you and Walker?"

"Nothing."

"Nothing, huh? You two seemed pretty cozy."

"He's a nice guy, but nothing is going on. He came to the brewery to have dinner with his uncle. They sat outside, and I waited on them. He told me that he thinks I'm cool and he's leaving for training camp, so he probably won't see me before I head to UCLA. He wished me the best of luck, we hugged, and that was it."

He was quiet for a moment. Then, "Why didn't you just tell me that?"

"Because I was mad at you."

"Don't play those games with me again. Did you want me to

think something was going on?"

"No, I..." Jesse's girlfriend had cheated on him, so of course, he'd be worried about something like that happening again. Not that I was his girlfriend, but regardless, I would never do that. I could barely handle one guy, let alone two.

"I'd never do something like that. I'd never cheat on you. Not that this is a relationship, but I wouldn't be with someone else." *Not for as long as I have you.*

Now that we'd gotten that out of the way, it was my turn. "Why did you agree to go along with Mason's plan to keep me in Texas?"

"I wanted to hang out with you," he said simply. "And it seemed like a guilt-free way to do it."

I wanted to hang out with you. That was before we even struck our deal. His words put a happy smile on my face. That must be the reason he kept showing up to work. Not because he had to, but because he wanted to hang out with me. Maybe he wanted to spend time with me just as much as I wanted to spend time with him. Not just for sex, although that was great, but just being in each other's space. Watching each other. Joking around. Sharing stolen glances. It was the very best kind of foreplay.

I was so focused on his initial response that it took a moment to register the rest of his words.

"You feel guilty?"

"Let me talk to Mason."

I sat up straighter. "Are you insane? No. No way."

He let out an exasperated breath. "It's better to be honest than to keep lying to him."

"We're not lying. We're just not telling him something that is none of his business. I'm his sister. It's not like I'm his girlfriend and I'm cheating on him. Besides, what would you tell him? Your sister and I have a deal. I'm fucking her—"

"Don't use that word."

"You say it all the time."

"I'm a guy. And I'm crude."

I rolled my eyes. Talk about a double standard. But that wasn't my main concern right now. "You can't tell him, okay? I mean… we're just hooking up. So when it's time for you to leave, it's over, right?"

"Right."

My shoulders slumped in disappointment. But what had I expected? That he'd deny it. That he'd tell me it's so much more than hooking up, and it didn't have to end when he went to California.

Jesse was quiet for a moment, and I thought he was still thinking about Mason. I listened to the rain falling wherever he was standing, and I held my breath, waiting for him to speak. I had a sinking feeling in my stomach that he wanted to end it. Maybe he'd tell me that it would be so much easier to find someone else to hook up with. A girl who was old enough to drink. A girl who didn't have to sneak around and keep him a secret from her overprotective family. A girl who wasn't his best friend's sister.

"Quinn."

"Yes?"

"Next time you get caught in a heavy downpour, pull over on the shoulder and turn on your hazards."

My brow furrowed, my brain scrambling to catch up with the sudden change of subject. "What?"

"You nearly gave me a fucking heart attack."

"What are you talking about?"

"When you hydroplaned… you nearly gave me a fucking heart attack." He exhaled loudly like I was testing his limited patience. "Which part of that didn't you understand?"

"But you were ahead of me. How… what…"

"I doubled back to make sure you were okay. Then, I followed you all the way home."

"You did? But why would you do that?" I hadn't even seen him. But I hadn't been able to see much of anything.

"Why do you think? Because I wanted to make sure you were okay."

"Oh."

"Yeah. Oh. If that ever happens to you again, don't slam on your brakes. Just ease up on the accelerator and steer into it."

"Okay," I said meekly.

He softened his tone. "Are you okay?"

I let out a shuddering breath, his words prompting me to relive that moment. My heart had been beating triple time, and I was so sure I'd end up crashing. My first instinct had been to hit the brakes even though I'd vaguely remembered it was the wrong thing to do. When I came to a stop, I'd been shaking so hard I could barely grip the steering wheel. "Yeah, I'm okay. I was kind of freaked out, but I'm fine now."

"I was so fucking pissed at you."

"Because of the thing with Walker?"

"Fuck Walker. I was so scared something would happen to you that I tailed you all the way home at fifteen miles per hour."

Oh, Jesse. There I went again. Tearing up. Everything was

making me cry tonight. My voice was so clogged with emotion that I was amazed I could speak at all, but I managed to get the words out, failing to sound as lighthearted as I'd strived to. "I bet that was hard for you. Being a speed demon and all."

"You have no idea," he said softly, and I got the feeling he wasn't talking about having to drive slowly.

Chapter Thirty-One

Jesse

When I went inside after my phone call with Quinn, which had lasted two hours, Ridge looked over at me from his spot on the leather sofa where he was cradling his acoustic guitar.

"Careful, bro. Looks like you're catching feelings."

"We're just friends." The look on his face told me he didn't believe it any more than I did.

Whatever Quinn and I were, it was more than *just* friends, and it was more than *just* sex. Yeah, I'd been pissed off when I saw her with Walker. But that was my problem, not hers. I had to get over being jealous of every guy that so much as looked at her, let alone talked to her.

But when her car skidded across the road and went into a spin, my heart was pounding so hard, I could barely breathe.

If another car had been coming or if she'd gone off the side of the road, I would have fucking lost it.

As it was, I'd been a safe distance behind her when it happened. Her car came to a stop on the shoulder, and she'd narrowly missed crashing through the guardrail. I'd expected her to wait a while. Catch her breath and gather her courage before starting to drive again. I was all set to go talk to her. Take the wheel and drive her home. But by the time I'd pulled over and gotten off my bike, she was already driving away.

Which confirmed something I'd known all along. Quinn was tougher than she looked. Stronger than anyone gave her credit for. I knew Mason worried about her, but he shouldn't. Quinn could take care of herself.

I grabbed my clothes from the dryer—I'd gotten soaked to the skin and was wearing one of Ridge's holey T-shirts and basketball shorts—and headed back to the living room to say goodnight.

Head bent over the guitar, Ridge started plucking out a tune that sounded vaguely familiar. After a few more notes, I recognized it. A botched version of "Jessie's Girl." To make matters worse, he started singing along. Cheesing it up with a stupid grin on his face.

I groaned. "I'm going to bed."

"Goodnight, old man."

I held up my middle finger as I walked out of the room. "Good luck at college."

"With skills like mine, I don't need luck," he called back.

His cocky response made me laugh. I had a feeling he was in for a rude awakening.

When I got upstairs, I nearly tripped over the duffel bags in the hallway. Tomorrow Ridge was headed to training camp. Not sure why the hell he thought it was a good idea to stay up all night when he was about to get his ass kicked on the field. But that was his problem, not mine.

An hour later, I was still tossing and turning, thinking about those moto forums and the girl who was getting under my skin, when I heard a female voice. Ridge's bedroom door slammed shut, and two minutes later, the wall behind my bed was shaking.

With a groan, I pulled a pillow over my head and tried to drown out the sounds of my eighteen-year-old cousin having sex against the wall in the room next door.

After a few hours of sleep, I woke up to more rain and a knock on the front door.

I pulled on my jeans and ran my hands through my hair as I walked out of the bedroom. The duffel bags were gone, and so was Ridge. I jogged down the stairs and opened the front door to Shiloh, who gave me a big smile.

"I brought breakfast." She held up two shopping bags, and I stepped aside to let her in.

"I brought eggs and stuff for breakfast smoothies." She unpacked her bags in the small kitchen and set everything on the counter. "Sound good?"

"Sounds perfect. Need some help?"

"You can peel the apples." She set two green apples, a peeler, and a knife on the chopping board in front of me.

I peeled and chopped while she washed the vegetables.

"How have you been, Jesse?"

I'd seen her almost every Sunday at my parents' house, but we'd never spoken privately, and even though her tone was casual, the question sounded loaded. "It's all good."

She side-eyed me as she added kale and ginger to the blender. "You seem a lot happier than you did in April."

"So do you. Good to see you smiling again." Using the back of my knife, I slid the chunks of apple off the cutting board and into the blender.

"Love does that to a person." She set two bananas on the board. "Sometimes, Brody drives me nuts. But he's a good man. The best I've ever known."

"You must have some pretty low standards," I teased, peeling and slicing the bananas.

She laughed and shoulder-bumped me. Her laughter faded. "Before Brody, I was in a really toxic relationship." She added blueberries, a squeeze of lemon, and the banana to the blender and whizzed it all together. "So I know the difference between good love and bad love."

I searched the cupboards and found mason jars but no glasses. "That's what Brody and Ridge use instead of glasses," Shiloh said with a shake of her head.

"Typical rednecks," I joked.

"I know, right?" She set a frying pan on the stove and whisked the eggs in a bowl while I poured our smoothies and toasted the multi-grain bread. "Brody would be complaining that there's no bacon, and the bread tastes like birdseed."

I laughed at her observation. Brody's idea of a well-balanced meal was a juicy T-Bone steak with a shot of whiskey and a beer chaser.

A few minutes later, we set our food on the breakfast bar and sat across from each other. We made small talk while we ate our breakfast, but I could tell she had something on her mind and had come over here on a mission. The women in my family—my mom, Lila, and now Shiloh—took it upon themselves to share their wisdom and advice, whether we asked for it or not.

Sure enough, as soon as we finished eating, she broached the topic I suspected was her reason for bringing breakfast.

"So I guess what I was getting at earlier...." I took a sip of my smoothie and eyed her over the rim of the mason jar. She pushed her plate away and leaned her forearms on the counter, her gray eyes on mine. "Okay, I'll just come out with it. When you and Alessia came to my concert and hung out afterward, I noticed a few things. It's probably not my place to say anything. I don't really know her and spending a couple hours with her probably doesn't give me room to judge, but...." She chewed on her lower lip.

I finished the smoothie and set down the mason jar; my curiosity piqued. "What did you see?"

"I saw enough to know that you can do better. You deserve better. Maybe I'm projecting. Maybe I'm thinking about my own experience with someone I loved who was emotionally abusive, but it's made me hyper-aware when I see it happen to other people."

My gaze wandered to the French doors. The rain was still coming down hard and heavy, the spring-fed lake barely visible through the line of trees. Talking about my relationship with Alessia wasn't high on my list of fun things to do, but I found myself wanting to talk about it for some reason. Or at least, I was open to listening.

I dragged my gaze back to Shiloh. "What are you saying, exactly?"

"She seemed like the kind of person who took joy in putting you down rather than lifting you up. It was almost like…" She squinted into the distance, trying to find the right words. "Like she was happy that you were having a bad season. And I felt like you had to work so hard to keep her happy."

Shiloh wasn't the first person to tell me this, but it was the first time I'd actually listened. Earlier on in my relationship with Alessia, my mom had made a few comments. I'd gotten pissed and told her to kindly keep her opinions to herself. Unless she had something good to say, I'd prefer that she said nothing at all. Which was probably why my mother had rarely spoken about Alessia.

It made me feel weak to think that I'd let myself be treated like that. Had done everything I could to make Alessia happy, only for her to throw that love back in my face. And even worse, I'd gone back for more.

"I was an idiot to get involved with her." The shame must have been written all over my face.

Shiloh reached for my hand and gave it a squeeze before she released it. "You're not an idiot. You're amazing, Jesse. And she saw that. She saw the light in you, and she wanted to bask in the glow.

She saw the good in you, and she fell in love with everything you are. Because how couldn't she? But she was jealous. So she tried to bring you down to her level." Shiloh sounded like she was talking about her own situation as much as mine. "I used to think there was something wrong with me. Like, why wasn't I enough? What did those other girls have that I didn't?"

"Your ex cheated on you?"

"He was a serial cheater."

"He was an idiot."

She gave me a little smile. "It's crazy to think about it now. How much I put up with. Every time he'd be so sorry, you know? And he'd beg me to give him another chance. He'd swear up and down that it would never happen again, that it didn't mean anything, and that he only loved me. And I always took him back. Until finally, I just couldn't do it anymore, and I walked away. But I was stuck in that pattern for seven years."

"Jesus." Seven years was a long time. Looking at Shiloh, a rock star with the world at her feet, you'd never guess that she'd put up with something like that.

"Sometimes, we just fall in love with the wrong people. I guess I thought I could fix him. But you can't fix another person."

That sounded so much like me. It was how I always felt about Alessia. She was damaged. She was fucked up. Because of her father. And her high school boyfriend, who had abused her. She'd been with him, off and on, from the age of fifteen until she was twenty-two. Then she met me. The first time I met Alessia's mom, she cried.

"*Finally, my baby has met a good man. I prayed for this every day, and now my prayers have been answered.*"

I thought I could show Alessia that men could be good. I thought I could show her what good love looked like.

"What do you see when you look at me?" Shiloh asked, jolting me back to the present. She squared her shoulders and looked me right in the eye.

I didn't even have to think about it. "I see someone who is strong, independent, beautiful, and talented. I see a badass with a good heart."

She gave me a dazzling smile. "That's funny. I see the same thing when I look at you. You have a big heart, Jesse. There's room for someone else."

"Nah. I'm good on my own."

"On your own, huh? So… who's the girl?"

"What girl?"

She grinned. "Brody and I were at the farmer's market last week… my idea, of course. I have to force-feed him vegetables." I laughed a little, but I had a feeling I knew where this was going. "Anyway, I saw you with a pretty blonde. You two were having a lot of fun with the cucumbers."

My body shook with laughter. Quinn practicing blow jobs on a cucumber had to be one of the funniest things I'd ever seen. But when she put those same skills to the test, I hadn't been laughing.

"You looked really happy. You both looked happy."

She was right. I was happy with Quinn. If only our circumstances were different. If only she wasn't my best friend's sister. If only she were older. If only I wasn't a chickenshit who was afraid to fall in love again.

Chapter Thirty-Two

Quinn

*E*ver since last week when I lost control of my car and Jesse had been so worried about me that he'd followed me home, it felt like something had shifted with us. We were spending the majority of our free time together now. Hanging out, laughing, talking, and doing everyday things like a real couple would.

But I had to be careful not to think like that because we weren't a real couple. We were still a secret, and I was still sneaking out late at night to ride on the back of Jesse's motorcycle. Midnight rides had become our thing. When the August heat wasn't as suffocating, and the back roads belonged to us.

This summer, being with Jesse was everything I'd ever dreamed of and more. But in a little over a week, he would be gone.

Jesse signed a one-year contract with the FMX team, so it was official. Yesterday, he showed me their website. When I saw the schedule of events, I was nearly hyperventilating. For the next year, he would be all over North America. I was happy for him. I really was. But it was so hard to imagine my life without him in it.

It felt like we'd been living in our own little bubble, and pretty soon, that bubble was going to burst. But for now, I was taking it one day at a time, and I wasn't thinking about the future.

Curled up on Jesse's couch, I peeked over the top of my laptop. "What do you think is sexy?"

He looked over at me from the rowing machine. He'd moved it into the living room to watch a Livestream of the freestyle team he'd be joining.

"More research?"

"Mm hmm," I said absently, my attention diverted by his laptop on the coffee table. A cable connected it to the TV, where the same action scene played out on the big screen. These guys were insane. But so was Jesse. I couldn't believe anyone would be brave enough or stupid enough to take those kinds of risks.

"Wow." My eyes widened as I watched one of the guys fly up a ramp and soar into the air. He must have been sixty feet above the ground. I counted one, two rotations before he did a whip, and that was all I saw before Jesse blocked my view.

"He's really good."

"So am I." He crossed his arms over his bare chest as if daring me to challenge him on it. Sweat glistened on his skin, and my eyes lowered to his crotch. He snapped his fingers in front of my face. "My eyes are up here."

With a snort, I dragged my eyes away from the bulge in his athletic shorts and met his gaze. "Can you do what he just did?"

I knew he could. I'd watched him do all kinds of crazy stunts, had even captured them on video last week, but I loved teasing him.

He leaned over me and planted his hands on the back of the sofa cushion. "Higher and faster, baby."

"But that Australian guy—"

He shut me up with a dirty kiss. "What were you saying?"

This was a game, and I was ready to play. "I was saying that the tattooed, pierced Australian—"

I shrieked as he whisked away my laptop and closed it, tossing it aside. "Hope you saved that."

"Hey! I was working on that." The words were barely out of my mouth when he lifted me up and tossed me down again. My back hit the sofa cushion, and he braced his arms on either side of my head. Jesse loved tossing me around and caging me in his arms. I was his favorite plaything. "What if I messed with your dirt bike?" I stuck out my chin. "How would you like that? Huh?"

"You can mess with my dirt bike anytime." He nuzzled the side of my neck. "Fuck, you smell good."

"You smell like you need a shower." He just laughed and covered my body with his sweaty one, rubbing his sweat all over me. He didn't smell bad. Not really. I loved his scent. Even when he was sweaty after a workout, I still wanted to lick his skin. That's how far gone I was. Hopelessly crazy in love with my brother's best friend. "I better not have lost anything."

"It'll be fine." He waved his hand in the air, dismissing my concern.

I saved the Word document about two minutes ago. I was constantly saving my documents to avoid losing my precious words, but he didn't know that.

"Now… where were we?" He rolled onto his side and propped his head on his hand, peering down at me.

"I was about to shove you off the sofa. Show you the same respect you showed my laptop."

He laughed, knowing I was all talk. "You're getting so feisty." He tapped his index finger against the tip of my nose, his brows furrowed like he was thinking. "Oh right. That's it. What do I think is sexy?"

"I don't care anymore." God, I hated when he did that. Squinted his eyes and bit the corner of his mouth like he was deep in thought. I hated it because it was unfair that he could look so sexy.

"I need to help you do your research, and I take my job seriously."

Apparently, helping me do my research required me to be naked. "Love this little skirt." He knelt over me, unbuttoned my frayed denim mini and slid it down my legs then tossed it across the room. "But it looks better on the floor."

A laugh burst out of me.

"These are sexy." He hooked his fingers into the sides of my white lace panties and slid them down my legs. "Deceptively innocent. Like you." He dangled them from his fingertip and held them up for closer inspection, studying the pearl gray satin bow with a tiny pearl at the waistband before he flung them aside. "Being yourself is sexy."

His hands skimmed over my thighs and up my stomach, dragging my T-shirt up and over my head. My skin broke out in goosebumps, the little hairs on the back of my neck rising as delicious shivers ran up and down my spine. This was what he did to me. All he had to do was touch me, and every cell in my body ignited.

I shouldn't have caved so quickly, but here I was, lifting my arms so he could undress me.

"Bare skin is sexy." He kissed my shoulder. My neck. My jaw. An arm snaked around my back, and he deftly unhooked my bra. One-handed without even looking, which got me wondering how many other times and how many other girls he'd done this with.

If I were braver, I'd ask. But I was too afraid of the answer, so I kept my mouth shut.

He pushed the lace material aside and cupped my breast, thumbing the nipple before taking it in his mouth.

"Oh God," I moaned, arching my back off the sofa and digging my fingers into his shoulders.

"The little noises you make when I'm fucking you… they're sexy."

His fingers slid through my folds and grazed my clit. "The way you're always so wet and ready for me…." He slid two fingers inside, making it hard for me to focus on his words, his eyes darkening while he watched me writhe beneath him.

"A fresh face without makeup…." He removed his fingers and spread me wide, sitting back on his heels to appreciate the view before he dipped his head and smoothly licked me from slit to crack. I jerked at the contact, releasing a loud moan as his mouth teased me, and his thumb rubbed my clit.

"Jesse," I whimpered.

It only took a few seconds before I fell apart, no match against his merciless tongue. I was still gasping when he stood up and pushed down his shorts, freeing his hard cock before he knelt over me again. I reached for him, but he batted my hand away. Warm hands coasted up my thighs and covered every inch of my skin before his mouth captured mine. Hot and demanding, his tongue lashed against mine, and he pushed my hands into the sofa above my head, entwining our fingers. "After ten thousand hours of research…."

"Ten thousand hours?" I asked breathlessly.

"I've concluded that Quinn Cavanaugh…." He swiped his tongue over my bottom lip then sucked on it. "Is sexy as fuck."

"Hmmm. Really?"

"Mm-hmm." With a groan, he pushed inside me in one powerful thrust, and I nearly choked on the fullness, but I met him thrust for thrust.

It was too much, but never enough.

And I thought there was nothing and no one sexier than Jesse.

The moto legend. The freestyler who was so reckless and daring, fearless on a dirt bike.

He was my friend and my soul mate. He was everything I'd always dreamed he would be.

Unforgettable. Irreplaceable. The love of my life.

If only I could be his too.

Chapter Thirty-Three

Jesse

It was raining again, and my backyard was a mud pit. Too risky to practice my jumps. My phone buzzed with a message, and I did two more pull-ups, my legs parallel with the ground before I released the bar, and my feet hit the rubber mat on the garage floor.

I snatched up my phone from the weights bench and took a seat while reading Quinn's message. **Are you hungry?**

Are you offering dessert?

Jesus. Why did I have to make everything sexual? I wanted her all the fucking time. I couldn't get enough. That was the problem.

I carved my hand through my hair and watched the dots on my phone, waiting for her response. They started and stopped. Started and stopped.

Instead of a message, she sent a photo. She was lying on her bed in one of my T-shirts, her hair spread across her pillow, biting her lip. Her eyes were hooded like she was coming down from an orgasm.

And that was all it took. Just a photo of her face, her pillow-soft lip clamped between her teeth, and my dick was at half-mast.

Nice T-shirt.

Quinn: I stole it from some guy. I can't even remember his name, but I do remember one thing about him…

What's that? His huge cock?

Quinn: I was going to say that he was good with his tongue, but okay, we'll go with huge cock.

Where did you learn to be so naughty?

Quinn: I've been schooled. Do you think I deserve a spanking?

Fuck. I was a bad influence. Not that I was complaining.

Are you home alone?

Quinn: Yes

I FaceTimed her, and she appeared on the screen with a smile on her face.

"What are you up to?" she asked, her gaze roaming over my bare chest.

"Just finished working out."

"I wish I could lick you." Her eyes widened, and she slapped her hand over her mouth. "I can't believe I just said that."

I laughed. "If you were here, I'd let you lick me. All. Over. Like an ice cream cone."

"Oh." She licked her lips and let out a little moan that shot straight to my cock.

"Show me what you do when you're alone."

"You want me... to show you?" she asked, her voice breathy.

"Mmm hmm." I didn't think she would do it, but Quinn constantly surprised me. I loved that about her. "Put your phone somewhere, so you have your hands free, and I can see you."

She thought about it for a moment, and then she walked her phone across her room and set it against something, checking that she was still on the screen when she returned to her bed and sat with her legs underneath her.

"Take off the T-shirt," I commanded.

She slid it over her head and tossed it aside, licking her lips. I took a moment to appreciate the view of Quinn in a lilac bra and panties that matched her nail polish. She made pastels look sexy. The thin straps and lace looked so delicate against her suntanned skin, and I could see her nipples straining against the fabric, her milky white breasts spilling out of the cups.

"Take off your bra."

She hesitated a moment, then reached behind her and unhooked it, slowly sliding one strap down her shoulder and then the other before she removed it and flung it across the room, exposing her tits to me.

I licked my lips, wishing they were wrapped around her nipple, sucking and biting the rosy peaks.

My cock swelled in my shorts, but I resisted the urge, the *need*, to wrap my hand around it and squeeze. The longer I waited, the more the tension would build and build, making the payoff that much sweeter.

"Play with your tits."

Quinn leaned forward a little bit and cupped her breasts in her hands, pushing them together and squeezing.

"Are you imagining those are my hands? Squeezing your tits? Making your pussy clench."

She panted, her lids at half-mast as she squeezed her tits in her hands. I stroked my cock a few times, just a light brush of my hand through the nylon, my stomach muscles contracting as the tension built up. I loved the sweet ache of holding off.

"Pinch your nipple between your fingers." She did as I said, squeezing and twisting her nipple between her fingers, and let out a low moan, her jaw going slack.

Fuck. My dick strained against my shorts, tenting the fabric. Painfully hard and so ready.

"I bet you're soaked, aren't you? I bet it's dripping down your thighs."

"Oh God, yes. I'm so wet for you," she panted, moving her hands down her stomach, caressing it before one of her hands slipped under the waistband of her lace panties.

"Oh no, you don't. You don't get to do anything unless I can see it. Take them off."

She disappeared for a moment and then reappeared on the screen, completely naked, pillows propping up her head and her knees bent, thighs open wide so I could see the pink glistening with her arousal.

It was all I could do not to say fuck it, I'm on my way over. But I wanted to see how this played out, and I was so turned on, my cock so stiff I couldn't move from this bench right now if I wanted to.

"Slide two fingers inside," I ordered.

With a sly smile, she ignored my words and dragged her fingers through her folds, then circled her clit as she rocked on the bed, breathing hard. "You said you wanted to see what I do when I'm alone, right?"

"Right."

I was a captive audience as I watched her hips roll and her heels dig into the mattress when she finally did as I'd asked and slid two fingers into her pussy.

I didn't know if I wanted it to be my mouth or my cock fucking her right now.

My dick jerked. It was throbbing. "What do you think about when you touch yourself? Do you imagine it's my cock sliding into your tight pussy?"

"Yes. I pretend it's you," she said, her chest heaving as she grinded against her fingers.

My grip on the phone tightened, and I was surprised it didn't crack in my hand from the amount of pressure I was exerting.

"You have to come with me."

I felt the blood rushing to my cock. I wasn't even touching myself, but I was so close already that it wouldn't take much to push me over the edge. I pushed down the waistband of my shorts and fisted my cock, squeezing it hard as she moaned and panted and writhed on the bed, her back arching off the mattress and her fingers where I wanted my cock to be buried right now.

"Oh God. Jesse… I'm going to…" I jerked myself harder. Heat flooded my body, fire spreading from my thighs to my groin, my balls throbbing as they tightened up. "I'm coming," she yelled.

I squeezed, pumping it harder and harder, spurts of hot liquid spilling onto my abs and the muscles in my stomach contracting. I slowed my hand, pushing out the last drops of cum as my muscles went slack. Shit. Fuck. I didn't want it to be over already. I wanted more.

I opened my eyes and met Quinn's smile. "Hi," she said, licking her lips.

I laughed under my breath and grabbed my T-shirt from the floor, wiping my abs before I tossed it aside. "Hi."

"Back to my original question. Have you eaten lunch yet?"

"That was your question?"

She laughed. "Are you hungry?"

"Starving. I'll pick you up in ten."

Her smile grew wider. "Sounds good. I've built up an appetite."

"And I'm looking forward to dessert."

Quinn was barely eating. She'd only taken a few bites of her burger, and now I watched her drag a French fry through the ketchup and drop it back on her plate. I'd brought her to her favorite diner. She loved the burgers, fries, and shakes, but the restaurant didn't exactly cater to vegetarians.

Their idea of a salad was a wedge of iceberg lettuce with a few anemic slices of tomato and shredded carrots, so I ordered an omelet that I'd finished five minutes ago.

"I thought you were hungry."

"I was but…" Her shoulders sagged, and she leaned back against the red vinyl booth.

I studied her face. She looked pale. "Are you feeling okay?"

"I got an email." She took out her phone and opened her emails, then held it out to me.

I took her phone, not sure what to expect. Results from a blood test or a note from her doctor. Whatever it was, if her face was anything to go by, she'd gotten bad news.

So I looked down at the screen and read the email, waiting for the bomb to drop. It was from UCLA, and it had all the information for her freshman year housing assignment. So I read through it, searching for the bad news. But nope. All good things.

"Is that a bad dorm?" I re-checked the name of the dorm as if that would give me a clue. Not that I knew the first thing about the dorms at UCLA or any other college.

"No. It was my second choice, but it didn't really matter to me. I didn't care which dorm I ended up in."

"So, what's the problem?"

She sighed and chewed on her lip. "Before this email, it just felt like a possibility. I mean, I knew I was going to UCLA. I got an acceptance letter. But this makes it real. They have a room for me. It's not just a dream in the distant future. This is really happening." Her brow furrowed like she couldn't understand how or why this was happening. "And it's… it's happening really soon, Jesse."

I looked down at her hands—she was ripping her paper napkin into shreds—then back at her face.

She was nervous, maybe a little bit scared. That's how it felt when you did something big and new. Even when it was something you've wanted for a long time, it was natural to feel apprehensive.

"What if I… what if I don't make any friends?" she said. "What if it's like fourth grade all over again, and nobody wants to hang out with me? And what if I… what if I fail? I mean, it's a really good school, and everyone is probably super smart, and I'm not… I mean, I got straight As and everything, but that's only because I worked hard and studied a lot. It's not like I'm a rocket scientist. It's not like it comes easy to me or I'm some kind of genius—"

"Quinn."

She lifted her head. "Jesse. What if I—"

"Quinn," I said again, reaching across the table and taking her hands in mine. I gave them a little squeeze, trying to reassure her. "First of all, you are smart, or you wouldn't have gotten in. And the fact that you work hard for your grades makes you that much more likely to succeed. And regarding friends… anyone who doesn't want to be your friend is missing out."

"But—"

"No more buts. Are you done eating?"

She nodded.

"Let's get out of here." It smelled like fried food and burnt coffee in this diner. We needed some fresh air.

When we got out to my truck, I opened the passenger door and waited for her to climb in before I closed it and rounded the hood.

"You're going to make friends." I rolled down the windows to let some fresh air in before pulling out of the parking lot. The rain had stopped, and the sun was burning through the clouds. I flipped down my visor to shield my eyes against the glare. "College isn't like grade school or high school…."

"How would you know? You've never been to college."

I winced. It was true, but I hated to be reminded of it. "Yeah, well, I'm not as smart as you."

She sighed. "I'm sorry. I didn't mean it that way."

"I know." It was my own stupid insecurity, and I knew she wasn't trying to make me feel bad about it. "But from what I've heard, college is a lot different. You'll find your tribe. Just by being yourself, you'll attract the right people into your life. And you won't fail. You're smart and determined, and you work hard for the things you want. It's going to be amazing. I can feel it. In the meantime, you still have the rest of the summer. Don't waste it worrying about things that haven't even happened yet."

"Okay. I just…" Her eyes lowered to her clasped hands.

"You just what?" I prompted.

"Never mind." She gave me a smile, but I could tell it was forced.

"Hey. Everything is going to be okay."

She swallowed hard. For a girl who had her sights set on UCLA, she looked pretty fucking miserable now that it was actually happening.

I ran my hand through my hair, trying to come up with the words that would make her feel better. Maybe she was looking for a way out. "Are you having second thoughts? Because if you want to stay here in Texas, I'm sure you could go to any college you want." I didn't want to let on that I knew for a fact she could go to college right here in Austin.

Quinn shook her head. "My dad told me about UT," she admitted. "He just wanted to make sure UCLA was what I really wanted before he paid the tuition."

She didn't sound angry about it, and I was relieved that her dad told her. There were already too many secrets and lies this summer.

"It's just kind of scary when your dreams come true."

"It can be. But it would be tragic if you let your fear stop you from doing the things you dream about."

"I won't let that happen," she stated firmly.

"Good." I glanced at her. She looked pensive, lost in her thoughts, and the atmosphere felt too fucking heavy for a summer day. "How about we go and have some fun?"

She looked over at me, and I licked my bottom lip suggestively, my gaze roaming down her body before returning to her face.

"What kind of fun did you have in mind?" Her lips curved into a seductive smile, and that sparkle was back in her eyes.

There's my sunshine girl. Ready to play.

I put my hand on her thigh and gave it a little squeeze. "You're not afraid to get dirty, are you?"

Chapter Thirty-Four

Quinn

Oh my God. We were going to die.

I let out a yelp, my arms tightening around Jesse. We caught some air before the wheels hit the ground, and we whipped around a curve in the trail.

Mud splattered my jeans and T-shirt. I ducked behind Jesse, using his back as a shield when he veered right so he could ride straight through a puddle. There was no help for me now. It was raining mud, and I was covered in it, laughing so hard as we flew down a hill.

But with Jesse, even when he was driving fast on his motorcycle or the quad bike, I always felt safe. Like he was in complete control and would never let anything happen to me. It was probably naïve to think that, considering all the injuries he'd sustained.

Either way, I felt safe, but I also felt like we were just on the edge of losing control and something was thrilling about that as he deftly maneuvered the quad through a narrow section of the trail that cut through the trees. One wrong move, and we'd crash into a tree.

I'd never felt more alive.

This was such an adrenaline rush.

When he'd asked me if I was afraid to get dirty, riding on the back of his quad through the mud was not what I expected. But it had helped a lot. It was a reminder to live in the moment and enjoy it while it lasted. No need to think about the future or college or the fact that Jesse would be leaving soon.

So I shoved those thoughts out of my head, and I hung on to him for dear life.

Jesse aimed the hose at me, blasting me with cold water. I screamed, laughing as I lunged for him, trying to grapple the hose out of his hand. He pulled it away just as I dove on top of him, knocking us both to the ground, the spray from the hose raining down on us. We were both laughing.

I stared down at his face and tried to commit it to memory. The smile that reached his summer sky eyes. His tousled brown hair messy and disheveled. The water raining down on us. I traced a drop of water down his cheekbone.

Kiss a boy in the rain.

Close enough. I kissed his lips under the spray of the hose, the water falling like raindrops.

Letting go of the hose, he flipped us over and braced his arms on either side of my head. I wrapped my legs around his waist and pulled him down to me for another kiss. I was greedy that way. Always wanting another kiss. Always wanting more. And more. And more. Of his everything.

He pulled away and got to his feet, offering me his hand. "Let's take a shower."

A shower. God, I loved this. I took his hand, and he pulled me to my feet. Being with him just felt so natural. Like it was perfectly normal for us to shower together.

We left our wet shoes outside the door, and when we got inside, we stripped off our clothes, and Jesse tossed them in the washing machine.

I couldn't believe I was walking around his house naked. I couldn't believe that I felt confident enough to do that. I followed him down the hallway, my eyes on his bare ass.

"Stop staring at my ass," he called over his shoulder.

"If you didn't walk around naked, I wouldn't be staring at your ass."

"So feisty," he said, stepping under the spray of the shower.

"You like me feisty."

He yanked me in with him and pushed me under the water. "I like you naked too." He poured shower gel into his hand and washed me before he washed himself and turned off the shower.

"I'm holding you hostage until your clothes are ready."

Like I'd fight him on that. I was a willing captive, not even putting up a fight as he dragged me to the bedroom like a caveman.

Later, breathless and lying next to each other, I couldn't help but smile.

"I'll grab the clothes from the dryer."

When he left the room, I grabbed one of his T-shirts that was hanging on the back of his door and pulled it over my head, inhaling his scent as I flopped down on his bed to wait for him.

His phone buzzed on the bedside table, and I rolled onto my side, checking the doorway before I looked at the name on his phone screen. Gina.

I had no right to snoop. So why was I looking at his phone?

And who was Gina? I stared at his phone until the call went to voice mail. Two seconds later, my phone buzzed with a message. My mom, asking when I'd be home for dinner. After texting my response, I tucked my phone back in my bag just as Jesse strode into the room with my clean clothes.

"I think someone was trying to call you," I said, trying to keep my voice casual.

While I got dressed, I watched him from the corner of my eye when he checked his phone. His brow furrowed, and he bit the corner of his mouth.

"Anything important?"

He pocketed his phone. "Nope."

"Just drop me off right here."

He exhaled loudly, but he pulled over in front of the tall hedges that bordered the front of our property. I knew he hated that we were keeping this a secret, but too bad. He had plenty of secrets.

As soon as the truck came to a stop, I pushed open my door and hopped out. "See ya." I went to close the door, but he leaned across the passenger seat and held it open.

"Hang on."

I looked over at him, my brows raised in question, the name Gina beating like a drum in my head. "What?"

He gave me a big smile that made my knees weak. Damn him. "I had fun today."

"Yeah, me too."

"See you soon, Sunshine Girl."

I forced a smile, and then I walked away, not even turning to look as he drove off. Maybe he was going to meet Gina, I thought bitterly. But no. He wouldn't do something like that. Jesse wasn't a cheater.

But why was he so quick to pocket his phone as if he didn't want me to know who had called him?

"Hi, honey," Mom said when I walked in the door and found her in the kitchen. She was in front of the stove, sauteing garlic in olive oil.

"Hey, Mom."

"Good timing. I'm making that pasta dish you love. Do you want to sit at the island or on the patio?"

"The island is good."

"The salad is in the fridge." She looked over at me when I

came out of the refrigerator with the salad and set it on the island. "Whose T-shirt is that?"

I looked down at the T-shirt I was wearing. I'd completely forgotten that I was wearing one of Jesse's shirts, the cotton so soft and faded, his scent still lingering and filling up my head every time I inhaled.

I grabbed the utensils and placemats from the drawer, my back to her as I set the island. "I'm not sure. Declan's, maybe? I found it in my drawer."

Oh my God. Why had I just lied to my mom? The lie had slid right off my tongue like it was the most natural thing in the world. I'd never been a liar. So why would I lie about something so stupid? I could have just said, "*It's Jesse's T-shirt.*" But then what? How would I explain why I was wearing Jesse's T-shirt?

"Huh. And why are you wearing Declan's T-shirt?"

"Just wanted something comfortable."

My mom gave me a funny look. Before she could see the lie on my face, I opened the cupboard and grabbed two glasses, filling them with ice and water.

A few minutes later, when we were seated across from each other, the food on our plates, she said, "Do you have anything you want to tell me? Anything you want to talk about?"

I shoveled a bite of salad into my mouth to buy myself some time. "Nope. Nothing's going on with me. Except for my housing assignment." Which we'd already texted about in our family group chat.

"I feel like I haven't been around much this summer." Mom took a sip of her wine and watched me a little too closely. "I feel like I missed a lot."

"Nope. You haven't missed much. Same old, same old."

"If there's anything on your mind, I hope you know you can talk to me. About *anything*."

"I know." I smiled and took a sip of water. My mom was cool, but there was no way I could tell her everything and anything. My mom liked Jesse, always had, but I didn't know how she'd feel if she found out about us. Not that there was an us. But still. If she found out I was having sex with Jesse *and* riding on the back of his motorcycle all summer, she would probably freak out.

I mean, maybe she'd be cool about the motorcycle. When she forbade me to ride on the back of Jesse's bike, I'd been a kid. Eleven or twelve. But I wasn't willing to risk it. Which was why my helmet and jacket were hidden in the trunk of my car.

What my mom didn't know couldn't hurt her.

Chapter Thirty-Five

Jesse

"We're going to pick up my friend first," I informed Noah and Levi, who were sitting in the back seat of my truck. I wanted to spend time with them before I left for California, so I told Lila I'd take them for the afternoon. When Quinn found out, she asked to join us.

"She loves ice cream," I told my nephews.

"Everyone loves ice cream," Noah said confidently as I pulled into Quinn's driveway. She was waiting on the front steps and gave me a big smile as she walked toward my truck in cut-offs and a faded orange T-shirt that said Life is Good. Sunglasses shielded her eyes, and her long blonde hair hung loose, framing her pretty face.

Quinn always looked like summertime.

And it suddenly struck me that in just a few weeks, she'd be out in California living her dreams. She wanted to learn how to surf, she'd told me. I could see her doing it, too. That determined look on her face as she paddled out for a wave. The joy on her face when she caught it.

I entertained other visions of Quinn in California too. Kissing guys who weren't me. College guys who wouldn't fully appreciate just how fucking amazing she was. Or maybe they would. Maybe she would find someone who treated her like a queen, and she would fall in love. Bring him home to meet her parents. Travel the world with him. Make him the hero of every story she wrote.

The fuck? Why was I thinking about this? I scrubbed my hand over my face to erase the vision of my sunshine girl with another guy.

"Hey, hot stuff." I gave her a wink and squeezed her thigh as she fastened her seat belt. She blushed a pretty pink. I loved that about her. How she could get dirty in the bedroom but still retain that sweetness and innocence.

As I pulled onto the road, she turned in her seat and greeted my nephews. "Hi, guys. Who's excited about ice cream and a nature walk?"

"Me!" they shouted in unison.

To show his enthusiasm, Levi kicked the back of my seat. He hadn't stopped kicking it since I'd picked him up fifteen minutes ago.

"I'm Noah, and this is Levi."

"It's nice to meet you. I'm Quinn."

"Are you Uncle Jesse's new girlfriend?" Noah asked.

"Um, no… we're…." Quinn glanced at me as if she wasn't sure how to answer.

"We're just friends." Guaranteed this would get back to my family and be the discussion at the next Sunday dinner. Good thing I was leaving on Sunday morning, so I'd miss it.

"Like me and Hayley," Noah told Quinn. I knew all about Hayley. Everyone in Noah's life knew about Hayley because he talked about her constantly. "She's my best friend. Someday I'm gonna marry her."

"Oh. Wow," Quinn said. "You must really love her."

"Yep. She loves me too. Daddy Jude says that me and Hayley must be soul mates. Just like him and my mom. He said he loved her ever since they were kids. And he loves her even more now. He even loves her when she's covered in baby puke. He told her so the other day. She was crying so hard she couldn't stop."

"Your mom was crying?" I asked.

"No. Well, yeah. She was crying too. Because Gracie wouldn't stop crying." He sighed loudly. "Babies are no fun. All she ever does is eat and poop and puke and cry."

I stifled a laugh. "Babies are a lot of work."

"Yep. And Daddy Jude says stupid things sometimes."

This I'd love to hear. Kids were so unfiltered, and I knew Noah would spill the beans. "Oh yeah? Like what?"

Noah sighed again. "Like how he wants more kids. That's what made my mom cry. She was covered in puke, and Daddy Jude was saying what an angel Gracie is." Noah snorted. "Sure she is. And he was saying he wants more babies, just like Gracie. Like, *a lot* of them. So Mom said that if he kept talking like that, she was gonna lock him out of the house and make him sleep on the back porch."

Quinn and I exchanged a look, and we burst out laughing.

Levi kicked the back of my seat again. I could feel the impact of each kick, and the more he did it, the more annoying it got. "Yo, Levi. How about you take a break from all that kicking."

Thwack. Thwack. Thwack. Should have known that would make him want to do it even more.

I reached around behind my seat and wrapped my hand around his ankle but not so tight that it would hurt him. "Stop kicking my seat, or you won't be getting any ice cream." It was an empty threat. I'd buy Levi as much ice cream as he wanted. But I could sure as hell do without all that kicking. It was hitting the exact spot where I'd broken those two vertebrae.

"I want ice cream," he shouted, his kicks coming faster and more furious. I checked the rearview. He was thrashing in his car seat now, trying to break free of the straps. Lila had warned me he was going through "the terrible twos," and tantrums were a daily thing, but he didn't usually act up around me.

"You know what we should do?" Quinn turned in her seat to face Levi and clapped her hands together like she'd just had a brilliant idea. "We should sing a song."

Levi was screaming now, his face an alarming shade of red, so I doubted that he even heard her. Noah plugged his ears with his fingers and shouted, "Be quiet, you annoying baby!"

"I'm not a baby!" Levi shouted.

"Do you know this one?" Undeterred by the screaming and crying in the back seat, Quinn launched into a song I knew, one that just about everyone knew, but she changed the words. "I see a silhouetto of a lamb, Scaramouche, Scaramouche, can you do the fandango?"

"A lamb?" I asked with a laugh.

Her brow furrowed, and she tapped her chin. "Actually, I think it's supposed to be clam."

"It's not clam or lamb. It's man," I informed her.

She scoffed. "Try telling the Muppets that."

Quinn was fucking hilarious. I laughed as she sang, using exaggerated hand gestures like an opera singer performing at the Met. "Thunderbolt and lightning, very, very frightening…. Galileo, Galileo, Galileo Figaro."

I checked the rearview and watched Levi's enraptured face. The kids loved Quinn. So much so that she got them singing along to her crazy version of "Bohemian Rhapsody."

By the time I pulled into a parking space near the town square and the nature trails, Levi had stopped kicking, and that tantrum was a distant memory. All thanks to my little magician.

"I don't think me and Hayley are gonna have kids," Noah announced as I hopped out of the truck and freed Levi from the confines of his car seat. I pulled him out of his chair and held him in one arm so I could close the door. We met Quinn and Noah on the sidewalk outside a honey shop with bees painted on the white stucco.

"Bzzzzz," Levi pointed at the wall, and then he pinched the skin on my arm between his thumb and forefinger.

"Ouch! I got stung by a bee." I grimaced, making a big show of being in pain.

That made him laugh so hard he was snorting. Pain was

hilarious to kids. Not that it had hurt. When he stopped laughing, he leaned down and kissed my arm. "All better," he said, smacking my cheeks with both hands. So damn cute.

"Thanks, buddy." I ruffled his hair. "It doesn't even hurt anymore. You kissed it all better."

I caught Quinn watching us, and she gave me a little smile before turning her full attention to Noah while he chatted a mile a minute.

"Down," Levi commanded, wriggling in my arms.

I knew what would happen if I set him down—he'd take off—so, instead, I swung him onto my shoulders. He patted the top of my head as if to say that he approved of our compromise.

"You might change your mind about kids," Quinn told Noah as we strolled past the boutiques and a cedar-shingled café and bakery with hanging flower baskets outside the yellow front door. "You still have some time to think about that."

Like she was talking to an adult, not a seven-year-old who was convinced he'd already met the love of his life. Ever since Noah was four years old, I'd heard about Hayley. He punched a boy in nursery school for making her cry.

"Anything can happen," I pointed out. "When you get older, you might fall in love with a different girl."

Quinn glared at me. I didn't even have to turn my head. I could see it in my periphery. Could practically feel the heat of her glare. That's how intense it was.

"I won't," Noah stated confidently. "I'm gonna marry Hayley."

"You have a special kind of love," Quinn said. "So, of course, she's the only one for you."

"Yep. My one true love," Noah said.

Quinn sighed and put her hand over her heart like that was the best thing she had ever heard. Should have known she would find that romantic.

"But my mom said we have to wait until we're older," Noah said. "Like, I dunno… I'll probably wait until I get my driver's license. Then I can borrow Dad's truck."

Noah was dead serious, but I burst out laughing at the thought of sixteen-year-old Noah rocking up in a pickup to propose marriage.

Noah scowled at me. "It's not funny."

Quinn reached over and smacked my arm. "Yeah. It's not funny. It's good to have a plan."

Come on, it was fucking hilarious. But Noah obviously disagreed. He stopped in the middle of the sidewalk, crossed his arms over his chest, and scowled at me. Quinn raised her brows, prompting me to apologize.

I wiped my hand over my face and got my laughter in check. "Sorry, buddy. Didn't mean to hurt your feelings."

His scowl deepened.

"I'll tell you what. How about I make it up to you with some ice cream?" It had been the plan all along, so it wasn't like I was offering him something he hadn't already expected.

He tilted his head and considered my offer. "Well, maybe ice cream will help. 'Specially if it's a double scoop."

"I think we can manage that." I swung Levi off my shoulders and set him on the ground before I opened the door of the pink and mint green ice cream parlor and ushered them inside.

"You can have a double scoop too," I told Quinn, giving her a smack on the ass as she walked ahead of me.

"Pfft. I plan on ordering *all* the flavors. With all the toppings."

"So feisty."

She winked at me over her shoulder. "You love it."

She was right. I did love it.

In fact, I couldn't think of anything that I *didn't* love about Quinn. So it was probably a good thing that I'd be gone in a week.

What we had right now was idyllic. A stress-free summer hook-up.

There had never been a time in my life when I'd had so much free time. Soon, that would change for both of us, and then we'd go our separate ways.

Chapter Thirty-Six

Jesse

We were standing next to my truck in Jude and Lila's driveway, and I was just about to tell Lila we needed to get going when she said, "Stay for dinner."

"I need to get Quinn home." Gracie wrapped her tiny hand around my index finger and squeezed. "You have a good grip, baby girl."

"It's only five o'clock. I can stay." Quinn said, rubbing Gracie's back and kissing the top of her head. As soon as we arrived, Lila asked Quinn if she wanted to hold Gracie, and she'd eagerly accepted.

Quinn and Lila had met all of ten minutes ago, and in that

time, they'd managed to cover a lot of ground. It never ceases to amaze me how much information women could share within a short time.

But I'd known Lila most of my life, so I knew she had an ulterior motive by inviting us to stay. This wasn't just a casual family dinner. She wanted the dirt.

"Your mom probably expects you home for dinner. So we should get going."

Quinn shook her head. "She has a business dinner."

"There. It's settled," Lila said with a smirk as Quinn handed Gracie back to her. I opened my mouth to protest, but Lila cut me off. "I'm not taking no for an answer. You're staying for dinner."

"Yay!" Noah raced over to us with Levi close on his heels. They'd been running around the front yard, and now Noah grabbed Quinn's hand and dragged her toward the house. Not wanting to be left behind, Levi chased after them.

Quinn looked over her shoulder and gave me the eyes as if she was silently asking for my help.

I shrugged and held out my hands. *You asked for it, baby.*

When Quinn disappeared inside the house with the kids, Lila handed me the baby, and we walked up the flagstone path to their stone farmhouse. It was a beautiful home, timber, and glass on the inside, with high ceilings and a wall of windows overlooking their land. When they'd bought the place, Jude had planted fields of flowers for Lila's floral design studio.

We stepped inside the foyer, and Lila gave me a sly smile that confirmed my suspicions. She wanted the dirt.

"So this is her."

I didn't know what she meant by "her" unless Shiloh had said something. "Quinn is just a friend."

"Uh huh. Sure she is. So she has nothing to do with you not being interested in Camryn."

"Nope." I hesitated a beat too long.

Lila laughed and smacked my arm. A natural reflex for her. She'd always been so physical. "You've never been a good liar, Jesse."

So I've been told.

It was a well-known fact that the McCallisters were highly competitive. We *hated* to lose. Growing up, *everything* had been a competition.

Now we had the next generation of McCallisters, and they'd obviously been drinking the same Kool-Aid.

"We have to beat them," Noah said, his hands balled into fists and his brows furrowed in concentration like we were competing for an Olympic gold medal.

"Don't worry," I assured him. "They don't stand a chance. We're gonna take them down."

"It's just a game," Quinn said. "It's about having fun, not about who wins or loses."

Noah and I shot her a look. "It's the Triple Crown," Noah said, his voice hushed. "We wanna win. We *need* to win. So make sure you don't miss," he told her.

"Go easy on her, Noah. She's not a McCallister."

Quinn glared at me. "You think I can't get this bag of corn in the hole?" She waved the rawhide bag in the air. "Is that what you're saying? Because I can get it in the hole. Just watch me."

I couldn't contain my laughter. "Say hole one more time."

She pressed her lips together, and I leaned in close and whispered in her ear. "Pretty sure I'm the only one who can get it *in the hole*."

Ignoring my comment, Quinn spun around and marched over to the chalk box Jude had drawn on the grass behind the opposing team's board.

"Watch and learn, racer boy."

I crossed my arms over my chest, and I watched her ass. No clue what the fuck she was doing—winding up her arm like she was on the pitcher's mound while simultaneously shaking her ass—but hey, I wasn't complaining. I enjoyed the view.

My gaze drifted to Jude on the opposite side, and he raised his brows. *Eighteen? Really?*

I knew he was thinking that because he'd cornered me right after dinner and questioned me. One of the reasons I hadn't wanted to stay. I'd never hear the end of it now.

"Isn't she a little young for you?" he asked.

"We're just friends."

"Just friends don't look at each other like that."

I hadn't bothered asking how we looked at each other. I already knew the answer. It had been a summer of stolen glances, and every time I looked at Quinn, it got harder to drag my eyes away.

Quinn missed the shot. Wasn't even close. The beanbag landed on the southernmost tip of Texas, somewhere around the mouth of the Rio Grande. "Almost had it," I said. "Next time aim for something north of Amarillo. That way, you'll have a better chance of getting it *in the hole*."

She rolled her eyes. "We still get points."

I wouldn't count on it. Jude was up next. And like I said, the McCallisters were competitive beasts.

He aimed for Quinn's bag, and big surprise, he managed to knock it off the board.

Noah sighed. "No points for us."

"Really, Jude?" Lila said, smacking his arm.

He held up his hands. "That's how the game is played."

"God, you guys are the worst."

"Like you're any better," Jude scoffed. Which was true. Lila was an honorary McCallister, had even lived with us after her mom died and her stepdad took off, and she'd always been just as competitive as the rest of us.

"Don't worry. You'll do better next time," Noah told Quinn, giving her an encouraging pat on the back. "I hope," he muttered under his breath.

Quinn didn't do better with her next pitch, but the view was just as good, so I wasn't complaining.

We lost the Cornhole Triple Crown to Jude's team, but by the end of the game, Quinn managed to get a few 'in the hole' and did a little victory dance after each one. As did Lila whenever she scored. Noah, on the other hand, did victory laps and shouted, "*We're the champions!*" every time he scored.

A bit premature, but I applauded his enthusiasm just the same.

Before we left, Lila pulled me aside and issued a warning. "Don't break her heart, Jesse."

I thought about her words on the drive home while Quinn sat in the passenger seat, her bare feet on the dash, her toenail polish the same color as the cherry popsicle in her hand. The consolation prize for the losing team.

The windows were open, and the breeze whipped her blonde hair around her face. My gaze kept drifting from the road to her lips wrapped around that popsicle and to her legs. Suntanned and toned, her calf muscles long and lean, skin silky and smooth. Two nights ago, they'd been wrapped around me while I'd rammed into her, her muscles clenching my hard cock, her nails scoring my skin, and my name ripped from her throat as we'd barreled into shared orgasms.

She leaned across the console and held the popsicle up to my lips, a little smile on her face as she looked up at me from underneath her dark lashes. "Want a lick?"

The way she said it sounded dirty. "Think you can get *that* in the hole?"

She laughed, and then she shuddered. "No way. I prefer something hot and hard."

"Like a sausage?" I teased, wrapping my lips around the popsicle and sucking on it.

"A pepperoni sausage. Hot and spicy." She made a sizzling noise and settled back in her seat. I put my hand on her thigh while I drove the winding back roads. We'd taken the scenic route, twice as long with better views.

The sun was setting over the hills and the valley, and the air smelled fresh and sweet. Quinn cranked up the volume on "T-Shirt Weather" and sang along. Slightly off-key, but it didn't matter. Not even a little bit.

Today was damn near perfect. I didn't think it could get much better than this.

Two minutes later, I was proved wrong when Quinn leaned over the gearbox, unzipped my pants, and pulled my cock out. She wrapped her hand around the shaft and guided it into her warm mouth, swirling her tongue around the head before running the tip of her tongue along the underside.

Jesus. It was a miracle I didn't drive off the fucking road.

"What are you doing, Sunshine Girl?" My voice was strained because, holy hell, she flattened her tongue and licked me from shaft to tip, hitting every nerve ending. She flicked her tongue over the slit, and my balls tightened.

"What does it look like I'm doing?"

I'd forgotten the question.

I held the back of her head and tried to focus on the road. Hard to do when she was sucking my cock, taking me deeper into her warm, wet mouth while she worked me with her hand like she'd done this a million times before.

I groaned when she brought her other hand into the action, cupping and squeezing my balls. I could barely see straight.

She hummed, with my cock in her mouth, sucking on it and her tongue flicking it and her hand squeezing my balls, and the vibration sent me over the edge.

"I'm going to come." It was a fair warning. The best I could do, considering I was on cloud fucking nine. But she didn't heed my warning and pull away.

Warm liquid spurted into her mouth, and she drank every last drop of it before she released me and scrambled back into her seat and fastened her seat belt.

It took me a moment to catch my breath enough to speak. I tucked myself back in my pants and looked over at her in the passenger seat, noting the smug smile on her face before she licked her lips like she didn't want to miss a drop. And that was so fucking sexy. My sweet, innocent sunshine girl with my cum on her lips and down her throat.

"I'd like to thank all those cucumbers you practiced on."

"Was it okay?" She sounded a bit shy and unsure now.

Was it okay? I nearly laughed. "It was better than okay. It was the best I ever had."

She smiled, and it was glorious. Like sunshine on a rainy day.

When I pulled up next to the hedges bordering Quinn's property, as per her instructions because we were still sneaking around like adolescents, I grabbed the back of her head and pulled her toward me for a kiss. She tasted like cherry popsicles and me.

"Thanks for today. It was fun," she said with a smile. I gave her another kiss before she pushed open her door and hopped out of my truck.

As I watched her walk away, barefoot in her tiny cut-offs, her shoes dangling from her fingertips, I thought about how easy it was to be with Quinn.

Easy, in the sense that it felt natural.

My phone buzzed, interrupting my thoughts, and I checked the screen.

Jude: Passing on a message from Noah: Tell Uncle Jesse that Quinn is pretty. And nice. And fun. I'm not even mad that we

lost. Well, maybe a little. But Quinn is still cool.

Jude: That's a thumbs-up from Noah. He approves of your cradle-snatching. Make sure you get her home before curfew.

I laughed as I read it and scrubbed my hand over my face, wishing I could dispute his words.

Me: You're an ass.

Jude: Good to see you happy again. But just for the record, if a 27-yo so much as looked at my 18-yo daughter, I'd beat the shit out of him.

Lila: Don't worry, Jesse. I'm on your team. And Gracie can be with any guy she wants. As long as he treats her right.

Jude: Over my dead body.

Me: Are you two reading each other's texts?

Jude: Rebel stole my phone and added herself to the group chat.

Lila: We're married. We have no secrets.

Jude: But I'm still full of surprises.

Lila: Keep it up, Devil Dog, and I'll lock you out of the house.

Jude: You can lock it up like Fort Knox, baby, and I'd still find a way to get to you.

Unsurprisingly, the texts stopped after that, thank God. I tossed my phone in the cupholder just as a matte black Dodge Charger pulled up alongside my truck. Because yeah, I was still lurking next to the hedges. I looked down at Declan in the driver's seat as he rolled down the window. This should be fun. Judging by the look on his face, he wasn't too happy to see me outside his house.

"I don't know what game you're playing, but if you fuck her over, if you *hurt* my sister, I will fuck you up. And that's a promise."

Two warnings in one night.

I tipped my chin to acknowledge that I'd heard him and waited until he pulled into the driveway before I took off.

I wasn't looking to break Quinn's heart. It wasn't like that with us. We weren't in a relationship, so no hearts would be broken.

Or, at least, that was what I kept telling myself.

Chapter Thirty-Seven

Quinn

I got out of my car and closed the door just as Carly rounded the side of the taproom. Mason was right behind her.

What was Carly doing here? I thought she quit.

"Come on, Carly," Mason yelled. She picked up her pace, hurrying toward her car parked next to mine. "How did you expect me to react?"

"I don't know, Mason," she yelled over her shoulder. "I guess you reacted exactly how I expected you to. So don't worry about it. I'll take care of it."

It was none of my business, so I shouldn't have been standing next to my car watching. But I couldn't seem to help myself.

Mason grabbed her arm and turned her around to face him. "What's that supposed to mean?"

"What do you think it means? I'll take care of it."

"Just give me a chance to think about this. You can't just spring something like that on me and expect—"

"You didn't need time to think before you fucked me." Yeah, definitely none of my business. "Just go back to your perfect little life. I'm not your problem."

She brushed tears off her cheeks, and I rounded her hood as she yanked open her car door.

"Hey. Are you okay?" It was a stupid question. Clearly, she was not okay. So I wasn't surprised when she just shook her head and didn't bother answering.

She jumped in her car and peeled out of the parking lot. When she was gone, my gaze swung to Mason.

He was pacing back and forth, tugging at the ends of his hair. Finally, he stopped pacing and kicked the tire of his Jeep. "Fuck." Kick. "Fuck, fuck, fuck." Kick, kick, kick. He smacked his palms on the hood and lowered his head. I moved closer just as Holden came out of the brewery and joined us.

"What's going on?" Holden asked me.

"I don't know. Mason…" I put my hand on Mason's shoulder. "Are you okay?"

He pushed off from the Jeep and turned around to face us, his eyes on the ground and his voice so low that at first, I thought I'd misheard. "Carly's pregnant."

Pregnant? He didn't just say that. He couldn't have. "Carly's pregnant?" I croaked.

Mason nodded and scrubbed his hands over his face.

Holden muttered something under his breath that sounded a lot like, *You dumb fuck.*

"Is it yours?" I blurted.

Mason glared at me. Holden burst out laughing.

"I'm sorry. It's just…." I cleared my throat. "I didn't know if you were exclusive or…." His eyes narrowed on me, a warning to stop talking. I clamped my mouth shut. This obviously wasn't the time to question his relationship status. And what did that have to do with anything? Accidents happen all the time.

Holden was laughing again. I elbowed him in the ribs and shot him a look.

"Shit. Sorry. No idea why I'm laughing."

"Probably because it's not happening to you," Mason muttered.

"I always keep it wrapped."

"So do I," Mason said between clenched teeth.

"Yeah, okay. Because pulling out is risky. You might think you got out in time—"

"I used a fucking condom," Mason gritted out. "I don't know how the hell this happened."

"Guess you have some strong swimmers that were just busting to get out."

I snort-laughed at Holden's observation. This whole conversation was so ridiculous. Mason glared at me again, and the laughter died on my lips.

This wasn't funny. Not even a little bit. Mason was going to be a dad. A *dad*. Holy crap. And Carly… I couldn't even imagine her with a baby. I didn't know her that well, but I'd been around her all summer, and I knew she liked to party. From the sounds of it, she and Tasha were always going out to bars and throwing parties. Not that there was anything wrong with that, but now she was going to be a mother.

"What are you going to do?" Holden asked.

"She said she's going to take care of it."

It took a moment for Mason's words to sink in, but Holden's response was immediate.

"Take care of it? Fuck, man. And you just let her leave? You need to go talk to her."

"Holden's right. If she thinks you don't want the baby, she might..." I didn't even want to think what she might do, but Mason had to stop her. He couldn't expect her to deal with this on her own.

"I *don't* want the baby."

My jaw dropped in shock. I *loved* babies. Who didn't? Only yesterday, I'd been holding Gracie. So innocent and adorable and trusting. I'd just wanted to inhale her scent and kiss her sweet cheeks all day long. "Don't say that."

"It's the truth. I don't want a kid right now."

Holden grabbed him by the shoulders and gave him a shake. "Get your shit together. Man the fuck up."

"God, that's so low, Mason. No wonder she's upset. She's pregnant with your baby, and she's hormonal, and you sent her away crying? If you don't do the right thing, I'll...." I crossed my arms. "I'll lose all respect for you."

"Bean. Don't say that." Mason sounded so weary that I instantly regretted my words. "You don't even know the story, okay?"

It was true. I didn't know the story. And I didn't know Carly that well, so I didn't owe her my loyalty, but I was fighting for the sisterhood. A guy should never feel like he's free to just walk away. It takes two to play, and now he has to take responsibility. "I know, but all I'm saying is that you're a good guy, so I know you'll do the right thing. You just need to get used to the idea."

To soften the blow, I patted his arm a few times. Which was obviously the wrong thing to do. He scowled, and I dropped my hand to my side. I wasn't sure how he would get used to the idea of having a baby with a girl he clearly didn't love. If he loved her, he would have had a different reaction. He would have still been shocked, but he would have been happy about it.

"Quinn's right. No matter how it happened, it's your kid, and you have to step up to the plate and deal with this."

Mason exhaled a breath, and then he nodded, struggling to come to terms with something that was obviously not part of his life plan. Ever since I could remember, Mason has been a planner. It was almost funny that he and Jesse were such good friends. They were total opposites. Mason was risk averse. He never did anything until he'd weighed all the options and considered it from every angle.

"Can you cover the bar?" he asked Holden.

"Whatever you need."

"Thanks."

Holden and I watched Mason drive away before we turned and walked to the taproom together. I couldn't believe Mason was going to have a baby. With Carly, of all people.

"Do you think he loves her?" I asked Holden.

"Judging by his reaction, I'd say that's a hell no."

I'd suspected as much, but it still made me sad. "What would you have done if Avery had gotten pregnant?"

I didn't usually bring up Avery, but it had been a year since she left, and I wondered if he still thought about her all the time. Or if he'd moved on and forgotten her.

"I would have been happy. I always wanted a bunch of kids. Not her, though. It's one of the reasons she left me."

"Avery didn't want kids?"

He shook his head no. "She wanted a career. She wanted to be able to pick up and travel whenever she wanted. And she wanted a beautiful, smudge-free interior that wasn't littered with toys." I heard the bitterness in his tone.

"Wow. I didn't know that. About the kids, I mean." Although it shouldn't surprise me. Avery was a perfectionist. She was also an interior designer. Beautiful. High maintenance. And entirely wrong for Holden. But people in love don't always see things as clearly as the people around them do. "You're better off without her."

"I know," he said, but there was no conviction in his voice.

Love made fools of us all. Why else would someone as smart as my brother fall in love with a woman who was so wrong for him? Guess I could ask the same thing about Jesse.

I had the table from hell. A middle-aged couple that bickered non-stop and complained about every single thing. Judging by the way they treated each other, I don't even think they liked each other. They ordered a bottle of cabernet sauvignon, and the woman wanted to taste it, so I poured a bit in her wine glass. She brought it to her nose and sniffed before she took a sip and promptly spit it back into her glass.

"This wine is corked. I should know better than to let you choose the wine," she accused her husband. "You never get it right."

"Let me try it," the husband said. I poured some in his glass and stood back while he tasted it.

"There's nothing wrong with this wine."

"You're only saying that because you chose it," she hissed.

"I'm saying it because the wine is just fine. If you don't want to drink it, I'll just have to drink it myself."

I took a couple steps back from the table. "So you're okay with the wine?"

"Bring her a cider. Good wine is wasted on her."

I walked away from their table mid-argument. When I returned with the cider, the couple was still arguing. "He's a lazy good-for-nothing. I don't know what she ever saw in him."

I set the cider next to the woman and cleared the table next to them, pocketing the tip before collecting the empty glasses.

"If you'd given him a job, they wouldn't have had to move in with us."

"Those kids need discipline. Shouldn't be surprised with the way you always spoiled our daughter. She doesn't know how to cook or clean, let alone look after her own kids."

"I paid my dues. I'm not looking after the grandkids too."

"Where is that waitress?" the man complained. "She just took off and left us here."

Taking a deep breath, I walked over to their table and plastered a smile on my face. "Are you ready to order?"

The man checked his watch and tapped his finger on the timepiece. "We've been ready for ten minutes."

They weren't ready, though. They hadn't even looked at the menu. When I suggested I'd give them a few minutes, they insisted I wait, *"It'll take us another ten minutes to flag you down."*

I tried my best to be pleasant, but these two were making it difficult. First, there was an issue with the appetizers. And now the main course.

"What's wrong with it?" Declan asked.

"The customer said she can't eat it. She said the meat is raw, and the cherries are too tart."

"Is this the same customer that sent back the stuffed zucchini blossoms?"

I sighed. "Yep."

"The duck is perfect."

"Apparently, it's not. She asked for a steak. Rare. Instead of the duck breast." The irony wasn't lost on me. She'd claimed the duck was undercooked, and yet she'd ordered a rare steak.

"The duck breast that is half-eaten." He pointed to the plate because it was, indeed, half-eaten. In fact, her plate was clean except for half of the duck breast. She'd eaten all the cherry sauce that she'd claimed was too tart.

"She's not getting a steak. I'm not serving her another damn thing. She obviously wouldn't know good food if it bit her in the ass."

"Declan," I hissed, tilting my head to the left and trying to send him a signal with my eyes. But he ignored my warning and kept up his running monologue, cursing out the woman who was standing to my left.

"Well, I never," the woman huffed. "It doesn't surprise me that the chef is rude." Declan snickered. He wore his rudeness proudly. "No wonder the food is barely edible."

Oh boy. Now she'd done it.

He glowered, his face murderous. You could insult Declan about anything, and he wouldn't give a shit. He'd just flip you off if he even bothered to respond at all. But if you criticized his cooking, you would feel his wrath.

"You can take your sorry ass and get the hell out of here. There's a McDonald's a few towns over." He reached into his pocket, pulled out his wallet, and slapped down a twenty. "There you go. It's on me. Go get yourself a couple Big Macs. Special orders don't upset them."

The woman's jaw dropped. "I'll be sure to leave a review," she huffed.

"You do that. Don't let the door hit you in the ass on the way out. Second thought, it might help to dislodge the stick that's wedged up there."

Oh my God.

"You owe my wife an apology," her husband blustered.

"Not happening."

The man's face turned an alarming shade of beet red. Thankfully, Aubrey intervened. "How may I help you, sir?"

She side-eyed Declan as she led the couple away. Aubrey had the patience of a saint and a knack for smoothing ruffled feathers. Declan, on the other hand, was a ticking time bomb waiting to go off.

"Really, Declan? Did you have to be so rude about it?"

He turned his wrath on me. "The fuck are you doing? You see this food?" He pointed to the two duck breasts on the pass, a popular item tonight. "It's cold. It's ruined. Because you've been so busy standing there gawking at me that you couldn't even do your damn job. How hard is it to pick up the food and deliver it to a table? Nobody's asking you to cook the food. All you have to do is carry it to the damn table." He grabbed the plates and threw them on the stainless-steel counter. "Now go explain to your customers why their food is going to take twice as long."

"You're such an ass," I muttered under my breath as I walked away.

This night couldn't be over quickly enough.

Turns out it wasn't done kicking my ass. Not by a long shot.

After I served the customers who had been kept waiting for twenty minutes and promised them a free round of drinks, I leaned across the bar and tried to get Holden's attention.

I called his name. Twice. He held up a finger, indicating that I had to wait a minute. Since he was the only one working, I had no choice but to wait. I tapped my foot, agitated. Tonight was taking its toll.

Holden was a good brewer, but he hadn't mastered the art of multitasking. How hard was it to pour two beers and talk on the phone at the same time? He wasn't even talking. He was just listening and nodding.

"I'll get the message to him, okay? I can't make any guarantees, but if I know Jesse, he'll make every attempt to be there." At the mention of Jesse's name, I perked up. "I'll tell him. Take care, Alessia."

Alessia?

Holden had been talking to Alessia? Why was she still calling him?

"What did Alessia want?" Just saying her name left a bitter taste in my mouth.

"She had no way to reach Jesse. She wanted to let him know that her mom died."

"Wow, she'll use anything to get Jesse back. How low can she go?"

I hadn't even realized I'd said that out loud until Holden frowned. "Her mom just died."

I immediately felt chastised. He was right. Her mom died, and that was horrible. Even though I couldn't stand Alessia, I still felt terrible for her.

But why couldn't she leave Jesse alone? They weren't even together anymore.

As if he'd read my mind, Holden said, "If something happened to Avery's mom, I'd want to know."

Holden had been close with Avery's mom. Her whole family, really. I guess that was all part of being in a relationship.

You get close with their family and friends, and when you split up, you lose them, too.

Chapter Thirty-Eight

Quinn

After my shift, I drove to Jesse's house. It had been a long night. Declan was still annoyed about those stupid duck breasts, and nobody held a grudge like he did.

Mason had gotten Carly pregnant, and I couldn't wrap my head around that. He was going to be a dad. He was going to have a baby with someone he didn't love, and something about that just seemed so unbearably sad to me. It happened all the time, I knew that, but I guess I always pictured my brothers finding true love before they settled down and had kids.

And Holden had been in a funk all night. I couldn't help

wondering if it was because I'd mentioned Avery. He'd been distracted and had barely spoken.

I was tired, and all I wanted to do was go home and crawl into bed.

So I wasn't sure why I'd driven to Jesse's house. He hadn't called or texted, and maybe he didn't even want me here.

I found him in his garage riding the Air Bike. He was shirtless and dripping with sweat.

It was ten-thirty at night, and I had no idea why he was working out so late. Knocking himself out like this.

I took a seat on the weights bench across from him. Our eyes met, so he obviously saw me, but he didn't stop cycling. If anything, he increased his speed. The news about Alessia's mom must have really upset him. Maybe they'd been close. I didn't really know what to think.

He was wearing AirPods, and I wondered what kind of music he was listening to that would help him set this punishing pace. I watched him for at least five minutes, maybe ten, long enough to question why I was still here before he finally slowed to a stop and climbed off the bike.

He wiped his face with a towel and removed his earbuds, but I couldn't read his expression. It was blank. He grabbed a bottle of water and drank half of it before he finally spoke.

"What are you doing here?"

Good question. I had no idea why I'd come. Curiosity? Fear? A gnawing sense of dread? "I just wanted to see how you are."

"I'm fine."

He wasn't, though. He had that same closed-off expression as he did at the beginning of the summer. Everything about his posture and flat tone warned me not to push for more information. But I couldn't help myself. We'd gotten too close for me to just back off and pretend I didn't care.

"I'm sorry about Alessia's mom."

He nodded once, that same shuttered expression on his face, and I wanted to scream. I hated that she still had this kind of power over him. One call from her, and he was right back to where he'd been a few months ago.

"Did you… talk to Alessia?"

I wanted him to say no. I wanted to hear that he hadn't called her, but somehow, I knew he would have when he heard the news.

He nodded, and I deflated. "Briefly." He raked his fingers through his hair that was matted down with sweat and looked over my shoulder. "I need a shower."

It didn't sound like an invitation. "Yeah, okay. I'll just…." I started backing away. "I should go. I just wanted to make sure you were okay."

I spun around and walked to my car.

God. Why did this have to be so hard? I thought we'd gotten past all this awkwardness. Maybe I'd been fooling myself all along. Maybe we hadn't gotten as close as I thought. Tears of frustration stung my eyes, and I just needed to get out of here. Hit the rewind button on this entire night and do it over again.

I yanked open my car door, ready to leave. Clearly, he had no interest in talking to me. If his body language was any indication, he didn't even want me here. So I wasn't going to hang around where I wasn't wanted. Or try to coax words out of him when he wasn't interested in talking.

"Don't go," he said brusquely.

It was hardly an invitation to stay. "I think I should. You probably need some time to yourself or—"

"Stay." He put his hand on my shoulder, his tone softer. "I want you to stay." He gave my shoulder a little squeeze as if to reassure me that he really did want me to stay.

I turned to look at him then, my eyes searching his face. I'd barged in on him, uninvited, and now I regretted being so impulsive. "Are you sure you want me to stay?"

"Yeah, I do." He sounded sincere, and I saw something in his eyes that gave me pause. Sadness. But there was something else there too. Something I couldn't identify.

"I just need a quick shower."

"Okay," I said slowly, still not entirely convinced that staying was a good idea. He must have noticed my indecision because he reached around me and closed my car door. Then, before I had a chance to change my mind, he grabbed my hand and led me up the stairs. His footsteps were heavy, and there was a weariness that hadn't been there yesterday when we'd hung out with his nephews and had dinner with his family.

We had such a fun day. Everything about it had been so natural and easy, just like we were a real couple, and it was perfectly normal to hang out with his family. Lila and Jude had been great, and over dinner, they told stories about Jesse when he was a kid. An adorable, fun-loving kid who loved to play practical jokes.

"How long have you been working out?"

"A while. My legs feel like concrete. Maybe I need a yoga session." He forced a laugh.

"Yeah." My own laugh sounded just as feeble.

He held the door open for me, ushered me inside, and left me in the living room.

"I'll be quick," he called over his shoulder.

I watched his back as he retreated. When he disappeared down the hallway, I flopped down on the sofa. Dropping my head against the back of it, I stared at the ceiling fan above my head.

Why was I even here?

My gaze landed on the laptop he'd left open on the coffee table.

I wasn't snooping. Not exactly. But I peered at the screen and saw that he'd been searching for flights to San Diego.

My stomach sank. It looked like he was leaving tomorrow.

It was bad enough that he was supposed to leave for California in less than a week—five days to be exact—but now I'd barely have any time with him. Would he just stay out there rather than coming back? I didn't think so. He planned to drive to California because he was taking his bikes and moving most of his things out there.

He returned a short while later, his hair damp and messy, in a T-shirt and shorts. "Do you want a drink? Water? Juice? Energy drink?"

He was playing host now, his voice cool and polite, like we were mere acquaintances and didn't know each other intimately. "No, thanks. I'm good."

Jesse grabbed an energy drink from the fridge and jerked his chin toward the door. "Let's sit outside. It feels stuffy in here."

It didn't feel stuffy. The air conditioning was on, and so were the ceiling fans, but he was already halfway out the door, so I left my seat on the sofa and joined him on the deck, where it was twenty degrees warmer than it had been inside. I took the seat next to him, a cushioned deck chair that overlooked the woods.

We were sitting close enough that when I inhaled, it was his scent that I breathed in—citrus and spice and woodiness. Masculine. Heady. *Jesse.*

If I moved my hand a few inches to the right, I could touch his arm. Run my fingertips over the thick veins and his golden skin and lean muscle. But tonight, it felt like an ocean separated us. So I didn't make a move to touch him.

Maybe it was my own insecurity, or maybe it was the standoffish vibe he was giving off, but I couldn't shake the sense of dread that had settled in the pit of my stomach. It had been there ever since Holden mentioned Alessia's name. I had a sense of foreboding that this would change everything.

"Are you okay?" I asked finally, desperate to break the silence and get some answers.

Jesse blew out a breath and took a swig of his energy drink. "Yeah, I'm just…." He squinted into the distance, those little lines around his eyes crinkling, and I don't know why that was so sexy, those little lines, but they were. And so was he.

And I had the overwhelming urge to cry.

God, I missed him already, and he hadn't even left yet. So why did it feel like I'd already lost him?

"Gina called me a couple times this summer. Alessia's mom," he clarified.

Gina. That's who had called him that day we rode the quad bike. It hadn't been some random girl. It had been Alessia's mom. I didn't know if that made me feel better or worse.

"But I didn't call her back," he finished.

Now I knew what I had seen on his face earlier. Guilt.

"I was so angry with Alessia that I didn't call Gina back. And it fucking kills me that I ignored her calls." He studied the bottle in his hand, and I got the sense that he was lost in his thoughts and maybe he just wanted someone to listen. So I didn't offer my opinion. I remained silent, and I waited, something I'd gotten better at this summer.

Waiting and wishing and hoping.

"She was a good woman. Whenever we went over there for dinner, she cooked all my favorite food. She's Italian. Was." He paused, letting the harsh reality sink in before he continued. "A lot of the food she cooked had meat in it. Bolognese. Meatballs. Chicken Parm. But she changed her recipes for me. Made them vegetarian. Gina was one of my biggest fans. Watched every single race. Before she met me, she didn't know the first thing about motocross. But she read up on everything she could, and she knew the stats better than I did." His lips tugged up at the corners, a small smile at the memory of Gina.

"You loved her," I said quietly.

Jesse nodded. "Yeah, I did. Alessia used to joke that the only reason I stayed with her was so I could eat her mom's cooking. She said her mom loved me more than her. Not true. But Gina spoiled me. Treated me like a son. I just wish like hell that I would have called her back."

I didn't really know what to say or how to make him feel better, so I said the only thing I could think of. "I'm really sorry, Jesse."

He looked over at me, and it felt like he was seeing me for the first time tonight. "Come here."

Jesse pulled me into his lap and held me close, my cheek pressed against his chest, his arm around my back, his hand wrapped around my thigh.

He wasn't looking for sex. He was looking for someone to comfort him, I guess. He pressed his nose into my hair, and I felt his chest expand on a deep breath before he released it.

"You always smell like summertime," he murmured. "My sunshine girl."

I wanted to ask him if I made him happy. I thought I did. But I didn't ask.

We sat in silence, and I held my hand over his heart, comforted by the steady beat, his chest rising and falling on each breath, and in the quiet, a tidal wave of emotions crashed over me. The feeling was so strong, so potent that it left me breathless.

I loved him so much. I always had, but over these past few weeks, that love had gotten stronger and deeper. It wasn't just a girlhood crush. My love for him was so deeply embedded that I'd have to rip out a piece of my heart to be free of it.

I wanted to say the words. But I couldn't. Not now. Maybe never.

Because I knew he would go to Alessia. I knew he would pay his respects to a woman who had treated him like a son. And he would try to comfort Alessia. Because that's who he was.

No matter how much I wished it could be different, you couldn't erase history. Jesse couldn't pretend he'd never loved her. He couldn't pretend that a part of him didn't still care about her.

My mom said you never forget your first love. You never really get over it.

He was mine, and she was his. So, where did that leave me?

The bubble had burst, and everything felt different between us. Like he was already pulling away while I was trying to figure out how to let him go.

But at this moment, he was still mine. So when he told me to look up at the stars and make a wish, his voice low and husky, his arms holding me tight like he didn't want to let me go, I did it.

I wished that he would find a way to let Alessia go and open his heart to someone else. To *me*. Even though a little voice inside my head warned me, *Love shouldn't have to be this hard. You shouldn't have to work so hard to make someone fall in love with you.* I ignored that voice.

Because love was a leap of faith, wasn't it? It was risky to put your heart on the line.

Love could heal you, or it could destroy you.

What was braver, or more foolish, than offering up your heart to someone and saying, *Take it. It's yours. Treat it with care. It's fragile and breakable.*

Nothing. Absolutely nothing. I knew that because I was that fool.

Chapter Thirty-Nine

Quinn

Two days later, I dragged Evie up to the lake. Jesse had flown to San Diego the day before and today was Gina's funeral. I hadn't spoken to him since the night I went to see him, and maybe that was for the best.

The sun was so bright as Evie and I stood at the top of the rocks under a big blue Texas sky. It was my idea. An attempt to fulfill a childhood wish. But more than that, even more significant, it was an attempt to get over Jesse. Although I wasn't sure how jumping off a cliff would help me do that. It was a symbolic gesture, maybe. A leap of faith.

Now I wrung my sweaty hands, my stomach churning as I stared down at the crystal blue water. It looked so impossibly far away. If we didn't jump out far enough, we might hit the shallows. Or there might be jagged rocks just beneath the surface that would break our bones and rip our skin to shreds.

This didn't seem like such a great idea anymore. In fact, it was a terrible idea.

"I can't do it." I turned to go.

Evie grabbed my arm to stop me. "Yes, you can. We're doing this."

My heart was so heavy I had visions of sinking like a stone and never resurfacing. "We could really get hurt. We might hit our heads and sink to the bottom and never come up. We might drown."

"Not on my watch. Nobody is drowning today."

As if she had the power to protect us. I looked over the ledge again. My skin felt clammy, and even though the sun was hot, I shivered. "What if we fall?" I whispered.

Evie grabbed my shoulders, her green eyes so fierce, and she gave me a little shake. "Quinn. What if we fly?"

Shock rendered me speechless. My eyes widened, my fears and heartache temporarily forgotten in light of this new development. "Are you… oh my God. Are you becoming an optimist?" I covered my mouth and widened my eyes in mock horror.

"No." She rolled her eyes. "I said that for you. Now let's do this. Don't make me push you."

"You wouldn't." But just to be safe, I moved a few feet away from the edge so she wouldn't be tempted to give me a shove.

"I wouldn't do that. But you want to do this. Otherwise, you wouldn't have dragged my ass up here. So let's do what we came to do. You need to do this." She looked down at the water, and I watched her face in profile. Still so beautiful but with a sadness that I hadn't noticed before. "Maybe we both need this."

"Are you okay?" I'd been so focused on my own crap and had been spending so much time with Jesse that I hadn't been the greatest friend. Evie was going through her own crap. But unlike me, she had never been the type to pour her heart out. So, I barely knew any of the details of what was going on with her. "I'm sorry I wasn't there for you. I've been a shitty friend."

"Don't talk like that. You're a great friend. My *best* friend."

"Do you want to talk about it? I mean… you haven't really told me what's going on."

"You know how it goes in my world. Shit's always happening. Nothing I can't deal with, though." She lifted her chin and hardened her expression like she was steeling herself against whatever the future held. Too often, people mistook Evie as haughty or, worse, a snob. She was neither. But she had a lot of pride. Too much pride to accept help or sympathy.

"You don't always have to be so tough, Evie," I said softly.

"And you don't need *him* to make your wishes come true. So let's do this."

She was right, of course. I didn't need Jesse to make my wishes come true. Not all of them, anyway. This was something I could do for myself. My California dream was my own too, and I didn't need him for that either. I'd go to college, and I would do everything I'd set out to do. I wouldn't let myself think about whatever Jesse and Alessia were doing right now. She was grieving her mother, so of course, he would be there for her. And by the time he got back, he'd only have enough time to pack up his house and leave.

So this thing, whatever we'd been doing, was about to end, and I needed to face that.

With a new resolve, I took a deep breath and squared my shoulders. "Okay. Let's do this."

She smiled. "On the count of three," she said as we stood on the edge of the cliff, preparing to take a leap of faith. "One… two… three."

And I did it. I dove off the cliff with my best friend right beside me.

We flew so high it felt like we could almost touch the sun.

But as everyone knows, what goes up must come down.

Chapter Forty

Jesse

I'm not sure how I expected to feel when I came face to face with Alessia again.

I hadn't come to San Diego for her.

I came to pay my respects to a woman who had treated me like a son.

Last year when I was in the hospital with two broken vertebrae, Gina visited me. She brought flowers from her garden, and she brought cannoli. Enough for all the nurses who were working that shift. The next day she brought lasagna. The nurses loved Gina Rossi. So did I.

When I told her that Alessia and I had called it quits, she was so heartbroken that I didn't have the heart to tell her why. So instead, I told her that Alessia and I wanted different things in life.

Gina called me a few times this summer but only left a voice mail once. She'd called because she knew she was dying. The doctors had only given her a few weeks to live. Not that she'd mentioned that in her voice mail. Gina wouldn't do something like that. She would never have guilted me into returning her call. Instead, she told me she loved me and still thought of me often. She hoped I was happy.

It killed me that I hadn't returned her calls, but it was too late now. She was gone and today was her funeral.

Last night, while I was sitting on the balcony of my hotel watching the lights shine off the bay, my mother called. She told me this would be a good opportunity to get closure. I didn't think I really needed closure. Alessia had fucked me over. What more was there to say that hadn't already been said?

At the funeral, Alessia sat in the front pew with her family— uncles and aunts and cousins—and I slid into a back pew undetected. The service was long, the church uncomfortably warm, and it smelled like incense and lilies. The eternal California sunshine streamed through the stained-glass windows as family and friends shared stories about Gina's life.

Afterward, I stood under a tree in the cemetery, a short distance away from the group gathered around the casket as it was lowered into the ground, and the priest gave the final blessing.

I considered leaving without speaking to Alessia. I owed her nothing, and yet, I stayed where I was, under the tree. The sky behind her was brilliant blue and cloudless as she walked toward me in a tight black dress that skimmed her thighs and stopped just above the knee. Sexy but tasteful.

Black sunglasses covered her eyes, and her lips were painted red. When she stopped in front of me, I shoved my hands in the pockets of my dark suit pants. She pushed her sunglasses on top of her head and smoothed her hands over the skirt of her dress.

"Jesse," she whispered. She was nervous. I could tell by the way her hands shook and her lip trembled. "I…" Her eyes lowered to the ground. "Thank you for coming."

"I told you I'd be here."

"I wasn't sure you would." She lifted her eyes, but they didn't meet mine. Instead, she stared into the distance, her eyes unfocused. "I wouldn't blame you if you hadn't." She smiled, but it was a sad smile, befitting the occasion. "She loved you so much."

I nodded once. "I loved her too."

"I know you did."

"I'm sorry about your mom." I could say this with complete sincerity. I was sorry that Gina was gone, and I was sorry that Alessia had lost her only real parent at the age of twenty-five. It was entirely separate from everything that had gone down with us.

"Thank you." She wrung her hands. "I'm sorry… about everything. I loved you so much, Jesse. I still do." She lifted her eyes, and her browns met my blues. "I look at you now… and all I see is everything I lost. You're just… you're so beautiful, Jesse."

I used to tell her the same thing. I'd always told her how beautiful she was. I'd always told her how much I loved her too. But it hadn't been enough.

"If you… if you give me one more chance, I know we can find a way to make it work."

I stared at her. At her beautiful face. Her flawless olive skin and dark, glossy hair. At the lips I'd kissed a thousand times and the body I'd explored with my hands and tongue and lips.

It had been a year since I'd been with Alessia. When she came back to me in April, we'd only been together for a few weeks. And at that time, I couldn't bring myself to touch her. So I hadn't fucked her. Not once.

It just went to show how delusional she was to ever think I'd take her back after everything she'd done. But this was her mother's funeral, so I reined in my temper, and I kept my voice even and measured, surprised that it wasn't as difficult as I'd expected. "We're not going down this road again. Not now. Not ever. I've moved on," I added.

It was true. I had moved on, and I hadn't fully realized that until I came face to face with the person I used to love.

Tears ran down her cheeks. She was crying for her mother, and for me too, maybe. But, unlike in the past, I made no move to comfort her.

"You've moved on?" she asked through her tears.

I thought about Quinn. And the freestyle team. But mostly, I thought about Quinn. My sunshine girl who had been there for me through my lowest of lows.

And I thought about what my mother had said last night. *"I just get the feeling that you're still hanging onto something, and until you let it go, you won't truly be free to move on."*

My mother was a wise woman. My brothers—Gideon and

Jude—and my cousin Brody had often called her a saint for putting up with my father all these years. I didn't think she was a saint. My father loved her in his own way. He couldn't live without her, and she felt the same. But my mom was used to dealing with a difficult man, so she always gave good advice. We didn't always take it, but I was grateful that she never stopped giving it.

So maybe she had a point. Maybe I needed answers. Or closure. A way to get over whatever the hell was holding me back from putting my heart on the line again.

"Why did you do it?" I asked Alessia. "Why did you throw it all away?"

I'd never asked the question, and it seemed crazy now that I never had. When I'd first found out, I was so hurt and angry that I couldn't even look at Alessia, much less speak to her. And in April, when she lied to me, I believed her. I'd believed that Nate Hutchins had forced her to have sex. By the time the truth came out, I wanted nothing to do with Alessia. So we'd never discussed any of this. But now, I was ready to hear it.

"I was lonely. You were never there, Jesse. All you ever cared about was your career and winning. You were either training or traveling to races."

In the beginning, she traveled with me to all my races, but when her own career started taking off, she couldn't pick up and go whenever she wanted. And I'd understood that. I'd *encouraged* her to follow her own dreams. "You knew from the start that's how it would be."

"I didn't think it would be that bad. You were *never* there. It was all about you and your schedule and your stupid races."

"My stupid races." I laughed harshly. Should have known she'd turn it back on me. "So you thought to yourself… I know, I'll find a way to sabotage that career I hate so much. Because that's what people do when they love someone. They try to fucking destroy them. They try to knock them down, and when they're on their knees, they come back and kick them in the fucking balls."

Her tears ran freely now. "I never meant to ruin your career."

"Did you think I would just let that go? Did you really believe that I wouldn't confront him?" My jaw clenched, and I tried to breathe. "You swore up and down that you were telling the truth, and I fucking believed you."

She wiped her cheeks. "I made a mistake. It was only once. I was only with Nate once. And I knew you'd never forgive me…."

So she'd lied to me. Because it was the only way to get me back. From the very beginning, I told her that I drew a hard line on cheating. She told me that she felt the same. But obviously, our values hadn't been as aligned as I'd thought.

As if it made a difference whether she'd been with Nate once or a hundred times. She still did it. And I didn't believe for a minute that it had only happened once. "Doesn't matter. You turned to him when you had me. You went behind my back, and you were texting with him for *months*."

Thanks to Nate, I'd read some of those texts. They were almost worse than the thought of her having sex with him. The flirting. The little shared jokes and innuendos.

That fucking asshole. I'd never liked the way Nate looked at Alessia, but she always told me that she couldn't stand the guy. Guess the joke was on me.

"I got scared," she whispered.

"You got scared. So you fucked my teammate."

"You were always surrounded by girls... all your little groupies... and Nate... he used to tell me things that put doubts in my head and made me think you were with other girls when you were on the road and I—"

I snapped. "You never had any faith in me, did you? I *never* would have cheated on you. I told you that a million times. I gave you my word, and that should have been good enough for you. But nothing I ever did was good enough for you, was it?"

She crossed her arms over her chest, on the defensive. "You weren't perfect either, Jesse."

Here we go. She was turning it back on me again. "Never claimed to be."

"You always acted like you put me first, but you *never* put me first." She threw her hands in the air, warming up to her subject.

"You never cared about what I wanted or where I wanted to live or what I wanted to do. I hated Temecula, but I lived in that boring town because that's where *you* needed to be to train. The only people you hung out with were moto heads and their stupid wives and girlfriends who trailed after their man. Those women had no lives of their own. No ambitions. Nothing. But I lived in that stupid town instead of L.A. even though you weren't there half the time. I did it for you. I sacrificed *everything* for you."

Holy shit. She truly believed that she'd sacrificed so much for me. This whole argument would be laughable if it wasn't so fucking sad.

When Alessia met me, she had nothing. No ambitions. No career to speak of. She worked at a coffee shop, picked up the odd modeling jobs, and couldn't even pay her rent. She was so deep in debt she'd maxed out her credit cards.

I'd bailed her out. Me. Like a fucking idiot, I paid off her debts because my *stupid races* had earned me millions, and my genius brother, Gideon, managed my portfolio and made smart investments for me. When I paid off Alessia's debts, Gideon was furious. "*Don't be an idiot. She's using you for your money.*"

"You're heartless," I teased. "I wouldn't expect you to understand the first thing about love."

"You're a fucking bleeding heart. Don't come crying to me when she buries a knife in it."

Should have listened to him. Gideon wasn't heartless. But he didn't wear his heart on his sleeve like I used to.

"If it had all been such a huge sacrifice and you hated everything about my life, why were you even with me?" I asked Alessia.

"Because I loved you. I just… I thought it would be different. I thought it would be more exciting to be with a motocross racer. But it got so boring, and I got so lonely…."

A thought occurred to me then, and I was shocked that it had taken me this long. I didn't think Nate was the only guy she'd cheated on me with, but it was the only time she'd been caught. "Right. So it all worked out the way it should. I made you miserable. You fucked my teammate, and God knows who else. Because you were bored, and you were lonely, and I was *never* there for you. You did me a favor, Alessia. So I should be thanking you. If I'd asked you to marry me, and God forbid you'd said yes, we would have made each other miserable. So why the fuck would you ever think you want me back?"

"I just… I know it can be different this time. In the beginning, everything was so good.…" Her tears had dried, and now she licked her lips and gave me that seductive smile she used to give me before we ripped each other's clothes off. Her gaze dipped, playing coy, and she looked up at me from beneath her lashes as she moved closer, running her tongue over her red lips. Alessia had missed her calling. She would have been a great actress.

Her scent, so familiar—vanilla and spice—washed over me as she smoothed her hands over the lapels of my suit jacket.

"We can have that again. We can find our way back." She slid her hands up my chest and looped her arms around my neck. "Remember how good it used to be?" She pressed her tits against my chest, and muscle memory had me wrapping my arms around her.

What the fuck was I doing?

Coming to my senses, I clasped her wrists and unhooked her arms from around me, pushing her hands down by her sides. "We were a mistake. I don't love you anymore, Alessia. Whatever good we might have had was destroyed. There's no going back."

She opened her mouth to speak, but I was done. I didn't want to hear another word from her lying lips, and none of this was appropriate at her mother's funeral.

Alessia didn't love me. She just loved the idea of me. The comfort of something familiar.

One time I'd asked her why she kept going back to the ex who had abused her. She'd said, "Because it was familiar, and I didn't think I deserved anything better. Until you came along. And now I know there is something better."

And so did I. There was something better out there for me.

And it sure as hell wasn't her.

So, for the very last time, I walked away from my ex-girlfriend.

"Jesse." I didn't turn around when she called my name, and she didn't chase after me, but I heard her words. "I have nobody left. Everyone leaves."

She was playing the woe is me card now. An attempt to get me to feel sorry for her and change my mind. She'd done this to herself, and knowing Alessia, she'd keep doing it. It was what she did. I'd bailed her out of so many bad situations in the past. But Alessia wasn't my problem anymore.

On the flight home, I tried to untangle my mixed-up emotions. Why had I fallen for Alessia? Had I been so superficial that I'd fallen for her because of the way she looked? Was it because of the way she'd always needed me to fix her problems? In all the time I'd been with Alessia, I'd never stopped to analyze *why* I was with her or what had made me think I loved her. When we met, I was twenty-three, and she was twenty-one. I'd been with plenty of girls before Alessia, but I'd never fallen for any of them.

We met on social media. She claimed she was a big fan—I'd later find out that was a blatant lie. She hated motocross or, at least, she grew to hate it. She messaged me on Instagram. After that first message, we messaged for weeks before we met in person at a coffee shop in Venice Beach. Coffee turned into lunch and then dinner, and we spent the night together.

She was different back then. Or maybe it was an act, I don't know. But she seemed so real and down to earth. In the beginning, everything was so damn good that I ignored the red flags. The resentment that grew every time I had to leave for a race. The way she'd accuse me of sleeping with other girls whenever I was away. She used to check my phone. Rifle through my bag, searching for evidence of my infidelity. And every time we argued, she would start crying and tell me that she had never loved anyone the way she loved me.

She'd make me feel guilty for shit I hadn't even done, and I'd always try to make it up to her. As if it was my duty to keep her happy.

Looking back, my reasons for being with her, for *staying* with her, were fucked up.

Quinn's words came back to me.

"Maybe I never really knew you at all. Maybe I was just in love with the idea of you. A fantasy I'd conjured up in my own mind, an ideal version of you that had never really existed."

The words had been aimed at me, but they applied to my relationship with Alessia too. I loved the idea of her. I'd fallen in love with someone who had played the part, had fulfilled my every fantasy, and had pretended to be something she wasn't.

This summer, I'd been with someone who was the opposite of Alessia in every way. Quinn never pretended to be something she wasn't.

But I don't think she was completely honest with me either. I think I'd known it since the night she offered me a deal I couldn't refuse. I don't think it was what she really wanted, but I'd gone along with it anyway. Why? Because it was what *I* had wanted at the time.

Would it have been better if Quinn and I had gotten together a few years from now? When I wasn't as fucked up, and she was older and had had a chance to experience more life. Hell yeah. But love doesn't always wait until it's convenient.

We'd both be out in California. So why did it have to end? On the contrary, this felt like a new beginning. A fresh start for a new life with someone who had always been special to me.

Despite all the odds stacked against us—the shitty timing, the age difference, the fact that she was Mason's sister–I'd fallen for Quinn.

Chapter Forty-One

Quinn

Despite my best intentions, I'd spent the past few days torturing myself with visions of Jesse with Alessia. Him comforting her while she cried on his shoulder. Or maybe she'd found a way to remind him how much he had loved her. Maybe he'd decided to give her another chance.

But no, he wouldn't do that, would he?

I didn't know. Sex with the ex was a thing, so maybe she came to his hotel room, and they reunited.

In two days, he would be leaving. He would pack up all his clothes and his bikes and drive to California, where he'd just returned from.

But now he was here, waiting for me at the end of my driveway.

I grabbed the helmet and jacket from my car and ducked under the garage door as it was closing. It was almost midnight, and my mom was asleep when I'd crept out, but Declan hadn't come home yet.

As I rounded the corner at the end of the driveway, I made out the shape of Jesse leaning against his bike. It was dark tonight, the moon a tiny sliver, and he was hidden in the shadows.

As I got closer, my footsteps slowed, and my pulse quickened. My heart was beating so hard it felt like it was going to burst through the walls of my chest. It had only been a few days since I last saw him, but it felt longer, and I shouldn't have missed him so much, but I had.

I stopped in front of him, and I inhaled his scent. It made my head swim.

"Hi," I tucked my hair behind my ear and gripped the helmet in my other hand.

"Hi," he said, his voice low and husky. He grabbed my hand and tugged me closer, so I was standing between his legs.

Out of nowhere, an overwhelming sense of loss washed over me. It made me feel hollowed out and empty. It made my heart ache too. It hurt so much that it felt like my heart was being squeezed, and I could barely breathe.

I wanted to tell him that I loved him. The words were on the tip of my tongue, practically bursting to come out, but I swallowed them down. It would be a stupid, stupid thing to do. A fool's mission to tell someone you loved them without any hope of hearing it back.

I could imagine the words suspended in the air between us,

just hanging there like a lead-filled speech bubble before it hit the ground with a heavy thud.

So I was going to do what Evie and I had talked about. I was going to let him go. After our motorcycle ride tonight, I was going to walk away.

"How was San Diego? Was it… are you okay?"

He nodded. "I'm fine."

Was he, though?

"Okay. Well, that's good." I waited for him to say more, but he didn't say another word.

"Are we going for a ride?" I don't know why I asked when that had been the plan all along. He'd texted earlier. Just a short text asking if I wanted to go for a ride. But now, he was studying my face so intently that I didn't know what to think. Even in the darkness, I could feel the intensity of his gaze.

"You never listen, do you?" His hand skimmed down my bare thigh, his rough, calloused palm on my much softer skin, and it sent a warm shiver through my body. "Wearing your tiny shorts and little dresses to ride on the back of my bike."

Tonight I was wearing a short white dress and my metallic gold Nikes, but unlike the first time I'd worn them, I didn't feel like I was walking on air.

"I think you like it."

He ripped the helmet out of my hand, and it rolled onto the ground as his hands cupped my ass cheeks, giving them a rough squeeze and pulling me closer. I was barely breathing. The air felt charged tonight like the atoms had shifted and rearranged themselves. I could practically feel the heat crackling between us.

His hand moved to the back of my head, and he fisted my hair, yanking on it to expose the column of my neck. His lips sucked and bruised, earning him a low moan. God, the ground beneath my feet felt shaky, and my core clenched as his hand skimmed up my thigh, and he slid his fingers inside my panties.

"What have you done to me?" he rasped.

I grabbed his shoulders to steady myself. In the dark, his voice low and rough and his lips leaving their mark on my skin, his fingers gliding through my folds, this felt dangerous.

More forbidden than it ever had.

"What do you mean?" I panted as he thumbed my clit, setting off tiny explosions.

"That deal we made…." He tugged my lip between his teeth and sucked on it before releasing it. "You promised me that it was all you wanted, right?"

Oh God. My stomach sank. I was hoping to avoid this. I was hoping he'd never question me. "Right," I whispered, praying that he'd just let it go.

"Were you telling the truth?" He slid two thick fingers inside me, and my knees buckled. He grabbed my backside to keep me from falling, his merciless fingers coaxing an orgasm out of me. "Were you being honest with me, Quinn? Was that all you wanted from me?"

I didn't know how to answer the question. I'd been lying, of course. Foolishly holding out hope that if he spent enough time with me, he'd fall in love with me the same way I'd fallen for him. But if I told him the truth, if I admitted that I'd lied to him, he would feel like I'd betrayed him.

"It was all I wanted at the time." Which wasn't really a lie. A little white lie, maybe, but not a total lie.

He considered my response for a moment and withdrew his fingers. I let out a little whimper.

"And now? What do you want now?"

"This." I moved his hand between my thighs again. "I want you to finish what you started."

"That's all you want? An orgasm? You want me to make your pussy clench around my fingers... is that what you want?"

Wordlessly, I nodded, not trusting my voice. I gasped when his fingers thrust inside me, reaching and curling, his thumb pressing my clit, and I buried my face against his neck as I came, breathing him in. My legs shook and held me up, so I wouldn't fall at his feet. Small mercy.

It felt like I was crashing and falling. It was so unfair that he'd questioned me about my motives while simultaneously giving me an orgasm. Cruel yet kind. And as I knew, Jesse could be both. I watched him suck on his fingers like the taste of me was his favorite food.

Now he placed his hands on either side of my face and tipped up my chin, so I was forced to meet his eye. "So when I leave here... when I leave *you*, it won't break your heart?"

Why was he asking it that way? What was he hoping to achieve? Did he want me to admit that I'd be brokenhearted? Was he looking for an ego boost? I didn't know what to think. But it was the way he'd posed the question and the fact that he hadn't told me anything about San Diego that gave me the strength to lie to him.

Lying shouldn't be something to be proud of, but there was no way I could tell him the truth.

"I'll miss you. It's been a good ride. But my heart won't be broken." I was relieved that it was too dark for him to read my expression because he was still studying my face so intently that if we'd been in the light of day, he would have seen what I was hiding.

I love you. I love you. I love you. And my heart's already breaking. You don't even have to be gone for that to happen.

"What if I said it didn't have to be goodbye?" He skimmed his hands down my arms and clasped my hands in his. "What if I said we could keep doing this when we got out to California?"

It was so tempting to jump at the chance, but he meant that we could keep hooking up. That was all he was offering, and suddenly it didn't feel like enough.

I swallowed hard and lowered my eyes so he couldn't see the tears that had gathered there. I wouldn't let them fall. Not yet.

"I'd say no," I said finally, surprised that my voice sounded normal despite my inner turmoil.

Because this hurt. It hurt so much to say no. But I didn't want to settle for so little. Not anymore. I wanted his everything, and he wasn't prepared to give me that. Maybe he never would be.

Sometimes you have to know when to cut your losses. You had to know when it was time to let go of a girlhood fantasy. And as much as it killed me to deny him, that time had come. He'd never promised me more than this, so I had nobody to blame except myself.

He released me abruptly and straddled his bike. "Let's go for a ride."

Why did he sound angry?

I pulled on my helmet and climbed on behind him, thankful that I could hide my face so he wouldn't be able to see my tears.

Chapter Forty-Two

Quinn

We took the winding back roads. I didn't know where we were going, but it didn't matter. I loved the freedom of the open road, the night air sweet and fragrant, cooler than it had been during the day when the temperatures had been in the nineties.

Tonight was so bittersweet. It felt like the end of something special. Something magical. Because it was. I loved Jesse just as much as I always had, even more now. But that was just it. I loved him, and he didn't love me.

I couldn't keep wishing and hoping that he'd change his mind about us. If he hadn't already, he never would. So I had to be brave and strong and tell him goodbye.

So I loosened my hold on him. I wasn't holding on as tightly. And then I let go of him altogether. I unwound my arms that were wrapped around him and slowly, ever so slowly, my thighs squeezing the seat underneath me to stay balanced, I sat up a little straighter, a little taller, and I held my arms out at my sides. I felt the warm breeze sift through my fingers, and I tasted the salty tears on my lips.

It made me feel a little wobbly, a little bit unbalanced, not holding on to Jesse. But I couldn't keep hanging on to someone who didn't want me the way I wanted him.

I didn't want to be that girl. I refused to be that girl any longer. Not even for the guy I'd loved all my life. Because I'd learned a few things this summer. I learned that someone could be kind but cruel at the same time. I learned that you never get over your first love, but you could eventually move on. And I learned that unrequited love was more tragic than the love story of the Sun and the Moon. Because at least the Sun acknowledged his love for the Moon.

Jesse must have realized that I'd let go because I could feel us slowing down. He was easing up on the throttle, and he was watching me in the side mirror. I couldn't see his face clearly, but I had a feeling he was angry. He'd always told me to hang on tight, and usually, I did, but tonight I hadn't listened.

I was so busy watching him in the side mirror that I didn't even notice the car.

One minute, I had my arms out to my side, the seat between my thighs, and the next thing I knew, I was on the ground, and all the air had been knocked out of my lungs.

"Quinn. Baby, can you hear me?" His voice sounded far away

like it was coming to me from the end of a tunnel.

I opened my eyes and blinked, trying to bring him into focus. "Jesse?" I tried to sit up. Pain radiated down my left arm. A sharp pain that made me dizzy and nauseous.

"Don't try to move, okay? Just tell me where it hurts." I squeezed my eyes shut. "Where does it hurt, Quinn?"

I sucked in a sharp breath and let out a whimper. "My arm."

"Your left arm?"

"Yes." I whimpered again. God, I hated that I kept doing that, but everything hurt, and I felt like I was going to throw up.

"How about your head? Does your head hurt?"

"I don't… I don't know…." I wasn't sure. How could I not know if my own head hurt?

"The ambulance is on the way," a man's voice said.

"Thanks," Jesse said.

"I didn't even see you coming," a woman's voice said. She sounded older, her voice warbling on the words like she was upset. "I'm awful sorry about this. I was trying to get to my granddaughter, you see. She needed me."

I didn't hear whatever Jesse said in reply. I broke out in a cold sweat, and my stomach was churning.

"Quinn," Jesse said so softly, his voice filled with so much pain that I wanted to comfort him.

"I'm okay. I just…" I tried to suck air into my lungs and get the world to stop spinning.

"I'm going to move you off the road, okay? I'll try to be as careful as I can, but if it hurts, tell me."

He slid one arm under my knees and supported my back with

the other arm, and then he lifted me up off the road and into his arms. I squeezed my eyes shut to hold back the tears. It hurt so much, and I was so nauseous.

"You're okay," he said. "Everything is going to be okay."

He was holding me now, cradling me in his lap like a broken doll, and he was trying to be so careful with me that it made me cry. He'd taken off my helmet, and I leaned my cheek against his shoulder.

"I'm so sorry." There was so much pain in his voice when he said that. "I'm so sorry, Quinn."

"It wasn't your fault. I let go. You told me to hold on tight, but I let go. It wasn't your fault." I studied his face and tried to focus on it even though I couldn't see it clearly through the blur of my tears. My body trembled in his arms, and I felt so shaky, I wasn't in control of my own limbs.

"It's the shock," he said, answering a question I hadn't asked. "The adrenaline is making you shake like that."

I could feel the adrenaline shooting through my veins, and for a little while, it dulled the pain.

"Are you hurt?" I finally thought to ask.

"No. But I wish it had been me instead of you." He took a ragged breath. "Does your leg hurt?"

"Kind of." That was a big fat yes. My leg felt like it was on fire.

"That's from the road burn. It's pretty scraped up."

The jacket had protected my arms, but stupid me had worn a short white dress.

"I'm so fucking sorry, Quinn."

I wish he would stop apologizing. It wasn't his fault. I don't know how it had happened, but I knew that Jesse would have done everything in his power to protect me.

Lights flashed across his face, and I looked over at the ambulance as two paramedics hopped out.

Still holding me, Jesse got to his feet. I had no idea how he was strong enough to do that. Core strength, I guess. I saw how strong he was in our yoga sessions.

My brain was fuzzy, and I felt broken as he carried me over to the paramedics. I probably could have walked on my own, but I didn't have the strength to protest.

It reminded me of all the times Jesse carried me up to bed when I was a kid and pretended to be asleep.

Jesse had always taken care of me.

"She's had two kidney transplants," he told the paramedics as he lowered me onto the stretcher. "She's on immunosuppressants."

Why did they need to know that? My arm hurt, not my kidneys.

"Is that your motorcycle?" someone asked.

Jesse nodded.

A sudden panic gripped me. He would leave me to ride in the ambulance alone, and I'd never see him again. It was irrational, but I couldn't help it. Mainly because I saw the guilt on his face when he looked down at me.

"Don't leave me," I pleaded, grabbing his hand with my good one. "Jesse. Promise you won't leave me." My voice had risen a few octaves higher and didn't even sound like my own.

"I'm not going anywhere. I just have to move my motorcycle, and then I'll ride with you in the ambulance." He dropped a soft kiss on my forehead and gave my hand a squeeze before he released it. "I'll be right back, and I'll stay by your side. Promise."

Chapter Forty-Three

Jesse

I couldn't stay with Quinn. As soon as the ambulance stopped outside the ER, they took her away to run tests and sent me to the desk to fill out the paperwork. I filled it out to the best of my knowledge, but there were some questions I couldn't answer.

I had Quinn's phone. It was in the pocket of her jacket, which they'd removed in the ambulance. I didn't know her password, and I didn't try to guess. It wasn't necessary anyway. I could access her emergency contact details without getting into her phone.

Getting a call like this was a mother's worst nightmare. Or so my mom had always told us. Abby answered on the second ring.

"Quinn? Where are you?"

"Hi, Abby. It's Jesse McCallister."

"Jesse? Why are you calling me on Quinn's phone?" I could hear the panic rising in her voice, so I rushed in to reassure her.

"Quinn is okay." I didn't even know if that was true, but I knew she'd race right over here, and I didn't want her to drive when she was panicking. "We had an accident. But she's going to be okay."

"An accident? What kind of accident?"

"She got thrown from the back of my motorcycle."

"Oh, my God. Where are you?"

After I gave her the information, she said she was on her way and cut the call.

I tucked Quinn's phone into my pocket for safekeeping and took a seat in the waiting area.

Fuck. I leaned my elbows on my thighs and held my head in my hands. If anything happened to Quinn, I'd never fucking forgive myself. She'd been so pale in the ambulance, and she'd been drifting in and out of consciousness, her body's way of blocking the pain, no doubt.

That car had pulled out right in front of me. The woman hadn't even looked before she'd pulled onto the road. And what were the fucking chances there would be a pickup in the oncoming lane? So I'd been left with no other choice but to make a dead stop. It had prevented a crash. But my rear wheel had lifted off the ground, and Quinn had flown off the back.

Fuck. I couldn't get the vision out of my head. Quinn lying on the road, looking so small and broken in her little white dress and gold Nikes.

Why the fuck had she let go? Why wasn't she holding onto me?

I should never have taken her for a ride in that damn little dress. It barely covered anything.

A woman's voice had me lifting my head and looking over at the desk where Quinn's mom was speaking to a nurse. I hadn't seen Abby since Thanksgiving, which was strange, considering I'd been spending so much time with her daughter.

When her gaze landed on me, I stood up from my seat and walked over to her. Like Quinn, Abby was petite, and tonight she looked much younger with her blonde hair in a ponytail, wearing a T-shirt and yoga pants.

"Abby." I tipped my chin. "I'm sorry—"

She held up her hand, indicating that she didn't want to hear my apologies. We moved away from the desk and stopped near the entrance. "Was she wearing a helmet?"

I nodded. "Yeah, she was. And a motorcycle jacket. It helped, but...." I cleared my throat. "She was wearing a dress, so her legs were exposed."

"How could you let her ride on your motorcycle in a dress? Or at all? I told you to *never* take her on your motorcycle. Do you remember that conversation? I told you to say no. I told you that, Jesse. You *promised* me."

I ran my hand through my hair. Quinn had always begged me to take her for a ride. Saying no to an eleven-year-old Quinn hadn't been easy. Saying no to eighteen-year-old Quinn was virtually impossible. "I'm sorry."

"You're sorry?" Abby cried. "After everything she's been

through… how could you?"

Abby shook her head in disappointment and started to walk away, but then she stopped and, slowly, she turned to face me again. "It was your T-shirt, wasn't it?"

"My T-shirt?"

"She came home in a T-shirt that was too big for her. She lied and said it was Declan's. I thought maybe… It was a boy from high school. When she was a little girl, she used to tell me everything. But now she's growing up, and she's keeping secrets. Quinn's always had a good head on her shoulders, so I never worried that she'd do something stupid. I thought she knew better. But you…" Her face twisted in anger, and I heard the disgust in her voice. "You're nine years older than her, Jesse. You're the same age as Mason. You've known her since she was a baby. *What were you thinking*?"

I opened my mouth to answer but didn't get the chance.

Mason came to stand next to his mom. "How's Quinn?" He looked from his mom to me.

"Did you know that your sister has been riding on the back of your friend's motorcycle?"

Mason winced and rubbed the back of his neck. "Yeah, I did. I thought it was a one-off, but—"

"You were so worried about keeping her in Texas, but you didn't stop to think how dangerous it was to ride on a motorcycle? Jesse has always been daring and reckless. And now look.…" She waved her hand at me. "He doesn't have a scratch on him, but your sister is—" She broke off on a sob and covered her face with her hands while I stood by, feeling like the world's biggest fucking asshole.

Mason pulled her into his arms and looked at me over her

shoulder. "Is Quinn okay?"

"They think her wrist is broken. So they've taken her in for X-rays."

Abby pulled away from Mason and pointed her finger at me, her voice shaking with anger. "You need to leave. I don't want you anywhere near my daughter."

"I promised I'd stay. I promised I wouldn't leave her."

"And you promised me you'd never take her on your motorcycle. So what's another broken promise."

"Mom. It was an accident," Mason said, trying to reason with his mother. But he didn't know the whole truth. If he did, he wouldn't be defending me. "Judging by the way he looks right now, he already feels like shit."

Abby crossed her arms over her chest. "So you're fine with the idea of your twenty-seven-year-old friend being with your eighteen-year-old sister?"

Mason's brow furrowed, trying to make sense of his mom's words. He didn't know what to think or believe. "They've always been friends." His gaze swung to me. "You and Quinn. You're just friends, right?"

I rubbed the back of my neck. It was time to come clean. "We're more than just friends."

Mason stared at me for a moment until my words finally sank in, and then, he clenched his jaw, and his hands curled into fists.

"I need to see you outside."

I nodded. Fuck. I knew this wouldn't sit right but worse than that, I'd been going behind his back all summer.

Mason strode out the front door, and I turned to Quinn's

mother, taking one more stab at an apology.

"I'm sorry. I never…" I blew out a breath, trying to find the right words to make this better, but I didn't think there were any. "I care about your daughter. I always have. I would never do anything to hurt her."

"And yet, here we are in a hospital. I always liked you, Jesse. But right now, I can't even look at you." She turned and walked away, and I let her go. This wasn't the right time to make amends.

I met Mason out front and prepared myself for whatever was coming my way. I didn't have to wait long.

"You son of a bitch," he gritted out, and then he punched me in the face.

Shit. I worked my jaw. Guess I deserved that.

"How long? How long has this been going on?"

"Most of the summer," I admitted. Although that was a lie. I'd kissed her on her eighteenth birthday. That was the day I stopped thinking of Quinn as Mason's little sister. But I didn't want to add insult to injury, so I kept that part to myself.

"Most of the summer?" Mason said incredulously. "I can't fucking believe this. You've been my best friend for twenty years. Twenty. Fucking. Years. I thought I could trust you with my life. I thought I could trust you with *my sister*." He gripped the back of his head with both hands and paced back and forth, trying to get his emotions under control. "Why her? Of all the girls you could have been with, why would you go after my sister?"

I'd been giving this a lot of thought over the past couple of days. There were a lot of reasons why I'd gone for Quinn, but I kept it simple. "Because she's special."

"Exactly why you should have stayed away from her." He shoved my shoulder, *hard*, the fucked-up shoulder that still gave me trouble. I winced, but I didn't even try to fight back. Not the first time he did it or the second. He knew it was my bad shoulder, but he was angry, and if I were in his shoes, I would be angry too.

So, if he needed to use me as a punching bag, then I'd let him. Because of me, his sister was lying in a hospital bed. The same sister he'd donated a kidney to without giving it a second thought.

"What were you trying to do? Get your ego stroked? Does it make you feel more like a man to know that an eighteen-year-old girl worships the ground you walk on? You were using her to get over Alessia, weren't you?"

"Maybe, in the beginning, yeah," I admitted. Then, before I had a chance to explain myself, he punched me in the shoulder.

Motherfucker. I grabbed my shoulder and staggered back, trying to breathe through the pain.

Mason wasn't a fighter any more than I was, but he was fighting because he thought I'd done him wrong. I got that, but shit, that had hurt.

"I hope it was worth it because you just shit all over our friendship. We're over. I'll reimburse you for the money you invested in the brewery."

"You don't have to do that."

"Yeah, I do. I want nothing to do with you." He stabbed a finger at me. "You'd better hope to hell this accident hasn't affected her kidneys."

I did hope like hell that it hadn't. I didn't want Quinn to be hurting at all. If I could take away her pain and make it my own, I would do it in a heartbeat.

Mason turned on his heel and strode into the hospital, leaving me outside on the sidewalk with my sore shoulder and a mountain of guilt.

"You and Quinn, huh?"

I turned at the sound of Holden's voice. He pushed off from the pillar and walked toward me. I hadn't even noticed him standing there, hidden in the shadows. "How long have you been there?" I asked, wincing as I rolled out my shoulder.

"Long enough. It felt like this was Mason's fight, not mine. So I stayed out of it." He rubbed his hand over his jaw, looking a lot cooler and more composed than Mason had. "He's going through a lot of his own shit right now. This sure as hell isn't helping."

Mason hadn't said a word to me. But then, I hadn't spoken to him in almost a week. "What's going on?"

His gaze drifted to the front door, then back to me. "Not my news to share. Do you love her?"

It was funny that Mason hadn't even thought to ask the only question that truly mattered. I nodded once, admitting it for the first time. "Yeah, I do. But it took me longer than it should have to figure that out." I didn't add that it might be too late. That was my problem, not his.

He nodded like he'd suspected it. "I'm surprised Mason didn't notice. It was pretty damn obvious to me. I figured it out that day we all went up to the lake. But sometimes we only see what we want to."

Wasn't that the truth? His phone buzzed, and he checked the screen before he pocketed it again.

"Quinn has a fractured wrist and a mild concussion. But her vitals look good."

I breathed a sigh of relief. "Can I see her?"

"I think you'd better let everyone cool down first. My mom's not too happy about any of this, and I have a feeling my dad won't be either. If you want to be with Quinn, you'll have your work cut out for you."

I didn't even know if Quinn wanted to be with me. Although, judging by her responses earlier, I'd say that was a no.

The only thing I need protection from is you.

Had she been trying to protect herself from me?

I'd been a coward. Instead of telling her how I really felt, I'd questioned her.

No wonder she hadn't felt like she could be honest.

One thing I knew with absolute certainty. If I let her go, I'd regret it.

She had made my life so much better, and what had I given her in return? Not a damn thing. It was time to change that. Time to show Quinn how much she meant to me.

Chapter Forty-Four

Quinn

My parents were arguing. I could hear them right outside the door of my hospital room, where all three of my brothers were at my bedside. Not that I wanted them here. I wanted to be alone, but privacy was a luxury I didn't have right now.

"Why didn't you know what our daughter has been getting up to all summer?" my dad accused.

"*Our* daughter," my mom said with a harsh laugh. "How convenient. You're never around. Do you have any idea what *our* daughter does with her time?"

"I don't live with her. You're supposed to be the mother. You're the one who keeps trying to cut me out. You don't tell me anything, Abby. If Holden hadn't called me last night, I wouldn't have even known our daughter was in the hospital, for Christ's sake. I don't even know when she has doctor appointments because you don't tell me."

"Well, maybe, if you hadn't cheated on me, you would know what's going on in our lives."

"Not this again. That was five years ago. When are you going to let it go?"

"You threw away our marriage like it meant nothing to you. How am I supposed to let that go?"

"Ignore them," Holden said like that was possible. Like I could just tune out their words.

A few seconds later, our parents' voices faded. Either they'd moved away from the door or lowered their voices, I didn't know. I squeezed my eyes shut, trying to block out their words. It brought back memories of them arguing when I was a kid. I always used to think my parents had the perfect marriage and my dad had destroyed it when he cheated, but now I remembered that it hadn't been perfect.

My brothers had always tried to protect me from bad things. They'd been doing it, each in their own ways, ever since I was born. Whenever my parents were fighting, they used to distract me, turn up the volume on a movie or take me outside so I wouldn't have to hear it. Declan used to let me play video games with him. We used to bake too. Which was funny to think about now. Big bad Declan baking cupcakes and brownies with me.

Holden used to take me on nature walks, on the same trails

where we took Jesse's nephews. Flora and Fauna were Holden's jam. His way to find peace in a world that was sometimes chaotic.

And Mason… he'd always worried about me far more than he should. Far more than what was healthy. I knew his heart was in the right place, but he needed to let me go. It wasn't his place to right every perceived wrong or to make decisions on my behalf. And, as far as I was concerned, whatever I'd done with Jesse this summer was none of his business.

It was a blessing and a burden to be loved as much as my family loved me. Sometimes, it felt almost claustrophobic. Like I needed to break away and do my own thing. Make my own mistakes without them feeling the need to fix things.

My family knew about us now. They knew about Jesse and me.

And he wasn't even here. He'd promised that he would stay. Instead, he left me with a fractured wrist, a mild concussion, road rash, and a broken heart. And I knew why he wasn't here, too. My family had sent him away.

"You're not eating your breakfast," Declan said, scowling at me from his spot against the wall, his arms crossed over his chest like my not eating was a personal affront.

"I'm not hungry. But thank you," I added. Because he'd made me a special breakfast—a fancy acai bowl that was so beautiful to look at, it really was. This morning, he brought it to the hospital, claiming that the hospital food was disgusting. Which it was. But I'd taken two bites just to appease him, and I couldn't force myself to take another one.

I wanted to leave the hospital and had begged to be released. I hated the smell—antiseptic with the artificial scent of soap and disinfectant that left a bitter taste on my tongue. I hated all the noise. Alarms and beeping and the sound of a patient down the hall yelling and moaning. I barely slept last night. The nurse told me I needed to rest, but every time I'd almost fallen asleep, someone came in to check my vitals. How often did they need to shine a light in my eyes and check my blood pressure to confirm that I was alive and well?

I wanted out, but they were keeping me in for observation.

Mason's gaze dipped to the orange cast on my arm, and I saw the accusation in his eyes. "I can't believe he fucking did this to you."

I let out a weary sigh. "I told you it was all my fault, not Jesse's."

"I don't believe that for a minute."

"Believe what you want. It's true. *I'm* the one who went after him. *I'm* the one who let go when I was riding on the back of his bike. And I'm the one who asked him to keep it a secret. So it was all on me." Which was all true. "So stop blaming him."

My words fell on deaf ears. Mason didn't want to hear it. He wanted to believe it was all Jesse's fault, that I was too pure and innocent to concoct a plan like that or go after his friend.

Everything was such a mess. My parents were arguing, and if it was up to them, I wouldn't even be allowed to go to California. But I wasn't going down without a fight. It was time for everyone to realize that I wasn't a little kid anymore and could make my own life choices.

So I fought tooth and nail, and I won that battle. Kind of. My father was coming to California with me. He was going to rent a place in Santa Monica so he could be there for me whenever I needed him. Unlike my mom, my dad hadn't been as angry about

Jesse and me being together as I thought he would.

"What about Camilla?" I asked.

He gave me a sad smile. "It didn't work out."

I wasn't sure if I should feel happy or upset. "I'm sorry."

"We're at very different places in our lives. She wants children, and I've already raised four amazing kids. I wouldn't trade that experience for anything in the world, but I don't want to go down that road again. Not at my age."

"So you're coming to college with me instead."

He rubbed his hands together like the prospect thrilled him. "Can't wait."

"You won't be popping up all over campus or anything, right?"

"Are you kidding? I'm planning to come to all the parties and sit right next to you in your lectures. I'll be like a barnacle, stuck to your side. You won't be able to get rid of me."

I laughed. It was the first time I'd laughed in days.

At first, I wasn't sure how I felt about my dad being out in California, so close by, but I was getting used to the idea. Maybe we'd get close again like we used to be.

Five days.

That was how long it had been since I last saw Jesse. For all I knew, he was in California by now.

Ever since I'd gotten released from the hospital, I'd been holed up in my room. My eyes were puffy from crying, my hair was a tangled mess, and Jesse's T-shirt smelled more like me and less like him, которая was enough to make me shed more tears. I'd already cried an ocean for him. I was surprised I had any tears left.

"What good is a king without his queen?" I said, trying to enunciate each word. "We belong together. You're mine, and I'm yours, and I'm never letting you go again. The End." I watched the words appear on my screen before I saved my work and closed my laptop. Sagging against the pillows behind my back, I covered my eyes with my right arm.

I did it. My story was done.

I'd tried typing one-handed, but my words were coming faster than I could type, so I finished it with voice to text.

Now I was drained. Mentally, physically, and emotionally exhausted.

But at least my fictional couple got their happily ever after.

Despite all the obstacles, Daisy and Ryder were in California, living out their dreams. Because Ryder fought for Daisy. He fought so hard to prove his love.

As I drifted off to sleep, I wondered, what if I had told Jesse the truth? If I'd confessed my love, would it have changed anything?

It was pointless to think about that now. I was done fighting for Jesse.

One week later, I said goodbye to my brothers and mom, who hugged me so tight I could barely breathe. I didn't complain, though. We shed a few tears, and then my dad and I boarded a flight to L.A.

Turns out, I didn't even have to cull my Nike collection. My dad shipped them to his new place in Santa Monica. I had my own room in his house—a three-bedroom Spanish Colonial close to the beach.

It was time to start a new chapter of my life.

My heartache accompanied me everywhere I went, like a dark cloud blocking the sun. But I was determined to live out my California dream.

Without the love of my life.

I hated him. I really, really did.

If only that were true.

Chapter Forty-Five

Jesse

It was my twenty-eighth birthday. Rock music was blasting, flames leaped up below me, and the spotlights were trained on us. It was my first show with the DirtDevilz, at an open-air stadium in San Bernardino, and tonight we were treated like rock stars.

It was a crazy way to make a living. Performing gravity-defying stunts and aerial acrobatics with a two-hundred-pound dirt bike on ramps so high we flew off the lip and soared into the sky.

Supermans, whips, and flips. We did it all for the thousands of spectators who filled the seats and cheered us on. I grabbed the seat of my bike with one hand and did a backflip, landing on the opposite ramp and flying down it with Knox so close behind me, I could feel him breathing down my neck.

It was a hell of a show, an adrenaline rush like no other.

When it was over, we autographed ball caps, T-shirts, and programs in the bowels of the stadium. One kid asked me to sign his moto jersey. He was around eight or nine and reminded me of Noah.

"Thanks," he said with a big smile when I handed his jersey back. "When I grow up, I wanna be just like you. I wanna do all the same stuff you do."

I wanted to tell him that he didn't want to be anything like me, but I knew he was talking about dirt bikes and stunts, not my shitty life choices.

"Work hard, dream big, and never give up. You'll make your dreams happen."

He grinned like I'd just given him the key to life. Which I guess I had. You couldn't make dreams come true without putting in the hard work, and you couldn't give up when the going got tough.

You couldn't run away either. But that was exactly what I did four weeks ago. The morning after the motorcycle accident, I showed up at the hospital to visit Quinn. I had her phone and a big-ass bouquet of flowers. Daisies. Dozens and dozens of cheerful yellow and white daisies.

I didn't even make it past the front desk. Correction. I didn't make it past Quinn's parents. They were arguing right outside Quinn's door. When they saw me headed down the hallway, they stopped arguing and walked over to me, effectively blocking my entrance to Quinn's room.

We went for coffee in the cafeteria. I didn't want coffee, but it was clear that they had something to say, and until they said it, I wasn't getting anywhere near their daughter.

They asked me to wait until Quinn was older, and if I still wanted to be with her then, they wouldn't try to stop us. Really big of them. Note the sarcasm.

"No disrespect, but this is Quinn's decision, not yours."

That's what I told them. I was prepared to fight for Quinn. She was worth it. Nobody was worth fighting for more than Quinn was.

"What are you doing with your life now, Jesse?" Mark had asked, his tone casual, although I suspected it was anything but.

Not sure it was any of their business, but I told them anyway. I didn't want to be combative with Quinn's parents. She loved them, and they were just trying to look out for her. Couldn't really blame them for that. If I had a daughter, I would do the same.

"So you'll be traveling a lot."

I nodded. Couldn't deny that either.

Long story short, they grilled me about my life choices for thirty minutes, and by the end of our conversation, one thing was blindingly obvious. For the next year, for the foreseeable future, really, I wouldn't be around much. I'd signed a contract with an FMX team, and we were set to tour North America and then Europe.

In the end, it was my decision to walk away from Quinn.

Not because I didn't love her, but because I did. I couldn't expect her to build her life around mine. To sit around and wait for me while I was traveling. That conversation with Quinn's parents reminded me of everything Alessia had said to me about the sacrifices she'd made for my career. In Alessia's case, that wasn't entirely accurate, but nevertheless, there was some truth in it.

It wasn't the life I wanted for Quinn. I didn't want her to give up anything for me. Not when she'd worked so hard to get to where she was.

So I walked away and told myself it was the best thing I could do for her.

I had been telling myself the same thing every single day for the past month.

I wasn't surprised that she hadn't responded to any of my text messages.

Until today. Today she sent me a text.

I reread it in the van on the way back to Temecula. Colby was passed out in the seat next to me, and the adrenaline rush had worn off. I loved the highs, but I hated the lows.

Dear Jesse, if I had your address, I'd send you a letter. Or a birthday card.

I typed and deleted this message so many times, and I'm still not sure if I'll send it. But I just wanted you to know that I don't blame you for anything. It was my fault that I fell off your motorcycle. I let go. I let go because I felt like that was what I needed to do. To stop holding on so tightly to a dream that was never mine.

And I lied to you. I just wanted you to know that too. I lied because I didn't want you to think that I wanted more. Which was stupid. Why should I feel like I deserved so little? But that's not entirely true either. You gave me so much. You really did. I've gone to the beach a few times, cast and all, and I wore a bikini top with shorts while I hung out with my new friends. It makes me feel like a badass. Like a brave warrior for baring my scars. You always made me feel beautiful, and that was such a great gift.

I finished the book I was writing. You helped me with that too.

So even though I'm angry with you, and sometimes I convince myself that I hate you, I'll never forget what you did for me. It was a good ride, Jesse. I don't regret a single minute. Happy Birthday from your sunshine girl

As if I needed further proof that Quinn was worth fighting for, she sent me that text.

Fuck it. I didn't want to go another day without telling Quinn how I felt about her. But that wasn't something you could do in a text or on the phone.

Chapter Forty-Six

Quinn

Last week, I kissed a boy who wasn't Jesse. A California boy with dirty blond hair and bronzed skin. He knew how to surf, and he said he'd teach me when I got my cast off. But I felt like I was cheating on my first love, so I said no. Which was so stupid.

Because my first love had left me, hadn't he? And God, I had cried for weeks over him. Meanwhile, he'd ghosted me. No, that wasn't entirely true. He'd texted me, but his texts made me so angry I hadn't even bothered replying.

I'm sorry. For everything.

As if to say I had been a mistake and he was sorry he ever

got involved with me. So no, I didn't reply because he didn't even deserve a response. But three days ago, I texted him for his birthday, and as soon as I'd hit send, I regretted it.

Now I stared at the two daisy chains hanging from the door handle of my dorm room. I looked up and down the hallway, searching for the person who could have put them there. Maybe they weren't even for me. Maybe Priya or Addison had a secret admirer. They were my roommates, and they were great. I'd lucked out in that department. We'd become fast friends. Which was lucky because we shared a triple and a bathroom.

But the daisy chains… who had put them here? It couldn't have been him. I couldn't even allow myself to think that, so I squashed my hopes, looped the chains around my arm, and opened my door with my key card.

As I tossed my backpack on my desk chair, my eye caught on a yellow envelope lying on the carpet. Like someone had pushed it under the door.

My name was on the front in bold print, the letters slightly slanted. My heart skipped a beat. That looked like Jesse's handwriting. But no, it couldn't be from him.

I sat on the bottom bunk below Priya's and slid the notepaper—white with a daisy border—out of the envelope.

Dear Quinn,

I'm not the writer, but I wrote a story for you. A fairy tale with an open ending.

Once upon a time, a princess asked a boy to marry her. He was, by all accounts, unworthy of the princess. But he couldn't believe his good fortune, so he said yes. They were married under an oak tree at the princess' castle. They wore daisy chains and promised to love each other until the end of time.

The boy pledged to be her knight in shining armor, to be loyal to her for all eternity. He would slay dragons for his princess and rescue her from every danger.

The princess grew up and she became a queen, and the boy became a man—a daring, reckless man. A selfish man. He returned home a broken knight with tarnished armor and a wounded heart.

You see, the knight had strayed, and in his travels, he'd lost his way. He was bitter and angry. He wasn't the same knight the queen remembered. But the queen was so good. So true and so brave that she was able to save the knight.

The queen breathed new life into her broken knight. Because that queen, she is the Sun. She shines so bright it's blinding. She shines so bright that the knight got greedy and wanted that light all to himself. But he never told her that. He never told the queen how fucking amazing she is. He never told her how special she is or how much she means to him.

Instead, he let her go, and not a day goes by that he doesn't regret it.

Without the Sun, that foolish knight was banished to a cold and lonely place, left to live a life without his queen for all eternity.

Yours,
Jesse

Oh my God. I reread the story. I read it so many times I knew it by heart. But what did it mean? What was he trying to say? It was so cryptic.

The door opened, and I looked up from the letter as Addison walked in and dumped her backpack on the floor. She was wearing basketball shorts and her high school volleyball T-shirt. Addison was nearly six feet tall, sporty and smart, with long blonde hair and big blue eyes.

"Oh my God, I'm so tired. My brain hurts." She massaged her temples as she walked over to the mini-fridge in front of the window. Our room was small, our quarters cramped, but we had an amazing view of Santa Monica and the ocean. Something I still marveled at, although today I was too distracted to notice the view.

"I need chocolate. Why did I think pre-med was a good idea?"

"Because you're a genius." She was, too. But the other reason was that her parents were doctors.

"I felt like the village idiot in Chem lab today. Then I got my ass handed to me on the volleyball court."

I half-listened but was still puzzling over the letter in my hand.

She rifled through our junk food stash and grabbed a bar of Ghirardelli—dark chocolate with sea salt. Addison was the only one who liked it. She plopped down in the desk chair under her bunk bed, moaning when she took a bite of chocolate before she turned her chair around to face me.

"Cute daisy chains. Did you wear them to class?"

"They're from Jesse."

Her eyes widened. Addison and Priya knew all about Jesse. I still couldn't believe it, though. Jesse made daisy chains and wrote a story for me. And not only that, somehow, he had found a way to get them to me.

Wordlessly, I handed her the letter, hoping she could help me make sense of it.

Later that night, Priya, Addison, and I spent hours dissecting it, trying to figure out what he was trying to say.

I fell asleep dreaming about a knight in shining armor.

Priya groaned and gripped the railing as we faced another set of stairs. "Give me strength." She held the back of her arm over her forehead in a dramatic display. Priya was a theater major, and drama was her middle name. A natural. Her mom used to be a Bollywood dancer, and her dad worked for Universal Studios. "Someone needs to carry me."

I laughed.

We lived on the Hill, where all the on-campus housing was, and there *were* a lot of stairs. "Come on. You can do it. Just think of the amazing things it will do for our calf muscles."

"You sound like my mother. 'Priya, you won't get anywhere in life by being a couch potato.'" She mimicked her mom's accent, pretty and singsong. "And here I was worried about the freshman fifteen," she said as we trudged up the stairs. "We lose a bucket of sweat and three pounds a day on these stairs."

Priya was a few inches taller than me and rail-thin. If she lost three pounds a day, she'd float away. By the time we reached the top, we had to stop for a moment to catch our breath.

"I wonder what he left outside your door today," Priya said, sounding just as excited as I was.

I didn't want to admit that I'd been racing home from class every day this week just to see what he'd left me.

We still hadn't figured out how he'd been getting inside the dorm to leave me little gifts. Priya thought he paid someone. Addison had questioned nearly everyone on our floor. But nobody knew anything about it.

"Maybe it's like the twelve days of Christmas," Priya said as we followed the sunlit tree-lined paths to our dorm. "What day is it today? The fifth, right?"

I nodded, and she started singing the Twelve Days of Christmas. Loudly enough to turn heads. "Oh my God. Today is the five gold rings."

On the first day, Jesse left the daisy chains and the story he wrote.

On the second day, he left a pair of Nikes. Not just any Nikes, either. They were custom Nikes with multi-colored Murakami flowers. Happy flowers with smiling faces. I hadn't taken them off since I'd found them outside my door.

On the third day, he left pink-frosted sugar cookies and a can of pink lemonade mix.

And yesterday, the fourth day, he left me a bracelet similar to the one he'd given me when I was twelve. This one, though, the gold bracelet I was wearing on my right wrist, said: The Sun and the Moon.

My pulse raced as we stepped off the elevator and walked down the hallway. When our door came into view, my shoulders sagged in disappointment. Even from the other end of the hallway, I could see he hadn't left anything.

"Maybe Addie put it inside the room. She only had morning

classes today, right?" Priya suggested.

"Maybe. Or maybe he's waiting for me to call him."

"I say, make him sweat."

That had been the consensus. I'd spoken to Evie last night, and she said it was a good start but not good enough. "We're talking some major grovel here, Quinn. Don't cave too easily. And besides, it's not like he's proclaimed his undying love or anything."

Which was true. He hadn't. Maybe the gifts were just another way to tell me how sorry he was. *About everything.*

"Oh my God." Priya checked her phone and stopped in her tracks. The look on her face made me think she'd gotten bad news.

"Is everything okay?"

"Oh yeah. Everything is great. But I totally forgot that I'm supposed to meet my friend at the… we have a thing. I have to run. Bye," she called over her shoulder as she hurried away.

Okay. Not sure what that was all about.

I let myself into our room and froze on the threshold, my heart thrashing as he turned from the window with a smile.

"Hey, Sunshine Girl."

Chapter Forty-Seven

Jesse

I found Quinn's jar of wishes. It was after one of our yoga sessions, a couple of days before I found out about Gina. Quinn was in the shower, and we were going to grab some food afterward. We were alone, but it hadn't felt right to take a shower with her in her mother's house, so I was hanging out in her room waiting for her.

I shouldn't have opened the jar. I shouldn't have read her wishes. But the temptation had been too great. I was curious, and the jar had been sitting on her bedside table. So I thought I'd just open one and read it. But I ended up reading half a dozen before I heard her outside the door and closed the lid.

Judging by the handwriting, Quinn was a lot younger when she wrote those notes. But she hadn't changed much. She was still a romantic with a big heart.

She loved daisies and picnics and kissing in the rain. And she loved me. Or, at least, she used to.

I fucked up. I'd been reckless with her heart, and I never should have let her go.

Now I was here to win her back. Hopefully, it wasn't too late.

"How did you get in here?" she asked. "How did you… do all this?"

Last week, I solicited the help of Holden, my only ally in the Cavanaugh camp. After swearing on my life that I wouldn't do anything to hurt his sister, he gave me the information I requested—Quinn's class schedule and her dorm room information. From there, all I had to do was convince someone from her dorm to let me in. Thankfully, I didn't have too much trouble doing that.

I winked at her. "I have my ways."

"I bet you do," she muttered, drawing a laugh from me. The laughter died on my lips when my gaze dipped to the orange cast on her arm. Fuck. It was a physical reminder of the way I'd left her. Broken and hurting. She was wearing the tiny skirt she'd worn the night she was waiting for me on the ramp in my backyard. The night we struck that deal.

"Did it leave a scar?" I asked, referring to her left leg where she'd had the road burn.

She shook her head. "No."

"I've missed you so fucking much."

"Why are you here, Jesse?"

"I have some things I want to tell you. Some things I should have told you a lot sooner. The night it happened… the night you got thrown from my motorcycle… I should have been honest with you. I should have told you how I feel about you. Instead, I questioned you. So we both lied that night."

She swallowed hard. "You lied?"

"Yeah, I did. I let you think that all I wanted was sex with no strings attached. I kept trying to tell myself that it was all I wanted. But like you said, I lie to myself all the time. I never used to. But I let that whole Alessia thing fuck with my head. Way more than I ever should have."

"I don't blame you for that. She didn't just cheat on you, she lied, and she ruined your career. That's a lot to deal with."

"But you made it all better, didn't you? You worked your magic, and before I even realized it was happening, you'd gotten under my skin. You're here." I tapped my temple. "And here." I held my fist to my heart. "And I can't get you out. You're here to stay."

"You left me, though. You promised you'd stay, but you took off."

"I thought I was doing the best thing I could for you."

She laughed harshly. "Wow. Okay. So you took it upon yourself to make a decision on my behalf." She shook her head. "I don't need anyone making decisions for me. Bad enough my parents and three brothers think they know what's best for me. It was the last thing I needed or wanted from you. I can't deal with these head games, Jesse. I'm trying to get over you. Can't you understand that? I need to forget you. But you're making that hard. You can't just show up and mess with my head all over again. It's not fair."

"I'm not here to mess with your head."

"You walked away from me like I meant nothing to you."

"You mean everything to me, Quinn. That's *why* I left you."

She shook her head, disputing my words. "That doesn't make sense. If I meant everything to you, you would have fought for me. And you didn't. You *never* did."

I winced, the truth of her words hitting me where it hurt. "I'm fighting for you now." I advanced on her and stopped in front of her, then wiped away her tears with the pads of my thumbs. "I thought I was doing the right thing. Because I'll be traveling so much, and I won't be around as much as I'd like. I've seen what that can do to relationships—"

"I'm not Alessia. I have *always* supported your dreams."

"I know that. I know you're nothing like her. And I just… I want to support your dreams too. I know it's selfish, but I want to be the one to travel the world with you. I want to be the one cheering you on when you get your diploma. I want to be the one who treats you like the queen that you are."

"Jesse." She looked up at me with her big hazel eyes, her lower lip trembling before she clamped it between her teeth. "What are you saying?"

"I'm saying that I love you, Quinn." They were the easiest words I'd ever said, and I cursed myself for waiting this long to tell her. "I love you."

Her eyes widened. "You love me?" she whispered, not quite trusting what she'd heard.

"So fucking much. And I should have realized it sooner. When I went to San Diego, that's when it hit me. That I loved you. And I should have told you that night. I should have known that you weren't telling the truth. But even if you had been, it shouldn't have mattered. Because when you love someone, you should tell them, even if they don't say it back."

"You believe that?"

I tucked her hair behind her ears and cradled her beautiful face in my hands. "I do. That's why I came here today. To tell you that I love you. I just wanted you to know."

"You drove to L.A. and waited in my dorm room just to tell me that you love me?"

I smiled. "I wanted to tell you a few other things too."

"Like what?"

"My mom once told me that when a McCallister boy falls in love, it's for life. When I met Alessia, I thought she was the one. But she wasn't. She never could have been. Because it was meant to be you all along. But you know, I had to wait until you got your driver's license and finished high school."

She laughed and brushed away a few more tears.

"But what my mom never mentioned was that the McCallister boys' road to true love is never easy. There are a lot of switchbacks and blind turns. A shitload of detours and blocked roads. But eventually, we reach the place where we were meant to be all along. The difficult journey to our end goal only makes the prize that much sweeter."

"Am I your end goal?"

"You are. And I'm prepared to wait for as long as you need. I'm prepared to make any sacrifice it takes to be with you. Even if it means giving up the traveling circus, I'll do it. That is… if you feel the same way about me."

"What if I said I don't?"

"I'd spend the rest of my life pining for you. You're worth it, Quinn. You're worth everything. And I should have told you sooner. I should have told you that you make my world a better place. Your smile… it's so fucking beautiful."

I traced her lips with my fingertip. "If I could spend every day waking up to that smile, I'd die a happy man." I skimmed my fingers over her nose. "I love the eight freckles on your nose. I love the sound of your laughter. The way you sing off-key and get all the words wrong. I love your strength and your bravery, and your eternal optimism. I love the way you light up every room you enter. I love how you go after the things you want in life and how you never give up. I can't think of anything I don't love about you. And I don't deserve you, I know that, but if you give me another chance, I'll do whatever it takes to be the man you deserve."

"Jesse. God, that was so beautiful. I've always loved you. And I still do. I love you."

"Thank fuck for that."

There was nothing left to do except to kiss her. I lifted her right off her feet, and she wrapped her legs around my waist as our mouths collided in a kiss that gave me life.

This was it. It had been Quinn all along. The girl of my dreams.

Epilogue

Jesse

Seven Years Later

I blink awake before the alarm goes off and look down at Quinn sleeping next to me. She's on her side with her back to me, blonde hair fanned across the pillow, the sheets pushed down to expose her bare thighs and white lace panties. She's wearing one of my old T-shirts—the maroon color faded and the cotton soft from so many washings.

Her hand rests on the pillow, the pink diamond and wedding band on her ring finger shimmering. She looks so peaceful, her brow unfurrowed, a tiny smile on her lush pink lips like she's in the middle of a perfect dream.

My sunshine girl is still a dreamer, spinning tales in her head and putting them down on paper. She still makes wishes on stars, but now she tells me that her wishes come true every day. I do everything in my power to make sure they do.

I hate to wake her, but the urge to touch her is so great that I can't help myself. My hand coasts over her warm skin, up her thigh, and over the curve of her hip. My dick stiffens when she lets out a breathy little sigh and grinds her ass against my erection.

"Good morning." My voice is low and rough from sleep.

"Mmm."

I'll take that as a *Yes, I'm up for morning sex.*

Encouraged by her response, I slide my hand under her T-shirt and cup her breast in my palm, brushing my thumb over the nipple. It hardens under my touch, and her little sighs shoot straight to my cock.

I'm two seconds away from pushing down my briefs and gliding into her when I hear the pitter-patter of little feet running down the hallway.

I groan and bury my face in the crook of Quinn's neck, inhaling her scent. She still smells like sunshine and summertime.

"Oh my God, how does she do that?" Quinn mutters.

"She's a little magician, like her mommy."

"She's a little daredevil, like her daddy."

True on both counts.

"Da-da. Da-da." Our little magician is smacking her palms against the door—our morning routine to let me know she's awake and ready to play.

"So unfair," Quinn mutters.

I laugh because, hey, what can I say? Fable Willow McCallister is a daddy's girl through and through. I kiss Quinn's hair before I reluctantly roll away from her. "I've got this."

"Are you sure?"

"I'm sure."

"Is everything packed? We have to leave soon," she mumbles.

"Everything's packed and in the car. We're not leaving until nine." We're headed down to Galveston for a two-week McCallister family beach vacation—a tradition we started a few years ago before Fable was born. It's going to be pure chaos. "Go back to sleep."

She's still half asleep, so it doesn't take much coaxing. "Love you," she says with a sweet little smile as her eyes drift shut.

"Love you more."

I hear Fable babbling as I get dressed in shorts and a T-shirt. She loves to make up stories, just like her mama does.

"Daddy's coming," I assure her. Satisfied with my answer, I hear her running back to her room.

A few seconds later, I head down the hallway past the framed photos. Quinn and I on our honeymoon in Bali, our Malibu beach wedding, the hot air balloon ride over Napa Valley when I proposed, our trips to Europe, Quinn receiving her diploma from UCLA, Fable's baby photos, and family photos grace our walls.

Our house was built on love, and some of our best memories are captured in these photos.

I find Fable in her fairytale bedroom, where she's dragging every stuffed animal she owns into the center of the rug. Her bedroom looks like Narnia, complete with a secret wardrobe and a playroom with a lifelike oak tree.

I'm not even biased when I say that our baby girl is the most beautiful baby in the world. No offense to all the other babies out there, but my girl has them beat by a mile. She looks like an angel with her halo of blond curls, apricot skin, and big blue eyes. Because she *is* an angel.

And don't even get me started on how smart she is. Pretty sure she's a genius.

How many other sixteen-month-old babies have cracked the code on how to escape their crib? My girl, that's who.

Pride swells in my chest as I lift her off the floor and swing her up into my arms. She's all smiles, but the smell nearly knocks me out. "Whoa, baby, you stink."

She giggles like that's the funniest thing she's ever heard.

"Keep it up, Chuckles. You're not the one who has to change the diaper."

That makes her giggle even more.

Five minutes later, diaper changed and dressed in shorts, and a T-shirt from Jude that says: *Sorry Boys, Daddy Says No Dating*; I carry her into the kitchen and sit her in her high chair while I make us some breakfast.

My baby girl and I are morning people. Quinn, not so much. Last night, she was up until two-thirty in the morning, finishing her book so she could meet her editor's deadline and not have to worry about it while we're on vacation. Quinn never misses a deadline, even if it means she has to forfeit sleep. I make sure she eats and has healthy snacks within easy reach because she has a tendency to forget.

I still help her with her research too. That's my favorite part of the writing process—the research. What guy doesn't want to hear: "I'm kind of stuck on this one part. What if they do Reverse Cowgirl? How would that work?"

Like a fucking charm.

Pretty sure that's how Fable was conceived. Not that she'll ever know that.

There's a pink Post-It note on the fridge, and I laugh when I read it: *Make sure we packed the floaties. And the inflatable crocodile. Did I remember the sunscreen? I'm sure I forgot something. Have I told you lately that I love you? I love you more than donuts with sprinkles. More than all the stars in the sky. You're my lobster.*

She punctuated it with a lipstick kiss.

I grab a pen from the drawer and scribble a response on an orange Post-It, then slap it on the fridge where she'll see it when she wakes up.

Quinn and I have been leaving notes for each other ever since we moved in together, the summer before her third year at UCLA. I was with the DirtDevilz for two years, and Quinn traveled with me whenever she could, but it was tough being away from her so much.

It was a good ride, but I was more than ready to settle down and start a new chapter of my life. Quinn never asked me to quit. She'd never do that. It was my decision. The truth was I wanted to spend more time with her. The other deciding factor was that my body couldn't handle the wear and tear anymore. So I coached up-and-coming new racers, and I set up my own moto and streetwear clothing line, which is more successful than I'd expected. I owe a lot to Gideon, who worked on the financials, and Quinn's dad, who helped me get the start-up off the ground.

Thankfully, I'm close with her family again. All they needed was the assurance that I loved their daughter and would do everything in my power to make her happy.

"We're going to the beach today, aren't we, baby girl?" I tell Fable as I set the cut-up fruit in front of her. She grabs a piece of mango and guides it into her mouth while I pour the wholemeal pancake batter into the pan. "You'll get to hang out with your cousins."

That gets her excited. My girl loves her cousins. She's babbling away and dancing in her seat while I tell her about all the exciting adventures she'll have at the beach.

We moved back to Texas a couple years ago when Quinn was pregnant. We loved California, but we wanted to live near our families, and we wanted Fable to grow up with her cousins. So we bought a rambling stone farmhouse with vaulted ceilings and tall windows.

Instead of ramps in our backyard, we have a swimming pool and giant oaks, and beyond that, acres of dirt trails through the woods. I still ride as much as I can.

I've been teaching my nephews—Levi and Zane, Brody and Shiloh's son. Zane was a foster kid, and Brody and Shiloh adopted him four years ago when he was almost three.

Mason's son, Jake, loves to ride too. But my star pupil is Gracie. At the tender age of seven, my niece is already a force to be reckoned with. Good luck to Jude if he thinks he'll be able to keep her locked up in an ivory tower. She's like a tornado. Every bit as competitive and stubborn as her parents and tough as they come. I love that girl.

But my two favorite girls are the ones I share a life and a home with, the ones I love above all others—the sunshine girl I married three years ago and the baby girl that was our greatest gift.

"Should we make your mommy a breakfast smoothie?" I ask Fable as I drizzle honey on her pancake and then set it in front of her. She'll be a sticky mess when she's done eating, but she likes to do everything for herself, so I don't try to feed her. Kids should be allowed to get messy.

She claps her hands together and rewards me with a big toothy grin.

"When you grow up, don't settle for anyone who doesn't treat you like a queen," I tell Fable as I prepare my queen's breakfast.

"She won't. She's too smart for that," Quinn says, wrapping her arms around me from behind. I turn to face her, and she smiles up at me. It's bright and glorious. Like sunshine on a rainy day. Still so fucking beautiful.

The smartest thing I ever did was not letting Quinn go.

She smacks a Post-It note on my chest before she wraps her arms around my neck. I capture her mouth with mine and palm her ass, pulling her body flush against me. Even after all these years together, I still want her all the time in every way imaginable. And believe me, we both have good imaginations.

"We still have time. If we're quick.…" I suck on her bottom lip, my dick swelling in my shorts, and now all I want to do is drag her back to bed and fuck her senseless. And her low moan gives me hope.

"Mama. Mama!" Fable shrieks. Not wanting to be left out, she's smacking her palms against the tray of her high chair and screaming at the top of her lungs now, demanding our full attention.

With a small laugh, Quinn pulls away from me. I groan, knowing there's not a chance in hell that I'll get lucky with my wife this morning.

"Read your note," Quinn says with a smirk as she lifts Fable into her arms and kisses her rosy cheeks.

I peel the Post-It note off my chest and read it: *Happy Anniversary (One Day Early). I love you more than words can say. You're the inspiration for every hero I write. Only you're so much better than any book boyfriend. You're my everyday crush and my dream come true. P.S. Last night, I had a dream... remember how I didn't want to try anal? I've changed my mind. I've packed the lube.*

I scrub my hand over my face and groan again. Jesus Christ. She's trying to kill me.

"You don't play fair."

Quinn just laughs and dances around the kitchen with Fable in her arms. She's singing an ABBA song, loud and off-key, but it doesn't matter. Not even a little bit. Her voice is my favorite sound. Quinn is my favorite everything.

My girls are laughing, their faces lit up with joy, and I don't know how it could get much better than this.

I haven't forgotten about our anniversary. I've already arranged a surprise for Quinn tomorrow. I know she's going to love it. When I asked her to marry me, I promised her a lifetime of adventure and love and of making each moment count.

It's been a hell of a ride already, and it's only just begun.

Quinn

"I can't believe you did all this." I drag my eyes away from the dolphins playing in the water and turn in Jesse's arms to face him. The evening sun makes his summer sky eyes look bluer against his suntanned face, and the breeze off the water ruffles his messy brown hair.

"I'm full of surprises."

"So am I." I give him an exaggerated wink that makes him laugh.

"Yeah, you are."

His eyes crinkle at the sides with his smile, and then we're kissing like two people who are madly in love and haven't seen each other for an eternity.

"Are you happy?" he asks a little while later. We have the perfect view of the sun setting over the water from our table for two on the private boat. Jesse chartered it for our anniversary celebration, along with a captain and crew and a waiter who had just served our dinner and disappeared to give us privacy.

"How can you even ask that?" Sometimes he still asks me, though, as if he needs reassurance. Alessia did such a number on his head. She didn't leave him alone after her mother's funeral either. No such luck.

She kept popping up in his life and, by default, mine. She showed up at a few of Jesse's stunt shows and tried to put doubts in my head. It didn't work, though. By then, I knew that Jesse loved me. He proved it to me every day, even when he was on the road and I couldn't join him.

Jesse used to work his magic, and I'd return to my dorm room to find little gifts letting me know he was thinking about me. We texted and FaceTimed whenever we were apart, and I never once doubted his loyalty. He was loyal to the bone, and after we got back together, we made a vow to never lie to each other again.

Now I lift my summertime cocktail in a toast. "Here's to many, many more years. Thousands and thousands of kisses and smiles and sunsets and memories." I wipe away a tear because I'm an emotional mess. Some things never change. "God, I love you. You're the best dad and the best lover and just… the best everything." He clinks his beer bottle against my glass, and we drink to that.

"I love you more. You and Fable are my world." I hear the sincerity in his voice, and I know he means every word of it. Jesse loves us so much and would do anything in the world for us.

"Happy Anniversary, baby."

"Happy Anniversary." How lucky am I? I found a man who treats me like a queen and who always puts me and Fable first.

I try to live each day like it's my last.

Life is precious, and I don't want to waste a single minute of it.

THE END

Acknowledgments

First, a huge thank you to the readers. Writing is a dream come true and I couldn't do this without you. As long as you keep reading, I'll keep writing. I have so many more stories to tell and I'm so grateful to each and every one of you.

To my daughters who are so supportive and understanding, even when I disappear for hours and days at a time and get lost in the world of my fictional characters. Love you to the moon and back. Forever and always.

To Jen Mirabelli—once again, I could not have done this without you. Thank you for believing in me and this story. For the daily chats, the tireless work you do to help make each story the very best it can be, and for organizing all the promo and marketing. You do so much for me and I'm so grateful and fortunate to be able to call you a friend.

To Aliana Milano—I wrote this book for you. Thank you for insisting that Jesse had a story to tell. I hope I did Jesse and Quinn justice. Thank you for making the Pinterest board so beautiful, for kicking my ass when I need it, and for all the midnight chats when we put the world to rights. Love you, boo.

To Ashley Estep—you have a gift for finding the best teaser lines. And thank you for getting me onto TikTok, although I might have to delete the app from my phone so I can actually get some writing done.

To Roxie Madar—for beta reading and for all your feedback that helped to make Jesse and Quinn's story the best it could be.

To Emery's Rambling Roses—my happy place on Facebook. Thank you for being so positive and keeping it drama-free. I appreciate you all. A special thanks to Emily Meador for doing such an amazing job of keeping the group going. You're an admin extraordinaire.

To Ellie McLove—for the editing and for always fitting me into your schedule and never getting upset about my shifting deadlines. I appreciate you so much.

To the book bloggers and bookstagrammers—for all the shares, tags, and support you've given me over the years. It doesn't go unnoticed. I appreciate everything you do for me and for the indie author community. Where would we be without you?

Much love,
Emery Rose xoxo

About the Author

Emery Rose has been known to indulge in good red wine, strong coffee, and a healthy dose of sarcasm. She loves writing about sexy alpha heroes, strong heroines, artists, beautiful souls, and flawed but redeemable characters who need to work for their happily ever after.

When she's not writing, you can find her binge-watching Netflix, trotting the globe in search of sunshine, or immersed in a good book. A former New Yorker, she currently lives in London with her two beautiful daughters.